Shane

IN THE COMPANY OF SNIPERS

Book 24

IRISH WINTERS

COPYRIGHT

Shane; In the Company of Snipers, Book 24

Cover design: Kelli Ann Morgan, Inspire Creative Services
Cover image: Paul Henry Serres Photography, www.paulhenryserres.com
Interior book design: Bob Houston eBook Formatting
Editor: Linda Clarkson, Black Opal Editing

ISBN Paperback: 978-1-942895-08-4
ISBN eBook: 978-1-942895-10-7
Library of Congress Control Number: 9781942895084.

In the Company of Snipers

You can find Irish Winters

On Facebook:
https://www.facebook.com/author.irishwinters

On Twitter:
https://twitter.com/irishwinters1

For news on upcoming releases, sign up for
Irish Winters' Newsletter at IrishWinters.com.

For more information about all my books, visit
IrishWinters.com.

IN THE COMPANY OF SNIPERS

This series revolves around former Marine scout sniper, Alex Stewart, and his covert surveillance company, The TEAM, home-based out of Alexandria, Virginia. An obsessive patriot and workaholic, he created the company to give former military snipers like him, a chance at returning to civilian life with a decent job, security, and a future.

This is not a serial with each book ending at a cliffhanger. *In the Company of Snipers* is a collection of passionate love stories involving strong women and men who are tough enough to take on the world alone. Each is a stand-alone read, complete in itself.

Spoiler alert: Every story contains adult scenes including sexual situations (some explicit), language, and violence. I don't write sweet romance, so be forewarned.

Book 1, *ALEX*, reveals how The TEAM came to be, as well as how Alex met Kelsey, how they fell in love and fought all odds to stay together. Each of the following books is a complete romance in itself, where, in the course of an active TEAM operation, one agent comes face to face with his or her demons. The men and women I write about are all patriots and warriors, dealing with what they've lived through or mistakes they've made.

It's my hope that you will come to realize along with my heroes...

Love changes everything.

"It is not the critic who counts; not the man who points out how the strong man stumbles, or where the doer of deeds could have done them better. The credit belongs to the man who is actually in the arena, whose face is marred by dust and sweat and blood; who strives valiantly; who errs, who comes short again and again, because there is no effort without error and shortcoming; but who does actually strive to do the deeds; who knows great enthusiasms, the great devotions; who spends himself in a worthy cause; who at the best knows in the end the triumph of high achievement, and who at the worst, if he fails, at least fails while daring greatly, so that his place shall never be with those cold and timid souls who neither know victory nor defeat."

- Theodore Roosevelt

Prologue

Current USA ROEs demanded a spotter accompany each sniper on every mission. Kind of a two-is-better-than-one concept. A failsafe protocol. The spotter attending USMC Sergeant Shane Hayes that morning was Staff Sergeant Carl Schnitzler. Carl was an older, smarter man, with a wife and two kids waiting back home in South Carolina. Hayes, on the other hand, was younger, a couple months shy of E-6, and hadn't yet decided how badly—or if—he wanted the hash marks on his soul that came with each higher rank. With every stripe, he'd lost a part of himself. Not so much lost, as given those pieces away. Little by little, he was losing the God-given soul he'd once believed he had. Not good for a guy who'd barely had a soul to begin with. No, being a Marine ended every bit of the wishful thinker he'd been before… *that day.*

Talk about a day that would forever *'live in infamy'.*

Since then, he'd been nothing more than a highly trained killer. An assassin for Uncle Sam. There weren't many jarheads who were better, and therein lay the quandary. As good a sniper as he was, he wanted to belong to something more than the Corps. But the simple truth was—He had nowhere else to go. No one waited anxiously back in the States for him. For that matter, no one waited anywhere on the planet for him. Well, except for his USMC buddies. Carl might keep in touch, but most of his buddies weren't real friends. They wouldn't keep in touch, and he didn't blame them. They weren't snipers. It'd be easier for them to acclimate to life after the Corps.

Shane hadn't left anyone behind when he'd enlisted, no girlfriend, father, or mother. No brothers or sisters. No long-lost uncles, aunts, or grandparents. Not even a dog. Sure, he could make the Corps his dysfunctional family of choice and spend the rest of his natural life snapping out loud and proud "Yes, sirs!" to every CO's orders. He could kiss butt and ante up, could devote that barely-there, shred of a half-soul to gearing up and marching out to take down the next high-value target on his CO's list. If the worst happened, if he were to die on one of these assignments, on some foreign piece-of-shit soil, his Marine Corps buddies might miss him—until his replacement arrived. Maybe.

Hayes doubted they'd miss him for long though. They had someone to go home to, and that made all the difference in the life of a sweaty, stinkin' grunt. He hadn't made friends in the Corps. Hadn't tried. Why bother? Snipers were born loners, and that was all he'd wanted to be. If not born that way, they quickly turned into unwelcome, impersonal pricks, if only to save face in light of their dark skillset. They stayed clear of stuff that could get a guy hurt. Relationships. Comradery. Women who meant something.

Hell, he didn't even carry a wrinkled *'if I don't come home'* letter inside his cap, pocket, or anywhere on his person. No sense in it. There was no one to notify if he ended up KIA, certainly no one who'd step up to bury him. There'd be no woman or child standing over his grave, weeping or angry, wishing he were there or... or shit, remembering him.

And that, he'd come to realize, had been eating at him the most since he'd enlisted. Not the lives he'd taken, intentionally or by accident. But that he was so damned alone in a country that didn't seem to care that he served to protect their outspoken, sorry, entitled asses. America's politicians had failed its rarest commodity—the men and women who served them, who protected them, indirectly allowing them to lie and cheat the American public and sell influence. If not by words, then by profiting through illegal insider trading. Or worse. Honestly, the more news from home filtered into mess halls overseas, the more ashamed of America Shane became. Because of failure at the highest government echelon, the entire USMC family was dysfunctional.

But once upon a time…

A long, long time ago…

Hayes had known what a real family felt like. The Corps wasn't it.

Hell, he wasn't even sure now why he'd ever thought serving America was honorable. Yet he had, and he honestly didn't regret taking the place of the man whose life he'd destroyed. Years ago, in a dumbassed stab at honor, he'd joined the Corps to repay that debt. A blood debt. But now, with each sanctioned hit, each HVT he'd put on the ground or in it, he wondered how many more lives he'd have to take to truly make amends for the awful thing he'd done. How many HVTs would ever be enough? Would the day come when he'd finally given enough of his soul to repay, at least decrement, a portion of that eternal debt? Real question, could he ever merit forgiveness for what he'd done? Could he forgive himself?

Not likely. Not that it mattered. Going back now would be starting over from scratch, which was all he'd done these past few years. But being stateside had to be a helluva lot better than living out of a rucksack in dusty, dirty, stinkin' Afghanistan, didn't it? God, he hoped so.

Both he and Carl were scout snipers with the Marine Corps Security Force Regiment, garrisoned out of Naval Weapons Station Yorktown, Virginia. Their assignment: Guard the high-value assets below, as part of what some USMC bigshot had coined *Guardian Angel Over-Watch*. Today, that meant eliminating the terrorist who'd successfully passed himself off as a day laborer, when in fact, he was armed with explosives and hunting the US contractors tasked to rebuild the runway below.

Green-on-blue attacks on Coalition forces and civilian contractors had increased steadily during this protracted war, more so after the USA announced the Coalition troops withdrawal from Afghanistan. Blue being all NATO, ISAF, and USA forces. Green being anyone associated with Afghan security forces, whether Afghan National Army, Afghan Air Force, or the local police. Basically, Coalition forces suspected anyone hired or vetted by Afghan authorities.

Despite US military expansion of counterintelligence at battalion levels, as well as requiring all US personnel in Afghanistan to carry loaded weapons on their persons at all times, Taliban infiltrators persisted. And along with those infiltrations, US soldiers and friendlies were continually being murdered.

Ironically, US contractors were only at the airport today because of a previous Taliban suicide bombing. Somehow, two idiots on their way to paradise and that age-old promise of seventy-two eternally young and beautiful virgins, managed to get their explosive-laden mini-truck onto the runway, but only close enough to die trying. Like so many ill-fated bombings, they missed their intended target, but instead, took out a large portion of concrete. They'd only *'killed'* the two vacant jetliners parked nearby. And themselves.

If Shane had his way, it'd be homegrown Afghan boys down there fixing their own damned tarmac and risking their lives for a change. Screwed up mess was what this country was. He was fed up with watching America's best die for nothing, worse for the scheming USA politics behind what had become an endless war. Hence, he and Carl were currently bellies down, scopes up, and sweating like pigs on the uppermost level of the scaffolding at this end of the terminal. It had been constructed for the Afghan workers replacing the plate-glass windows blown out in that same failed bombing. Fortunately, it was some kind of holy day today, so no Afghanis were on the job. Only those USA contractors below, Shane, and his spotter. Only the wind and the stink and...

"Got him. Shaggy dark hair, but neatly trimmed beard. Interesting combination. Pressed denim jeans. Long-sleeved, ragged, brown shirt. Olive-green shemagh around his neck. Just dropped out of sight behind the stacked bags of concrete mix to your far left."

Carl's calm words jerked Shane out of his depressing reverie and back to the job at hand. "Copy that," he replied, his attention now focused on the stacks hiding the assassin and waiting on Carl to tell him precisely when and where to fire.

Yes, bags and bags of concrete mix, a veritable mountain of it, all to be mixed, poured, and troweled the old-fashioned way—by hand. Why not? Manual labor built this country with its current forty-plus percent unemployment rate among common laborers. They needed work? They got it by way of paid slavery. But that was daily life in Afghanistan for the masses. Only the rich lived the modern, digital, refined life, and much of that was sustained by sweat labor. Just not theirs.

Flapping sheets of opaque plastic hung over the scaffolding. That was all that kept Shane and Carl out of sight. No one knew they were there, not the construction workers they cared about, the assassin they were here to eliminate, the few airport personnel working today, nor the Marines on the ground standing guard over the contractors.

While Carl repeatedly calculated trajectory factors: wind, distance, temp, etc., Shane zeroed into his sniper bubble, the state of calm that preceded the incoming chaos he'd eventually create. His cheek welded to the top stock of his bolt-action rifle. His neck muscles relaxed as he let his rifle and that cheek weld support the weight of his head. Automatically, his inner sniper took over, controlling his breathing, making everything slow and easy, his mission pure and true. His direction of aim was right then holding into the slight breeze coming south-by-southwest to his location. As soon as Carl gave the word, he'd make the shot. The assassin below would be one and done, and those American workers would be safe for another day.

Only problem was that Carl was right then fielding stupid orders by radio from their safe-in-his-office-with-his-feet-up-on-his-desk idiot CO. Which was no damned help. Seemed Captain Clinton wanted Carl to shoot actual live footage of this hit. The jerk was loud enough Shane could hear him bellowing, "Use your gawddamned cell phone to take the pictures, for fuck sake!"

Not going to happen. Not with Carl as spotter. Especially not while Shane's eyes were glued solely on his target.

Ensuring they both didn't end up dead was the spotter's primary job. What was Clinton trying to do? Get them killed to make himself look good?

Shane bit his tongue and let his annoyance go with the breeze. Carl was the true genius here. He had the wider scope of vision, not Clinton and sure as hell not Shane. His entire focus was limited to what he could see through his scope, which was a lot like looking through a cardboard paper-towel tube. Clinton could go to hell.

"Understood, sir. Copy that. Got my cell up and ready, you bet." Carl ended the call. It sounded like he'd slapped the mic on his collar and turned Clinton off. "Steady, dead-eye," he murmured, his voice low and firm in the way of all good spotters. "Reference farthest edge of left cement bags—"

"Are you sure those Marines down there know not to shoot back?" Shane interrupted without shifting position or giving up his cheek weld. "Did Clinton warn them we'd be here?" *Like he said he would.*

"No worries, Shane. I told Rowdy myself. Think I'd rely on a fuckwit when our asses are on the line?" Carl grunted like that was a no-brainer. "Forget Clinton. This isn't Hollywood and I'm not that kind of dumb."

Shane thanked God that Carl was older, wiser, and refused to kiss ass. Shane let what almost felt like a smile curl the corners of his lips. If he had his way, he'd only ever work with Carl, no other spotter. Carl made a damned good staff sergeant, but he wasn't staying on. Even he had higher aspirations—like getting to know his wife and twin daughters again. Shane just wanted to be back on American soil.

"Thanks," he told the man who was probably his one and only friend.

"No thanks necessary. Okay, again, reference the farthest bag to your left. Bottom of the stack. That rounded, black bump at ground level is the tip of our friendly assassin's boot. From that point, adjust a half meter to your two o'clock. Wait for it."

"Waiting," Shane breathed evenly, the adjustment made, the tip of the boot accounted for, and his universe narrowed down to whatever Carl said next. For now, Shane was looking at a round circle of empty space a half meter at his two o'clock, which put his aim barely above the stacks of concrete. He counted his heartbeats, and let his mind relax in what snipers called *'bubble compartmentalization'*, the ability to block everything in the world but his spotter's next command.

He didn't wait long. When the barest edge of that olive-green shemagh rippled above the stack, Carl ordered, "Send it."

Shane's right index finger depressed the ribbed curl of his rifle's trigger, and sent a .308 Lapua round on its way. "Sent."

"Direct hit," Carl confirmed through his rangefinder. "Assassin down. Let's move."

Shane didn't look for the body of the man he'd just tagged or the red mist a head shot incurred. Didn't want to know. Didn't care. Sniping wasn't sexy or cool like Hollywood made it seem. It was hard, dirty work, simply a necessary evil that hard men did in a world full of depraved and unnecessary cruelty. Whatever role that Taliban soldier had played in his family, home, or mosque was now just another bloody footnote in the story of Shane's life.

With this kill, his role of *'guardian angel'* was officially over. He'd decided. A smart man didn't need to see blood on the tarmac to know what he'd done. And Shane had done enough.

Together he and Carl stowed their weapons, gathered what little gear they'd brought with them, and dropped like shadowy wraiths behind the opaque, wind-buffeted plastic to ground level. Shane's boots had no sooner hit the concrete when Carl's radio squawked an incoming.

"Good shooting, boys," USMC Sergeant James 'Rowdy' Wayne relayed. "Had my eye on that asshat all morning. Just a bad vibe, you know, but damn, you were right. The fucker had three weapons on him, two pistols under his shirt, one in his belt. He'd just taken aim when you ended him. He was gunning for the foreman, who's a father of three little kids, damn it!"

"Glad we could help," Carl replied, his tone as emotionless as Rowdy's was amped.

"That Hayes working with you? Was this his work?" Rowdy wanted to know. "Fuck, I'd like to meet that man someday."

"Could be." Carl gave nothing away. Sniping wasn't about setting records or one-upmanship. Shane never wanted to be another Chris Kyle. He didn't want the notoriety. He'd joined the Corps simply to replace the man whose USMC career he'd cut short. This was his way of paying back. Or forward. Whatever.

"Well, hell. Tell whichever USMC bastard took that shot thanks from all us guys!" Rowdy exclaimed. "Whoever he is, he's one helluva guardian angel. Glad he's on our side."

"Copy that," Carl replied smoothly as he stuffed the radio into his gear bag. "You got time for a beer before you take off?"

"Sure." Shane had no more than answered when Carl's radio squawked again.

"Shit. Clinton," Carl cussed. His chest heaved as he tugged the entire radio out of its Velcro pouch on his hip, hauled back, and smashed it into the concrete. "Oops," he growled as plastic pieces flew. "Guess they don't make Velcro like they used to."

"Yeah, but that radio'll still work," Shane told him. "It's ruggedized. Better pick up the pieces and face the music."

"Not as far as it fell, it won't. Didn't you notice? It dropped all the way down, from the top of the scaffolding. Dropped like a rock, and shit if I'm apologizing to that pompous prick for not filming you kill that jerk." Carl landed a solid kick that sent the battered radio into one of the many concrete barricades erected to ensure airport security. "You saw it slip. I'll swear to it, and so will you, but no way I'm picking up those pieces."

Grabbing Shane by the back of his neck, he pointed back the way they'd come. "Besides, live-action shots would identify you to anyone who'd view that clip. What if the Taliban got hold of it? They'd be hot on your ass, and you don't need shit like that."

Hard to argue with an intelligent man. "Clinton's a prick. I'm done. My contract expires today, and I'm not re-upping."

By then, they were at their MATV, their MRAP All-Terrain Vehicle. "I'm gonna miss you, kid," Carl admitted. "But I'm sure glad you're leaving this shithole behind. About time."

"Yeah," Shane replied, his eyes forward but his heart already in the air somewhere over the Atlantic. "How many days for you?"

"Twenty-one, and trust me, I'm counting the hours. I'll look you up as soon as I'm home. After I spend a couple months with my wife and kids, that is."

"See that you do. I should be settled in by then." *Somewhere. I hope.*

"You got a good job lined up?"

Shane shook his head. He knew a guy but asking this particular man for a job wouldn't come easy. Not this job. Not that guy.

"Any plans? Any leads?"

Shane opted for diversion. "Yeah. Not to be here."

Wasn't that the truth? He had nothing to look forward to but leaving Afghanistan behind, and the only thing on his to-do list was finally facing the man whose life he'd ruined. Because that was what he'd done all those years ago. It was time to go back and face the music that had been playing since that day in Alexandria, Virginia.

Chapter One

Everlee Yeager jacked the steering wheel of her unmarked TEAM SUV hard to her left, squealing tires, and narrowly missing the oncoming delivery truck as her vehicle hit the left shoulder of State Road 522, east of Sperryville, Virginia. Man, that delivery driver's mouth looked like he'd just said some not very nice words when he'd seen her coming at him in his lane. Oh, well. Surprise, surprise. Emergency vehicle coming through.

"Easy, Ev," Walker Judge growled over her Bluetooth earpiece. "We want him alive."

"I'll sure give it the old college try," she returned gallantly, careening between two lanes of oncoming traffic, following Webster Finch, the creep who'd killed those two little eight-year-old third graders last week. In a school zone. Everlee hated drug dealers. They thought everyone was expendable but them, the bastards. Well, not today. The dirtbag's battered yellow sedan was in her sights. Finch wasn't getting away this time, and if she 'accidentally' ran over him in the process of capturing him, well, too bad. One way or the other, his baby-killing, drug-dealing days were over.

"There is no try, Ev," Walker said extra quietly. Which meant he was getting through to her.

"And now you're channeling Yoda?" she scoffed.

"Think about what you're doing. What if you're the reckless one who kills an innocent today?"

Well, damn. Walker had a way of taking all the fun out of this take-down. But he was right.

Lowering her speed to just above barely legal, Everlee kept to the far-left side of the highway, bouncing along the gravel shoulder while Finch hopped the median and returned to the eastbound lanes. She waited until she had a clear shot, then accelerated and did the same.

By then Finch was ten cars ahead and veering right. That son of a bitch meant to take the last exit into Culpepper. She could intercept him before then. She had to! Drastic times called for drastic measures, right? If she couldn't take him out before, she'd sure catch him after.

Putting her boot into it, she left the highway in the dust, hopped the irrigation ditch alongside, and sped diagonally across some farmer's dusty, old field. Thank you, Jesus! No big-eyed cows were in her way. Or fence posts. Just weeds and dirt.

Faster. Faster. Finch was just pulling right at the yield sign, taking it slow, acting like a law-abiding citizen when he was anything but. She set her trajectory to intercept. He hadn't yet seen her coming through the field at his right. The fool was only watching his rearview mirror. He thought she was behind him. Well, guess again.

"No, no!" she yelled at the semi-trailer that had just lumbered into the slow lane between her and Finch. But wait. That kept her out of Finch's sight a little while longer. Change of plans. She adapted quickly, hit the gas, cranked her wheel, and aimed for a point of intersection a mile farther south. There he was. Cruising past that eighteen-wheeler on

Highway 15 like he owned the whole damned road. Wrong again!

Everlee pushed her SUV for all it could handle. Blinked the sweat out of her eyes. Gritted her teeth. Clenched her jaw and prepared for impact. Contemplated angle. Gawddamnit.

BLAM! Touchdown! Smackdown! Whatever!

She t-boned that yellow POS in the passenger door and caught Finch completely by surprise. Revving her engine, she pushed his ride into the concrete barrier that separated southbound traffic from northbound and ensured both she and he were away from that eighteen-wheeler careening around them.

The trucker's brakes screamed bloody murder as it passed them. Since Finch hadn't yet braked or come to a complete stop, they were still moving. Man, that truck driver had skills! Good on him. With a masterful swerve, then another hard brake, he righted his rig without jackknifing or spilling his load. Way to go!

"So there!" she yelled at the baby-killer finally in her sights, even though she knew damned well Finch couldn't hear her. She had him, dead to rights. He wasn't going anywhere, and he couldn't get away. She'd done it! She had this jerk by the short hairs!

Until Finch lifted his arm and pointed a gun at her through his dirty passenger window. Everlee ducked low to her right and sent her SUV into a wicked side drift that once again, slammed the side of her vehicle up against Finch's sedan. The impact jolted his car. The weapon flew out of his hand. Finch had no choice but to brake. Perfect!

She had a warrant for his arrest, courtesy of The TEAM's connection with the Virginia Highway Patrol. But if he fired at her, even took one shot, she'd end this son of a bitch and her dashcam would prove it was self-defense.

"Everlee…" Walker said quietly. He had a way of not saying much, but her quietly spoken name over the earpiece inside her head was enough. Damn it.

With that one word, he'd expertly corrected her extraordinary sense of what some would call vigilante justice while, at the same time, he'd punched a hole in her overinflated ego and ended her plan for ending Finch. Instead of shooting him like the animal he was, she slammed her brakes and, within seconds, blasted out of the passenger side door of her still-rolling vehicle and ran straight for the grill of his POS sedan.

"Drop it, Finch!" she bellowed, her Sig Sauer P-210 on target—namely, the middle of his ugly face. "It's over. Hands where I can see them. Now!" Her heart hammered in her chest as if Thor were in there playing with his lightning and thunderbolts. The punch of adrenaline in her system was off the charts, but this was why she loved her new job. The thrill! The takedown! This, right here!

By then, her VHP companion escort, Trooper Ralph McKay, rolled to a stop in front of Finch's sedan, further trapping him. Slapping his VHP Smokey Bear hat onto his head, McKay scrambled out of his cruiser and ran to her side.

"You heard Agent Yeager, Finch!" he bellowed, his service revolver aimed at Finch and backing Everlee up like she knew he would. "Drop the weapon and put your hands on the steering wheel. Keep 'em where I can see them." Dropping his volume, McKay asked out of the side of his mouth, "That is what you told him, right Ev?"

"Yup, sure did." McKay was a good foot taller than Everlee, so she didn't mind that he'd said, *'where I can see them,'* instead of *'where we can see them'*. They'd worked together often enough. She knew he always had her back.

Instead of following orders, Finch tipped forward. No hands were in sight as his forehead hit the top of the steering wheel. His long, straggly hair draped like a curtain over his face, covering his cheeks and muttonchop sideburns. His hands were nowhere in sight. Not good.

Like the aggressor he now was, Officer McKay took a man-sized step forward. Everlee two-stepped with him. She and McKay were two parts of the same force of law. Finch didn't stand a chance. Not today. Not until an ugly vibe lifted the tiny hairs up on the back of Everlee's neck, and she knew, she just knew Finch wouldn't go easy.

"Don't do it! Finch! No!" she yelled, then screamed, "Gun!" Because sure as hell, Finch did it.

But she was too late. Finch's arm had already snapped up. He had another pistol aimed at McKay's bigger body mass. The son of a bitch fired. Once. He got off a shot but he jerked his weapon at the very last moment and missed McKay. Didn't miss Everlee, though. The impact struck her chest with what felt like the power of a freight train. She jerked backward, every last breath in her lungs squeezed out. She was a limp ragdoll with its strings in that asshole's fist. She went down on her back, wheezing, "Damn you, Finch!"

Which was good for McKay. It got her out of his way, but the sudden slam of her body onto the highway hurt like a bitch. Shit! If she didn't have bad luck, she wouldn't have any. Finch had taken her out of the game. One minute she was in her zone, triumphant! A winner! The next, she was a shooting vic with a pounding migraine from bouncing her head on asphalt. Not only out of the game, she had a bullet stuck in her chest. WTF!

"Not fair!" she wheezed, because, hey, even one bullet messed up a girl's day, and yeah, breathing really hurt.

Thunder erupted as Officer McKay returned fire. Two shots—she counted. But no answering volley. Good. McKay hadn't been hit, but she was willing to bet her paycheck that Finch had. And yeah, her.

Jiminy Christmas! She could hear Alex. He already thought she was a hazard to herself and his TEAM. What would he say now? Man, she had the worst luck of all TEAM agents.

"Officer involved shooting!" McKay yelled into the radio Velcroed to his vest shoulder. "TEAM agent down! Mile marker sixty-nine on Highway 15. Request EMT and TEAM support, STAT!"

Great. Just freaking great. No doubt Walker was already on his way. He knew I'd mess up.

"Not... down, down... R-R-Ralph," Everlee wheezed, her lungs spasming back into working order, but her heart pounding so hard, it felt like there wasn't enough room in her chest for both organs to do their thing at the same time. "Bullet hit my... my vest. Not my h-head." *No, I did that all by myself when I fell on my ass.*

McKay rolled his big, hazel-green eyes at her like he thought that was the stupidest comeback ever, which it might've been. But there was down, and then there was way, way dowwwwwn, as in kicking up daisies six feet under down.

"Shit," she hissed at herself. "Breathe, Yeager. Just… Christ! Breathe!"

Easier said than done. The force of any shot to the chest was a rib-busting powerful jolt of super-charged kinetic energy. Just what she didn't need, another OTJ injury. If this run of bad luck didn't end soon, Alex would fire her for sure.

While McKay jerked Finch's passenger door open, secured his weapons and checked for vital signs, Everlee focused on trying to catch a full breath. She needed to be on her feet before Walker or the medics arrived. But the dynamics of any gunshot created enough muscular trauma to a body, even a body with a tactical vest, to stall quick recovery.

Too bad people didn't take a hit and just bounce back up like make-believe heroes in Hollywood action films. Uh-uh. Even with Kevlar tactical vests the same rule applied. For every action, there was a guaranteed reaction. And a bullet in the chest was nothing to laugh at. Mainly because she still couldn't catch enough air to get her right lung to inflate so she could laugh properly at Finch's demise like she'd planned to.

Alex made sure his men and women were protected by something better than Kevlar. Whatever it was, Everlee was glad for it now. She blew out a hiss and studied the robin's egg blue Virginia sky overhead. Might as well. She wasn't going anywhere. The sun was still mostly in the east, making the blue even bluer instead of washed out like it would be later in the day. It was a beautiful summer morning. But she had to go and get shot. *Damn it!*

The EMTs were Johnny-on-the-spot and arrived before she could pull herself up into hey-I'm-okay, leave-me-alone-land. As if they would. Not these guys.

"Humor me," EMT Rich Slavich, another Virginia buddy she'd made since she'd left Seattle, instructed. "You know the drill. When you take one to the chest, tactical vest or not, you come with us. Mr. Stewart's orders. Stop whining like a spoiled brat."

"Not whining." Damn it, she whimpered even when she tried to sound tough. "Just want to finish what I started, you jerk."

Everlee curled her fingers into a fist and gave his bulky biceps the weakest knuckle smack ever. No way she'd hurt Rich. The guy was built like a bull, his biceps thick and tight inside that short-sleeved shirt.

Like the good sport he was, he played along, rolled with the punch, even had the nerve to wince as if she'd hurt him. "Anyone ever tell you that you hit like a girl, Yeager?"

"I *am* a girl, moron. Anyone ever tell you most women are tougher than most guys?"

"Yeah, yeah. How's that working for you?"

She strained to suck in a decent breath. "Honestly, that hit hurt a little, Rich. But only a little. I'm okay. Honest."

Rich nodded, patronizing her even as he slipped the cold end of his stethoscope down her TEAM polo and placed it over her breastbone. He cocked his head to listen and reverted into the highly-trained first responder he was. Until then, she hadn't noticed he'd unbuttoned her shirt. She tried not to notice how warm the tips of his fingers were on her skin. How his Adam's apple bobbed when those manly fingers grazed the pillowy tops of her breasts. He was a good-looking guy, but he was married. All the good guys were.

"Hey, watch it, Romeo. That thing's c-c-cold and…" Her heart skipped a beat, as in, it really jumped inside her chest. Kinda like it wanted out. Or it was playing hopscotch.

"You felt that, didn't you?" Rich asked, his baby blue eyes flashing to hers.

"Yeah. I did. What was it?"

"A minor palpitation. Nothing to worry about unless it keeps happening or it gets out of control. I'll pass that detail along to the ER doc so he or she can take a listen."

"Do you have to?" The big jerk was smiling. "Stop patronizing me, damn it!"

Rich grinned. "Wouldn't think of it. Just taking care of my best girl."

"How many best girls do you have, anyway?"

He had the nerve to shrug those huge shoulders, which made his shirt tighten across his chest even more. His eyes sparkled with mischief. "Guess you'll never know, will you?"

"Damned straight because I don't care," she shot back at him, pissed that he and his buddy were now wrapping her in a blanket, then strapping her onto their gurney, and trundling her off to the rear gate of their ride. Like she was an accident victim. Which she was not! The urge hit her to yell at the nosy rubber-necking drivers passing the scene, to tell them she was the good guy there, to stop gawking! That because of her, Virginia's children were safe again. Well, safer. That she wasn't really hurt.

Shit. A shiny black TEAM SUV pulled up alongside the EMT's wagon. Walker Judge had arrived, and Everlee hissed at the injustice of her accidental takedown. He'd report every last detail back to Alex. Didn't it figure? *And Jiminy*

Christmas! He'd brought his buddy Brimley Scott along for the ride, wasn't that just peachy?

Short answer, no!

"Aren't you supposed to be in China or Thailand, Singapore or somewhere else?" Everlee bit out before Walker opened his mouth.

Brimley tipped his head as he strode by and went to talk with McKay. He was a kindly older gentleman with a thick, gray, street-sweeper mustache on his top lip. Usually, he'd have a white, Labrador-sized mutt trotting at his side, but he must've left Rover behind in the newly built TEAM kennels. Which was too bad. Everlee could really use a wet, furry kiss and a puppy hug. Her eyes were watering.

Walker had picked up Brimley and Rover on his wild-assed adventure in the Azores a while back. Unjustly targeted by his USN command, Walker had been falsely accused of a lot of shit before Alex intervened and ultimately, tracked down the real mastermind behind the false accusations made by the Navy. Despite his trials by some seriously shitty Navy politics, Walker was one of the steadiest snipers on Alex's payroll. He was everyone's friend, and he had the damnedest way of getting people to share things they'd ordinarily not talk about. He alone knew about Everlee's biggest past mistake— her one and only marriage—and she intended to keep it that way.

Walker grinned that calm, cocky grin of his and walked up to the back of the EMT's wagon, his gunslinger swagger down pat. Damn, she loved working with a sexy bunch of alpha males, but this one in particular was a pleasure to watch. The way his hips rolled with each step. The way he scraped his thumb nail along his jaw, like he was wondering what on Earth to do with her. He almost made getting hit worth it.

"Ev," he said quietly once he came to a standstill. "You okay, kid?"

Her head bobbed. "Yeah, but my v-v-vest's got a big old d-d-dent in it." *And I still can't catch my breath.* No need telling Walker that. He'd figure it out.

Everlee was used to working with mostly men. She'd been Air Force, stationed out of Anchorage, Alaska, Joint Base Elmendorf-Richardson, Major Command PACAF, as in Pacific Air Force, home of the 673rd Air Base Wing. Not only that, she'd been an officer, a lieutenant, not just A1C, airman first class. She'd been LT Everlee Yeager, Chief of Security Forces. She might not be a SEAL or a sniper like Walker and the rest of the guys, but she gave every last one of them a run for their money at the shooting range on certification days, by hell. Ask Ember Dennison. She was in charge of weapons certification. She knew.

By then, Brimley had helped Ralph drape a large camouflage-gray tarp over Finch's sedan, hiding the death scene from John Q. Public, as well as the local news helicopter now hovering overhead. Brimley and McKay were on their way to her to witness her defeat.

"What'd he hit you with?" Walker asked.

"A thirty-eight." Trooper Ralph McKay stretched a hand out to Walker. The men acknowledged each other in one of those arm-gripping handshakes guys did. "She's lucky she was wearing a vest."

Walker's lips pursed into a whistle. "Damn, that's a big round, Ev."

"Yeah, but really, the ER, guys? I was just there," Everlee complained, still working an angle to not have to ride anywhere with Rich and his buddy.

McKay's brows lifted to the brim of his Smokey Bear cover. "You were? Why?"

"She fell up the front stairs at work." Walker's fist flattened against his smirking lips. The jerk was trying not to laugh but sure didn't mind telling McKay that Ev had, "Sprained the hell out of her ankle. This is, err, was, her first day back on active duty."

"And if you make me go to the ER, Alex will sideline me again." Everlee crossed her arms over her chest, which did not hurt at all! Much. "This is a waste of time, guys. I don't need the ER. Not for one little tap."

"Better safe than sorry, little lady," Brimley told her in that gruff, grandfatherly way he had. If anyone else had called her little lady, she'd have ripped their heads off for being sexist. But Brim was from a different generation, like Murphy Finnegan, her boss at the Seattle TEAM office. Neither were truly sexist. They just were who they were. She respected them for their service and their kind, gentlemanly ways.

"See you at the ER, Ev," Walker replied.

Rich closed the rear gate, ending further discussion—or argument.

Officer McKay smacked the roof and waved Everlee goodbye.

Men!

Chapter Two

Jarheads made up most of Alex Stewart's TEAM. Shane knew that because he'd Googled The TEAM and found nothing substantial from the source, as in from its CEO, former USMC scout sniper, Alex Stewart. But he had found plenty of third-party media bullshit, and hopefully some of it was true. It was damned hard to know these days.

Researching The TEAM was like following a stubborn thread of events around the world and through the past few years. Instead of a simple *Wikipedia* link that would lead to partial truths sprinkled with facts, Shane had been forced to track down and research newspaper and magazine articles instead. Seemed wherever Stewart or his men and women went, the media followed like a relentless pack of propaganda spewing trolls. Would've been easier if Stewart had maintained an informative website. At least the facts there would've been true—from Stewart's perspective. But the man didn't advertise and had not once extolled his TEAM's extraordinary successes. Worse, he'd made the FBI look bad the few times he'd worked with them. Had done so for years. Of course, the press jumped on that nugget and magnified it into sensational bullshit.

Since the first article published in the *Seattle Post Intelligencer,* of the attempted murders of Stewart and the abused woman who had eventually become his second wife, to the next by-line in the more palatable and believable, *News Herald,* out of Marshfield, Wisconsin, the press had hounded Alex Stewart at every turn. If they weren't bitching about the unsafe and inconvenient location of his TEAM Headquarters building, which he owned outright, in historic downtown Alexandria, Virginia, they'd outright invented shit that slandered the man, his wife, his TEAM, and their spouses, for hell's sake. Typical of the amoral propaganda machine the right-to-free-speech press corps had devolved into. Truth was an elusive characteristic in the media business.

Shane scrubbed a hand over his chin, prickly stubble already present on a face he hoped Stewart wouldn't recognize. Or be on the lookout for. He'd been about to turn eighteen that fateful day, and Shane hoped he'd aged enough these last years to make an impression—or something.

The latest unsubstantiated rumor Stewart refused to address publicly had garnered momentum since Vice President Mason's recent death from stage-four Hodgkin's lymphoma. Shane hoped that rumor was the by-product of some idiot reporter's imagination. But it made honest to goodness sense that President Adams would ask Stewart to serve as his VP. He'd worked closely with Adams on a covert mission a couple years back, the one that had ended Adam's first VP's treasonous attempt to dirty bomb Washington, DC. President Adams had made it clear that Stewart was not only a smart businessman but also a loyal friend. What President wouldn't want a man like that standing with him in the Oval Office?

But Vice President? If Stewart accepted, that'd make him the third VP under Adams. It'd also make him a target, because VPs sure didn't last long in this administration.

Guess the guys and gals of the media weren't liking the possibility of a no-kidding honest man, a former sniper, holding public office, though. Not if the quantity of bullshit and outright slander coming out of the local rags was an indication. The press was afraid of Stewart, and they should be. He'd personally destroyed one of the worst news outlets on the entire Eastern Seaboard, as well as their so-called *'topnotch reporter,'* the now deceased Crosland Webster of defunct Channel 16. Webster had made the fatal mistake of asking Stewart for protection from another victim he'd slandered, when, in fact, Webster was solely responsible for smearing Stewart's wife when she'd been kidnapped. Which told Shane that Stewart was doing something right. In Shane's book, pissing off the intolerant press was precisely what they deserved and what America needed. And maybe, just maybe, three times was a charm, and America would again rock the world under Vice President Alex Stewart's patriotism, care, and vigilance.

Shane swallowed hard and let that wish go. Truth was Stewart hired Navy and Army vets, some decorated heroes, and he relied on several damned smart civilians. But jarheads comprised the core of The TEAM, and every last one of them came with that cocky, in-your-face, *I-dare-you,* testosterone-filled attitude that irked other military guys and gals right out of the starting gate.

Word was he'd recently hired a couple of former SEALs, the latest a SEAL whose crooked trial and illegal confinement had outed several Navy commanders and a dirty-as-shit admiral. Ended the Black Dragon Syndicate, too, one of many perverse child smuggling operations strangling the world today. A guy didn't have to be military to appreciate the uproar that caused the country. Walker Judge, wasn't that the guy's name? Shane nodded to himself. And now Judge worked for Stewart. So yeah. Stewart's TEAM was the best. Hands down.

Christ, you could almost smell the bullshit and testosterone wafting out of the newly finished TEAM buildings a couple miles from the eastern gate of the Shenandoah National Park in western Virginia. At least from the few buildings visible from where Shane was standing. Most of Stewart's complex was underground. Again, Shane had to give the guy credit. Unseen was damned smart thinking for a dumbassed devil dog running the country's most successful covert ops team. What people didn't know couldn't hurt them, right? And what they couldn't see kept them oblivious of the kind of men and women now installed in their fair countryside. Kinda like Disneyland with all its underground tunnels for comings and goings and shit. The land Stewart had situated his TEAM on looked damn near passive.

Passive aggressive was more like it.

Shane snorted. He'd already been inside the brand-spanking-new TEAM Headquarters as part of the blue-collar construction crew. He'd helped frame, then sheet-rock the building, as well as most of the underground tunnels. Shane enjoyed sweat labor. It left him tired at the end of a productive day and proud of what he'd done. All of it. Unlike his last job.

Being a valued USMC scout sniper had turned him into a hired gunslinger and an assassin, not that he regretted any of the bastards he'd offed on his various overseas deployments. But he was done with that life, and the soul-suck that came along with taking lives wasn't anything like the Hollywood highs depicted on the big screen. At its best, it was cancer. The more people a guy killed, righteous or not, the more the cancer spread until it ate him from the inside out.

Caught like a distant cousin between Sperryville and Nethers, Virginia, a person could miss TEAM HQ if they didn't know where to look. Stewart had done a fine job concealing most of his mega-complex. His choice of underground bunkers that served as an office, natural terrain, and total lack of landscaping left a lot to be desired for the elite and very successful business he'd built from scratch. But that was Alex Stewart for you. The number one, most dangerous sniper in the world operated his covert business humbly and kept a low profile in this pretentious world gone bat-shit crazy.

Most of his neighbors probably had no idea he was here or what he did. Or if they knew, they weren't talking. Hence, the by-lines coming out of the District's pack of wanna-be celebrity reporters had gone damned near silent. Even the feeding frenzy over the rumored VP's successor had quieted down somewhat. Not that it'd stay quiet. Successful people like Stewart tended to attract the wrong people. Like Shane.

He stood nearly at attention by his pickup's open tailgate, listening to the quiet songs of red-winged blackbirds and meadowlarks along the ditch bank, wishing this morning was already over. That somehow in his wildest dreams, he belonged inside that prestigious, cloistered TEAM of outstanding repute. He had a no-kidding appointment, an employment interview with some guy named Mark Houston, part of Shane's plan to fake it until he made it. Why not? A man never knew what he was capable of until he tried. Asked. Begged. Whatever it took.

He wasn't stupid. If he did nothing but face Mr. Stewart, man-to-man, finally, like he wished he'd done back when everything had gone so horribly wrong in both of their lives, Shane wouldn't be here today. He'd already be dead and buried because Stewart would've killed him. At least he would've died with a clear conscience then, knowing he'd done all he could to make amends.

But now…

After all these years…

All the things left undone and words unspoken had turned to poison, and that poison had fermented into the shitload of unbridled self-hatred Shane still carried.

He puffed a vaporous cloud of carcinogens toward TEAM HQ and prayed that, at first sight, Stewart didn't send him to hell with a double-tap between his eyes. The man could surely do it.

Fuck, why'd I ever think this was the right thing to do?

His two rowdy English Springer Spaniels had both picked up a scent, no doubt of a muskrat, raccoon, or pheasant, and were running like boisterous, look-alike twins through the weed-choked ditch alongside this country highway. All Shane could see was their fluffy black and white tails, which was okay with him. The two-year-olds needed to burn off some of their natural-born hyperactivity before he put them back in the truck.

Shane would rather join them if he could. But while they were happy-go-lucky critters, always busy tracking something, or roughhousing for the fun of it, he was the pitiful third-wheel to their happy. He was the murderer come west to beg for a job from the very man who might kill him on sight.

The chicken-shit come back to roost. To at least meet Stewart, talk to him, explain things maybe.

Maybe not.

Things might go south before he got to the job interview. But that was a chance worth taking. Maybe then, Shane could sleep nights, knowing he'd at least tried. That was why he'd come here today. To clear his conscience and hopefully, give Stewart what he needed to heal.

The first thing Shane intended was to ask Houston if he could arrange a quick meeting with Stewart. All Shane wanted was a couple minutes with the man to tell him what happened that day. Getting hired would be a bonus, but it wasn't Shane's first priority. Stewart's peace of mind was. Sounded like a damned good plan when Shane had first thought of it. But now...

He blew another poisonous puff out of his lungs and into the air. Decent, fulfilling employment was hard for vets, particularly former snipers to come by. Which had put Shane where he was, between a rock and a gawddamned hard place. There was no future in selling used cars, pumping gas, frying burgers, or working maintenance for Kroger's industrial-sized bakeries. Hell, no.

He'd swallowed his pride enough. It was time to man up.

Stewart specifically targeted USMC snipers for his TEAM. The best of the best and Shane fit that bill, damn it. He did. He was a Marine. Forever would be. He'd fought hard for his country, and he'd served honorably in what had become a dishonorable war. Unbeknownst to anyone, he'd done everything these past years in an honest effort to atone for his sins. Yet not once had Stewart reached out to Shane for employment like he'd done so many other scout snipers. Hell, some he'd even hired before the Corps was finished with them.

But if those other men and women were good enough for Stewart's almighty TEAM, then, by hell, so was Shane. He had enough meaningless medals to prove it. If those weren't good enough, he had the scars. He just wasn't sure he'd survive a face-to-face with Stewart. Hell, he might not make it past the front door. Stewart probably had a kill order on him. Shoot on contact. A BOLO. Because there was no way Stewart would've forgotten Shane's name.

He flicked the ash off his smoke, pinched the glowing ember on the end of his disgusting, filterless treat, and whistled for his dogs to hightail it back to the truck.

"Come on, Molly! You too, Dolly! Time to go." Yup, you got it, his only friends were these two bitches, and he'd paid big bucks for them. Trained comfort dogs didn't come cheap, but they'd saved his life since he'd returned to the States and made closing his eyes in the dark easier. He actually slept most nights now.

Like little children, the dogs dilly-dallied along the ditch bank, so he whistled a piercing warning to turn those fluffy butts around. That did it. Within seconds, his girls were once again leashed in tight and panting in their places on the covered rear seat of his king cab. They'd had their drinks from the bottled water and collapsible bowls he kept under the seat for them. Drooling and bright-eyed, Molly sat at the left window, Dolly at the right. They were mostly obedient and always smiling, Shane knew that for sure. He'd only had them a couple months, but these two service dogs were his most loyal companions since he'd left the Corps.

Shit. It was time to head into the interview. Shane hoped for the best. But whether he left this place with or without the job he honestly wanted, he would always wear the names of the two innocents he'd killed that day. They were inked over his heart. **SARA** and **ABBY.**

Please God, let Stewart forgive me.

Chapter Three

Everlee tapped her fingertips on the keyboard, not hard enough to enter anything into Mr. Stewart's calendar for the day, just needing to do something. She'd been stuck on boring desk duty for five weeks now, and it was killing her. Killing, with a capital K. Guess one too many near misses wasn't looked upon kindly here at TEAM HQ. First near miss: spraining her ankle by falling up three measly steps on her way into TEAM HQ on her first day of work. Second: the ruckus she'd unintentionally caused when she'd taken down Webster Finch, the jerk. Alex ended up paying that farmer for damages she'd 'allegedly' caused his dusty, old field. Yeah, right. Lastly, and this was the most embarrassing, she'd recently tripped up those same damned steps and sprained her other ankle!

Alex said she was an accident waiting to happen. His sidekick, the handsome, debonair, and, okay, so he was married, too, Mark Houston, called her a gorgeous klutz. Of course, he'd chuckled with that deep baritone of his, which all by itself was enough to melt a girl's panties.

Well, duh. Newsflash! Accidents were what happened when people lived fast and hard. They took risks, and because they did, sometimes they messed up. *Get over it, guys!*

A person had to actually 'do something' to make mistakes. It sure as hell wasn't the know-it-all, big-mouthed do-nothings quarter-backing from their comfy, padded, Laz-Z-Boy recliners in the middle of their safe living rooms. No, it was the bloodied, wounded players on the actual field, the guys and gals being criticized and called names for fumbling the ball those arm-chair quarterbacks couldn't catch on a good day. Everlee was that man in the ring from President Theodore Roosevelt's speech, damn it. She was the guy in the arena. The one whose face was marred with dirt and blood and plenty of sweat, damn it. Of course she fell down a lot. She was the person actually running the race, wasn't she?

Everlee had long ago committed Roosevelt's comments to memory. Okay, so she was a bit of a klutz. No one ever said that man in the ring had to be an athlete. But honestly, there *was* something wrong with those three steps leading into TEAM HQ's entrance. Too bad no one believed her.

Her ride-or-die race-car driving father had always said life wouldn't be easy. But the only way to live it was head-on, straight into traffic, and without apology. And as much as she hated him now for what he'd done, the little girl inside of her still followed that sage advice. It was people like her who weren't afraid to stand up and take risks. They were the ones who made a difference in the world. Not some mama's boy who still lived in his parent's basement. Of course, there was another reason she was a klutz, a good reason, one she'd kept hidden for years and would never reveal until she was forced to. Ha, like anyone could make her do something she didn't want to do. But one of these days she'd have to tell Alex about her ADHD. Just not today.

"Jiminy Christmas, grow the hell up, why don'tcha," she grouched at all the big-mouthed, do-nothing idiots in the world.

It was crazy weird that she and her teammates who'd moved from Seattle—the bustling, enterprising, and beautiful Emerald City of the great Pacific Northwest—had ended up in the middle of Hicksville, Nowhere, Virginia. The change of pace, or total lack of pace, was stifling to the city girl she'd become. Utterly boring. And driving Everlee crazy bonkers. For a woman of her intense drive to be all she could be—not to mention her penchant for getting things done in too big of a hurry—country life in western Virginia was as slow as molasses in the dead of an arctic winter. Worse, there was no Starbucks within driving distance in any direction! WTF?

That had to change. She would've written to whoever the pretentious CEO of Starbucks was—she still had to look him or her up—but Alex, in his all-wise and all-knowing way, had already installed the most divine little gourmet coffee kiosk right in TEAM headquarters lobby. That by itself proved he was a genius. Who wasn't enamored by the scent of coffee? Or the scent of him?

Everlee rolled her eyes at the thought of possibly encountering her dream man again today. No wonder he'd recently been voted most successful entrepreneur on the Eastern Seaboard for the year. Again. Everlee would've voted for him herself if she could have, just based on the fragrance of whatever body wash he showered with or men's cologne he wore.

Yum!

Speaking of Alex… Unbeknownst to him or anyone else, he'd become Everlee's major crush. Yes, she'd liked a few of her Air Force buddies in the past, and she adored Mark Houston. But none compared to the man she would eagerly give her heart, body, and soul to—if he would only ask. And if he weren't already married to his pretty wife Kelsey, who Everlee also adored, just not in the same way. *Sigh.*

Her heart skipped a silly beat at her foolish infatuation with her boss. She loved Ed Sheeran, too, more so when she imagined herself dancing with Alex. They'd make such a good couple, him with his older way of leading a younger woman onto the dance floor. Her with her eyes aglow on him and nobody else. He had to have dance moves, didn't he? A man as tall, debonair, and sexy as Alex Stewart? She'd bet her last dollar on it, err, him.

But Everlee knew damned well better. The man might be a total knock-out, true. But he'd never, not even once, semi-flirted with any of the women he worked with, strayed from his marriage vows, or hinted he was anything more than just everyone's boss. She'd honestly tried not to gawk at him whenever he showed up, which wasn't very often now that construction was finally done on this complex of TEAM HQ buildings. But gah! That man was a rockstar. He was so handsome that he turned women's heads, all of them, not just hers. And he didn't even know it.

Of course he was happily married, and it showed. But that was part of the allure of the guy. He truly loved his wife, and Kelsey might as well work here, as often as she brought breakfast treats or other homemade goodies into TEAM HQ. It was the fact that he was an honest, loving, and faithful husband that made Alex all the more attractive. It was his rock-solid personality, his drive to succeed, and his written-in-stone moral compass that made him desirable.

Too bad it also made him off-limits. Everlee wasn't that kind of dumb. She would never do anything to come between

Alex and Kelsey. But a girl could dream, and when Everlee dreamed, it was always Alex she dreamed of.

She took a quick sip of her first piping hot Caffè Vanilla Frappuccino for the day and—

"Excuse me, ma'am—"

Everlee spat a volcanic stream of liquid at the silent intruder who'd effectively destroyed her idyllic, if imaginary, moment with her unattainable boss. "Who the hell are you and what the hell do you want?" she spewed along with her coffee.

The moment those unkind words flew out of her mouth, it registered where her Caffè Vanilla Frappuccino had landed. All over the shirt and tie of the very tall but unfortunate man standing on the other side of the TEAM's customer service counter.

Hurriedly, she followed that snarky question up with a sincere, "Oh, shit! I spit my coffee on you! I'm sorry! Stay right here. I'll grab some napkins."

Did he just glare at me? She wasn't sure. The big guy had yet to say anything else.

Shit, shit, shit! Jumping into action, she hobbled her ass around the customer service desk as fast as her big, black orthopedic boot allowed. Damned thing made her sound like a peg-legged pirate all the way across the lobby to the coffee kiosk. Jerking a handful of napkins out of the holder, she whirled on her rubber-soled, plastic boot heel and—*Whoa there, big guy*—ran smack into a solid, manly chest that—*oh, my gosh*—had to be made of pure granite. Or marble. It was that hard and solid—and warm. So warm. Quite lovely in fact.

Even as he gripped her biceps to keep her from falling backward, which was also really nice, Everlee couldn't help but sigh as the fingers on her napkin-less hand flattened over the eye-popping pecs beneath this guy's damp shirt. They enjoyed every bit of what they were feeling. Oh, did they ever. At the same time, they assessed the perfect rib structure and sturdy musculature beneath what had once been a crisply ironed, white business shirt. She'd spit coffee on his black silk tie, too. Damn, damn, damn. What a lousy first impression. For him and for her.

"I'm so, so sorry," she said again, contritely, as if repeating herself could make time rewind and let her start over again. Suck back that scalding Frappuccino. Take back those bitchy words. And let this nice man make the impression he'd obviously dressed for.

But those muscles. That chest. Everlee could barely breathe as her eyes traced the placard of this stranger's shirt all the way to his square-as-a-brick chin, which was already sporting the beginning of a heavy five o'clock shadow. This guy was no boy, uh-uh. He was all man. Every last bit of him, from the way he now controlled her body to the dark piercing glare that came along with his brooding personality. His current close proximity set her girly parts buzzing.

Oh, my hell. Her fingertips itched to fondle that stern chin, just to feel the roughness of it abrading her skin. Just to make this magnificent male specimen smile.

His dark hair, she couldn't decide if it was dark brown or black, was too long for military, but perfect for the brooding attitude he had going. The ends of it curled at his neckline, just above his collar, while the rest was combed neatly over his skull. His sideburns were precisely trimmed. Judging by his stiff, proper stance, his posture, and his obvious athletic condition, this man was most certainly former military.

His Adam's apple bobbed as he glowered down at her. Everlee didn't mind—or take the hint that he might not appreciate her scrutiny. Man, those midnight eyes of his were positively dangerous, like the dark blue shade under the curl of a killer wave off Hanauma Bay. Everlee was standing so close she could see tiny glints of green that reminded her of sea-glass flaring out from pupils so black that a girl could fall into them.

Yikes. A shiver raced up her spine at the magnetic connection she felt with this guy. The space between them crackled with electricity. Her throat worked just to swallow. Did he feel it too?

Oh, Jiminy Christmas, will you look at those lips. They were firm and right then pinched into two flat lines that declared utter disdain and disapproval. He hadn't yet offered one word to lessen her acute embarrassment. Not one. But her nostrils still flared at the old-fashioned scents of starch and spicy, masculine deodorant, mixed with a heady hint of cigarette smoke, wind, and what she was pretty sure was whiskey, coming off this guy.

Drinking already? So early? Meh. Who cares.

"H-how may I assist you?" she asked, her voice as hoarse and breathy as if this guy, whose name she didn't yet know, had just blessed her with an orgasm instead of a deathly glower. Even the manly disapproval on his face radiated enough sexual attraction to make her knees weak. Not what she needed, considering her well-deserved rep as a fall hazard. Which made her sound old and feeble, which Everlee most definitely was not. She'd just had a string of bad luck and that was over. Bad things came in threes. She'd filled the cosmically defined quota, damn it. In spades.

Clearing her throat and intending to sound stern, certainly more professional, Everlee's mouth ended up asking, "Whatz up?" as if he were just one of the TEAM guys. Which he wasn't. Them, she knew.

"I'm here for a job interview," he answered as he released her, his deep voice flat and emotionless. Sticking two thick, long fingers behind the Windsor knot at his throat, he loosened his coffee-spattered tie and ripped it from his collar. The thing snapped like a tiny whip, which only served to heighten the crazy, inappropriate sexual attraction Everlee was feeling.

Taking her wandering fingers back, she covered her mouth and coughed, then handed over the napkins and let this guy wipe the mess off himself. She could act just as bored as he was. To prove it, she turned her back and hobbled to her temporary workstation. "Your name?" she tossed indifferently over her shoulder.

He growled a throaty, "Shane Hayes."

"Hmm. You're not on Mr. Stewart's calendar this morning." At least she'd thoroughly scrutinized that before this disastrous meeting.

"I was told Senior Agent Mark Houston handled employment interviews."

"Mark. Right. He does," was all Everlee's steamy, scattered brain could come up with, as she settled her butt into the chair behind the customer service desk again. Damn Mondays. Of course Mark handled interviews. Everyone knew that. "Let me check Mark's calendar. Your name?"

This guy had followed her and was right then standing in her frag zone—or maybe she was in his. Thick, masculine brows lifted over those gorgeous eyes, creating a corresponding set of manly wrinkles across his forehead that only added to the caveman sex appeal he had going. He cleared his throat. "Already told you, ma'am. Shane. Hayes," he repeated extra slowly, like she was a dolt.

But oh, yeah. He had said that, hadn't he? By then, Mr. Hayes was standing nearly at attention on his side of her counter. He'd taken his suit jacket off. It draped over his left arm and his tie was wound around his right fist. That magnificent stubbled chin of his dipped low to his clavicles while he patted the Caffè Vanilla Frappuccino stains on his chest and down his centerline and…

Oh. My. Hell. He wasn't wearing a t-shirt. Everlee's throat went bone dry at the sight of two dusky, flat nipples revealed through the wet, white shirt. *Dayam.*

Embarrassed she was openly ogling this stranger, she squeezed her eyes shut to break the connection that had no business sizzling between them. Not like he'd felt it, because if he had, he wouldn't be acting like such a prick. She had no idea why she'd considered this guy handsome in the first place, not as stuffy as he was. Man, she needed to get laid.

Everlee forced her eyes back open and pulled up Mark's Monday To-Do-List on the computer without glancing even one more time at Mr. Stuffy Hayes. "I really am sorry, but you startled me. You're early. Mark hasn't come in yet."

"I'll wait."

Still avoiding eye contact, Everlee nodded toward the corner of the coffee kiosk and the adjoining sitting area of comfy chairs around a coffee table scattered with shooting magazines. This guy had as much personality as a post. "Please take a seat, Mr. Hayes. I'll let Mark know you're here the minute he arrives. And please let me pay to have your shirt and tie dry cleaned. It's the least I can do."

He glared out the front entry as if watching for somebody. Man, this guy was as tense as a post, too. Downright rigid. Didn't he know he'd score higher if he relaxed before job interviews?

"Never mind. I'll take care of it myself."

Of course you will.

"At least let me get coffee for you while you wait, okay?" Everlee poured sincerity into the question. Alex was right. She *was* an accident waiting to happen, and apparently, she'd happened all over this poor man right before an important interview. She'd ruined his first impression.

But what a sight. Tall, dark, and incredibly handsome, this man moved with the smooth grace of a lethal predator. Those dark blue eyes of his parsed the front lobby as if he were judging it on sight and finding everything in it insignificant. He acted like he owned the place. As if he ruled The TEAM, and Alex was merely an interloper keeping his seat warm until he showed up.

From this safe distance, Everlee could better appreciate the bespoke suit of gunmetal gray Shane Hayes was wearing. His shirt was more silver than just plain white, and she wouldn't be surprised if its buttons weren't stamped with Winchester or Remington. Whoever this guy was, he was thickly muscled, built like a boxer, thin hipped, long legged, but arms and hands loose at his sides. He was light on his feet, considering the bulk of his neck and shoulders and…

Man, that chest. Heat unspooled at Everlee's core, and she was pretty sure she was drooling. She ran her fingers over her lips just in case. This guy's biceps strained the sleeves of the jacket he'd just put back on, and damned if hiding that chest under a jacket wasn't a crime. Shane Hayes was simply thicker and taller than Alex. Where Alex had an elegant, gentlemanly build, this man was built like a brick wall. Not even his expensive suit could hide that.

Hayes shook his head when two gorgeous Springer Spaniels appeared at the front door, their long, pink tongues hanging out, their entire bodies waggling like they thought he'd be thrilled to see them.

"Are those your dogs? They're beauti—"

"Yes, damn it," he hissed, cutting her off. "I'll be right back."

Chapter Four

Shane was halfway to the door when that gorgeous, but addle-brained woman at the front desk called out, "Bring them inside. They'll fit right in. We love dogs here."

Yeah, that'll never happen. He shot her a terse look that was half-annoyance, half-angry disbelief over his shoulder. Stewart's secretary was a pretty thing, but flighty as hell, and her babysitting his dogs while he fucked up his one shot at joining The TEAM would only add to the shitty way this morning was headed. Downhill, damn it.

"No, thanks. They should've stayed in the truck." *Where they belong.* But no, they'd wiggled out of their harnesses. That was how they'd gotten free, clever girls. All they'd had to do then was squeeze out the window he'd left partially open for them, and here they were. Happy as hell to see him. "I'll be back in a minute."

"Stop right there, Mr. Hayes," the secretary ordered with a titch of stern authority in her voice. "Bring those adorable dogs inside like I said. Please. I'll be glad to watch them while you successfully handle your interview. Mark just got in, and you're precisely what he's looking for. Hurry up! You don't have time to waste. He's waiting for you. Chop, chop!"

Damn, she was bossy. Shane turned to tell her no. Flat no. This day had already gone to hell. With that blast of her coffee, he'd lost the edge a good impression could've made. Imposing his dogs on her was the dumbest idea ever.

By then, she was thumping her way over to him with plenty of attitude and noise. Well, guess what? If this was a test of wills, she'd lose. Until her lips curled into a genuine smile, and the sparkle in her coffee-brown eyes challenged the golden light of the sunbeams breaking through the plate-glass windows behind him.

"I… I…" He started to shut her down, to tell her he didn't need anyone's help, least of all hers. Especially *not* hers. But the stubborn rebuttal his brain came up with got stuck in his throat, and, shit. "I don't know your name," came out instead of, *'You've already helped more than enough.'*

Her hand came forward. "Let's start over, shall we?" she asked demurely. "Good morning, Mr. Shane Hayes. I'm Everlee Yeager, formerly Lieutenant Yeager, Chief of Security Forces at Joint Base Elmendorf-Richardson in Anchorage, Alaska. It's very nice to meet you. May I please get a decent cup of coffee for you before you head in for your interview? And for your information, I'm not Mr. Stewart's secretary. That would be Paige; she's on leave. I'm only filling in for her until I'm cleared for active duty." She waggled her booted foot at him. "As you already know, I can be a bit of a klutz."

Shane nodded, aware that the palm his fingers were wrapped around was much smaller and definitely more slender. Feminine. Soft and tender. But firm. LT Yeager's grip was quite solid in fact. She might be more than he'd first assumed because she was giving back as good as she was getting. Her eye contact was impressively direct, and judging by her grip, she truly believed she was in charge.

He tipped his head to her, just once, released her fingers, and let her think whatever she wanted. In the end, it wouldn't matter. Once Stewart kicked him out, he'd never see her again. "Good morning, Ms. Yeager. Pleased to meet you. Any relation to Chuck?"

"Ha!" And just that fast, she ditched the polish and changed back to the energetic spitfire he'd first met. "I wish I were related to America's number one Flying Ace, but no, darn it. I'm not even a distant relative. I did get to meet Brigadier General Chuck Yeager at Air Command Staff College, though. Bright, charming man, a hero our nation should be damned proud of."

The warm glow on this woman's face increased along with the sincerity in her wide-open smile. Her lips were lush and pink and wet, damn it. No lipstick, only the barest hint of make-up, and none of that charcoal-smudged crap most women did to their eyes. Her copper-colored hair was cut short and framed her oval face perfectly. Didn't they call that a pixie style? Her lashes were clean ebony feathers over clear skin the color of that mocha latte thing she'd spit on him. Not Spanish, though. But definitely some other enchanting country mingled with her European white.

"Agreed," Shane replied hoarsely.

When the phone on the desk behind her rang, Ms. Yeager released his hand. "Listen, while you go meet Mark, I'll handle your dogs. Tell me their names, so I can make friends."

Shane hesitated. "Are you sure?"

"I love dogs, and Paige keeps treats in her desk for our four-legged visitors. Come on, give. Now please, what are these cute babies' names?"

Of course, Molly's and Dolly's bodies waggled like they'd just found their new best friend.

The phone kept ringing, but Ms. Yeager seemed more interested in him and his dogs. Which actually said something about her, that people who were live and in-person were her first priority. She'd chosen to let the phone system handle the incoming call instead of putting him on hold and making him wait on her caller like some insignificant lackey. She'd put him first. Shane liked that small nuance to this klutzy woman with big, brown eyes.

"Molly and Dolly. They're two-year-old littermates and trained service dogs, but they can still be a handful. Are you—?"

"Sure? Yes, positive. Go, go, go." Ms. Yeager shooed him toward the hallway at the left side of her desk—her left, his right—and headed for the entry. "I'll let your girls in. Mark's office is second on the right. His door's always open. He's waiting for you. Hurry!"

While Ms. Yeager thumped around him to open the door, Shane obeyed. She was good for her word since neither Molly nor Dolly tracked him inside like they usually did once they spotted him. He gave them one quick backward glance and saw that they were both busy impressing LT Yeager, umm, Everlee, wagging their tails and sitting like good girls, while she cooed and baby talked at them.

Shane hurried. The hallway he entered was brightly lit with recessed overhead lighting. Plush, red carpet covered the floor. Four rosewood office doors on each side, but only the second was open. The brass name-plate on the first closed door declared: `Alex Stewart`.

A chill raced up Shane's spine as he passed it, and his inner chicken-shit was glad for the temporary reprieve. That closed door meant Stewart was either already occupied or he wasn't in for the day. Either way, it gave Shane time to ask Mr. Houston when would be the best time to set up a face-to-face meeting with the guy. Later. Tomorrow, maybe. Next week? Next month? *Next year?*

Yeah, no. Shane refused to accept any job offer provided he'd even get one, until he'd had his chance with Stewart. No sense being hired only to get fired the same day. Before he stepped into Mark's view, he ran a hand over the still damp, coffee stain down his front, sucked in a deep breath, and ventured into Mr. Houston's office looking like the loser he was. Damn it.

"You must be Shane Hayes," Mark said from behind his desk, his arm outstretched over it and his hand reaching out like a friend. "Good to meet you."

Shane swallowed hard, feeling like a liar and a betrayer all wrapped up into one nervous mess of shit. At least, Mr. Houston was kind enough not to draw attention to the coffee stain. "Good to meet you too, sir," he replied, returning the handshake. "Appreciate you taking the time to meet me."

"Sure, no problem. And it's Mark, not sir. We don't do titles here, and we're always looking for a few good men, a few good gals, too. I see you've met Everlee." The man was pleasant, dark-haired, and built like a beast. Dressed like he was, all in black, he could've passed for a nightclub bouncer. Or a Marine. And he eyed the coffee stain on Shane's shirt with a teasing smile instead of sharp disapproval.

"Ah, yeah. She's a pistol."

"You have no idea." Mark gestured to the wooden chair alongside his desk.

Shane had done his homework. Mark hailed from Ohio, had served honorably in the Corps, and was one of the first men Stewart had lured away from active duty when he'd started his business. That either said something about Houston or Stewart. Or it said a helluva lot about Shane, since he was the one still looking for decent work.

"Before we begin…" He cleared his throat. "Would it be possible to speak with Mr. Stewart first? Prior to our interview? I should've made that clear when you called, and I'm sorry I didn't. But I've had time to think, and if it's at all possible—"

"No problem. Turn around and meet the boss. Alex Stewart, Shane Hayes. Shane—"

"I know exactly who he is," a terse male voice hissed at Shane's back.

Ah, shit. He pivoted to his left, not sure how he'd missed the assassin seated in the corner behind the gawddamned open door. Clever asshole.

"Mr. S-S-Stewart," he choked, his throat and tongue as dry as a sandstorm outside Kabul. "Sure. Yeah, I've heard of you." *Cough, cough.* "Pleased to meet you, sir." *Oh, God, I'm dead.*

Damned if Stewart's left eyelid didn't twitch. Shane cringed all the way to his toes and his heart damned near climbed out of his chest. He'd pissed Stewart off with that one stupid word: *Sir.* Shane knew better. Stewart was non-com, a sergeant, an enlisted grunt, not an officer. And Shane— *shit!shit!shit!*—had committed the unforgivable sin of calling a man who had actually worked in the Corps, *sir.*

He stumbled over himself to rectify the fatal error. "I mean, yes, I've heard of you, Mr. Stewart. Who hasn't? Didn't mean to lump you in with asshats like my CO. Won't happen again." *And now I'm talking too damned much.*

"Sit," Stewart hissed.

The guy Shane had thought he could work for was mean-eyed, dark-haired, and dressed impeccably sharp in a light-tan suit, a crisp, white—and impeccably clean—dress shirt, and brown silk tie. His blue eyes were daggers, though, sharp as the arctic wind. Right then, the cold rolling out of them drilled Shane like a thousand frozen arrows, all fitted with titanium, razor-sharp tips, and hitting the only dumbass target in the room. Him. But beneath that dressed-for-success business apparel, lay a very cold, lethal sniper, and Shane was as good as dead.

He nodded once and took the seat by Mark's desk, but turned the chair enough that he faced Stewart on his left and Mark behind the desk on his right. Stiffening his spine, Shane dropped his palms to his knees and studied the sniper in the corner, wishing he could start this morning over.

On his reputation alone, Shane had expected Stewart to be bigger and wider. Certainly not the elegantly dressed professional who looked more like he'd just stepped off some high-class business magazine instead of a gun range. There was no mistaking the killer vibe shuddering off the athletically built, clean-shaven owner of The TEAM, though. If Shane had met Stewart in a dark alley, he would've considered him lethal at first sight, and he might've turned tail and run. Then. Not now. He'd come here today to speak with Stewart, and he wasn't leaving until he did. Despite his arrogant glare, this man deserved to know what only Shane could tell him.

"Boss, here's everything you need to know about Shane." Mark slipped a file folder across his desk to his boss. "He's perfect for The TEAM." Houston was everything Stewart wasn't. Friendly. Relaxed. Kind.

For now.

Stewart waved the offer off. "Why are you here?" he clipped at Shane, his tone nasty and his glare full of more killer arrows.

By then, Shane's heart was rat-a-tat-tatting in his chest like an overheated fifty-cal. He swallowed hard, but shit. Nervous or not, this was why he'd come here today, to finally meet Alex Stewart. Face time, damn it. This was all Shane had wanted—and so much more. Too much. *Kiss that shit goodbye.*

Summoning his courage, he raked his fingers over his hair and faced the bastard who still might kill him. "I need a decent job, that's true. But I really came here to tell you what happened that morning, Mr. Stewart. You need to know I wasn't drunk like the papers said, and I wasn't texting or distracted. The accident, it just happened and—" And there was no way Shane could gauge what was going through Stewart's mind. No expression. No reaction to his words. Just the stone-cold stare of America's deadliest sniper bearing down on him.

"What are you talking about?" Mark asked. "What happened that you need to explain?"

That was an unexpected development. Stewart hadn't ranted to everyone about the shithead who'd killed his family? That might be good news. But it also let Shane know there was no TEAM hit list with his name at the top. *Yet.* He took the only opportunity he expected would come his way and broke eye contact with Stewart. Turning to Mark, he asked, "You mean you don't know?"

"I guess not, so tell me. What's going on, Shane?" That was the other thing Shane liked about Mark. He relied on first names, not ranks or stuffy salutations.

"I'm…" Shane swallowed hard and tried again. "I'm him, Mr. Houston. I'm the guy who killed his wife and daughter. Me. I'm the bastard that destroyed Mr. Stewart's life and ruined his USMC career." He licked his lips before he could go on. "It was me."

Mark groaned. "You were driving that delivery truck? God, the one that—"

"I was, yes."

Mark shoved his chair back, his fingertips firmly planted on his desk "Boss, I'm sorry. His records are stellar, but I had no idea he was that guy."

Crap. The way Mark said, *'that guy,'* sounded a lot like a death knell. Shane thought Mark might be an ally. Guess he'd thought wrong. Tremors began deep inside his already tense body.

"Of course you didn't know," Stewart snapped out like a whip. "It wasn't your business. It happened before we met."

"I'm sure sorry, Mr. Stewart," Shane said before he found his ass kicked to the curb. Might as well get it over with. His voice wavered like a chicken-shit coward's, but that was just nerves. He'd tried his best to prepare for this meeting, just hadn't expected he'd be ambushed right out of the gate. He'd thought he'd have more time. Also thought he'd have more courage.

Deep down, Shane knew he hadn't set out to hurt anyone that morning. He hadn't been charged with vehicular manslaughter, hadn't even been ticketed. Several witnesses had stepped forward and verified everything he'd told the police. That he'd already applied his brakes before Mrs. Stewart's car had swerved into the intersection. That he wasn't to blame. Hell, even the utility guys working the electrical nightmare in Alexandria that day weren't to blame or no one was held liable. They'd taken all necessary precautions, had posted more than enough hazard cones, blinking barricades, and warning signs. That there was no intent, just dumb bad luck on everyone's part that morning.

But Shane suspected Stewart already knew everything. Still, he explained, "There was a power outage the night before. A severe wind storm. It lasted most of the next morning. There were four-way stops all over Alexandria to handle the morning rush. But traffic was heavy, and every street was a mess, and..." Shane couldn't bear to look at the man whose wife and daughter he'd killed. He kept his head down, his gaze fastened on the hardwood flooring. But he now knew there was no future for him here. Not anymore. Stewart wasn't that kind of stupid. As soon as he said what he'd come to say, Shane was out of there.

"It was early, still dark," he went on. "Lots of tour buses on the streets. Lots of tourists on the sidewalks and crosswalks. People were jay-walking everywhere. You know how bad rush hour traffic in Olde Town gets. Traffic lights were flickering greens, yellows, and reds, then not working at all. Someone got confused, thought he had the right-of-way. Didn't even slow down. I don't know, maybe he was in a hurry or something, but he ran the four-way stop. I'd already entered the intersection. I slammed my brakes to miss the guy. Thought I got off easy. Only thing in front of my van was an iron lamp post on the corner. No great loss there. But then your wife's car—"

He swallowed hard, the rest of the story agonizingly hard to tell. The man who'd run the four-way stop had also clipped Sara Stewart's vehicle and sent it careening like a bullet into Shane's path. There was no way for him to stop in time. He'd already been standing on his brake pedal. Didn't matter. The much heavier delivery truck he'd been driving broadsided the driver side of her much smaller, cheaper car with enough impact to flatten the passenger side against that iron light post. Her airbags went off. Just the front airbags. There were none in the sides and nothing but seatbelts in the back.

Sara and Abby Stewart took a hard hit. A lethal hit. Abby had been sitting right behind her mom. She'd had her seatbelt on, for all the good that did. Shane still remembered the wide-open surprise on that little blonde girl's face at the precise moment of impact. How her slender, little-girl body had flopped sideways within the confines of her seatbelt. How her neck had snapped. How her mother had screamed. How the crushing silence afterward became the biggest, loudest noise of his life.

He couldn't, didn't dare lift his chin and look Stewart in the eye. Didn't want to see the pain in those wicked blues. Or shit, the tears, if the man's heart was breaking all over again. Shane's was. But it should. He was the transgressor, would never be anything more. Not a day went by he didn't wish he'd never been born. His heart couldn't heal from what had happened that awful morning. What was one more blow to a pulverized organ that had been leaking blood for years?

But Stewart needed to know what happened from the man who'd been there, who'd stolen his family. So Shane continued. "I was the first at her side. Ah, your wife's side," he explained quickly, needing to get this done, his ass in his truck with his dogs, and his truck back on the road. "I'd already reversed my truck away from her car so I could reach her. But the driver's door was mashed inward, and the passenger side had curled around the l-l-lamp post. I couldn't get either door open. Not even Abby's d-d-door." Saying that little girl's name would forever tear Shane's resolve to shreds. "The things wouldn't budge."

How he'd tried! There was no reason to tell Stewart he'd bloodied his hands trying, or that he'd broken his knuckles when rage at his impotence took over and he'd punched the lamp post.

"Your van was a heavier than her son of a bitchin' car," Stewart said hoarsely. "She had to have that gawddamned car. They never stood a chance!"

There was so much rage and pain in those few words. So much hate. Shane would've agreed, but he knew who'd really killed Stewart's family. Him. He was responsible. Blame him. Not the car. Only—him.

He closed his eyes, determined to weather this wicked storm from which there would be no relief. Not today. Not ever. He should've stayed home that long-ago morning. Sure as hell wished he had today.

"Your wife talked to me," he explained quietly, the misery in his heart suffocating him all over again. "Her window was shattered, but I talked to her. I did. And she talked with me. I asked if she was okay, and she said she was, and then I asked your daughter how she was doing, but she wasn't answering. I thought the crash just knocked her out. Your wife thought so, too. Sara kept telling me everything was going to be okay…" And there it was, another heartbreaking name that never failed to stab Shane again and again… "I… I wanted to believe her," he stuttered. "She sounded so sure, but I was scared I was going to lose them both, and the cops weren't there yet, and neither were the paramedics, and then it started to rain, and I—"

"They were never yours to lose!" Alex boomed. "They were mine, you asshole! They were all I had!"

I know. I know. God, I know.

Shane bit the inside of his cheek, wishing his mouth would stop with the running monologue. Because of that morning, Sara and Abby were not just names of people he'd never met nor cared about. They weren't just light reading in the evening newspaper. Stewart might never understand, but because of that cataclysmic meeting, Sara's and Abby's deaths were just as real to Shane as his mom's. They were his special angels, and he talked with all three of them every gawddamned day. They were inside his head and heart to stay, wedged in tight like their car had been wedged between his truck and that damned light post. Which was why Shane was here. Alex needed to know Shane loved his wife and daughter like the sisters he'd never had. They were part of him. Too. A devastatingly sad part, but a part nonetheless.

"I do know that, but Sara—your wife—she asked me to get Abby out first, and by then, some guy showed up with a crowbar, and we tried to open Abby's door. Only it wouldn't budge. No matter how much weight we put into it, we couldn't make it open, and then the fire department showed and the cops, and she still wasn't answering us or her mom, and we got pushed out of their way, and—"

"They used son of a bitchin' jaws-of-life to get my wife out," Stewart snarled, his voice breaking. "Son of a bitchin' worthless piece-of-shit car!"

"I know, I know." *Because I was there and I watched everything until the ambulances arrived and took them away. Until I knew I'd killed them... That they were dead because of me...*

Shane took a deep breath. There would be no forgiveness today. All he'd done was cause Mr. Stewart more pain, and that wasn't what he'd wanted nor why he'd come here. "Anyway, you know the rest, I know you do." Another dry swallow refused to go down. "I never should've come here today." He licked his parched lips. "I'm sorry. I rescind my job application. I don't want to work here. But honest, I only came because I felt I needed to face you, Mr. Stewart. To tell you that I'm so gawddamned sorry for what I did to you that morning. I'd do anything to change what happened. I am so, so gawddamned sorry."

Blinking through the blur gathering in his eyes, Shane lifted to his feet, ready to escape, but intending to at least shake Stewart's hand before he did. Lifting his arm, which felt like it weighed a ton, for the last time he faced the man whose life he'd destroyed. Shane stuck his hand out and said, "I appreciate you taking the time to at least see me. I'll just go, and you'll never hear from me ag—"

"Why don't you tell me what really happened?" Stewart was on his feet now and fighting mad. "All you've shared so far is what's in police and insurance reports. I already know that crap. I also know the lies the media spread that you were drunk, but you weren't. I damned well know that, too! Why don't you man up and talk to me instead of running away with your tail between your legs like a gawddamned coward?"

Shane blinked and stared into the pit of utter misery. His arm was still stuck out like the damned thing was frozen. It might've been, because Stewart's eyes were glacial. But there was something else glimmering in them that Shane couldn't quite define—or didn't want to face. It was hard to see past the agony he'd created. Again. It seemed all he did was cause this man pain. What a stupid idea to think he could ever work here, for Stewart. Shane wished he were back in Kabul fighting assassins. Death there would be honorable.

He dropped his hand. Like a shot, Stewart squared his shoulders, immediately putting Shane on the defensive and blocking the only way out. Stewart was more formidable on his feet. His shoulders were broader, his chest was bigger, and his thighs were thicker. His top lip curled into a wicked sneer. His nostrils flared as if there wasn't enough air in the room for both of them.

"Boss," Mark said quietly.

"Stay out of this!" Stewart spat.

Instinctively, Shane's fists clenched, but he'd never fight Stewart. Instantly, he relaxed his fingers and shook them to loosen the Devil Dog urge to strike first and hit hard. If Stewart needed to beat him to a pulp to feel better, Shane meant to stand there and take every last punch, kick, and slap. He deserved it. But he had no idea what the hell Stewart had meant or what he wanted. What else was there but facts?

"Your mother died that morning," Stewart hissed. "Tell me about that, why don't you? I want the gawddamned details, every last son of a bitchin' one of them. Why were you even behind that wheel?"

"Boss," Mark said again.

Stewart shut him down with a nasty, "No, Mark. He started this. I'm finishing it. I want to know every gawddamned thing, Hayes. Every detail! Answer me! You weren't in a decent frame of mind to be driving. You couldn't have been. You might not've meant to kill them, but you sure as hell shouldn't have been behind that son of a bitchin' wheel!"

Now he was getting personal. And mean. This wasn't how Shane had seen this meeting going, not at all. Every protective instinct inside slammed the walls to his heart down and locked the sweet memories of his mom up tight, far away from this dangerous killer. Stewart had no right. Except he did, and Shane understood. Stewart was right to be angry. But he'd never gain access to the memory of Shane's mom.

The nasty inquisition continued. "How gawddamned old were you? Fifteen? Sixteen? Did you even have a gawddamned driver license?"

"Almost eighteen, Mr. Stewart. I was nearly of legal age and I was gainfully employed and—"

"Alex! Stop calling me Mr. Stewart! Wake up and talk to me like a man. Really son of a bitchin' talk, gawddamn you! Isn't that why you're here? To get everything off your shoulders and pile the shit you're sick of carrying on mine?"

"No, sir!" Shane yelled back, his hands still at his side, but pissed at the pompous jerk squaring off with him. "I had a killer migraine that morning! I didn't sleep the night before, because Mom…" *Jesus, I don't believe I'm going to tell him this, but…* "My mom, my poor, sweet Mom, died at twelve-thirty-two that same gawddamned morning! I couldn't close my eyes and sleep because all I saw was what I… Did. To.

Her! I'm the one who let her die. She had breast cancer, or did you already know that, too?" *You ornery asshole!* "She thought it went into remission. We both did. But it came back, okay? It fuckin' came back like fuckin' cancer always fuckin' does!"

Shane sucked in a breath to compose himself. He'd never used so many fucks in any conversation before. But he was running on adrenaline and there was no way to calm down now. Stewart asked for this and he was going to get it. All of it. "Only it came back in her brain, and by the time we found it, there was nothing anybody could do to stop it or keep it from spreading. So I stayed with her every minute of those last two weeks of her life, and I never left her side. I couldn't, *Alex.*" He threw as much venom into the bastard's name as he could. "I sang every last one of her favorite songs to her. I read the newspaper to her every morning." *And I cried my heart out the whole damned time.* "She was blind by then, but she never—not once—ever complained. But none of that changed anything, did it? She still died—*Alex!*"

Shane twisted the man's name with enough sarcasm to kill a horse. "What do you want from me? Yes, I went to work that morning. I had to! I was a stupid college kid with a fuckin' funeral to pay for and a two-bit job to make sure it was good enough for... My. Mom!" He stabbed his chest with his thumb. "You think you know everything? You think you lost everything that day? Well, so the fuck did I! Only one death wasn't enough shit for me to deal with, was it? No! I get to live with three innocent deaths on my head. Three! For the rest of my fucked-up life! I killed three people that day!"

"You didn't kill your mother—"

Too late, you pompous asshole!! "Shut the fuck up!" Shane roared. "I'm not talking about Mom with you anymore." He was done. He'd lost his composure and his mind for ever thinking this meeting was the good and right thing to do. If he stayed one more second, he'd either have to fight his way out or he'd break down.

Suddenly, Mark squared off beside Alex.

Great, now he had to fight both of them. *Well, bring it on!*

But there was no sense explaining that morning to anyone else ever again. Kindness and honor were never their own reward. What a shittin' lie. Shane licked his dry lips, swallowed hard, and blew out a gut full of regret that would never die.

"This was the stupidest idea ever," he told the floor. "I thought I could give you closure or" —he shrugged— "something. I never meant to hurt anyone or to cause you more pain. I'm sorry I was in that intersection that morning, and I'm sorry I'm here today. Thanks for…" God, for what? Nothing? Another slap in the face?

"Sit," Stewart hissed, then to Mark he bit out, "Hire the son of a bitch."

Before Shane could refuse the nasty offer—because there was no way in hell he'd work for Stewart now—the man stalked out of the office and slammed the door behind him.

Shane sank to his knees then, broken again and so damned tired of the fight. All he'd wanted was to give Stewart some measure of peace. He'd never expected Stewart would forgive him. He shouldn't. That would've been asking too much, and Shane had never expected that. With all his heart, he wished Stewart had beaten the shit out of him.

It couldn't hurt any worse.

Chapter Five

"Well, that went to shit in a son of a bitchin' hurry," Alex snarled as he slammed himself into his office. He was flaming pissed that he'd lost his temper—again! More pissed that he'd all but attacked the young man who'd had guts enough to face him after all these years. Who'd been smart enough to come here for a job, instead of accepting less from anyone else. Who'd had to be one brave son of a bitch to confront the bastard that might hate him, or want to kill him on sight. Requesting this job interview had to have been the gawddamnedest, hardest thing Hayes had ever done in his life. And like the ass he obviously could still be, Alex had rained hell all over the man. Real brave, that. Real stupid was more like it.

Alex slammed his day planner onto his desk, sending it skidding across the polished, slick surface as he circled behind the elegant chunk of marble to the window. He was so angry! Like a crazed lion protecting his kill, he stared over his credenza at the scenery but didn't see a damned thing. Only the two blonde, blue-eyed sweethearts he'd buried before their time.

The pain of losing them never went away. It couldn't. Not because he hadn't tried to let it go and move forward, but because he still and would forever miss his first wife and his oldest daughter. Sara and Abby. God, he still loved them, and he missed them savagely.

Looking up at the ceiling, a roar sprang up from deep in his gut, the need to scream at God and swear and cry and… *Son of a bitch!* He hadn't been this out of control in years. But he would not give in to that level of rage again. He refused to backslide or relent. He was not that man, that desperate lovesick fool anymore.

Son of a bitch! Remembering was hard.

Forcing himself to recall the positives in his life, to count them one by one, Alex calmed the cruel side of his nature into restless, uneasy submission. Nothing today was as bleak as it had been back then. Those first years after their deaths had been Hell on Earth. He'd been the *Walking Dead,* no doubt about that. But he had Kelsey now, and she'd brought a wellspring of quiet wisdom and gentle knowledge into his life. She'd showed him better ways, more logical ways to vent and, ultimately, to heal. He didn't curse God anymore, and most of the time he wasn't the ass he used to be.

And Alex didn't hate Shane Hayes. Never had. Hadn't even considered it. He'd hated that Sara and Abby had died, sure. But the only person he'd truly blamed and hated for years had been himself. That because he hadn't been with Sara and Abby when they'd needed him most. A husband and father should never live when his wife and little girl didn't. Yet even that was a false negative, one of those sucking black holes grieving people often dug themselves into and spent the rest of their lives trying to escape.

Taking another calming breath, Alex rolled his shoulders and popped his neck, staving off the killer migraine he'd come to expect after temper tantrums like this one. Taking another slow, steady breath, then exhaling just as slowly, he did as Kelsey had taught him. It seemed a useless, small thing for a hard-charging man like him to do, but Kelsey was right. Controlling his breathing helped. The red-hot anger dissipated into aching nothingness. The self-incrimination in the center of his chest left like the ghost it had always been.

Hayes should sure as hell hate him, especially now that Alex had shown his true colors. His old true colors. Alex wouldn't blame Hayes if he did. But he deserved better, and Alex was finally the man Kelsey had always thought he was. God, he adored that woman.

Because of her he wasn't hateful, mean, or resentful anymore. Couldn't remember when it happened, but he had really moved on. Didn't even hate himself like he used to. He'd healed, and he liked who he was today. Well, most days. Not this morning, but…

That was the son of a bitchin' problem. Alex couldn't explain why he'd gone off the rails so quickly, or why he'd all but attacked Shane Hayes. For what? It wasn't as if he'd bragged or rubbed those untimely deaths in Alex's face. The poor guy hadn't done anything but confess to murder. Three murders, for the love of God. Three murders he sure as hell hadn't committed.

Turning away from the scene outside that he wasn't seeing, Alex took another breath and sank into his chair. Just as quickly, he dug his heels into the carpet and shoved the chair back from his desk. He needed to get a grip, march back into Mark's office and face Hayes, like a man this time instead of an asshole. The kid deserved respect, not bullying.

Better yet, Alex needed to talk with Hayes, really converse and get him some help. No one should waste the rest of his life stuck in the past, worrying what he should've done differently or better. Shane Hayes wasn't a murderer, and he deserved a second chance. That long-ago morning had simply been a mix of unbearably tragic accidents for everyone involved.

Not just for Alex. Hayes was right; he was still carrying those three deaths. Blaming himself for things that were out of his control. Son of a bitchin' survivor's guilt. It never gave a guy a break, but if he let it, it could surely destroy the rest of his life.

Alex ran a hand over his chin. Mark was right. Hayes was a good fit for The TEAM. Just looking at him told Alex all he needed to know. Thickly-muscled up top, but lean through his waist and thighs, Hayes was obviously self-disciplined. A self-starter. He didn't mind hard work or manual labor. Alex saw his hands. They were callused, the nails chipped, the cuticles ragged. Shane was earnest, honest, tried, and true. A damned good sniper and a man of integrity, according to his after-action reports. That he'd joined the Corps immediately after he'd buried his mother was troublesome, though. Why would any guy follow in the footsteps of the man whose wife and daughter he'd accidentally killed? Alex needed to know.

The hint of whiskey on Shane's breath worried him, too. He'd gone down that same road to nowhere after Sara's and Abby's deaths. Had Shane? Was he a closet alcoholic like Junior Agent Renner Graves had once been? Did he carry a flask everywhere he went? And if he drank, was he a sloppy drunk, or did he know when to say enough? Could he handle his liquor? Was he worth the risk?

Hell, yes. Alex already knew that. Any man brave enough to face him after all these years was precisely who he wanted on his TEAM. And if Shane had a drinking problem, it was none of Alex's business. The truth would out. If Shane was as smart as Alex knew he was, he'd find a way to handle it himself. That was what men did. They manned up, by hell.

Son of a bitch, Stewart. First impressions count, damn it. On both sides of the fence. And now you proved you're an out-of-control asshat, while he proved he was a damned good man. What were you thinking?

Truth was, he hadn't expected Shane would show up today. More than anyone, Alex understood the misdirected sense of responsibility that came with survivor's guilt. For years, he'd carried a gut full of self-hatred for not having been with Sara and Abby that morning. *He* should've been the one driving that day. *He* should've been in the country with his family where he'd belonged. Not on the other side of the globe doing Uncle Sam's dirty work.

But he hadn't been there. He'd been a world away. And those were the immutable facts. He didn't have to agree with them, and he sure as hell didn't like them. But facts were rigid sons of bitches. They were what they were. Reality. And a stupid, hard-headed man could waste the rest of his life blaming himself for things he couldn't change and hadn't been responsible for. Or he could get on with the art of living, and in doing so, honor the people he'd lost. Like Sara and Abby. Like Kelsey's two innocent sons. She'd suffered an incalculable loss, too. And because of her pain, she was the one—the only one—who'd gotten through to him. Who'd saved him.

Alex let his lungs and belly fill with another deep cleansing breath. It had taken years, but he understood now that he wasn't to blame for everything that went wrong in the world. Neither was Shane. Accidents happened, damn it. And the only relief Alex had found in all those police and insurance reports was in understanding that fate was just a damned fickle bitch.

Understanding that Sara and Abby had died quickly, that his wife and daughter were together at the end brought some measure of comfort. There was peace in that knowledge, and that was precisely what Shane needed now. A measure of peace in his soul, a hand up, and the comfort that came with belonging to a family like The TEAM. It still wasn't enough, but that was another one of those damned facts. The people you loved the most would still die. That didn't mean you should stop living. If anything, you should live better.

Alex stuck his knuckles in his eyes and wiped the annoying glimmer of tears away. He wasn't the angry, bleeding, belligerent, grieving son of a bitch he used to be. Well, he was still grieving—always would be that—and Hayes had certainly stirred up a hornets' nest of bitter, wretched memories that Alex would rather leave in the past.

But the kid needed help finding a way out of his own survivor's guilt, and he'd come to the right place. The TEAM was made up of a bunch of survivors. Hell, look at Beau Villanueva and Maverick Carson. Look at Harley Mortimer and Jameson Tenney. *Shit, look at me.*

The phone on his desk rang, startling Alex out of his melancholy. He glared at the damned thing, daring it to ring again. Of course, it shrilled right back at him, right on cue, like phones did, damned annoying things.

Oh, Kelsey. Good. Just seeing her name on the lighted caller-ID strip sent a shot of relief straight to Alex's gut. The woman always seemed to know when to reach out and touch him.

His greedy fingers latched onto the receiver like a lifeline. "Hey, sweetheart, whatcha need?" he asked, keeping his tone neutral. His fingers were shaking, what the hell?

"Just want you to know Maverick will be in late today because he's here changing my tire. Guess I picked up a roofing nail yesterday, maybe when I took your dad in for his weekly appointment. There was a lot of construction going on there, and flashing barricades were all over the parking lot. Nothing major. Maverick will check in with you as soon as he gets to work."

"Sure, no problem. Harley's already down at the barns. A nail, huh?"

"Yes, but it's nothing you need to worry about. Maverick will run my tire over to Stark's garage on his way in. We can go get it later tonight, and tomorrow I'll be good as new." She always sounded so damned upbeat. It was hard being even a few miles away from her when he was feeling this ornery and mean. One kiss was all it would take to set him right.

"No problem," he told her. "For you, anything."

"What's wrong, honey?"

Alex ran a hand over his face. There was no sense lying. Kelsey knew him too well. "Nothing really." *Just me being my usual dumbassed self.*

"But something. I can hear it in your voice. You're not angry, you're… you're hurting. What's going on, honey? Did somebody die?"

And now he'd frightened her. "No, sweetheart. Everyone's fine, well…" He rolled his shoulders to shake off that damned migraine before it ramped up any worse. "I just met the young man who was driving the delivery van the morning that—"

"Oh, no. Alex, I'm so sorry. I'm on my way. Don't go anywhere."

"No, sweetheart, stay home with the kids. I'm fine. Really. It just hit me harder than I thought it would and…" He pulled the receiver away from his ear and stared at the thing, sure he was talking to dead air. "Kelsey?"

Yup, she'd hung up on him, and she was on her way to him. He loved her so much that sometimes the link and love they shared physically hurt. He replaced the receiver in its cradle, finally sucked in a full breath, lifted to his feet, and headed his sorry ass back to Mark's office. If Shane Hayes could summon the courage to face him, by hell, he could look that man in the eye and treat him civilly.

Damn it, sometimes Alex was best at making an ass of himself instead of handling delicate, sensitive situations, well, delicately. With one more cleansing breath, he palmed Mark's door open and faced Shane Hayes again.

Mark looked up from his desk, his brown eyes so dark, they'd gone completely black. He wasn't smiling. Neither was the young man sitting alongside the desk. Shane's dark blue eyes were red-rimmed, and he looked like a pile of warmed-over shit. Especially with those stains down his shirt. Looked like someone threw up on him.

Way to go, Stewart. Kick a man when it's obvious he's already down.

Alex shut the door quietly this time, pulled the chair he'd been sitting in from the corner, and joined the huddle at Mark's desk.

"I was just telling Shane that you needed more time, that you'd come around," Mark explained quietly, his voice uncommonly firm. Not accusing, but stern, as if he dared Alex to act like an idiot again. "But like it or not, Boss, Shane's USMC record is impeccable, and The TEAM needs him. I strongly recommend you hire him today."

Alex ran a hand up the back of his neck, cracked his jaw, and calmly replied, "Already told you to hire him."

"But you didn't sound like you meant it."

"And I don't need any job that bad," Shane declared. "I only stayed because Mr. Houston asked me to, but I've got other offers. I'm not desperate, you son of a bitch."

Alex nodded, taking that angry hit as graciously as he could. He had to give this guy credit. Shane wasn't taking anymore shit, but Alex truly doubted that *'other offers'* dig. Shane's demeanor radiated desperation, else why would he risk coming into TEAM HQ to ask the man he thought hated him for a job? If not desperate, then why'd he apply?

It was an employer's market these days. With all the men and women coming home from the sandbox, the covert security market was glutted. There were too many good guys and gals for all of them to end up at TEAM HQ. Decent jobs with benefits as good as Alex provided were damned hard to come by, especially for the uniquely skilled former military snipers he targeted.

But Alex didn't call Shane's bluff. This man had just gone above all expectations. He didn't need any more crap. Instead, Alex swallowed his pride with a long, audible sigh and told his newest employee, "Shane, I apologize. What I said before wasn't fair to you, nor was it necessary. Truth is, you hit a tender nerve I didn't realize I still had. I was a mess for years after I lost Sara and Abby. And now that I've had time to calm down and think, I can see that you're in the same dark place I was then. When I first lost my family, I believed there would never be any relief for me. I blamed myself for everything that happened, and I… Shit, I honestly hated everything and everyone for a few years. I took out my anger on my employees, and I hated the two women, the ex-wives" —he cleared his throat after admitting how stupid he'd been— "who I tried to replace Sara with. I know now I did that because I hated myself most of all."

"You think I don't know how that feels?" Shane asked more softly, his head cocked and those ocean blue eyes taking stock of the man Alex truly hoped he was now.

And there it was, the truth. Alex had thought he'd lost everything back then. Well, Shane had lost everything, too. Maybe more.

"No, I think you know precisely what I'm talking about." Alex moved to the edge of his chair, reached one hand out, and laid it on Shane's shoulder. That was some shoulder, damned near as wide and as hefty as Mark's. This was no young kid at his fingertips, but a war-hardened Jarhead with the persistent growth of a heavy five o'clock shadow, and it wasn't even noon. A man Alex admitted he respected. "Mark Houston's my second-in-command, Shane, and he does all the hiring. If he says you're good, you're hired. Simple as that. I trust Mark with my life, and because he trusts you, I trust you with my life now, too. Deal?"

Mark dipped his head, acknowledging that he understood how difficult this was for Alex. "He is that good, Boss. If you don't snap Hayes up, some other security company will, and it'll be our loss."

Alex appreciated that Mark said, "our loss," not "your dumb-assed fault."

"Then do it," Alex said, his angst completely gone instead of just buried, and his head on straight once again. To Shane, he said, "My wife's on her way in. You'll like Kelsey, and I know she'll like you. Are we square?"

Shane nodded, but there was no hint of a smile on his rugged face, no relief at being employed shining in his eyes. Well, Alex figured he deserved that. Next step: Prove to Shane how well he would fit in The TEAM. How much he was needed. Fitting in was one thing; belonging was another. It was time Shane Hayes found his place in the world, and it was with The TEAM, damn it.

Imagine an eighteen-year-old with the weight of the world on his shoulders. Still navigating his way through his first year of college. Then faced with arranging and paying for his mother's funeral. Top that off with a tragic vehicular accident that ended in two deaths and…

Son of a bitch. What was God thinking to put that heavy load on a kid still wet behind the ears? Alex had been eight years older than Shane the day of that fateful accident, and eight years was a helluva difference between a kid fresh out of high school and a dumb-assed grunt who'd thought he had to save the world. Hell, Alex hadn't been able to save himself. Kelsey had done that. Alex knew that for damned sure.

Now, twelve years later, four of them spent banging his ornery head against every brick wall that came along, including two divorces and enough Irish whiskey to drown a team of draft horses—or asses, depending on how you looked at things—Alex wasn't the mean bastard he'd been back then. Well, he was still a bastard. A man could only change so much.

But he'd married Kelsey and loving her made all the difference. Sure, he still had bad days, and he would forever miss the blonde darlings he'd had to bury. There was no replacing the people he'd loved and lost, not ever. But he had Kelsey to wake up to each morning now; his darling Lexie Rose and Baby Bradley to play with and read to when he went home. To kiss goodnight.

His family was Alex's second chance, and Kelsey was his guiding light, the one, true bringer of life into his sour, old heart. If not for her positive outlook on life and her forever annoying habit of forgiving everyone—including him—well, he'd just be a bitter old drunk. Still cursing God, the world, and himself, like the loser he'd been after the funeral. Those had been some damned dark days. But they were safely buried in the past, and honoring his first wife and daughter by living was the best kind of comfort. Somehow, Alex needed to teach Shane that.

He squeezed that bulky male shoulder again. "If you came here to ask me to forgive you, Shane, you came to the wrong man. I never blamed you. There's nothing to forgive. Accidents happen, and cancer is a son of a bitch. I'm sorry you lost your mother, but you can't carry those three deaths with you for the rest of your life. Sara and Abby are at peace now. So's your mom. Do you think they want you to suffer for something you had no way of preventing?"

Alex never thought he'd be the one sitting here talking to anyone like this or about those deaths like he was. But it felt good being the only one who truly understood how Shane felt. It'd feel better if he were able to help this younger man recover from what had been a helluva blow.

Forgiveness was never meant for the person you wronged. Most times, they didn't even know what they'd done to you or that you were bitterly condemning them behind their backs. Forgiveness was simply the grace you needed to let go of the things you could never change. It was the wisdom to forgive yourself for being human and the permission you gave yourself to start living again. It was a built-in escape clause when tragedy struck and you thought all was lost or everything was hopeless. According to Kelsey, God was the most perfect Father of all fathers. If Alex, as flawed as he knew he was, could love his imperfect children as much as he damned well knew he did, how much greater did his Heavenly Father love every last one of his children? Even the sinners...*like me.*

Shane nodded, sniffed, and rubbed a hand under his nose. His eyes fluttered until he finally looked up and met Alex's gaze. "I do know that, Mr. Stewart, err, Alex. But it's damned hard to forgive myself. Sounds easy, but..." He brushed his hand over his face again. "I still see them, then I see you, and then I... I..."

"Have you been to grief counseling?" Mark asked.

Shane shook his head. "No. Wasn't time. I enlisted right after I buried Mom."

"Why?" Alex asked. "Why'd you enlist so soon after you'd lost everything?"

Shane's nostrils flared and his chest heaved. He swallowed hard, his neck muscles working to make something go down. "Because... I ruined your life. I took everything from you. And I read somewhere that you'd left the Corps, that you quit because I took your family away from you. I had to do something to make it right, so I became—"

"You became a scout sniper because you thought you could pick up where I left off."

Shane nodded. "It seemed smart at the time. I mean, I saw you in your dress blues at the funeral. I was there. I saw what I did to you. I needed to pay it forward somehow."

Enough! Alex closed the distance and pulled Shane's hard head into his shoulder. It was either that or bust out bawling as that day crawled all over him again. "You've suffered enough. You've given enough," he declared, his voice husky as hell. "Let it go. What's done is done. It's over."

"I did it for you. I paid it forward for you." The guy was shaking, and Alex was so damned humbled. He sucked in a belly full of air and slapped the back of Shane's hard head. "You're an idiot, you know that, don't you?"

"Guess that makes two of us then," Shane said as Alex let go and Shane sat back in his chair.

Alex nodded and, damn it, he had to brush a damned tear off his lower eyelid before it got away from him. He grunted because remembering still hurt, then sucked in another breath and let the last of his own angst fizzle away. Luckily, Mark's intercom buzzed, and Everlee's voice came across with a bright and cheery, "Do you know where Alex is, Mark? His wife's here, and this place is too big to send Kelsey on a scavenger hunt looking for him."

"And she'd do that, too," Mark replied, his voice still devoid of his usual lighthearted humor. "Alex is with me and Shane. Send her in."

"Thanks, Mark!" Everlee's voice was muted as she must've turned and told Kelsey where her ornery husband was. Everlee came back with, "Great! She's on her way. Let me know how things go with Shane, will ya? I really like that guy. Just my opinion, but you'd be smart to hire him."

"Later, Ev," Mark replied, a definite tone of chastisement in his voice.

"Gotcha. Can't tell me anything, understood. My lips are sealed. Can't blame a girl for asking, though. Bye, big guy!"

Mark shook his head and rolled his eyes at her nosy enthusiasm, and Alex had to smile. Over the years, he'd unintentionally surrounded himself with positive go-getters. Like Mark and Everlee. And Kelsey. Knowing her, she'd probably been halfway to his office before Everlee had even disconnected.

Sure enough, Kelsey rapped on the door, then peeked in and said, "Oh, there you are."

Alex held out his arm and invited her to join them.

She came swiftly to his side with an anxious, "Are you okay, sweetheart?"

He stood. Putting one arm around her waist he admitted, "I am now. Kelsey, I'd like you to meet my newest hire, former USMC scout sniper, Sergeant Shane Hayes. Shane, this is my wife and the biggest blessing in my life, Kelsey."

Kelsey's eyes widened a fraction at hearing that name. Shane Hayes. She knew who he was, but she had the grace and good sense not to react or make things more difficult for the guy.

Shane and Mark were on their feet by then. Shane leaned around Alex, offered his hand to Kelsey, and said, "I can't tell you what an honor it is to meet you, Mrs. Stewart." Poor man's voice was still tight as shit, and if he stiffened that spine any farther, he'd make a good flagpole.

Kelsey untangled herself from Alex. Unlike him, she walked up to Shane, brushed his hand aside, and pulled him into a welcoming hug. Tipping up on her toes, she told him quietly, "I'm so glad to meet you, Shane. But you're so young. I thought you'd be an old troll like Alex, but you're just a baby."

The guy choked, but he didn't pull away from the amazing woman hanging onto him and patting his bulky shoulder, holding him close like his mother probably had once upon a different time. But when he squeezed his red-rimmed eyes tight, Alex gritted his teeth and turned away.

There. That thing Kelsey was doing right then was what Alex should've done in the first place. Instead of barking like a rabid dog, he should've welcomed Shane at first sight and let everything work itself out. He'd known most of what had happened the day of the accident, and he'd known the man behind the wheel of that delivery van had been barely out of high school, just a freshman at a local community college.

Until he'd seen Shane's name on Mark's roll of interviewees and prospective new-hires, Alex hadn't dug any further into his history. He hadn't realized until today that Shane had been dealt a devastating blow earlier the same morning, nor that he had no family to lean on afterward. Made Alex feel like an ass now for ever believing his loss was worse than Shane's. If anything, the pain and losses not yet dealt with in Shane's hard head were still eating him alive. Whereas Alex was whole and calm these days. Most days anyway. He could lend a no-kidding helping hand to this youngster. He just wished he'd done it sooner.

Alex shook his head, amazed he still had so far to go to be as good and kind as his wife. He was so damned thankful for Kelsey. Somehow, she'd smoothed over his jagged edges, at least made them less cutting. "I'm not a troll, damn it," he teased to lessen some of the sting he'd led with. "You ought to hire my wife as our welcoming committee, Mark. She's better at this than I am."

Shane licked his lips and released Kelsey, but she didn't step back, just kept looking up at him, holding his wrists like he was a little boy. Kelsey was like that. Alex knew damned well that she believed all men—didn't matter how scary-big they were, how mean they looked, or how many tattoos they had—were just little boys in grown-up disguises. That if she stood there long enough and looked hard enough, she'd see past the defensive mask Shane led with, to the hurting person behind it. There was no denying she was light-years ahead of Alex when it came to seeing through bullshit. His in particular.

Shane hadn't broken eye contact with her yet, but he kept blinking. Before the poor guy broke down, Alex tugged his wife away and settled her under his arm. At the same time, he extended his right hand in friendship. "Welcome to The TEAM, Shane," he said sincerely. "You're right, I know most of what happened that day. Just wasn't as prepared to meet you as I thought I was."

"Thank you. I think." Shane had a good strong handshake, but what Devil Dog didn't?

Alex felt stable again. With Kelsey at his side and the herbal scent of her shampoo in his nose, he was a better man. Her being here this morning sure as hell proved that.

Mark blew out a breath between his pursed lips. "You might as well know I was prepared to fight you for this guy, Boss. Congratulations. We've just hired one of the best."

"Well, of course we did. He's a Marine, isn't he?" Alex replied quickly. "Not sure if you've heard Mark's spiel already, but plan on staying the rest of the day, Shane. He'll show you around, introduce you to whichever other agents are in, maybe even take you over to the barns. You got a dog?"

Shane held up two fingers. "They're in the lobby with LT Yeager."

"Great. Harley's got a good set-up, complete with kennels for visitors if you'd rather not have them underfoot while you're working."

"You'll be perfect for this band of roughnecks, Shane," Kelsey added.

She hadn't taken her pretty, brown eyes off him, and Alex knew damned well she'd tuned into the guy's ragged emotions. Not like anyone could miss them. They were written all over his face. No doubt Kelsey had also homed in on the fact that Shane was alone in the world, that he just might need an invite to dinner. She had a knack for finding lost boys and bringing them home.

Alex beat her to it. "My place," he ordered his new hire. "Five pm sharp today. I know Kelsey, and I can see she'd love to cook for you."

"Err, but I've got—"

"Stuff to do. Yeah, yeah, I doubt that, and this is not a request. Let me show you what Stewart hospitality's really like." Alex knew he'd hit the mark the way his wife's eyes glistened.

Shane rubbed a hand up the back of his neck, a sure sign he was still stressed, that an invite to his boss's home might stress him out more. Well, too bad. He'd get over that as soon as Lexie climbed up onto his lap and ordered him to read her favorite book of the week to her.

Alex was finally understanding that life was just one beginning after another. Which unfortunately, also meant there were plenty of tear-filled endings between each of those awesome fresh starts. That was the key, the mystery, and the damned difference between living and living well. A guy had to learn the hard way how to weather painful endings before he could move on to his much-deserved new beginnings. Before he could find his Kelsey.

At last, Shane replied, "I'll be there. Thank you."

"You said you left your dogs with Lieutenant Yeager?" Alex teased. "With Everlee? The only TEAM member to sprain both ankles within months of each other?"

"And both on the job," Mark added playfully.

Shane's chest expanded with relief. "I didn't think bringing my girls into an interview with me would go over too well. Besides, they're smart," Shane replied, the barest smile curling the corners of his lips. "They might've kept Everlee from falling in the first place."

Alex nodded, suddenly aware he was seeing Shane through Kelsey's eyes. Shane was all man, and he'd been a damned good sniper. Alex knew that for certain. He had a copy of Shane's military records. But there was a whole lot of kid beneath the hard, manly façade Shane led with. Reminded Alex of himself when he'd joined the Corps. He'd been straight out of high school, too.

"Well, go get them," he groused. "Bring your dogs to work with you, every day if you want. Other agents bring theirs. You might as well get used to having plenty of service dogs around. They're welcome in any section of the complex." He looked over at Mark. "Make sure he meets Harley. Maverick, too. Harley handles our *Puppers-for-Vets* program, Shane. Maverick runs the therapeutic riding program we offer for special needs children and vets, *Everyone's a Cowboy*."

"*Puppers-for-Vets*?" Shane asked.

"One of Harley's boys came up with the name," Kelsey explained. "Oh, just wait until you meet everyone." She clasped her hands together under her chin. "I think I'll serve roast beef, mashed potatoes, and gravy for dinner. Would you like that?"

He gave her a head nod. "Yes, ma'am, sure would. Been years since I've tasted home cooking."

"You're going to love it here," Kelsey replied, but Alex caught the drift in her voice. He'd bet odds she was thinking the same thing he was, that Shane's last home-cooked dinner had been when his mother was still alive.

Alex scrubbed a quick hand under his tie and over his heart, hurting for the pain he'd unintentionally caused this brave combat veteran. God, it was true. There was something to be learned every damned day.

Mark jerked his chin at his door. "Welcome aboard, Junior Agent. Let's get you oriented. I'll discuss TEAM benefits while we walk."

"Thanks, sure," Shane replied and then turned to Alex. "Thank you, too, Mr. Stewart."

Alex growled. No sense being lead dog if you couldn't keep the *puppers* in line.

"I meant, err…" The cords in Shane's neck worked until he finally spit out, "Thank you, *Alex*."

"You bet. Welcome back. Better yet…" Alex grabbed Shane's hand and squeezed the hell out of it. "Welcome home."

Chapter Six

Shane couldn't believe how much better walking back to Everlee's desk felt. He'd expected Stewart to be hard-assed. Had thought he'd mentally prepared for it, especially given the bombshell Shane dropped on him. Marines fought dirty, and Stewart wasn't above hitting below the belt. Neither was he above admitting he'd been wrong, and that, right there, made one helluva difference between him and the commanding officers Shane had worked for in the Corps. They'd only been interested in two things, getting another star or stripe, and making themselves look good to their superiors. Stewart's sincere apology still amazed the shit out of Shane. No one had ever treated him so good, and that welcome home? And the sweet hug from Stewart's wife?

He brushed a hand over his eyes before he choked. For the first time in years, Shane felt like he might just enjoy this job. But man, Stewart's wife looked younger than him. A lot younger. She was stunningly beautiful, with her chocolate-brown hair tied up in a messy bun, while Alex was gray at his temples. He might dress like he belonged on Capitol Hill, but his nose had been broken a time or two. What the hell was a classy woman like her doing with a street-fighting bastard like him?

Guess opposites did attract.

Shane shook the puzzle off. He had a plan for the evening. The dinner invite was going to be short and sweet, over and done before the sun went down. This game he knew how to play. Show up on time. Be respectful. Schmooze a little. Keep his opinions to himself. Eat small portions of what was offered. Then leave.

But wow, he couldn't shake the lovely image of Stewart's wife out of his mind. For a moment there, when Kelsey'd grabbed him into a hug, she'd rocked Shane's world. Not in a sexual way, but in a way that was so damned motherly. He'd missed the tender touch of a good woman, and she'd hugged him exactly like his mom used to. He could've bawled like a baby.

Because life had been damned miserable after his shitty father deserted his mom and him when he was thirteen. With her working two jobs while Shane finished junior high, they'd been sinking fast. But once old man Swanson hired him to stock shelves at the neighborhood grocery store, well, Shane worked his ass off to impress the guy. Eventually, the after-school job included Saturdays. Never Sundays. Swanson closed up shop on Sundays, said smart people didn't shop nor work on the Lord's day. He must've known something. Because within a year, thanks to Shane's weekly paycheck, his mom was able to quit her second job. From then on, Shane made attending the Catholic church on the corner of his street an every Sunday morning habit. And after Mass, he fixed dinner for his mom.

God, he missed her. She was why he'd never hooked up with loose women for one-night stands. His old man had cheated on her with one woman after another until it broke her heart and damned near broke her spirit. Shane wasn't made that way, had never wanted to be anything like the bastard who'd fathered him. Still didn't. Yeah, he'd had a few close encounters with women, but none lately. He'd never felt he was good enough for the nice ones, considering his profession. What lady wanted to hook up with a professional killer?

"Girls," he called out as he rounded the corner. "Time to go. Come," he said, slapping his thigh to get their attention. Molly and Dolly charged him, two furry bundles of energy. They were just like little kids. No matter what he did, they loved him, and their smiles proved it.

"Well? Are you leaving or are you staying?" Everlee asked.

"Staying," he replied. Man, it was good to be able to say that. He had the job he'd wanted.

"Congratulations!" Excitement glittered in her eyes. "You actually look like you're going to live now."

"Yeah, being employed helps, thanks." He ran a hand over his head. "But I've got to go with Mark for a while, and these girls get to come with me." *How great is that?*

"May I come, too?"

"I guess. Sure. Alex said something about the barn and Harley and Maverick, though. Sounds like it might be a lot of walking. Are you sure you're up for it?"

"I meant to dinner at the Stewarts. May I ride with you? We all just got a blanket email invitation, and" —she waggled her boot at him— "I can't drive. Give me a ride over?"

Blanket invitation? "Everyone will be there?" Stewart hadn't said anything about inviting a crowd. But he had recently closed his Seattle office. It made sense. "How many are you talking about?"

"Everyone. Definitely four dozen or so, give or take a couple missing wives or husbands. But kids. Lots of kids. Did you know Mark and his wife have *five* children?" Everlee's eyes widened and her brows lifted nearly to her hairline. "'Course the twins are adopted, but five. Can you even begin to imagine having all those kids? The Houstons are a party all by themselves."

Shane zoned out somewhere between *blanket invite* and *party*. He hated crowds and now Everlee wanted a ride. Which meant he'd be driving her home. Maybe walking her to her door and dealing with the awkwardness that went with it. "I, ah, I've got dogs. My truck's full of dog hair and—"

"So? In case you haven't noticed, this place is the most dog-friendly place you'll ever find, and there's plenty of dog hair here. Get over it, Mr. Hayes. Shane. What'll it be? Do I have to call a cab, or will you let me tag along with you this one time? It's not like I'm asking for a date. Just a ride."

"Ride," he answered gruffly. "Sure, yeah, no problem."

Big problem.

"I'll call when I finish with Mark, and we'll go from there. Sound good?"

No, sounds bad, really bad. She's pretty and I don't see a ring. She'll expect something, only I don't have anything to offer.

"Great!" Everlee handed over a business card. "Here's my contact information. Call when you're ready to leave. I'll meet you out front."

He tucked the card into his shirt pocket. "Yeah, sure. I'll call as soon as I'm able."

Damn it.

"See that you do. Be there or be square!"

Her excitement was annoying as hell and hard to miss. He nodded, then walked back to Mark's office with Molly and Dolly tagging behind, not at all sure about Stewart's invite. If anyone had a reason to duck and run for cover, it was Shane. He hated crowds, but mostly, he was a lot like Stewart had been. He hated people. Too many hidden land mines in a large gathering at an unfamiliar home, and what if he lost control? What if he panicked and did something stupid? Like curse or scare the kids or… *that.*

What if he fell off the thin line between forgetting and remembering? Some of the shit he'd done for the Corps had a sneaky way of coming back at him. Nothing was stable in a world where every corner and shadow could hold a hidden terrorist, a suicide bomber, or an IED that would shred a man's boots, feet, and legs to bloody mulch. Never mind what it could do to the rest of him.

He inhaled a deep breath to get the terrors of all he'd lived with, seen, and done off his back. Scout snipers might do their best work from a safe distance, but the carnage they created through their scopes was always up-close and too damned personal to forget. There was a time Shane had been new at his hunter/killer job. From that day forward, he'd zeroed down on every sort of mass murderer the Taliban or ISIL had thrown his way. His scope had focused mostly on men ready to kill themselves for their causes, but there was the occasional woman who'd been willing to kill herself or her children. Plus, there were still Sara and Abby and Mom and…

WHOOSH. Damn. Fuck!

Nightmares flooded back on him en masse, each fighting to be seen and remembered, all of them elbowing forward, the stench of rotted flesh suffocating the shit out of him. They poured into his mind like swarming wasps. Too close and too fast. Too painful…

No longer able to see past or through them, he closed his eyes and slapped a palm to his breastbone to keep his heart from pounding its way out of his chest. The buzzing anguish of all those yesterdays crescendoed into louder screams and bloodier mayhem. So many tears and so much—

"Shane!" Some fiend screamed at him through the black cloud sucking the life out of him.

How'd these shadows know his name? "No!" he barked, needing them to stand down and back off. "Hell, no! Keep away from me!" His gawddamned heartbeat matched the agonizing volume of all those buzzing, terror-filled memories. There was no escape. No way to fight all of them.

"Shane! Son of a bitch, you're not alone!" The same asshat grabbed his biceps and shook him like a limp, wet rug until the back of his head knocked against something as hard as granite. He was on a floor?

"Come back to me right gawddamned now!"

He turned his face toward the slathering beast at his side, wishing he'd brought one of his pistols and—

What the fuck? He *was* on his back. He *was* on the floor inside TEAM HQ. In the lobby. Looking up. Sweating buckets. Watching for terrorists hiding up in that stupid, retro-industrial ceiling of painted-black pipes and tiles and—*Shit!* Whose bright idea was that black-splattered ceiling? It camouflaged anyone up there perfectly. Damned if his eyeballs weren't frantically rolling from side to side, forever searching for the terrorist assholes and hidden IEDs and—

"Snap out of it, damn it. You're at TEAM HQ, Shane," the asshat growled like Beowulf. "Nothing to worry about here. You're among friends."

"I know, I know," he huffed, gradually letting the suffocating nightmare go. Gathering his senses and moving out of the dark shadows. Sliding into the present, forward into the here and now. Instead of backward into—the horrible then. Shane swallowed, at least he gave it his best shot. But there wasn't enough spit in his mouth to make that bodily function work. Funny how he always tasted dust and blood after these panic attacks.

But then everything got so much worse. He blinked the nightmare off and found himself staring up at—Alex. His boss. *No, no, no!*

Shane jolted upright, damned near banging his head into the man's chin. Sticking both palms to the floor behind him to steady himself, he licked his lips and forced the panic back to its rightful corner in his mixed-up head. He'd no more than sucked in a deep breath of *'I am so fucked,'* when two cold noses and wet tongues lashed up his neck and his chin and over his face.

Molly and Dolly to the rescue. He pulled his girls in hard to his chest, wrapped his arms around his lifesavers while they crowded in. He let them slobbery kiss him, needing them. Not needing Alex or anyone else huddled on the floor with him.

Shit! He'd drawn a crowd. They'd all seen. Even Kelsey. Now everyone knew.

After-tremors came fast and hard and…

Gawddamn his screwed-up brain to hell! Why couldn't it let go of all the crap his eyes had seen? Why throw it back in his face now, when he'd finally had something to look forward to? A decent job! Jesus Christ, always one baby step forward, and right on that measly success, ten fuckin' giant, panicked steps backward.

Shane wiped his hand over his mouth in case he'd bitten his lips and that was his blood he was tasting. Thank God, it wasn't. Just drool. Not like that was any better. But how was a guy supposed to deal with persistent, stupid, walking, talking nightmares? He had no idea. Of all days, today was the moment he'd needed to project himself as the hard-assed warrior he was. But now, sitting there on the floor, his heartbeat felt like one gigantic throbbing kettledrum stuck inside his chest. Because he was shaking like a beast, he kept his face buried in Molly's thick mane, hiding, taking time to regain some measure of normalcy and composure and—

Oh, what the fuck? Everyone knew. Everyone who mattered. This was Shane's normal, and he couldn't fix the problems in his head. Even his girls could only help so much. This—this broken sweaty mess of a man was who he really was. Not the tough, confident killer he wanted everyone to see. But this quivering piece of chicken shit. He growled like a beast at the fucked-up quicksand he was stuck in.

And suddenly, it was Everlee bulldozing Alex aside. She was in Shane's face, ordering him to, "Breathe, buddy. Nice and easy, just focus on breathing right now and hang onto those girls of yours as long as you want. Damn, they know just how to help you, don't they? And they're so gentle about it, too. Not like my pittie. Blade thinks he has to French kiss me whenever I'm having a bad dream, and trust me, the slobber from that guy is enough to drown a girl."

Yeah, okay. Okay. I can do that. I can breathe.

Instead of wishing she'd back off, Shane focused on Everlee's bright brown eyes and the sparkling black pupils at the centers. Man, she really was pretty. Her short, coppery hair bounced into her eyes, but he knew what she was doing. Distracting him. Helping him through the latest motherfucking panic attack to unman him, here of all places, gawddamnit. At TEAM HQ. In front of everyone he'd thought he'd just impressed. Alex. Kelsey. Mark. Kick that bullshit illusion to the curb.

God, just kill me now.

Alex didn't need men like him, and wasn't that the shits? Especially since it was men like Shane who'd done the dirtiest work for Uncle Sam, the bastard.

"Hey, there you are." That sweet voice had to be Kelsey. Of course. "You're not alone, Shane. I still have panic attacks, too." She was kneeling between Alex and Everlee. Her palms were on her thighs, but she'd tipped forward as if she'd hug him again if he'd let her.

Shane closed his eyes to shut her out. He had his girls. They were all he needed. Another womanly hug would only hurt.

"So do I," Everlee declared loudly, almost as if she was proud of it.

He had to open his eyes to see if she'd really meant that.

"No one comes home unscathed, buddy." That was Mark's rumbling baritone. His hand landed on Shane's shoulder, his thumb digging into Shane's collarbone. "My wife and I deal with ours by holding onto each other when things get bad. Looks like Molly and Dolly understand you need that. They're hugging the hell out of you. Did you train them to do that or did it come naturally?"

"Yeah, naturally," Shane huffed, wondering what sort of traumas Kelsey or Mark and his wife had to deal with. "They… help." He slammed his eyes shut again, so damned embarrassed. He loosened one hand from Molly's or Dolly's fur and—

Hell, he didn't even know which of his girls was sitting on his legs and which was kissing the hell out of his neck and chin and whining. But their possessive positions helped disguise the quick as lightning brush over his zipper his fingers made—just to be sure. Just to be safe. He actually inhaled a real, no kidding speck of relief then. He hadn't completely lost control and unmanned himself—that way. But a guy stuck in the throes of hellish nightmares often lost control of everything. Even his bodily functions.

Still too weak to get to his feet, Shane heard quick, light footsteps, as well as the heavier stomp of boots, coming at him across the tiled floor. *Of course. Join the party!*

He nearly ducked for cover until a pretty blonde wearing a white jacket, like she worked in some kind of a lab or something, materialized on her knees beside him and Everlee. Right off the bat, she put her cool fingers on his forehead and said, "Hi, Shane. I'm Doc Fitz. I work for Alex, and this is my husband, Beau. What's going on, honey?"

He stared at her like a fool without a brain. *Honey? Me? Man, have you got the wrong person.*

The dark, messy-haired, behemoth glowering at her side stuck a callused hand in Shane's face. It was his words that broke the hold of his embarrassment. "Been there, buddy. Done that. Time to get off the cross. Somebody else needs the wood." With a manly hand up, Beau jerked Shane to his feet, then locked one arm onto his shoulder and made sure he didn't face plant. "Staying down thinking about shit makes it worse. Always get back on your feet and in the saddle as fast as you can. Just like riding a horse."

"S-sorry," Shane stuttered at the floor.

Alex smacked the living shit out of his back. "Don't be. Happens to the best of us. Hell, you just watched me make an ass out of myself."

Shane had the nerve to lift his head and face Everlee then. Not Alex. Someone gentler. She was still at his side, standing close up, smack inside his personal space like she belonged there. Within touching distance but not touching. Her lips were pursed into an O, as if she thought she needed to show him how to breathe in and out. Which she kinda did.

He nodded as he licked his lips and followed her example, letting her know he appreciated the support. Funny, but her support seemed different from everyone else's, and he didn't understand why. Maybe because she'd already spit all over him? Yeah, somehow that indiscretion helped more than everyone else's kindness.

Not a hint of disdain glimmered on her face, not even a tone of superiority in her voice when she told him, "You should've seen me the first day I hired on. I—"

"She keeled over and damned near knocked herself out on the stairs," Alex deadpanned. "Little did I know I'd hired an—"

"Accident waiting to happen," Beau finished with a gravelly chuckle.

"Shut up, you two jerks," Everlee shot playfully over her shoulder, her focus still entirely on Shane. "You know damned well you were thrilled I accepted your offer to move here, Alex. What would you do without me?"

"I don't know," Shane murmured, even as Alex tossed back, "Pay out less workman's comp."

Shane shook his head, shocked he'd said that out loud. But he had. He liked Everlee Yeager. For whatever reason, she felt safe. Despite her being the only one who'd spit on him. The sight of her pretty face when she'd realized what she'd done was fast becoming one of his better memories. He damned near smiled.

Would have, but Doc Fitz and her hubby were still standing too close for comfort. Everyone was. Beau had let go of his shoulder, but Everlee was the only one who'd gotten inside his force field. She was treating him like a normal grunt, just one of the guys. And that was a problem. As perky and bossy as she was, she was dangerous. She needed to back off.

Kelsey leaned in, her fingers circling his wrist. "Have you eaten today?" She might be timid and quiet, but she'd gotten to the root of the problem.

"No, ma'am, but I've got sandwiches in my truck and—"

"My treat!" Everlee exclaimed. "Breakfast in the cafeteria everyone. Now, big guy! Let's go."

By then, Shane knew he was standing in a circle of, well, people who might become friends. No name-calling, except for Everlee calling Alex and Beau jerks, and him big guy, which was weird. There was no judgment on any of these people's faces. No pity in their eyes, either. Only relief that he was okay, and that was, well, different.

Doc Fitz was standing behind him, shrugging Beau's hand away and growling at him to, "Back off, honey. I'm working," as she ran her gloved fingertips up the back of Shane's neck. "He's got a knot the size of a golf ball back here, and its bleeding. Might have a concussion." She torqued her body around Shane's shoulder to peer up at him. "Did you hit your head when you fell? Did you black out?"

She had to know he hadn't just fallen. More like checked out and collapsed like a damned sissy. But the second he answered with a definite, "No, ma'am," Everlee piped up with, "Yes, he did, McKenna. His head bounced. I saw it and I heard it. He hit the floor so hard I thought he cracked it. And he definitely blacked out."

"Did not." And now he sounded childish. But Jesus, she was getting up in his grill. The woman needed to cease and desist.

"Did, too," Alex growled.

Well, damn. There was no winning with these people.

"That does it," Doc Fitz declared, her hand firmly cuffing his wrist. "You're coming with me, Shane. Beau, please make sure he doesn't fall again."

Oh, for shit's sake. "No, really. I'm not going to fall, everyone. I'm okay. Just need to catch my breath," Shane insisted, needing his girls to stop clinging to his legs like they did after his meltdowns. That would make his lie more credible. He didn't like being the center of attention. He was a loner. Didn't these people understand that about former snipers? He eased away from Doc Fitz and Beau and shook his dogs off his leg with a firm, "Sit."

"But you need to eat, big guy," Everlee reminded him. "If you're not going with Doc Fitz, I'm taking you to the cafeteria. My treat. Buckle up and prepare to pig out."

"No, thanks, ma'am. I'm good," he told her in no uncertain terms. Hell, he'd come in here a badass and was walking out a pansy ass. How'd that happen?

She cocked her head back like she was prepared to argue, but Doc Fitz beat her to it. "Are you sure you're okay?" The stethoscope from her neck was now stuck in her ears and she was sliding the business end of it between the buttons of his shirt like she had a right to examine him in public. Cocking her head while she gave a listen, she told everyone to, "Shush people. Give me a few seconds of silence, will you?"

Shane obeyed and kept quiet along with everyone else. No sense in arguing with the doc.

"I'm not hearing any irregularities," she told him after a long, quiet minute, her eyes incredibly intense. "But rules are rules. Come to my office for a thorough check-up, as soon as you're done with whatever Alex wants you to do, today. He thinks he's the boss, and we let him think that, but we all know better, don't we?"

Shane had no idea how to answer that loaded question, so he kept inhaling and exhaling as steadily as he could, wishing everyone would go back to work and leave him alone. But then he thought better. He'd been living the solitary life since his last missions with Staff Sergeant Carl Schnitzler. At the time and considering the country, he'd been okay with his solitary life. But these people were his new TEAM. Which meant they were one step away from becoming his one and only family. Yeah, they weren't blood relatives, but neither was Carl. Yet he'd been the closest thing to a friend Shane ever had.

Begrudgingly, he admitted his biggest hang-up. "I'm still back there, some days. Back in Kabul. At the airport. Triggers are…" He cast his gaze at the ceiling where a terrorist dressed in black might still be hiding behind all those sprayed black pipes and shit. "God, they're everywhere. Even… up there."

And around corners.

Beneath freeway overpasses.

In shadows.

Hell, even in sunlight.

When everyone's gaze lifted upward, Beau chuckled darkly, his eyes half-closed as if he too saw the same potential threat. "Fuck, that ain't nothing. Try watching your brother drop through what looked like a solid concrete floor and then land on a bed of rusty fuckin' spikes." He dropped his chin and his fierce gaze stabbed Shane. "Thought Maverick was a goner that day. He had filthy-as-shit rebar sticking through his gut, for Christ's sake, and his leg, and… and shit!"

Shane nodded, having seen worse atrocities, but so damned thankful for the angst pouring off Doc Fitz's husband. Even his f-bombs spelled camaraderie in harsh, bold caps. It offered a link between the newbie Shane was and the war-hardened TEAM warriors these men and women were. They were him. They understood.

Beau shook his head as if that helped get his brain back on track. "Seeing him down there bleeding to death still comes back on me sometimes, and I can be a mean, stupid son of a bitch when it does. Next time I lose my shit, you have my back, okay? Remind me that Maverick's okay. That he's alive today, and that bitch Catalina Montego is fuckin' dead. Understood?"

Wow, the vehemence. That Shane understood. "Yeah, yeah, sure, I will." *Once I know who Maverick and Catalina Montego are.*

"And…" Doc Fitz breathed. "Understand you're not alone, Shane. Every single one of us has been through one or two levels of Hell in our lives. We don't judge because we know exactly what you just went through. Traumatic events leave imprints on human psyches. On everyone's, not just yours. Yes, setbacks are hard, and sometimes we think we'll never forget what we've seen or forgive what we've done. But brains do heal, and in time, yours will, too."

"And we're all here for you," Kelsey added timidly. "We've got your back."

"Anytime," Alex growled.

"Any day," Beau declared.

"Any-damned-where," Mark added gruffly. "That's the best part of working here, Shane. Alex might've started off with a rag-tag bunch of misfits, but he—"

"I ended with a damned good family," Alex interrupted evenly. "Do what Beau said. Climb off that cross you've been dragging and don't think you're the only one who's got demons. I'd be surprised if you didn't. Now get the hell to work, people. I'm not paying you to stand" —his blue eyes zeroed in on Shane— "or lay around. You are coming to dinner, right?"

"Right. Me and my girls," he answered without hesitation this time.

"And me!" Everlee piped up.

That earned her a spiked brow from Alex. "Please don't hurt Shane. We just hired him. We need him."

Her pretty face split into a grin. "Copy that, Boss. Might as well get the good stuff out for us tonight, cuz we'll be there."

"Always do," Alex said as he latched onto Kelsey's hand and headed back down the hall with her. "Later, people," he called out as he lifted a hand over his shoulder and gave them a thumbs up.

"If you can't come see me tomorrow, at least make an appointment," Doc Fitz told him.

"I will, thank you," he replied.

Shit, this might be hard, being part of a civilian team instead of the military. Shane hadn't belonged anywhere for years, not since he'd let the lease on his mom's—on their—apartment go. For a change, he was looking forward to dinner. Kind of.

Chapter Seven

Everlee kept an eye on Shane from her corner of the Stewarts' massive stone patio, where she sat enjoying her second helping of Kelsey's decadent chocolate mousse dessert. He'd thrown back two shots of Jameson when they'd first arrived after Alex and the guys cornered him. But he'd switched to ice-water during Kelsey's magnificent feast, what she'd called just another 'family' dinner. She must have an in with some pretty good local caterers because this impromptu meal included not only huge slabs of tender, juicy roast beef, a ton of buttery mashed potatoes, and buckets of rich, brown gravy, but enough yeast rolls, spicy hot wings, fries, pizza, and coleslaw to feed an army. Kelsey sure knew how to take care of her guys. What man didn't like hot wings?

Shane seemed to fit right in with this hardcore, former military group. He'd sure made a statement after everyone sat down to eat when he bowed his head, though. Everlee had stopped talking, hell, everyone had, even Alex, when Shane offered a short, but unexpected blessing over the food. Nothing fancy, just a quick *'thank you, Heavenly Father for this food. May it strengthen our bodies and refresh our spirits.'*

But no one had ever done that before, and Everlee knew for a fact that most of these guys went to one church or the other. Dayum, that fierce looking man might be fighting

PTSD, but he had one helluva backbone, to pray in front of everyone like that, even his boss.

She'd worried about him after the episode in the lobby. It had been frightening to see a man as hefty and muscled as Shane collapse. But it had also brought everyone together, including Shane, in a way he hadn't seemed to realize. Yes, falling made him look weak, but once Beau showed up, Shane seemed to connect with his new team in a deeper way than most agents. That was what every veteran needed, to fit back into the America they'd fought for once they returned home. Better yet, in Beau, Shane found a fellow warrior suffering with his own boatload of PTSD demons.

At the moment, he, Connor Maher, and Maverick Carson, all with mugs of after-dinner coffee in their hands, were discussing the latest football scores over by Alex's dogs' kennel, which was empty. The spring sun was setting. Pretty soon everyone would leave or migrate inside. Both Whisper and Smoke, Alex's former EOD dogs, were prowling between chairs, around people, and under tables. Like the Stewarts' personal clean-up crew, they snarfed tidbits that had fallen, as well as helped themselves to low-lying goodies in any unwary child's hands.

Harley Mortimer, one of Alex's four senior agents, was seated on a barstool at the outside kitchenette, joking as he fixed root beer floats in fancy, frosted mugs for the kids, and there were dozens of them. Lexie Stewart, Alex's oldest, was somewhere inside with the younger set, while Alex had his baby boy, Bradley, on his hip while they made rounds and chatted with everyone.

Everlee guessed Harley's wife Judy must be inside too, which stood to reason. Her twin boys—well, Georgie anyway, not so much Little A—was a holy terror. At last summer's TEAM picnic, the one Alex threw together to welcome the Seattle agents moving to Virginia, Georgie faked drowning. No kidding!

At first, he'd played at spraying everyone with the hose he'd found near the deep end of the pool. Then, after he'd ditched the hose and was horsing around with Little A back at the shallow end, everyone stopped paying attention. That was when, with all the noise and activity, Georgie had snuck along the wall of the pool, then ducked underwater and out of sight, and made it back to the deep end beneath the diving board. There, he'd dived down, then sat cross-legged on the pool's floor, unseen and breathing from the same hose, waiting to be noticed. The little shit. No one realized he'd unhooked the hose and left it dangling a few inches in the water.

He got noticed all right. Never before had Everlee seen so many men and women dive into a pool at the same time after Judy screamed, "Harley! He's drowning!"

Even Alex.

But Harley got to Georgie first. By the time he'd stormed out of the pool with his naughty son laughing hysterically and draped over his arm, Judy was in tears and the picnic was ruined. And right there, in front of everyone, Harley turned Georgie over his knee and spanked the little guy's bottom. Harley cried while he did it, but with every smack, he explained the spanking was for Georgie scaring his mother to death. Truth was, Georgie had scared the hell out of Harley, too.

After a while, when everyone's heartrates had settled back to normal sinus rhythm, Harley'd made Georgie go person-to-person and apologize for being thoughtless. By the end of his teary mission, he'd had to face his mom. That ended up being the hardest apology of all. Judy had cried throughout his entire punishment. But when her turn came for an apology, Georgie sobbed in his mother's arms. Guess he'd never realized how much his death would've hurt the people he loved. He'd wanted to leave the picnic then, said his stomach hurt. But Harley'd made him stay for the fireworks show Alex always ended his picnics with. By the time the Mortimers begged off and went home, Georgie was one docile, repentant, little lamb.

So, yeah. Judy had to be inside riding herd on her troublemaking son. Unfortunately, for tonight's impromptu dinner, many agents were absent. Zack Lennox for one. He was out of the country, along with Persia Judge, David Tao and his wife, plus a couple others. Walker Judge was probably on his way to join them in China again, God bless them all. They were Alex's Asian Child Smuggling Task Force.

The new guy, Cord Shepherd, was right then tipped back on two legs of his chair across the patio, laughing heartily at something either Seth McCray or his wife Devereaux said. Everlee was pretty sure Cord and Devereaux were brother and sister, just hadn't confirmed it yet. But they looked so much alike. What else could they be to each other?

Scottie stayed close to his dad, and Everlee noticed how Seth kept one arm on the back of his son's chair. How he'd reach over and ruffle Scottie's hair every so often, or lean into Scottie's ear and say something that made him laugh. Like most of the men here, Seth was a darned good father, the kind of man who made a woman sit up and take notice. Like Deveraux was noticing Seth right then, him whispering in

Scottie's ear, continually drawing him into the conversation. Everlee could swear Dev had stars in her eyes.

Sigh. What woman didn't want a man like that? Not that Everlee was looking for a man. She most certainly was not. She was good with being alone. In fact, she was better by herself. Less drama. Fewer lame-assed excuses to put up with. No lies to deal with, either. People were wrong, alone did not mean lonely, nope. It meant living her life the way she wanted, without answering to anyone or having to explain her actions. Alone meant she had no one to be afraid of. Not that she was afraid. She wasn't that woman anymore. And if all else failed, she had Blade. Her pittie might be her very own snuggle bunny, but he was hell on steroids with strangers, even with one particular creep who wasn't so much a stranger as a persistent stranger-danger.

Forcing those sneaky, uncomfortable thoughts of past dramas out of her head, Everlee looked around, took a deep breath of springtime in Virginia, and allowed herself to savor the moment. Man, there was a lot of handsome male eye-candy to behold in the Stewarts' backyard, all of it broad-shouldered, tall, tanned, and stand-out-in-a-crowd damned-good-looking. Her tongue ran a quick lap over her top lip, then paused at the corner of her mouth. This rare view of so much masculine beauty in one place at the same time was one of the perks of working for Alex.

There was magic in watching her boss in his natural environment, too. It made Alex a hundred percent more attractive knowing he doted on his kids, how he sprang to attention without being asked whenever Kelsey needed an assist. Even if she didn't. How those two lovebirds eyed each other and how kindly they treated each other. Men who respected their wives instead of belittling them or using their shortcomings to make themselves look better were few and far between in Everlee's experience. Who would've ever guessed the abrupt, sharp-tongued man Alex was in the office, the guy who could make anyone back down with just a word or one of his famous glares, was a pussycat at home? Didn't that make him an even hotter commodity, to see him so wrapped around his pretty wife's pinkie finger?

Sigh. Yeah. It did. Problem was men like him were always married. They'd found their happily-ever-afters. Too bad for Everlee. But that was the breaks, wasn't it? Bad decisions made in haste led to consequences that lasted years. *Drat.* Her chocolate mousse was gone and, judging by the happily married couples scattered across the yard, the world had gone on without her. Like always…

As if! Like a rockstar, Everlee tore her eyes off the unattainable TEAM quarterback standing over there with his Kelsey, and let that foolish daydream go. Everlee wasn't a homewrecker, damn it. And it was obvious to anyone with two eyes that Alex was well-spoken for.

Everlee killed the stupid high-school-girl crush. Just snuffed it out like pinching the flame on a candle she'd had no business lighting in the first place. She'd entertained the silly daydream long enough. Alex definitely had the whole alpha-male vibe going for him, but Kelsey had cornered that market. Like Libby had Mark, Mei had Zack, Dev had Seth, Judy had Harley, and Everlee had—

Damn. Showing up at these TEAM dinners, parties, and picnics sucked. Everlee knew damned well where her daydream had come from. Despite loving who she'd become and where she was going, there was a hollow space in her chest that ached like a cold fireplace at get-togethers like this. Everyone here had someone to go home with. Even Shane had made plenty of friends, that whole brothers-in-arms bonding guy-thing. The TEAM had certainly welcomed him like a long-lost brother, and that was good. She was happy for him.

So why was she sitting by herself, feeling sorry for herself? Because everywhere she went, Everlee was the third, fifth, or seventh wheel. Forever the good sport and always the odd man out. Yeah, she was really rocking the whole self-pity vibe tonight. Definitely time to leave. Where the hell was Shane?

Setting her empty plate aside, she scanned Alex's backyard one last time. Mark was still sitting with his wife Libby at one of the twenty or so round tables. Beau Villanueva and Doc Fitz, newlyweds Jameson and Maddie Tenney, as well as Renner Graves and his wife Tara, and Tripp and Ashley McClane were seated with Mark at his table. Renner's kids, Jessica and Tanner, were two of the many gathered around Harley waiting their turn for root beer floats. He had a knack for handling children and keeping their attention. The three super-trained but loveable Malinois puppies he'd brought with him helped. Kids loved his dogs, and damn, those pups were smart.

There were days Everlee wished she'd hooked up with one of Harley's pups instead of her pittie. Less drool. But she loved Blade, and he'd proven himself adept at protecting her, as well as heading nightmares off at the pass. Either by sticking his slobbery snout in her face or by sprawling his heavy, muscled body over hers like one of those weighted blankets. Only he whined, which she guessed was his way of telling her she'd be okay. Considering the alternative—

sweating, shrieking like a banshee, and fighting her blankets—snuggling a heavyweight like Blade was a relief to wake up to in the middle of scary nights. He always made her feel safe, and, in his way, he grounded her, too.

Her traitorous eyes strayed back to where Shane stood with his arms folded over his chest, his legs spread in that dominant way men stood. Still by the kennel, Alex and Kelsey were talking with him now. Shane's back was to Everlee. Alex was facing her, not focused on her, though. Instead, focused on Shane.

Bradley was now asleep on his mom's shoulder. Alex's black GSD sat at rapt attention at his knee, but just like Alex was attentive to Shane, Whisper's shiny black eyes were definitely fixed on Kelsey. Which made Everlee smile. Alex might rule the world at work, but here at home? Even his dogs knew better.

She let her eyes scroll down that stiff spine to Shane's slender waist and from there, to his ass. Just like the rest of him, it was taut and muscled. Was probably as hard as his chest. Or his biceps. Or his forearms. An inkling of attraction sparked to life deep in her gut. What would he be like in bed, bossy or willing? Generous or selfish as shit? Would he think he had to compete with her? Would he respect her?

She blinked those foolish thoughts right out of her head. Respect was a hard line for her. Kindness, too. As for love and all its romantic lies? She'd given up on that fairytale long before she'd ever left home. As much as she had adored her dad, he was a selfish prick who'd never had a problem leaving her and her mother behind while he cruised every last hotrod race between the Evergreen racetrack in Washington to the

Daytona in Florida. But after he'd snapped and did what he did? She'd never forgive him.

That Alex had somehow garnered the devotion of gentle, honorable men like himself, said a lot about the guy. He had no tolerance for men who didn't respect women or women who didn't respect men. He expected honor from his TEAM and, by hell, he got it.

Just then Shane glanced over his shoulder. His sharp-eyed gaze pierced Everlee as if he knew she'd been watching his ass, which she had. Although, his very masculine front was pretty good eye-candy, too. She fluttered her fingers at him and gave the standard it's time to leave head nod toward the street. Most guys understood that. But it still surprised her when he nodded politely to Kelsey, said something to Alex, stepped back, excused himself, and headed straight for Everlee.

"Are you ready to go?" he asked quietly, as he folded his lean, muscled body onto the empty bench beside her. His hands fell loose between his knees, and his elbows landed on his thighs. With its top two buttons undone, his shirt stretched in all the best places. Across his taut, wide shoulders and impressive chest, giving her a glimpse of crisp, black chest hairs. Why that sparked her libido said a lot about how long it had been since she'd had sex.

Which was, *let's see... Well over two years ago. That ought to make me damned nearly virginal, right?* Probably not. Virginity was one of those seals that, once broken, could never be restored. Like indelible ink, if you chose unwisely, you carried the stain of your stupidity for the rest of your life.

"I am if you are," she replied.

Automatically, her gaze strayed to his left hand, to his ring finger. Nothing there, not even an indentation or untanned line where a ring might've been. Good. Not that all married men wore wedding bands. Not that she cared one way or the other. Shane could do whatever he wanted.

But rule number one in a single woman's life was: *Never date married men.*

She hadn't appreciated being cheated on; she'd never do it to another woman. Daydreaming about her boss was different. That was just stupid, life-is-boring-at-the-moment infatuation. Alex was a dynamic, damned good-looking man, but not once had he been anything less than professional, and she'd never—ever—made a move on him. Hadn't even flirted. Wouldn't think of it. Because cheating on your spouse was underhanded, stupid, and just plain mean. Besides, Alex was an extra-happily married man. Blowing out a breath of pent-up sexual frustration, Everlee was done being an idiot. *Alex belongs to Kelsey. Case closed. Moving right along...*

"And no, I'm not married," Shane said as he rolled his sleeves up his arm into halves, which showed off his impressive tan, and damned if those forearms weren't as solid as the rest of him. Even his biceps seemed too bulky for his shirt.

"Well, aren't you the cocky one?" was all Everlee could come up with. She knew her neck had turned red with embarrassment. She could feel the heat. A flaming crimson tide would soon creep up and over her cheeks like a blazing beacon for all to see. Darn her red-headed complexion. Despite being half Puerto Rican, the fair-skinned Irish in her ruled her emotions.

"Relax. I caught you checking me out, that's all. How about you? Single, engaged, or still looking?" he asked, his tone indifferent, and his gaze across the yard.

She fluttered the bare fingers on her left hand. "You forgot divorced."

He shrugged the bulky shoulder nearest her. "You're kidding. You're way too young to have been married, much less divorced."

"Biggest mistake of my life." Everlee tried for distraction. Her failed marriage was the last thing she wanted to talk about. "Bet you've got a girl in every port and every post you've been stationed in."

"Nope. Never played fast and loose. Never had time." Whatever that meant.

He flexed both hands into fists, then relaxed them, and again, they dropped between his knees. And like the sex-starved fool she was, Everlee's gaze scrolled over the impressive build of the man beside her. What was it about the dark hairs on this guy's tanned arms and the purplish veins on the insides of those muscular arms that made her mind wander? There wasn't one part of Shane that didn't scream All American Male. His build. His bulk. The scent of him. Yet there was a vulnerable side to him, too. She'd seen it just this morning. How could a man so obviously strong and capable, so capable and fit, ever fall prey to PTSD? He seemed put together. Confident and lethal. Not broken, but okay, maybe fractured a little around the edges. But that just made him like everyone else here tonight. *Even me.*

Everlee blushed at the semi-still-there, light brown stains down the front of his shirt. Man, she'd gotten him good. He hadn't bothered to stop at his place to change on their way to the Stewarts' house, and she knew Mark gave him at least a week's worth of TEAM polos like he did with new hires on their first day. Yet Shane hadn't changed into one of them, either. Why not? Was he just that confident that he didn't care what anyone thought? Seemed like it.

"Alex wants us to tackle a mission."

She wiggled her boot in case he'd forgotten she was temporarily sidelined from active duty. "Must not be a walking mission," she teased.

"No. Nothing OCONUS and nothing too difficult. He wants us to locate a Ms. Tuesday Bremmer in Dallas, Texas, and bring her back to DC for questioning. That's all."

"Why?"

Shane hmphed. "Because apparently, the FBI has worse ROEs than Alex, and The TEAM can get things done they can't. Alex'll send the brief to your email as soon as he—"

Her cell phone pinged an incoming notification. "And there it is. So, what's Ms. Bremmer wanted for?"

"For murdering Atchison Bremmer, her husband of five years, their three-year-old son Toby and two-month-old daughter Betsy. Allegedly, last month in New York City, she disabled the smoke alarms in their Fifth Avenue apartment, poured charcoal lighter fluid throughout the rooms, then lit the place up. As if that wasn't bad enough, on her way out, she chained the apartment doors from the outside hall to keep everyone locked inside. She burned them to death while they slept, and the apartment manager has the security footage to prove it."

Everlee gasped. "She killed her own children?" Like killing anyone's child made her less of a monster.

Shane nodded grimly. "Oddest thing though, she'd purchased five-hundred-thousand-dollar life insurance policies on each of the kids and increased the payoff on her husband's policy to a million before she killed them. But then she let herself be filmed chaining the only exit, the double doors, while the fire alarms went off. FBI thinks they've got an alibi-proof case. They're investigating her first husband's death now, too. But Alex isn't convinced."

Everlee let that slide. Alex had been at odds with the FBI forever. He'd made a few friends, including FBI Director Zachary Strong, the man President Adams appointed. Also, Tucker Chase, the director of the Bureau's one and only Paranormal Unit. But for the most part, he had nothing good to say about the Bureau.

"She was married before?" *Amazing*.

"Yeah. Her first hubby, Frederick Lamb. Also in New York."

"Was she the beneficiary on his life insurance policy, too?"

"Not sure. Alex only knows he was quite a bit older and he died of a heart attack about six years ago. According to the FBI's ME who examined Lamb's body, no one suspected they were looking at murder. Guess Lamb had a history of minor cardiac events, so there was no suspicion. But with these last three deaths, the Bureau's exhuming the body to do a more thorough examination."

"How old are you talking?"

Shane's lips pursed. "Forty-two years difference. Ms. Bremmer's only twenty-six now. She was seventeen when she married him. Talk about a winter/spring romance."

Everlee shivered at the image that honeymoon invoked. *Yuck.* A creepy old guy with a seventeen-year-old child-bride who'd probably never had sex. Did she and Lamb even consummate their marriage? Worse, Ms. Bremmer had gotten pregnant pretty damned fast the second time around, if that three-year-old boy was hers. Was insurance fraud her plan all along? And for that, she killed that boy and a two-month-old baby girl? What a sicko! "She's a black widow is what she is, and she's been busy. How old was she when she married Atchison Bremmer?"

"Twenty-one."

"Criminy, she didn't even let her first husband's body get cold. How long was she married to Lamb?"

Shane grunted. "You're gonna love this. They'd only been together a little over three years before he died."

"Jiminy Christmas," Everlee breathed. "She was so young. Do you think she might've had a psychotic break?"

"That would make sense, but I get the feeling Alex doesn't think so, nor does he trust the Bureau's intel. We may not have all the facts."

"Alex doesn't like most Bureau agents. He's been burned too many times. When does he want us to leave?"

"Tomorrow morning if Doc Fitz clears us for duty. He thinks you're going stir-crazy, that this mission'll get you away from the customer service desk. Sounds easy enough if you ask me."

"That's because this isn't Afghanistan, and we won't be in combat. Of course it sounds easy, but there's no such thing as an easy op, big guy." She fist-bumped his biceps for emphasis. "The instant you even think the word, everything goes belly-up. So lay off the easy op crap."

"I'm sure we can handle whatever pops. What do you think? You game or would you rather baby that ankle another week? It's been what, a month or so now?"

Her hackles lifted. He'd taunted her on purpose. "Six weeks, Hayes. My ankle's fine. The real question is, can you pass Doc Fitz's exam? Huh?"

He shrugged at her less than gracious comeback. "Guess we'll find out tomorrow. Alex said he'll have someone called Mother take care of our travel arrangements." Shane turned back to the Stewarts and gave Alex a thumbs-up. Alex acknowledged him with a stiff chin nod.

Shane turned back to Everlee and asked under his breath, "Does his mom seriously work for him?"

Everlee snickered. "Heck, no. Mother is Sasha Kennedy, The TEAM's master techie. She goes by Mother or Mom, and except for Alex's, she handles all TEAM reservations. Maddie Tenney, Alex's protocol officer, handles his schedule and travel affairs. I'll bet Mother already has everything lined up for us." Everlee tugged her cell out of her jeans pocket as another notification hit. "Yup. Did you get it?"

Shane was on his cell, too. "That was fast. Looks like we're leaving after we meet with Doc Fitz and Alex. Darn, that won't give me much time to make arrangements for my girls."

"Don't worry. Us agents with dogs just drop our fur babies off with Harley before we head out to wherever we're going. He runs the kennels, which includes boarding, training, and whatever Molly and Dolly need while we're gone. Cool, huh?"

"Incredible," Shane murmured. "Mr. Stewart really takes care of his agents, doesn't he?"

"That's what makes his TEAM the best to work for." She tipped back a bit to look closer at him. And damn, her breath hitched like she was some star-struck Chippendale fan. Which she would never. But sitting this close to Shane was… was… yeah. Breathtaking. The alpha vibes rolling off of him matched Alex. His meltdown earlier magnified the sharp edges to his face, neck, and… those arms.

"L-looks like you had a good time schmoozing tonight," she muttered to get her brain back on business.

"Hard not to. Alex has a solid team. Everyone here's been easy to talk with."

"Plus…" She hesitated. Sharing her PTSD stories was hard, which is why she hadn't shared any. Didn't need go to any shrinks, either. "I suspect everyone's been telling you their own personal PTSD stories. You do realize we've all got it, one way or another. What happened to you this morning probably encouraged everyone else to open up. Look around. Dinner at the Stewarts is group therapy at its best. Some of these guys' wives have lived through some pretty awful crap, too. See McKenna over there?"

"You mean Doc Fitz?"

"Yes. Her mother's sisters, her aunts for Pete's sake, tried to kill her. That's when she met Beau."

"Sounds like he's been through some real shit, too."

Everlee nodded. "He has. Scuttlebutt says Alex almost fired him. You heard Beau mention how Maverick fell through a concrete floor. Well, Beau's the one who jumped down into that hole after him, did heart compressions until EMTs arrived, and pretty much saved his life. Us guys from the Seattle office heard it was touch-and-go for a while, and I think that happened during the same time Mother lost her daughter. So yeah, like Alex says, we're a banged-up bunch of losers, but we're all he's got."

"He really says that?"

"He's a Marine. What'd you expect him to say? Something sweet?" Everlee chuckled. "That'd be the day."

Shane scratched the back of his head. "Guess not. He's one powerful son of a bitch, though. Almost didn't believe it when he told Mark to hire me. Not the way he stormed out and slammed the door behind him."

"He can be a hothead," Everlee said thoughtfully. What she wouldn't give to have been a fly on Mark's office wall during that interview. She'd heard a door slam. But why had a simple job interview pissed Alex off? That was the real question. As much as she wanted to ask Shane what happened, she opted instead for, "Have you ever thought of taking something for anxiety?"

His brows slammed together, and she had to stop herself from licking the pad of her thumb and scrubbing those adorable lines out from between his brows. Hot damn. This guy had the thickest eyelashes, but those testy brows were masculine as hell. When he frowned, the winkles between them turned him into an indisputable alpha. The five o'clock scruff shadowing his jaw didn't hurt his sex appeal none, but those deep, dark blues and the worry lines between his brows shot a healthy dose of lust to Everlee's core, one that was downright intoxicating. In another place and time, she might just—

"I already take crap for migraines," he declared with conviction, completely oblivious to what had to be her glassy-eyed stare. "And I've got my girls. They work just fine."

He leaned forward and looked around Everlee, so she turned and looked, too. She'd forgotten both Dolly and Molly were lying beneath the expansive shade cast over most of the yard by the maple tree in the opposite corner. Their attention was solely on Shane. When he snapped his fingers, they bolted across the lawn to him, then sat like twin statues at his feet, their bodies quivering as they waited for his command.

Everlee put her fingertips to her lips and laughed. Man, if only Blade behaved as well as these two Springer Spaniels. If only he obeyed as quickly. But he tended to be more creampuff than obedient, and he was built like a snuggly, warm tank. These two happy girls made her big bad boy look like a roly-poly pansy, but she wouldn't have him any other way.

Shane's dark eyes scrolled from his dogs back to Everlee. "Something funny?"

She shook her head, loving the picture of this damaged warrior with his *'girls.'* "They adore you, don't they?"

"I guess. I'm the one who feeds them, aren't I?"

Everlee curled her fingers into a fist and smacked his biceps, fully aware how solid this man was. How close he was. How good he smelled, outdoorsy with a hint of cigarette smoke. No scent of whiskey though, despite the shots he'd tossed back before dinner.

"It's more than that, and you know it. They love you, Shane, and I'm a little jealous. Blade doesn't look at me like that."

"Yeah, well…" He lifted the arm closest to Everlee. For an instant, she thought he might hug her. But he just reached over his shoulder and scrubbed that big hand up his neck, as if his muscles were tense. Hers sure were.

Flash. The erotic image of her straddling Shane's bare butt while she massaged that stiff neck—and anything else that might be stiff—ignited a blazing grease-fire in her sex-starved brain pan. Everlee's mouth went dry at her nearly virginal body's fiery reaction to the heft and bulk and nearness of this man. She knew, just knew, he'd never hit her. But mixed with that stab of panic was the very real notion that he could've hugged her. He still could.

For a second, her heart drummed a lickety-split two-beat dance of anticipation, and wet, slick heat melted her core. Not good. Well, good, yeah, a hug from this man would be, oh, so good, but no, no, no. Shane was off-limits.

Rule number two for any smart single woman: *No office romances.* They were hard on a woman's ego. Just as hard on office morale when you still had to work with the jerk who dumped you or who you dumped. Just. No.

Everlee jerked her eyes off Shane and shook the wayward but totally erotic image of the man she barely knew out of her head. Had to be all the sugar she'd indulged in tonight. Not once had she pictured Alex sans clothes and she'd been crushing on him forever.

Mental note to self: *Lay off the calories, girl. No one likes a fat ass, so no more chocolate mousse, and no more stupid crushes. You were an officer, act like one.*

Thank heavens, Molly whined and jumped onto Shane's lap. Then Dolly kind of crawled, mostly begged up his leg for a hug. "You ready to go home?"

When Everlee didn't answer, he nudged her with his elbow. "Hey. I was talking to you."

"Umm, sorry, what?"

"I asked if you're ready to get out of here." His voice had turned deep and demanding. "My dogs have had enough and tomorrow comes early."

Everlee doubted those were the real reasons he wanted to leave, but she let it slide. Slapping her palms to her knees, she jumped to her feet and replied, "Anytime you're ready, big guy."

They said their goodbyes, and an hour later—because, hello, this was a big crowd and there were a lot of goodbyes to be said—Everlee walked to the curb where Shane had parked his king-cab pickup. Black, of course. While he opened the backseat door for his girls to jump in, praised them, and snapped their harnesses onto the two short leashes fastened there, she grabbed hold of the suicide handles inside the front seat passenger door. Planting her big, black boot carefully on the running board—because hey, she was a fall hazard—she hefted her butt up and into the front seat, shut her own door, and fastened her own seat belt. She was independent and proud of it. Why wait around for some guy when she could do everything herself. Smart thinking, huh?

Dog safety was important, and Shane took extra good care of his girls. He should. Dogs were like children. You took care of them, or you had no business getting a *'cute widdle puppy'* in the first place.

But once, just once in her life, Everlee wished he'd opened the door for her like a gentleman did for the woman he cared about. What would it feel like to be the center of someone's whole world? To be cared for as much as Shane cared for his girls?

Honestly? She had no idea.

And apparently, Shane was no gentleman.

Chapter Eight

Shane couldn't put his finger on it, but there was a definite buzz inside his truck while he followed Everlee's directions to her apartment complex, Arlington Heights. Which was an odd name for anything, since Arlington, Virginia, was way east of the new TEAM HQ and Alex's castle-like home.

"Next left, then take the first right, and you're there," Everlee said quietly. "You can't miss it. Second building straight back. Let me off by the Dumpster. Gives me less distance to walk."

"Sure. No problem." Shane cast a quick sideways glance her way.

Seemed like most agents lived nearby TEAM HQ. Several had recently moved from Seattle, and the others had given up their homes closer to Washington, DC, for the lazy life of western Virginia. Everlee, along with Paige Royal, the Seattle's TEAM office manager, and several guys, were some of those Seattle transplants. Only Everlee had been at the picnic tonight. The rest of them were still on extended leave, moving households.

But Shane was pretty sure that off-kilter buzz was coming from her. Except for her succinct directions, Everlee hadn't said much since they'd left the Stewarts. Her bossy, energetic other half was nowhere in sight.

Shane was drawn to Everlee. Had been since she'd spit coffee in his face. How could a recluse like him not be drawn to a woman with as much fire in her gut and attitude as Everlee Yeager? She was a good foot shorter than him, which made him feel taller and bigger, meaner, and okay, for some reason, protective of her. Wasn't that a kick? Him feeling protective of a former Chief of Security Forces, which made her an officer to his enlisted rank? Not that rank mattered now that they were both civilians again. But neither did a trained police officer with plenty of attitude need any guy's protection. She could take care of herself, and he was a sexist for even thinking she couldn't.

Plus, Everlee was carrying. That might explain why she'd kept her distance from everyone else tonight. Shane wasn't, hadn't been all night, not with so many kids around. He'd left his holster in his truck and his pistol stuck to the magnetic strip under his dash, where it was still safely secured. But accessible.

More than once he'd thought about joining Everlee on that lonely bench tonight. But each time he'd headed her way, he'd been sidelined, if not by one of the guys, then by the kids or one of the Stewarts. He'd had a great time meeting everyone, hadn't felt an inkling of tension, which was surprising in a crowd that size. Maybe because everyone there was former military, married into the military, or was born under the flag. They all spoke the same language. Yet Shane couldn't help thinking he should've paid more attention to Everlee.

Obediently, he made the left turn, took the first right, and drove easily through the deeper than normal gutter at her apartment complex entry. Arlington Heights was a collection of rectangular, colonial-style buildings. Decent. Tidy. Painted white with large, black-stamped eagles at the center front of all buildings. Doric columns lined the rear porticoes. The glass entrance doors were tinted black, and judging by the keypads at each entry, only residents were allowed access.

Sixteen multipaned windows lined both first and second levels, front and back. Well-cared for and colorful flowerbeds bordered each building. Sidewalks ran between the grassy areas between the buildings. Covered numbered parking stalls lined the rear section of the eight-foot-high brick wall that encompassed the entire complex. A rear driveway offered additional egress. The place seemed quiet and calm tonight, and it was good knowing Everlee lived in a secure, safe facility. Just as good as knowing where both exits were.

He refused to just drop Everlee off at the Dumpster, though. Like hell. That unsettling buzz had grown stronger, so he pulled into the nearest visitor stall, shifted into PARK, and turned to his too-quiet passenger. "Here we are."

Yup, the buzzing was coming from Everlee. She all but radiated tension. The cords in her neck were tight and stiff. Her head was down, and her gaze was on the floor. Her body was wound as tight as a rubber band about to let a spit wad fly. Was she scared? Why?

Shane reached out and laid a hand on her forearm, in case there was something she wanted to tell him. "What do you need me to do?"

She jumped at his touch. "Nothing. Can't we just" —her throat worked hard to make that swallow go down— "leave? Maybe take a long ride around the block or something?" She cranked her chin up, looked him in the eye, and added, "Please?"

It was the faint tremor to her usual cocky tone and the un-Everlee-like shine in her brown eyes that spurred Shane to action. "Yes, ma'am," he declared. She was afraid, and he didn't need to know why. Slamming his truck into reverse, he pulled a short, sharp K-turn out of the parking space and aimed for the rear exit. Easy in. Just as easy out. Well, except for another steep speed bump. Because his truck sat so high, he had to slow down and crawl over the humongous thing.

They were nearly out the rear exit when some jerk in a universal-camouflage-patterned uniform—otherwise known as the US Army's digicam crap—jumped out from behind another Dumpster and waved his arms for Shane to stop.

Shane slammed on his brakes to avoid hitting the guy.

"God," Everlee whispered. "Why can't he leave me alone?"

Good question, one Shane was pretty sure she hadn't meant to ask out loud. But GI Joe there might explain the tension in Everlee. "Who is this guy? Were you expecting him?"

"Not exactly,'" she answered even as she shook her head, then nodded. "But yeah. I knew he'd show up one of these days. Sorry." Everlee unsnapped her seatbelt.

Shane wasn't about to let her face this jerk alone. He put the truck back into PARK right there in the middle of the exit, shrugged out of his seatbelt, and jumped to the ground. In a few quick steps, he was in the guy's face. "Can I help you?" he asked, keeping his tone civil and his body language relaxed. For now.

Anger suffused the air between him and this guy, who had his fists up. "Where you been with my wife?"

Your wife?

Shane kept his cool. Didn't react. Didn't get mad. This guy had to be her ex. Everlee'd said she'd been married, not was married. No wonder she'd divorced the jerk. He reeked of body odor and something sour, like he'd recently slept in his own vomit and hadn't bathed. His long, blond hair was greasy and thin, wispy like the scruff on his chin. Not on his face, just on his chin, like a teenager's face before his balls dropped and his voice changed. Before he could actually grow anything a man would call a real beard. Or a pair.

Everlee didn't deserve being ambushed in a semi-dark parking lot even if they were married, and Shane didn't owe this belligerent any explanation other than, "Not your concern."

"Oh, yeah? You been fucking my woman? You have, haven't you? I can see it on your face, you pig." The man's head tilted as he yelled around Shane, "Ev! This who you're sneaking around with now? Jesus, woman! Can't trust you for shit, can I? Get your ass over here!"

Shane went for broke, just stuck his hand out, needing to tone down the rhetoric. "Shane Hayes. Who are you?"

The man's chest puffed out. "None of your business. 'Sides, I already told you, shithead. That woman sitting her ass in your truck is my wife! Which makes me her gawddamned husband, and you're a cheating son of a bitch!" His eyes popped over Shane's shoulder at the sound of the truck door slamming. "There she is, now get out of my way, asshole. Me and Ev got things to discuss, and they don't include—"

"Get out of here, Butch," Everlee ordered, her voice even. She was in her Air Force LT mode, her shoulders back and her face set to give orders. "You're drunk. Go home to your mom. Sleep it off."

"But I need you, not Ma," he declared, his chin up and his red-rimmed eyes bleary as shit. He took a stumbling, sideways shuffle to get around Shane.

Shane cut him off, blocking Everlee's view. Instead of pushing Shane aside, she replied from behind him, "You never needed me, Butch. You just used me. Like you use everyone else in your life. Go home. We're through. Have been for two years and—"

"And three months and a couple days! Gawd, you don't think I know that? I can count, damn it! Git your ass away from this bastard so I can get a good look at you!" Butch swiped the back of his hand under his nose, then smeared a line of snot from his hand across the front of his shirt. Which was just plain disgusting. "I miss you, Ev, I do," he bellowed, "and you're wrong."

The guy stomped his boot like a two-year-old about to have a full-blown temper tantrum. "I really, really need you! Can't you see? Always did. You never shoulda left me because I can change. I know I can. Just need you and another chance and—"

"And another and another and another..." Her words faded as she stepped forward and bumped against Shane's right side. When she turned to look up at him, her hand went to his chest and his automatically fell to her hip. "I'm all out of second chances. I've told you before, you and me are done. We've been done for years. You picked booze, pot, drugs, and cheating over me. I was just too stupid to see it soon enough. Go home to your Ma. She'll feed you. Take a bath. Eat something, for hell's sake."

"Not 'less you come with me!"

Way to impress a woman, Butch, Shane thought as he shifted his hand from her hip to her shoulder and pulled her in tight against his side. *Scream. Whine. Act like the snot-nosed addict you obviously are. Ev's right. Go home.*

"I'm not going anywhere with you, and you know it," Everlee said. Despite the tension in her body, her voice remained uncommonly calm and controlled, like the professional she was. "You need help, counseling wouldn't hurt. Get it before it's too late."

"'S already too late, Ev, baby!" Tears trickled down the guy's dirty face and into the sparse whiskers on his chin. "If you can't find it in your heart to forgive me, what else do I got? I got nothing! You took everything I was when you left me behind and moved to Alaska!"

"I didn't leave you," she said, confronting his pity-party with the same calm indifference. "You did. With Georgette and Lucy and Kalli and…" Everlee waved her hand as if that list went on and on.

"But this time I really, really" —Butch's belly expanded with a full breath before he bellowed— "need you!"

Everlee turned to Shane. "Thanks for the ride. See you back at the office."

Her eyes were still a clear crystal brown, like black coffee. For the first time, he noticed her pupils were huge. She still presented a calm demeanor, but there were cracks in her composure. This confrontation might be a rerun of a hundred others, but it cost her.

The urge to carry her back to his place and hide her and make love to her stormed Shane's common senses. Everlee was no damsel in distress, and he refused to reduce her to that old-fashioned stereotype. "Uh-uh, Ev. I'm not walking away and leaving you out here alone with this guy," he told her under his breath. Shane crooked his elbow, inviting her to grab hold of him. "Not until you're safely inside. Which place is yours? Point the way, and I'll get you there."

He didn't think she'd do it. Everlee was still a puzzle who needed someone willing to take the time to unravel. But she did, just slipped her small hand into the crook of his arm, offered a wan smile, and said, "Thanks, Shane. I appreciate it."

Poor thing was trembling and that pissed Shane off. "How long's he been showing up here?"

Her lower jaw widened, stretching her bottom lip into a grimace. "This is the first time since I left Seattle. Guess he heard about what happened on Highway 15. Timing's about right."

"What happened?"

"The usual. Ended a pervert's crime spree. Finch won't be killing anyone's little kids anymore. But it made the news and you know how they are," Everlee hadn't looked at her ex since she'd turned away from him. Good strategy.

Shane arched back to really see the woman on his arm. "That was you? You're the one who took down Webster Finch over in Culpepper?"

She shrugged both shoulders like it was no big deal. "Paper got the deets wrong as usual, but yeah. That was me."

"You sideswiped his car." *Unbelievable.*

"Sideswipe, nothing. I meant to hit that piece-of-shit, and I hit it square on like I planned. Highway Patrol Officer McKay boxed him in after the impact, but I'm the one who stopped—"

"Local news said Finch got one shot off." Shane dropped his arm to take hold of her shoulders and turned her to face him. "My God, where'd he shoot you?"

"It was nothing. I was wearing a vest. I survived. It happens. Let it go."

"Where?" he persisted.

She tapped her chest up high on her breastbone, damned near the hollow of her throat. "Here. Nothing to worry about."

"Hey, guy-zzzz!" Butch hollered, dragging that last word into two, long, annoying syllables. "Enough whispering. I ain't dumb, ya know. If you're gonna talk about me, do it louder."

Everlee took hold of both Shane's wrists. "Would you mind if we went somewhere else?"

He didn't need to be asked twice. "You bet."

Like a man on a mission, Shane escorted Everlee back to his truck, opened her door, put his hands around her tiny waist and lifted her up over the running board and onto the passenger seat. "Sit back," he told her as he deftly reached around grabbed hold of her seatbelt, and fastened it snugly.

She sat there smiling down at him, a funny glow in her eyes. "Jiminy Christmas, Shane. What'll your dogs think?"

"You like ice cream?" he asked instead of answering her silly question. His dogs only ever got the back seat. Riding shotgun was for someone special and here she was.

"Doesn't everybody?"

"I know a place." For some crazy reason he couldn't explain, Shane's face cracked into a big grin. It'd been so long since he'd really smiled that it almost hurt. He peered around the back of Everlee's seat to his girls and asked, "Want a treat?"

Molly and Dolly both let loose excited yelps, and Everlee laughed. She probably couldn't help it because the enthusiasm of those two crazy dogs was contagious. Shane ran around his truck, climbed in, and threw one arm over the back of his seat. Deftly, he backed his rig out of Arlington Heights the same way he'd driven in, and he and Everlee left What's-His-Name screaming his guts out in the rear parking lot.

For a day that had started out embarrassing as fuck, it was ending pretty great.

Chapter Nine

"He's not even a veteran," Everlee told Shane. "Butch never served anyone but himself, and he's been an addict for years. He's a thief. Stolen valor. None of those medals he's wearing are his, neither's the uniform. His mom probably bought the stuff for him at the Army/Navy surplus thrift store. She's an enabler, treats him like he's still her baby boy. Guess that's what happens to moms when they only have one kid."

"Not so," Shane said quietly. "I was my mother's only child, but we were always a team, the two of us. It was us against the world, and I'm no baby."

That was for sure. "Where's your dad?"

"Don't know. Mom never said. He left when I was a little kid." Shane shrugged like that was no big deal. "How about you? Did you live in Washington all your life before you moved here?"

"Yes, born and raised. Lived in Fife with my parents until I joined the Air Force. First assignment was JBL, Joint Base Lewis McCord. Married badly, as you just saw." She ran a hand through her bangs, then over her head to the back of her neck. "Divorced quickly. Had a chance to start over at JB Elmendorf-Richardson up north, so I took it. Best decision I ever made."

Well, second best. Leaving home was first, always would be. But there was no way she'd ever tell Shane why she'd really joined the Air Force, or how thrilled she'd been to finally put on Air Force blues. The day she'd enlisted was the day she'd put the past behind her, and in the process, gained a real family she could rely on, and saved herself. All those Disney princesses had it wrong. Waiting around, pining for some Prince Charming to stumble by was stupid. Smart women did not do that.

"You liked Alaska?"

"Loved it. I'd go back in a second, but there's not much decent work for civilians up north, and nobody has benefits or pays as good as Alex."

"So now you run down bad guys."

It might've seemed like a trite thing to say, but Everlee caught the ring of pride in Shane's statement. "Yes, and I'll do it again, anytime, anywhere. Finch had it coming. He killed two little kids while fleeing arrest. Just ran them over like they were garbage in his way. No slowing down. No remorse. And they were in a school crosswalk! The bastard was on the street selling his shit the same freakin' night."

"That's something to be proud of, what you did."

"Well, of course. And I am. I'm not always a klutz, you know."

Shane slowed his truck, then turned into the overflowing parking lot of a small barn painted white and black, Holstein cow colors. The neon sign in the shape of a giant ice cream cone that commandeered the peak of the barn declared: Farmer Boyz. Best Ice Cream in the State.

Strings of Christmas-colored lights glowed from the eaves, outlining the repurposed barn in dazzling reds, blues, yellows, and greens. Even the black spinning rooster weathervane at the uppermost point of the roof was fitted with tiny, sparkling white lights. A small crowd waited patiently in lines at the four front windows.

"Sit tight," Shane said as he pulled around the building to the opposite side.

Well, hello there, drive-up window. "I had no idea this place was even here, and it's so close to where I live. How'd you find it and I didn't?"

"Maybe because I'm parked over there." He stuck his chin at the RV park across the street. "My rig, I mean."

Interesting. Shane lived less than a mile from Arlington Heights. That put him less than ten minutes from TEAM HQ. "You live in a trailer? Like an RV?"

"No, like a fifth-wheel rig. It's on blocks for now. Got the wheels covered to protect them from sun damage, even installed skirting this time. Where'd you stay in Anchorage? Officers' Quarters?"

"Nah, nothing as fun as a travel trailer, either. I had my own apartment."

"What's up with your ex?"

She blew out a tired breath. "Long story, short, we met just before I joined the Air Force. Didn't take long to wise up. We were together six and a half months, only married five. After the divorce, I got myself reassigned to Alaska, and he stalked me to Anchorage. You'd think he'd learn. Hell, you'd think I'd learn. We're over, but he keeps whining and trying."

"He ever hurt you?"

Everlee ran a hand over her hair, fluffing the coppery-colors at the same time she wanted to tear it out. "Not a conversation for tonight, sorry." Her marriage and her messed-up family were the last things she wanted to discuss with Shane. Talk about buzzkills.

After waiting behind three cars full of kids, Shane pulled up to the take-out window. The freckle-faced teenage girl there handed him a stack of napkins and cheerfully said, "Hi, Shane! I was hoping you'd come by tonight." She nodded at Everlee. "He's one of my favorite regulars. Are the dogs with you?"

Everlee liked this girl. "Sure, they're in the back seat. Hey, I'm Everlee. Nice to meet you."

"Nice to meet you, too. I'm Hailey. His dogs are so cute. Hi, Dolly! Hi, Molly!" She handed Shane two dog biscuits. "What'll it be? The usual?"

He passed the dog treats to Everlee. "Yes, one medium vanilla cone, please. Also…"

With one knee on the seat, she leaned across his lap and told Hailey, "One small chocolate fudge brownie on a waffle cone, please."

"Coming right up!"

In the short time it took to give the order, Shane's much larger hand landed on the small of her back as if he thought he needed to steady her. Which he didn't. Not really. Everlee wasn't in danger of slipping, but the warmth of his hand was too good to ignore. And somewhere along the line, her palm had ended up on his muscular thigh.

A thrill ran up her spine. Everlee froze where she'd perched. They were so close. Eye to eye. Nearly mouth to mouth. Shane was so much larger than her, and man, was he beautiful. The familiar scent of starch mingled with manly deodorant lifted up from his body and wrapped around them like an inviting, intimate bubble.

This was that magic moment when one of them should either back off or dive in. It wasn't going to be Shane. He hadn't moved a muscle, but he was still looking at her. Sharing her air. Holding her still. Her heart skipped a beat. The color of his eyes was such a deep, dark, intoxicating blue that a girl could get lost in there. Without thinking, the tip of her tongue snuck a quick taste of her lips. Wetting them. Teasing him.

Everlee was caught between doing something incredibly brave and kissing him, or chickening out and tipping back to her butt and out of his comfort zone—like she should. But what would his lips taste like? And why was he still touching her? Holding her? She wasn't falling, but he hadn't yet pulled his hand back. Instead he'd splayed his fingers. Did he want more? She was certainly willing to explore whatever was happening between them. Ever since he'd collapsed from that panic attack, she'd been dying to hold him and—

"That'll be seven dollars and thirty-seven cents!"

As if he hadn't felt anything, Shane jerked his hand away, and Everlee sank back in her seat. There. Over and done. Magic moment gone. *Pffft*. Just that fast they were teammates again. Nothing more. *Darn Hailey.*

While Shane handed a credit card over and chatted with the teenager with a crush, Everlee turned around and gave his girls in the back seat their treats. Both were waggling their tails, a hundred percent focused on Shane. Everlee knew how they felt.

That did it. The second she got home, she was losing that darned orthopedic boot, and tomorrow, bright and early, before work, she'd start running again. Maybe not her usual five miles, but she'd long enough to work up a good sweat and feel the burn in her thigh and posterior muscles again. She'd been sitting too much. All this recovery time was killing her, making her crazy and lazy. It was time to get her life back on track.

After Shane passed the gooey fudge cone to Everlee, he drove across the street and slowly through the RV park. Impressive. The individual camping sites were clean, shady, and private. There were only ten parking pads on each of the five, narrow one-way asphalt loops. It was more like driving through tunnels of giant sycamores lining the roads. Freshly cut green grass surrounded each long asphalt pad. Thick shrubbery separated them. There were enough trees that, except for the bright yellow and black welcome sign, the RV park was nearly hidden from the street. Everlee hadn't known it was there until Shane pointed it out.

"This here's my rig," he said as he pulled alongside a twenty-something foot-long fifth-wheel and shifted into PARK. Two empty dog crates sat side-by-side on the wooden porch. A green-and-white striped canvas awning extended from his rig over the crates. The fifth wheel's porch light was on, making everything look well-kept and homey, not traits she usually attributed to men.

"Looks nice," Everlee offered indifferently.

He wasn't inviting her in and this wasn't a date. They were teammates, that was all. Even if he did invite her in, it wasn't because he wanted her in his bed. She wasn't falling for this guy. Wouldn't even consider it. Nope. Teammates. Just teammates.

He kept the truck running while they finished their treat. She refused to play with her food in any way that might be suggestive. Didn't swirl her tongue over the tip. Didn't lick it, suck it, or pucker her lips over the melting blunt mass of it. Didn't look to see if Shane was watching, either. Nope. Just bit into all that rich, gooey goodness, and swallow by swallow, she ate that cone as fast as Molly and Dolly had eaten their dog biscuits. While she looked out the window.

Because Everlee knew men. She'd worked around them all her Air Force career. Every little thing a woman did with her mouth and lips could be construed as a sexual come-on. She suffered through a killer brain freeze, but at last, her ice cream was gone. Only the waffle cone remained when she turned back to Shane.

He wasn't watching her. Wasn't even turned her way. Just sat staring at his rig, licking his ice cream cone slowly, the tip of his tongue flattened to catch any drips before they melted over the edge.

Big mistake. Now it was her mind imagining all the things he could do with his tongue and those straight, white teeth. Those nimble fingers. Unfastening her seatbelt, she turned to watch him. He had no idea of the suggestive show he was giving her. There was something melancholy about the way his tongue lapped over and around the ice cream. He wasn't enjoying the treat. Just licking it out of habit, just because it was there.

"A penny for your thoughts," she murmured before she crunched the last of her cone into her mouth and swallowed it.

He shook his head, not telling her no, as much as shaking his mind out of wherever he'd gone. "Just thinking. I need to fill the propane tanks, but it can wait until we get back."

"Let's do that now. I've got time."

He shook his head again, still not facing her. "No. It'll wait." It was as if something heavy was now sitting between them. "I should get you home. Think your ex is gone by now?"

Shane turned to her then, his lips full and shiny and just-kissed wet. Okay, so he'd done the licking and she hadn't kissed him, but the moment was gone, and he was right. They had a job to do. It was time to go home.

So she told him, "Yes, Butch never hangs around for long."

And Shane drove her back to her apartment. When he dropped her at her building's rear entrance instead of the Dumpster, Everlee didn't wait for him to open her door. Just climbed out of the truck, put both boots firmly on the ground, then looked across the seat and told him, "Thanks for the ride. See you tomorrow."

"Alex's office," he reminded her.

She gave him a curt nod. Shutting the truck door firmly, she hurried around the rear of it in case he wanted to drive away. She wouldn't blame him if he did. The whole damned day had been one disaster after another. By the time she was on his side of the truck, Shane was on the ground waiting for her.

"Goodnight," she told him in passing. "Thanks for the treat, too. Next time, my turn."

He fell in step alongside her. "Glad your ex decided not to hang around."

"Yeah, I'll have to warn the complex managers he's been here. That ought to be fun."

"You can always stay at my place."

Everlee shook her head. "Nope, I'm good. Been dealing with Butch for years. He's not going to hurt me." *Because I'll shoot him the next time he does.*

Chapter Ten

He wanted to walk her to her door, but Everlee acted like she'd rather be alone. So, Shane left her at the apartment complex's secure entry instead of the Dumpster, then walked back to his truck. His ears perked up to catch anything going on around him. He scouted the fenced-in Dumpster enclosure and the back gate as he drove away. No sign of Butch. Good enough.

The next morning's meeting with Doc Fitz and Alex went smoothly. Doc Fitz approved Shane for duty, and he left Molly and Dolly with Harley. He'd packed before driving into work and was ready to travel.

The afternoon before, Mark had explained the ins and outs of TEAM employment: life and health insurance, the investment tracker all agents were automatically signed up for, as well as the on-site gym, medical clinic, the TEAM armory, range certification, and well, everything else. Shane listened, but honestly, he was on information overload by the time Mark finished. TEAM HQ was just too much.

Alex hadn't built just a couple office buildings. He'd also built what resembled an upper-class, fully staffed resort for veterans and a private retreat for handicapped kids, complete with the companionship of well-mannered service dogs and gentle therapy horses. And cats. Lots of friendly cats roamed the property. Guess Maverick's daughter Kyrie ran her own

Adopt-A-Kitty program out of the same barn where he kept his horses.

It was a helluva place to work. Helluva TEAM to get to work with. Some of these former snipers were legends. Not only Alex, but Walker Judge, Jameson Tenney, Lee Hart, Adam Torrey, Hunter Christian, Connor Maher, and Eric Reynolds. And those were just some of the guys from the Virginia office who Shane had met.

Hell, there wasn't a TEAM agent he hadn't read up on or heard about at one time or another. They all had bragging rights, but the ones he'd met so far hadn't been smug nor arrogant. Well, except for Alex. But Shane didn't blame the guy. If anything, he and his boss had a scary lot in common, which was disconcerting as hell. Turned out Alex had also joined the Corps straight out of high school. He'd lost his mom early, too, and until he'd met Kelsey, he'd been alone in the world. Just like Shane was now. Yeah, scary.

At the moment, he and Everlee were in transit to DFW International Airport in Dallas/Fort Worth, Texas. A flight attendant came through with a cart of refreshments. Shane accepted a bottled water and a pack of chocolate cookies, but she winked and handed over two more packs of cookies and another water. "We don't see a lot of nice guys like you these days," she murmured. "Let me know if you need anything else."

"It was the right thing to do," he replied quietly. Shane wished she'd drop it. All he'd done was give up his seat to an Army PFC flying standby whose wife was in labor. Understandably, he'd been on pins and needles. Shane only wanted to get the poor guy to wherever he needed to be before he became a father. Being there when your kid was born seemed a lot more important than flying first-class. Staff Sergeant Schnitzler would've done the same thing.

So, now Everlee was sitting by herself in first-class while Shane sat dead last in the plane, back by the rear galley and restrooms. No big deal. He'd flown worse flights.

They were both dressed in look-alike, casual TEAMwear: black cotton-knit polos with the gold TEAM logo embroidered high on their left chests, over black jeans and work boots. Shane wore the only boots he owned, a scuffed pair of dark-brown, composite-toed Ariats he'd gotten at half-price years ago. The soles still had enough cushioning that, at the end of a hard day marching, his feet weren't flat and he wasn't crippled.

Interestingly, Alex hadn't designated either of them to be Agent-in-Charge, which made them equal partners, although Everlee was the take-charge, bossier of the two. Shane didn't mind. He was the newbie, and she wasn't that bossy. He wasn't worried.

As soon as they touched down at Dallas Fort Worth International and deplaned, she handed him her ticket and asked, or more like ordered, him to collect her luggage while she grabbed a rental car. Signage was great at DFW. Shane had both their bags at ground level and on the curb near the taxi stands when his brand-spanking new, ruggedized TEAM cell phone buzzed an incoming.

"Junior Agent Hayes," he answered crisply.

"Listen to you, all professional and everything," Everlee teased.

"Where are you parked?" he asked at the same time he spotted her waving from the sunroof of a shiny red SUV that did not say 'covert' at all. "Yeah, I see you. Be right there, hotshot."

Shane hoofed it across the one-way shuttle and taxi lanes to the passenger pick-up zone. Leaning across the front seat, Everlee opened the passenger door for him. He loaded their bags onto the rear seat and climbed aboard. "Nice car," he said instead of *what the hell were you thinking when you chose this flashing neon sign?'*

"I like it," she snapped.

Everlee had that defensive look in her eyes again like she expected a dig and was prepared to fight back. Maybe because that was what her bonehead ex did, criticize and dig at her? Shane had no doubt Butch was behind most of Everlee's angst. He let it go. "I take it you've been to DFW before."

"Yes. Murphy sent Leisha and me into Mexico last year to rescue Heston Contreras and Asher Downey. Man, those guys were glad to see us, but I think two women saving their asses rubbed Heston the wrong way. All that tough Spanish machismo pride, you know." A wide-open grin broke out over Everlee's pretty face. "That was a fun mission," she purred. "He was so upset he didn't talk to me for weeks after we got home."

Shane could've sat there and stared at her for hours. Once he'd gotten past her prickly side, Everlee was another woman altogether. She liked her job, the people she worked with, and it showed.

"Plus, the guys in the office won't let Ash or Hes forget who rescued them. Men." She shook her head and giggled. "Don't they know that anything they can do, us women can do better?"

"Most of the time," Shane agreed. "I don't believe in role assignment, but women shouldn't have to do what an able-bodied man can and should do for her."

Shane now knew that Murphy Finnegan had been chief of the Seattle workforce before Alex consolidated both offices into TEAM HQ in Virginia. Murphy had also hired a more diverse group of agents, fewer Marines. Counting Paige Royal, his secretary, Murphy's team included several women. Everlee was former Air Force, but Murphy was an Army vet from the Vietnam Conflict era. Asher Downey, Heston Contreras, and Leisha Warner were also former Army.

"Oh, yeah?" Everlee asked. "Like what can't I do better than you?"

"Knock a man my size out with one punch," he answered quietly. "Put your fist through rotten wooden walls. Jump from a fifty-foot-tall tree without breaking any bones or spraining your ankles. Walk thirty miles carrying a full ruck, while carrying a wounded buddy, who weighs damned near two hundred pounds. And his gear. In the pouring rain. Shit like that."

"You've done it?"

Shane shrugged. "Had to. Wasn't leaving him behind."

"Where? Afghanistan?"

"No, that time we were in the Hengduan Mountains, in the southern region of Myanmar, near China. He got hung up in his chute when we dropped in. Never accomplished our mission because it turned into rescuing him instead. No big deal."

"Hmmpf," Everlee breathed through her nose. "You might be right."

Might? She seemed determined to prove she was every bit as good as a man. Truth was, in a lot of ways, women were hands down better than most men. Any guy worth his salt knew that. But they were still the fairer, lovelier sex, and Shane hated that she might one day be in a position where some asshat knocked her down or bullied her. Or killed her.

"If Heston's smart, he'll come around. Just takes a while for some of us guys to admit you girls are damned capable." Shane tugged his gear bag over the rear seat, then put it on the floor between his feet and unstrapped it.

There wasn't much room on the floor for the bag and his size thirteen Ariats, but he didn't go anywhere without his pistols, two Smith and Wesson Bodyguards with True-Touch laser that stayed activated as long as his hands were on the grips. All four magazines were loaded with .380 ACP, the popular self-defense cartridge used by law enforcement.

Shane pulled out one pistol after the other from his bag, unlocked the cables that ran through their open slides, down and out their empty magazine wells, and slapped full mags home. While Mark had made sure Shane had the proper federal licenses to carry aboard aircraft, Shane had made certain his weapons were safe to travel. Life was easier when you were a smart gun owner.

"Are you prejudiced?" Everlee shot him a sharp glance as she pulled onto the busy interstate.

Shane shouldered into the double. "Nothing to be prejudiced about. But I do think we're all biased one way or another. Each of us only knows what we know, right? And if you're brought up in a strictly male or female, white or black or brown, or whatever color, household, how can you possibly know how differently other kids and people live or think?

Older people tend to be more set in their opinions. That's not a bad thing, it's just the way life was for them when they grew up. Why fight it? Women being in combat-related jobs is a fairly new advancement. I see the pros and cons, but you've got to remember that most moms still teach their sons to be considerate and polite around women. They're raising gentlemen, not knuckle dragging heathens. Like it or not, part of that early parental training means most of us guys are gonna look out for our sisters-in-arms."

She huffed. "I'm no damsel in distress, and it's an outdated mindset."

"It might be, but I was still surprised when I faced off with an armed female recruit after I enlisted. She was a helluva lot tougher than I expected any woman would be. And she was quick as lightning with a pugil stick. Knocked me on my ass a few times."

"I didn't think male and female recruits mingled at Parris Island."

"They don't. This was an off-site competition, and Jessie Krankowski damned near cleaned my plow that night." Shane smiled, remembering Jess. "You'd like her. Jess is a red-haired dynamo and covered with freckles, least as far as I could see through all her protective gear. But I swear, she's more driven to succeed than most male recruits I worked with, probably because of her gender and her family background. She's proud as hell to be following in her father's, mother's, *and* her grandmother's footsteps. They were all Marines, her grandmother in World War Two. No way could she'd allow herself to fail. And she hasn't. Last I heard, Corporal Jess is now Lieutenant Krankowski, and she's graduated from IOC, Infantry Officer Course. That puts her on track to become one of damned few female USMC infantry platoon commanders. I think she'll do it."

"You sound proud of her."

"I am. Wouldn't mind serving under her, either. She's a ballbuster, but she's as honest as the day is long. You should meet her someday. Where to? Are we dropping our gear off at our hotel now or later?"

"Later. I figured we'd drive by the last known location the FBI had for Bremmer. Case the place, you know?"

"I was hoping you'd say that." Shane loaded the pistols into the leather cups under his arms and slid the extra magazines into his pockets. A six-inch Ka-Bar slipped easily into its boot sheath. The hard knuckle tactical gloves went into the passenger door's side pocket. No sense carrying them if he wasn't walking into a brawl.

Finally geared up enough to feel like himself again, he returned his bag to the rear seat and watched the streets go by. Many were lined with strip malls, Mom and Pop restaurants, gas stations, and convenience stores. In a few miles, those businesses faded into an older residential neighborhood, where elegant brick houses had been set back beyond large, well-kept lawns, trimmed privet hedges, and horseshoe-shaped driveways that took visitors right up to their front doors.

Branches of well-established live oaks bowed over the unmarked asphalt thoroughfares, creating shady tunnels to drive through. No sidewalks. No cars parked on the streets. Not much traffic. Basically, Bremmer lived in a quiet bedroom community, which seemed odd for a black widow who'd killed her husband and children. Unless she was already hunting her next target.

Everlee's glance strayed from left to right as if she too was trying to figure out why a killer would choose this little piece of domestic suburbia. "Does she have family here? Relatives?"

"None that I know of." He'd read the mission brief late last night. For some reason, Shane felt a kinship with the diabolical woman he hadn't yet met. He had no idea why. Bremmer was either a monster or a victim, and as much as he didn't want to admit it, he was the same. Still a victim of his mother's death, also a monster trained by the Corps. Neither by choice, both more through fate. Was that the only difference between Bremmer and him? Would he kill again? Absolutely. Would she? Shane wished he knew that answer.

The information in her file portrayed her as an insignificantly normal teenager until she'd turned sixteen. Tuesday Bremmer had been born Tuesday Smart. She'd been a serious straight-A student, also team captain on her high school volleyball team. But within weeks of her sixteenth birthday, her parents, Ray and Riki Smart, were killed in a one-car traffic accident. Alex had that woman named Mother check over the details of their deaths. Shortly after her parents' joint funeral, Tuesday dropped out of school and disappeared from her hometown of Duluth, Minnesota. Didn't surface again until she'd married millionaire Frederick Lamb in a lavish ceremony at The Hamptons and moved into his NYC penthouse. Where she had allegedly killed him.

"You've read her brief," Shane assumed. "How do you think a sixteen-year-old even met a man forty-two years her senior? They couldn't have traveled in the same circles, not some big shot from New York City and a kid from Minnesota."

"The brief didn't go into that much detail, but who knows how these types think? Freddie could've been a friend of the family or one of her dad's business associates. Maybe that's all their marriage was, a way for Bremmer to get out of town and get herself into the lap of luxury. I mean, what's worse, living unknown and alone in Podunk, Minnesota, for the rest of your life or whooping it up on the arm of a good-looking millionaire? Especially one so much older."

"I take it you've read the media reports included with the brief then."

"Yeah, lots of speculation, and everyone's got an opinion, but no real proof of anything, anywhere. No personal interviews with Bremmer, either. At least one would've been nice," Everlee answered. She'd slowed the arrest-me-red SUV into the curb on the opposite side of the street from where Bremmer allegedly lived. A for-sale sign marked SOLD dominated the middle of her front yard, but the place didn't look vacant, and the yard was too well-kept if it were. The home's owners were listed as Val and Sharlett Coogan; their real estate agent marketed himself as Dan-the-Man Greenberg. But the lawn had recently been trimmed, and the flowerbeds were full of pink and yellow flowers.

"Damn, this place is a little too Ozzie and Harriet for a killer like Bremmer, don't you think?" Everlee asked.

"She could be in the process of buying. She's rich enough. Let's sit and watch a while. Keep the car running and the a/c on. Springtime in Texas can make sitting in a parked vehicle uncomfortable. No sense sweating if we don't have to."

"Good call." Everlee put the SUV in PARK but kept it idling.

Shane leaned forward to look past her at the house in question. He had to admit, it was homier than he'd expected. Maybe the *Addams Family* mansion would have served her better?

They sat in front of the house for three hours and did nothing but make small talk and watch the grass grow. While there was little more activity from Bremmer's neighbors and their families as the hours dragged by, there was absolutely no sign of life inside her house. No one came or went. Not even the mailman. There were no Amazon or UPS deliveries, either.

"She could be in the wind," Everlee murmured. "She's smart enough, probably knew we were coming and took off."

Everlee had grown restless, and Shane didn't blame her. Most people couldn't sit still for very long. But then, most people weren't trained snipers hunting their latest high-value target. "True. Or she could be hiding in plain sight and we just haven't spotted her yet."

"She's got balls if she is," Everlee said to her side window. "But I guess a woman smart enough to kill two husbands and her kids would know how to get away with murder."

"She hasn't gotten away with anything yet."

"Hmmpf," Everlee breathed again.

Bremmer's brick home was older, built generations earlier when porches were large, wide-open places where families gathered at the end of the day, where neighbors paused for gossip or company. Two white rocking chairs made the place look inviting and lived in, although Shane suspected they might have been added for curb appeal. Bright yellow daffodils danced along the front walk, all the way from the curb to the wooden porch steps. There were no sidewalks in this neighborhood, just plenty of green between the homes.

Both Bremmer's steps and porch were built of wide wooden planks, and from where Shane sat, the lumber looked like stained redwood. No fancy gingerbread gables adorned the eaves. The window frames were modern aluminum, not old-fashioned wood. Just clean lines and minimal upkeep everywhere. He kept his eyes on the curtained, multi-paned picture windows at each side of the front entry. The sheer panels to the left of the door fluttered at the far right, lower corner. Probably a nearby vent creating the subtle disturbance in the air, but it gave him something to look at.

They'd landed at DFW at three pm. By six-thirty, the spring sun had set and the curtain was still moving. Not regularly. Just often enough to make Shane suspicious. There were no lights on inside, but there was only one way to make sure Bremmer wasn't home.

"I'm going in," he told Everlee. "I'll take the front. You take the back. Head her off if she bolts."

"You bet," Everlee replied as she tried to grab her gear bag, the black one with three gray smiling skulls across the front flap, from the rear seat.

"Here, let me get that for you."

"I can take care of myself."

"But my arm's longer, and you can't reach it."

"Well, yeah, there is that," she finally admitted when she couldn't extend her arm or fingers any farther. "Okay, all right. You're right this time, Hayes, but I'm no pansy. I pull my own weight."

"Never said you didn't." He couldn't resist the smile that tweaked his lips.

"I open my own car doors, too." She seemed determined he understood that.

"Yup, got it." Shane took firm hold of her bag, lifted it into the front, and set it on her lap, then waited while she armed herself. He was impressed. The woman carried a damned nice Sig Sauer, P365 Nitron Micro-Compact pistol, and judging by how adeptly she checked the chamber and chambered a round, she knew how to use it. A weapon that small would never fit his hand. Maybe two fingers, but it fit Everlee's palm like it'd been made for her. Pushing back into her seat, she tucked it into an inner pants holster just left of her centerline, which made it easy for her to reach with her right hand when needed, then bloused her polo over the barely noticeable bulge. No one would guess she was carrying unless they knew where to look.

"How's the ankle?"

"Fine," she snapped, her door opened and one boot already on the street. "You ready, Hayes?"

Shane took that for the shut-up-and-mind-your-business it was. "You bet. Let's go meet our suspect."

"Soft entry or hard?" Soft meant knock, approach politely with care. Hard meant break and enter with surprise, speed, and force.

"Soft," he replied. "No sense starting a war. I'll just tell her my car stalled and ask if I can use her phone to call roadside service. Only I'll call you. Sound good?"

"Yeah, let's get this done. I'd like to be on our way home by morning."

That word, home, caught in Shane's throat. He ducked his head in response but wondered if that was what Virginia truly was. It had been home once. Could it be again?

Chapter Eleven

Something wasn't right. Everlee could feel it. While Shane approached the front door, she'd walked up Bremmer's nicely edged concrete driveway and into her open backyard. No gate, no fence at all. With every step into what appeared to be a commonplace, all-American backyard, complete with three apple trees in blossom lining the back border between her property and the neighbor's, Everlee's spidey senses tingled. This wasn't the disorganized home of a psychotic murderer, not at all. Not unless Bremmer paid a gardener. Or she was just that intelligent and evil...

Which she might be. Everlee hated that nothing about this assignment was lining up like it should. Ms. Bremmer had honestly thought she could just move to another state, buy a family home outright, and never have to worry about the long arm of the law knocking on her door? And another thing, if Everlee and Shane had found her this easily, why hadn't the FBI arrested her by now? *Jiminy Christmas*, there were several FBI field offices in Texas, one a few miles away in Dallas. If the Bureau could pass Bremmer's whereabouts along to Alex, surely they could've parked on this street and apprehended the woman themselves.

So, yeah, there was something fishy about this particular contract. Office gossip was that Alex and the FBI hadn't always gotten along, that he'd pulled their bacon out of the fire more than once before. Most notably was the mission in Wisconsin, the time they'd gotten Libby Houston's sister killed during an all-out war between the Bureau and some Russian gangsters. Alex had made the Bureau look pretty bad when he'd taken over their operation and saved Libby's parents' lives. Was this just another screwed-up FBI contract that would force his hand? If so, how? And why? What did the Bureau have to gain by offloading their federally assigned responsibility to a private contractor?

The Bureau's mission was to protect Americans and uphold the Constitution. But when they failed, like they had against David Koresh and his followers, a bizarre religious sect known as the Branch Davidians, in Waco, Texas, back in 1993, they failed spectacularly. That time, the federal government had thrown the full force of the Bureau of Alcohol, Tobacco, Firearms and Explosives, aka the ATF, as well as the FBI, a division of Texas Rangers, *and* the National Guard, against Koresh and his followers, which amounted to just ninety-one people. Ninety-one! And yes, the sect had had run-ins with civil authorities before. Lots of them. But against all that federal manpower?

During the initial ATF attempt to serve a search and arrest warrant on Koresh, a gunfight ensued, and four ATF agents had been killed. In the end, after a fifty-one-day siege against the sect by the full weight of the United States law, seventy-six members of the Branch Davidians were dead, including twenty-five children and the cult's leader, David Koresh. Public sentiment ran strongly against the government's heavy-handed treatment of so few civilians and the unconscionable loss of so many children. To this day, people called the disaster the *Waco Massacre*, not the politically correct *Waco Siege*.

That the FBI and ATF had previously bungled a similar eleven-day siege in Ruby Ridge, Idaho, in 1992, wherein the son and wife of suspect Randy Weaver, were killed, cast the Bureau in particularly inept lighting. The killing of civilians, especially Randy Weaver's wife by a long-range FBI sniper, horrified Americans. But in the end, the damage was done. Randy Weaver's wife and only son were dead and civil lawsuits ensued. The government ended up paying millions to Randy Weaver and his three surviving daughters. But not one cent of those dollars brought his family back.

More recent ill-fated FBI shortcomings were just as telling. Which were all on Everlee's mind as she stepped onto Bremmer's backdoor step and alongside the wrought iron railing beside the rear exit. The sun had set and the house inside was dark. The back door was solid wood, painted white with a window inset in the upper panel. A single motion detection light flickered on over the door at her approach, which made Everlee a well-lit target, damn it. Her heart skipped a beat and her throat went dry. She would've felt better if Alex had sent four agents, not just two. But two was better than one and there she was.

With her pistol in her right hand and pointed up, she lifted her chin and peered cautiously through the backdoor window. Another light had just flashed on somewhere inside. Or that golden glow could simply be from a motion detector light at the front door. It was hard to be sure, since the glow was coming from, or at least through, the front room. Everlee had no way to know if Bremmer had answered Shane's knock or not. The narrow band of light lit the dark hallway that stretched beyond the kitchen. There wasn't any movement inside, not even a shadow most likely cast by that motion-activated front light.

She stepped to the side of the rear door, breathing hard but keeping an eye out for activity, in and outside the home. So far this day had been a bust. There was nothing suspicious about Bremmer's place. Even the backyard was pleasant and inviting. Taking one last glance over her shoulder, she stifled a yawn, bored with a mission that seemed to be a waste of time. Until—

KABOOM! The house shuddered. The sky overhead filled with fire and brimstone. Debris exploded out the backdoor's single window in one long, fiery belch that damned near scorched Everlee's hip when it passed. The ensuing backdraft sucked the air out of her lungs, like a dragon taking another breath before—

Jiminy Christmas! The dragon blew the door off its hinges. Even the concrete steps bucked, rolling her forward and backward as if she were on a ship at sea. She grabbed hold of the railing. There was no way to return fire, no one to fire at.

"Shane!" she yelled as she caught her balance when the ground stopped shuddering. She'd been lucky. If she'd stood directly outside the rear exit, she would've been skewered by the broken window. Tightening her shoulders, she tucked her head into the arms she'd raised to shield her face and eyes from the heat emanating from the burning house and from the shrapnel ricocheting into the backyard like a fireworks display gone crazy. The hellish dragon inside Bremmer's home still spewed plenty of red-hot spears across the neighboring yards. Booms, growls, and groans sounded deep inside what was left of the damaged structure.

But all Everlee could think of was Shane in front of that all-glass entry door and the two giant plate-glass picture windows beside it. He had to be dead or severely injured. She bellowed again, needing him to answer her, damn it. "Shane!"

She didn't dare move, not with hellfire raining down on the entire neighborhood. Poisonous vapors swelled around her. So many items that homeowners decorated with were flammable and downright toxic. Couch cushions. Carpeting. If she stepped out of this narrow safety zone, she'd risk death and pain and—

Forget that. Everlee was Air Force, not Chair Force. Not a damned scaredy-cat woman waiting for a big, brave man to come save her, either. Decision made. She jumped away from the blown-to-Hell rear egress, sure some exploding piece of glass or metal could still nail her in the back. Who cared? She chose to fight to her last breath, not to die quivering in fear like a civilian. Dodging fire and streaming debris, she hustled her ass around the house to—

God, no. Shane was on his back in the street. The soles of his boots were smoking. So were his jeans. Most of the front of his shirt was gone. His double holster was still intact, and he was lying there, pointing a pistol skyward. Everlee glanced upward as she ran to him, in case he knew something she didn't. Like maybe a house was falling?

Big mistake. In her haste to reach her partner—and because she was watching the sky instead of where she was going—Everlee stumbled, not sure on what. Probably on her big feet. Might've been debris. Whatever! She lost her balance and ended up skidding sideways on her thigh and butt over the last stretch of dew-laden, smoking grass. Nothing hurt, not even her previously sprained ankle, when, at last, her slide dropped her on the street. She scrambled to Shane's side.

He wasn't on fire, and up close, he didn't look burned, at least his face wasn't. But the front of his shirt was scorched into pieces. Black sooty smudges covered his face, and every inch of him was steaming. His blue eyes were watering plenty. That fine head of dark hair was now feathered and singed. His eyebrows were, too.

"Jiminy Christmas," Everlee breathed when she finally had her hands on him. "Are you okay?" she asked as she lowered his stiff arm and peeled his rigid fingers from the pistol's grip. He was alive but in shock. Damn Bremmer! She'd planned for this! "Look at me. Tell me what hurts, big guy. Did you hit your head again?"

He laid there blinking up at her, and she was remembering how he'd unraveled so quickly at the office yesterday. This wasn't a good time or place for him to have another panic attack, but she wouldn't blame him if he did. She was near to panicking herself, but only because she'd been worried about him. Yeah, right. They both could be dead right now. Hell, she might just join him in one, great big panic attack. They could cry on each other's shoulders.

Instead, Shane curled his torso forward, the muscles of his bare abdomen taut but wrinkling as he forced his body into an impressive sit-up. Turning his head, he looked straight at her, but his eyes were spacey. He wasn't dead, but he was hurt and—

"Damn Tuesday Bremmer to Hell!" Everlee spat as she took firm hold of Shane's hefty biceps and tried to ease him back to the ground. "You're hurt. Not bad, but you hit your head again, didn't you? Lie down. The EMTs, firemen, and police are on their way."

"What?" he yelled, pushing her hands away and refusing to stay put. Confusion and maybe a bit of hysteria darkened his deep blue eyes as he sat back up.

"Can't you hear the sirens?" She could barely talk over them emergency responders screeching up the street. It was then she saw the ink on Shane's left pec. In caps adorned with light green vines and tiny pink flowers. SARA and ABBY? Who were they? His mother maybe, and who else? A girlfriend? Two girlfriends? Not like it mattered. Everlee stored that detail away, saving it for another day—when she could think.

"What?" he asked again, louder this time and blinking like that might help his ears work.

Muscling him onto his back one more time, Everlee shook her head. There was no sense talking to a man whose eardrums must've shattered from that blast.

Shane shook his head at her, then signed in ASL, "You okay, Ev? Are you hurt? You're scaring me."

Will wonders never cease? Everlee knew American Sign Language, too. She'd learned early because she had two deaf friends, also because ASL actually helped her thinking process work a little slower and a little better. Quickly, she signed back, "I'm scaring you? You're the injured one here, buddy. I'm good. Just worried about you. How bad are you hurt?"

He shrugged, then signed, "My shirt's scorched, and I can't hear for shit, but otherwise, I'm good. Just out of breath." Shane rolled his neck, lifted both shoulders off the ground, and stretched forward, testing for injuries. "Looks like I got a little toasted."

Everlee ran her hand over his head, searching for blood or bumps or… Oh, what the hell? She just needed to touch him, to make sure he wasn't bleeding or lying or dying. Guys tended to fib when they were hurt, and every one of them said they were good when they were anything but. She didn't need that kind of macho crap, not today.

At last satisfied that he wasn't badly injured, she allowed a deep breath, then settled her brain and signed, "I thought you were dead. When I first saw you, you were smoking, and on your back, and..." She ceased signing before she signed something dumb, like how scared she'd been that she might have gotten him not only hurt on his first mission but killed.

"No such luck, Yeager," he signed enthusiastically, "but Tuesday Bremmer" —he nodded his chin at what was left of the damned witch's latest hideout— "if she did what it looks like she did, then we're looking at another crime scene. Maybe attempted murder. Of us."

"Yeah, I know, but I'm just glad you're okay," Everlee signed, her heart pounding in her throat, high enough that her eyes were watering like crazy now, too. He could've been killed, and that would have been her fault. Alex told her not to let him get hurt, and right out of the gate, this happened. She signed furiously before her emotions betrayed her. "She just tried to kill us, Shane. This was a trap. One that she set, damn her. She's mine!"

He shook his head, as the first of what eventually became five police cars, three fire engines, and two ambulances, screamed up to the scene, their blue, red, white, and yellow lights flashing. Dazed, he took his pistol back and returned it to his left holster cup. He'd only drawn the one, Everlee guessed because he'd probably been polite and rang Bremmer's doorbell with his other hand.

"Did you open her screen door? Is that when everything blew?"

He bobbed his head and signed, "She didn't answer her doorbell, so yeah, I opened the door to knock, thought maybe—"

"That's what triggered the bomb." Damn Bremmer. She'd known someone would come looking for her. And damn the FBI, too, for offloading this nightmare to The TEAM.

A neighborhood crowd had already gathered on the opposite side of the street beyond the fire trucks. The rental SUV's side windows had been turned into cracked safety glass and the windshield was gone. Something small burned on its roof. Several men, probably the homeowners, were spraying both houses on each side of Bremmer's with garden hoses to keep the fire from spreading. The homes' windows were broken and both lawns were checkered with blackened or burning spots from where the debris landed. What a disaster.

Shane's fingers were still flying. "We need to talk with her first, Ev. We don't have any proof she did this. Can't condemn a person without evidence and a fair trial. Alex didn't send us here to be judge, jury, and executioner. Our job is only to take her back to DC."

"Yeah, but..." Everlee stopped signing. She had no words, in ASL or otherwise, that could express the turmoil churning in her head and her heart. She'd never lost a partner, but she'd come damned close tonight. The thought of Shane dying was ripping her up. He was a brand-new hire, one of

America's best, and she'd almost gotten him killed. Her, someone who'd never seen combat, but who thought she knew everything.

Jiminy Christmas… So much carnage. Here. In what should have been a nice quiet neighborhood. Not wanting Shane to see her meltdown, Everlee looked over her shoulder at the glowing shell of brick where Tuesday Bremmer had 'allegedly' lived. *Allegedly, my ass.*

Every last one of Everlee's suspicions flamed brighter now. Was there any chance in Hell Bremmer was innocent? How could she be anything but guilty? After two vicious murder sprees that resulted in four deaths, her home exploding just when Shane and Everlee approached her? How could she not be behind this disaster? Everlee had seen the security footage from the latest fire Bremmer had set. She'd kept looking over her shoulder while she'd chained her apartment door handles. Sure as hell, she'd known what she was doing, yet she'd done it anyway. Just like she'd rigged this house to explode.

Everlee was a firm believer in the three-strike rule. And by hell, Tuesday Bremmer'd just had her last chance. Just for killing her kids, she needed to go down and go down hard. Three-year-old little Toby and two-month-old Betsy, for the love of God. Their deaths rankled the worst. Killing children was the most unforgivable sin in Everlee's book. But man, killing Shane would've been just as bad.

EMTs were on the scene now and taking charge. Two fired questions at her, and shined their annoying little flashlights straight into her eyeballs. "I'm not the one who's hurt, damn it. Let me be," she snapped, batting the nearest one's attempt to help away. She signed to Shane, "Stay here. I'm calling Alex."

He nodded, not like he was going anywhere. Two EMTs had already manhandled him onto a gurney and were seriously fussing over him. He seemed okay with it, and that worried Everlee. He might've been hurt worse than she thought and was just acting tough like guys did when women were around. He might've landed harder than he realized. Might have internal bleeding after being blown off the front porch. That was a good twenty yards or so. Shit.

Stepping into the middle of the street, she made her way over to their bright red and ruined rental. Everlee tugged her cell phone out of her pants pocket. Before she called home and unleashed the Armageddon that Alex would surely rain down on her for getting Shane hurt, he needed another shirt. She located his gear bag in the front seat where he'd left it and, just as she'd expected, found a neatly rolled extra set of pants, a shirt, socks, and underwear beneath the dozen or so boxes of .380 ACP ammo. *Sweet*. Then she dialed home.

Of course, Alex picked up on the first ring with a terse, "Stewart."

What'd he do, sleep in his office? So much for his *'alleged'* retirement.

"Boss," Everlee said, her heart suddenly squeezing the single word out of her vocal cords. Making her sound weak. She and Shane were alive, but Shane was hurt, and...

Damn. This was going to be hard, but Alex had to know, and she had to tell him—everything. Fighting tears, she cleared her throat and said, "Bremmer's house blew up when we approached, Boss. I'm okay, but..." She blinked to see straight. Everything had gone blurry. Had to be from all the smoke, damn it.

"Sh-Shane's hurt," she finally spit out. "Police and fire are here, and the EMTs are taking good care of him, and he thinks he's okay, and the fire department's here, and… oh, shit, Boss!"

"What is it?!" Alex barked like the Rottweiler he could be.

Everlee stopped whining and babbling. She was repeating herself anyway. But only because three firemen had materialized through the smoke billowing from Bremmer's scorched front entry. Something lay on the gurney between them. Something long and black and charred and…

"Looks like a body," she answered. Everlee blinked, shocked she'd said that last thought out loud. "Boss…" Her heart fluttered like it had that day she'd ended Finch. Too! Much! And too hard! "The firemen just exited Bremmer's house. Looks like they found a body inside," she answered, her voice still weak with shock. "Someone was inside Bremmer's house when it blew, Boss. Might be h-her."

Might not be…

Probably wasn't, knowing Bremmer.

But Everlee couldn't keep the quiver out of her voice.

"She blew herself up?" Alex asked, his tone calmer now. Gentler. Which meant he recognized the shock in her tone, damn it. Everlee hated sounding wimpy, especially to her boss.

"Not sure. I hope not… I mean, I doubt it." Everlee had already jumped past the conclusion that the body was Bremmer to the very real probability that it was another innocent victim. "I think she planned this, just like she's planned everything else. Bremmer's been one step ahead of the FBI all along, and now she's ahead of us. She knows she's a wanted fugitive. She set a trap in this house and waited for someone stupid enough to come looking for her. For us. For someone to knock on her front door. God, what if that had been a kid? A paperboy or someone lost or—?"

"How bad's Shane hurt?" Alex interrupted evenly.

With the rolled pack of Shane's clothes under her arm, Everlee leaned to one side to see past the line of firemen manning the hoses and into the street where the EMTs attended Shane. "He caught the worst of it, but he isn't too badly burned. Just a little scorched, you know. We split up. I was going around the house, you know, while he took the front. You know, in case Bremmer ran." Everlee wanted to kick herself for her repeated use of *'you know'*. But she was frazzled, and her mind was jumping all over the place. Every time it landed, it landed on the very real possibility that she was responsible for whatever happened to Shane. That she could've gotten him killed. "After the house exploded, I found him on his back in the middle of the street. Whatever she used blew him off her front porch, you know?" *Damn, I can't stop saying it.* "I thought he was dead." *You know?!*

She lowered her gaze to the ground and bit her lip. Her ADHD was killing her. There was no going back from this. Everlee would never forgive herself for the fact that Shane had nearly died tonight.

"Is he conscious? Can I talk to him?"

"Not right now. He's a little spacey and the front of his shirt's g-g-gone." *And I can't stop stuttering!* "But he was signing plenty when the EMTs took over and m-made him lie down."

"Signing?"

"His ears, you know? He can't hear, so yeah…" Might never hear again as hard as he'd hit his head. Everlee swallowed her guilt down one more time. "We've been communicating by ASL. American S-s-sign Language."

"Son of a bitch!" Alex's relief was tangible over the phone. Harsh, but sincere. That helped.

"This is my fault, Boss. I sh-should've taken the front door. We shouldn't have a-approached until we did more recon. I shouldn't have—"

"Stop."

Everlee shut up despite the hissing command from Virginia, or maybe because of it. Her gaze dropped to her boots. For the first time in a long damned time, she was submissive and scared Shane was now damaged for life. Wouldn't that suck? His first TEAM op and he'd never be able to hear again? He'd spent years in the Corps and had come home safe, but one day with her, and she'd gotten him injured. Her eyes teared up again. Damn all this smoke!

"There's no sense jumping to conclusions, Everlee," Alex said quietly. "Shane's a big guy, a lot bigger than you. He's built stronger and sturdier." *Yeah, that's what he said.* "And I'm sure he's thinking he's glad he took the hit instead of you. Go see what the medics say. Find out what they think about his condition before you fall apart."

She nodded, listening to the kinder side of her boss. Alex was the first one in a fight, and he could be brutal when brutality was needed. But he had a tender side as wide as the ocean and twice as deep. Which was the real reason she'd crushed on him all these months. Once—just once!—it'd be nice to have a gentle man, a no-kidding thoughtful male, in her corner. A guy who would actually put her first once in a while, like Alex did with Kelsey all the time. Just because. Not because he wanted something out of her, like breakfast or dinner or sex or mothering or… or whatever. But just because he liked her as a person, because he actually saw her. The real her.

"Are you still with me?"

"Yes," she murmured, then swallowed again, trying to work up enough spit to keep talking. "I can see them from here. They're still working on Shane. He's not bleeding, but he's shaken up, and they've already inserted an IV in his arm, and I… I'm so, so sorry."

"Stop blaming yourself," Alex told her with what sounded a lot like understanding. "Shit happens, and you of all people know that. Trust Shane. Trust the medics. Go check on him, then call me back if he needs to be hospitalized. He's your first priority. Get him sorted, then find out for sure who that dead body is. Talk to Bremmer's neighbors. Find someone who's spoken with her face-to-face. You've got to find her before someone else does."

That wasn't what Everlee expected to hear. She cocked her head at the worry in his tone. Not nasty anger or suspicion, just worry. For a killer like Tuesday Bremmer? Her moment of self-pity faded into righteous wrath. "Why should I? Who cares who finds her first, us or the FBI? As long as someone stops her murder spree, what does it matter?"

"Because I said so," Alex growled. And there he was, the volatile man she'd grown to love—in a purely platonic way. But then he coughed and backed off all that male arrogance with a quiet, "Son of a bitch. Belay that last order. Didn't mean it the way it sounded. You're not an idiot, Ev. I trust you and Shane. I've just got a bad feeling about this entire mission."

"Go on," she encouraged. It was rare anyone got the upper hand over Alex. Had the FBI?

"Think about it. Why send a highly skilled team like ours into a state with more than one FBI field office? Hell, there's one in Dallas."

She liked that Alex said *'team like ours'* instead of just *'his.'* "Go on."

"Why hire private contractors to locate anyone in the first place? What's so difficult about finding a murder suspect—if Ms. Bremmer is in fact the killer everyone thinks she is—that the Bureau can't do it themselves? They've got some of the best agents in the country. Thousands more than I do. And they knew precisely where she was."

It sounded as if Alex didn't think Bremmer was guilty. That gave Everlee pause. "Yet they've sent us straight to her last known residence."

"According to the Dallas County Assessor's office, it is. The property title hasn't transferred yet, but Ms. Bremmer did, in fact, buy it from her aunt and uncle, Val and Sharlett Coogan, two days ago. Mother's already double-checked."

"You think something else is going on, don't you? You think she's innocent? So why'd the FBI hand this case off to us?"

"To be honest, I can't reach FBI directors Zachary Strong or Tucker Chase to get confirmation. But when you catch up with Ms. Bremmer—and you will—place her in protective custody, yours and Shane's, and get her to the nearest safe house. Keep her safe, Ev. Don't talk to anyone, not even the FBI. Just bring her back to Virginia alive."

Whoa. "A safe house? Virginia, not DC? You want us to bring her to you now? Not to the FBI?" Everlee asked, her heart fluttering again at the three hundred and sixty degree turn this seemingly simple case had taken. Sure sounded like Alex wanted them to protect Ms. Bremmer from the FBI.

"Yes, a safe house, and yes, bring her to TEAM HQ. Call me when you get close. Once you find her tonight, take her to Smoke Montoya's ranch. You know where it is. But look around now while you're at the scene. Sometimes the safest place to hide is in the open. Check the crowd that's watching her house burn. Look closely at any women in emergency responder uniforms, police, fire, or EMT. Use your head, Ev. Find Tuesday Bremmer."

"Copy that," she replied, her gut back online and her head once more in the game. "I've got to get back to Shane. He needs a shirt. We'll be in touch."

"Stay safe."

"We will. I promise." Everlee ended the connection. A safe house meant going off-grid. Once they were securely inside the one Smoke Montoya provided, they'd be shielded from the Bureau, the National Security Agency, hell, even from the USA's geosynchronous satellites that watched everything and everyone on the planet from above. But first, she had to find that dirt bag, Tuesday Bremmer.

Alex might be convinced she was innocent, but Everlee wasn't.

Chapter Twelve

Shane had lost track of Everlee when she'd stepped aside to talk with Alex. All the noise—and there had to be a lot of it—was nothing but subdued mumbling. Made Shane feel as if he were deep underwater and out of touch with reality. Which he was. Thank goodness for ASL. One of the medics tending him knew the same language. He was good enough at signing to keep up a running conversation about what he and his buddies were doing while Shane lay there and let them do their thing. He used the time to catch his breath and his bearings.

Until Everlee came back into view. He didn't have time for medical care then. He had work to do, and, like it or not, she needed protection. She was what, five foot nothing? Brushing his entourage of efficient—and pushy—EMTs aside, Shane ripped the blasted blood pressure cuff off and lifted to his feet. His ears popped when he stood, which brought on a wave of dizziness. Like that was any reason to lay around.

He shook it off and jogged over to his partner, dodging firehoses, charred debris, and feeling pretty damned lucky that he and Everlee were alive. Man, she looked good. Pissed but good. Things could've been worse. He could be one of those gawddamned survivors, and Ev could be on her way to the morgue. Nope. Not going down that slippery slope. She was alive and still as bossy as hell. That was what mattered.

As if she meant to prove it, she tossed the bundle under her arm at him, and he was pretty sure she'd said, "Think quick, big guy."

He caught it one-handed. Holy shit, it was one of his three extra sets of clothes. Good thinking. Shane shook it out, stuffed the socks and underwear in his rear pockets, then draped the jeans over his arm. He looked down at the bandages covering his slightly toasted chest and belly. If the hair on his head was singed, the hair on his chest was burned off and gone. Oh, well. It'd grow back. He shrugged into another new TEAM polo that smelled fresh and clean. But it hurt like a mother sliding over his scraped shoulders, and he now knew the tips of his ears were blistered.

"What's going on?" he asked out loud, though he was close enough to sign. What he hadn't expected was to hear his own voice. He'd spoken louder than he'd intended. Temporary hearing loss, that was all he'd had. But man, the cacophony of heavy engines, men shouting, and hoses spraying was deafening. One of the fire engines had extended a ladder over the far end of Bremmer's roof, and a hose was secured to the top rung. Several firemen on the ladder tended the hose, drenching the flames in the cavern of what was left of a nice family home. Hence, all the racket.

Everlee's jaw was working. Shane took hold of her wrist and pulled her in close to hear her.

"Are you sure you're okay?" she yelled.

"I'm good," he assured her, speaking just as loudly. There was no choice. A person had to shout to be heard.

"Look at all those people, Shane."

"Lots of onlookers," he agreed, glancing over his shoulder at the crowd that had gathered. "Lots of worried moms and dads, little kids, too."

"But look at the crowd. Really look at them. At their faces. You'd think this was a circus show or something."

"In a way it is. It's a disaster, right here on their home turf. Of course they're watching." He forced her head back around to face him. "You're scaring me, Ev. Are you okay?"

She nodded even as she fell into him and put both hands flat on his chest. Her weight on his burned skin hurt, but he stifled the automatic wince and looked down at her. She looked up at him. "No, Shane, I need you to really look at these people, study everyone, not just those behind the police tape. The firemen found a body in the house. Alex doesn't think it's Bremmer's work. But he thinks she's still here, watching her home burn. He wants us to find her and get her to a safe house."

That brought Shane's head up. Just as quickly, Everlee's hands went to the back of his neck and pulled him down until they were nose to nose. He stifled another shudder at the pain she didn't seem to realize she was causing. "Don't be so obvious, big guy," she said firmly. "We don't want to spook her. But are you sure you're okay? No headache or... or anything?"

Shane knew that *'or anything'* crack meant she was worried he'd freak out again. Not happening. Despite the explosion, he was solid. Despite the pain of her touching his neck, he made no effort to pull away. He hadn't been this close to a woman like Everlee in a long time. Hell, he couldn't remember the last time he'd held any female. She'd pressed her entire body against his, and she had one leg between his knees. She'd lifted her hands from around his neck and her fingers were at the back of his head now, combing through his hair. All her plush softness was now flush against him, and that was an unexpected, hot-damned-nice position to be in. A man could endure any pain for this much feminine attention.

She ran a hand over his head, a teasing light in her eyes. "Your hair's singed, big guy. Looks like you sprouted feathers."

"Needed a trim anyway," he replied even as comfort flowed from her body into his at their intimate position. Her brown eyes were dark but sparkling, full of life and excitement. What he wouldn't do to run his hand over her short hair, to feel the silk of those penny-colored strands and the darker brown strands sliding between his fingers.

Everlee thrived on adrenaline, Shane could see that clearly now, and he had a feeling she knew precisely what she was doing. He liked the way she'd taken charge of their mission and of him. These days a guy never knew what women wanted, to be treated like ladies or just another one of the guys. He'd worked with female jarheads before. But things were different in the civilian world, and he was, after all, the new guy on The TEAM. What did he really know about Everlee Yeager? Other than holding her in his arms right now made it hard to breathe, harder to think. Just hard, damn it.

Didn't matter if he knew her well or not. Shane liked her inside his comfort zone. He shifted his feet, strengthening his stance to better hold her. As sharp as she was, she wouldn't stand like this for long. Certainly not once she felt what was going on beneath his zipper.

"You can trust me. I'm good," he answered. *Good at holding you.*

Everlee didn't step away. Didn't ease back or move her fingers from his head. Didn't act the least bit annoyed that he might be taking advantage of the situation. Which he was. He thought that twinkle in her eye meant she'd wised up. Instead, she leaned her head into him with a sigh. Which put her cheek against his chest, the top of her head under his chin, and her hair in his nose. He inhaled a bellyful, thankful for this small reprieve of—what was that delightful scent? Smoked coconut and ash? Yeah, he'd stand here all day and night if it meant breathing her in.

Her hands shifted to his shoulders, her thumbs stuck in the hollows above his collarbones, her fingertips fluttering like gentle butterfly wings over his shirt. "I thought I got you killed. I'm so sorry, Shane."

"Not hardly." His voice was husky for some reason. Must be the smoke. But there was no way Shane could ignore the feminine body snuggling against him. He circled her tighter inside his arms and let himself enjoy the moment. Because that was all this was—a moment, not a lifetime. An event that wouldn't last nearly long enough, nothing to take too seriously. Nothing to misinterpret. There would be no kiss, no magic moment where time stopped. Everlee was only making an emotional scene because she was as shook up as he was and because she was tracking a suspect. The damned hard truth, but still—the truth.

Even as he luxuriated in the warmth of her body against his, Shane kept his eyes open. The place was crawling with emergency responders, every one of them busy, but most obviously bigger, wider males. The EMTs who'd helped him were now standing over the charred remains the firemen had pulled from the house. A van marked CSI had arrived on scene and was parked between two firetrucks. That added three more people to the scene, all males. DFW's Medical Examiner was right then backing into Bremmer's driveway. That added two more uniformed professionals, one a tall and fit Black woman, the other a skinny white guy in round Harry Potter glasses, both in light gray uniforms. But no sight of Tuesday Bremmer.

Shane let his gaze scroll over the scene, dismissing first responders one by one. He was a trained spotter. This was what he did. He would find Bremmer.

Oddly content in the middle of the mayhem, he let his nose drop deeper into Everlee's sweaty hair. His nostrils flared at the sweet scent of shampoo against her scalp. Even mingled with the sting of ash and smoke, it was still the distraction he needed. Was she feeling the same peaceful sensation? Shane wondered as he held Everlee while he parsed and quartered the scenes around them.

Yellow police tape fluttered from temporary orange barricades set along the opposite curb. Several officers patrolled the perimeter of the quiet crowd, talking to some, nodding to others. Again, those officers were males. The neighbors looked concerned, and Shane wanted to think that concern was for their new neighbor. That someone standing here gawking tonight was actually worried about Tuesday Bremmer, not just their property.

One of the local news channels had a reporter on site, but she'd been sequestered far from the fire with the civilians on the opposite curb. Even now, she was going from one of Bremmer's neighbors to another, sticking her mic in their faces and asking questions. Cocking her head. Actually listening.

Interesting.

Shane stiffened at what he was seeing. There was no accompanying cameraman trailing her. For that matter, there was no support team anywhere in sight. He hadn't seen any news vans. He'd only assumed there had to be at least one, which most people would assume when they saw someone who looked like a reporter with a mic. But if a real reporter was here, she wouldn't be across the street talking with spectators, would she? No, she'd be puffed up with self-righteous ego, demanding to speak with someone in command, the fire marshal maybe. She'd be loud and rude and throwing around her First Amendment rights to free speech and to print sensationalism—or lies—which seemed to be what the press did best these days.

If that reporter actually was Bremmer, she was damned nervy—and smart. Despite the hour and the hubbub, she'd partially hidden her face behind extra-large sunglasses that hid her eyes and most of her cheeks. Her long, brown hair, streaked with chunky blonde streaks and parted down the center, fell casually over her shoulders. She acted perky and interested, friendly, like the typical girl next door, not stressed or worried. Dressed in a dark-pink trench coat that looked more brown than pink beneath the flashing lights, and matching heels that put her at nearly six feet tall, she smiled generously at her neighbors like they were best friends. At least, they should've been. Maybe one or two were friends, but there was something off about the reporter.

A pain tweaked Shane's heart at the very real possibility that Bremmer was like him, acting as if she were fine, while in reality, she had no one in her life who really cared, no one to go home to. That she'd been fighting the world alone, without anyone at her six since her parents died. He'd been like that after he'd lost his mom. He knew how grief and tragedy made a person act rashly, without thinking of themselves or the repercussions of the rash choices they made. That rule about holding off on making major decisions until a year after a death or a major life event was damned straight advice. Should've been a law, not just a good idea.

The hem of her trench coat fell below her knees. The belt was undone. The flapping sides of the coat covered a plain white t-shirt and a good portion of stone-washed jeans, the kind with those trendy horizontal slashes everyone was wearing these days. If that was Ms. Bremmer, she sure had a lot of guts to fake interviews while her home crackled and burned behind her. While someone else died in her home. Unless that person had already been dead. Guess there was always another possibility. But the dead body certainly fit her MO. Even if whoever that person was had already been dead, it was a damned solid plan. Plant a body. Watch it burn. Then waltz away and create another identity. Anyone who watched crime shows on TV knew it'd take months, maybe years, for the forensic evidence from a fire to be processed, longer for DNA. If there were any. By then, Bremmer'd be Mrs. Somebody Else and on her way to another insurance scam.

"Got her," he told Everlee with a certainty born of a man who knew damned well what he was seeing.

Sure enough, Everlee looked across the street despite her telling him not to. "Where?"

"On the curb. Your two o'clock. The reporter in the pinkish, brownish trench coat. See her? Over there by that mother and her two kids. Reporter but no cameraman. Want to bet she's our target?" Shane set Everlee away from him, turned, and took his first step toward Bremmer.

"Let's find out," Everlee replied evenly. If she'd felt anything during their close encounter, she wasn't feeling it now. "I'll go long, big guy. You go short. Don't let her see you coming."

"Copy that," he said as he walked toward the woman he absolutely knew was Ms. Tuesday Bremmer. He could feel it. Take away those outlandish heels, which were a damned good disguise all by themselves, and that long trench coat, and he guesstimated her height at five seven, her weight a hundred or so pounds. Just like her file said.

To maintain a casual meander that wouldn't attract Bremmer's attention, Shane paused at the rear gate of the ambulance and made it look as if he were looking inside for someone. What he really wanted were his pistols back. But the medics had taken them the moment they'd arrived and handed them off to the police. Who knew where they were now? He sidestepped a couple fire hoses on his way across the street, keeping his head down but his eyes on his target.

Someone's little girl squealed, "Mommy, look at that funny man!"

My God, people had actually brought their children to watch their neighbor's house burn. And they were catching what was essentially another person's worst nightmare on their cell phones like it was nothing but a circus event.

To disguise his disgust at this new generation of entitled voyeurs, Shane made a silly bow at the little girl, which allowed him to track Bremmer as well as Everlee. She'd taken the long way up the block, and was right then on the opposite sidewalk, walking straight for the lying reporter.

"You're funny!" the little girl yelled.

"Wait until you see my next trick, little lady," Shane jokingly replied.

That brought the phony reporter's head around. Shane looked her in the eye, at least into her glasses, and knew—he just knew—he was looking at Tuesday Bremmer.

She knew it, too. Bremmer dropped her fake mic, kicked out of her mile-high heels, and ran like the wind—straight into Everlee. Shane took off after her, dodging spectators and neighbors. By the time he caught up, Everlee had Bremmer face down on someone's freshly mown lawn. Her knee was in Bremmer's back while searching her for weapons.

"Good take down," Shane said.

Everlee looked up at him, breathing hard, her eyes bright and shining. "Yeah, not bad if I do say so myself. Thanks to you, she never saw me coming."

"Ouch, you're hurting me. Let me go. You can't do this," the reporter/murderer hissed. Without glasses, the whites of her eyes were wide with fear. "I have rights. Who the heck are you guys, *'Dumb and Dumber'*?"

Shane got the movie reference, but he wasn't playing. He dropped to one knee alongside the struggling prisoner while Ev cuffed her wrists behind her back. "Settle down, Ms. Bremmer. We're only here to help."

Of course she pitched a fit. "You call this help? And I'm not Ms. Bremmer! Stop calling me that. Now you're putting handcuffs on me? You idiots just made everything worse. Get off me. Let me go!"

"Not happening, Ms. Tuesday Bremmer or should I call you Diane Sawyer?" Everlee asked with sarcasm. "Seeing as how you think you're a reporter."

Shane agreed. "Do you even know any of the people you were talking with? Your neighbors? Don't you care about anyone but yourself?"

"I'm… I'm…"

"You're a liar is what you are, ma'am," he said quietly, his eyes on the crowd in case anyone decided to come to her aid. "Now, we can do this the hard way or you can come quietly, but you *are* coming with us. We're not turning you over to the police. We're taking you somewhere safe."

That took the wind out of her sails. "Really? You're not? You can? How… how can I be sure? Show me some ID."

Shane leaned back far enough to let her see the bright, shiny, federal contractor, TEAM badge clipped to his belt. "I'm TEAM Agent Hayes. My partner's Agent Yeager. We're not the only ones looking for you. You're on the FBI's most-wanted list, but we're not the Bureau if that's who you're worried about. We're private contractors who only want—"

"You're bounty hunters?" she hissed, struggling and kicking as if she could get away. Which wasn't likely.

Ev wasn't much older than Bremmer, but she had police training and experience on her side. She knew precisely where to exert pressure. Her knee in the small of Bremmer's back instantly ended the fight. "Nope. Not even close," she said as she rolled Bremmer over and jerked her up onto her knees. "But right now, we're the best chance you've got at staying alive. You didn't set that explosion, did you?"

That right there was the perfectly worded question. It offered Bremmer a way out, even as it stated her crime and her dilemma. The starch went out of her. She stopped resisting and swallowed hard, her chest heaving like a blacksmith's bellows. "No, I don't know how to do stuff like that. Even if I did, I wouldn't have blown up my own house. What good would that do?"

Which begged the question: Who did? And did she know how to set fire to her flesh-and-blood children while they slept? Did she know how to taser a stupid old man just because he fell in love with her, file fraudulent insurance claims, or make a buck off the deaths of others?

Everlee waved Shane away like she didn't need help. Which was true. With an unladylike grunt, she lifted to her feet, and, while keeping a hand on the flex cuffs now behind Bremmer's back, she hoisted their prisoner off her knees.

"I didn't know my house was going to blow up, and I don't know for sure who did it."

Everlee scoffed. "And yet here you are, in disguise pretending to be a reporter while your alleged home burns to the ground. Is it a coincidence that you just happened to have a trench coat and a mic handy? I doubt it."

Bremmer's eyes darted up and down the street. Everyone and everything at her home's end of the block was cast in an orange glow against the dark night's shadows. She kept licking her lips, a sure sign she was nervous, but not a sign of innocence. "I had to be ready. Some guy's been following me. He's built like a weightlifter, and every time I've seen him, he's been in a black suit and black dress shoes. I don't know what he wants, but he looks like he's from the mob. I suspected he'd flush me out eventually, so I kept a go-bag in my car, just in case. That's why the coat and mic, but now you guys blew my cover, and he'll—"

"Who?" Shane asked.

She bit her lip. "I don't know. I haven't gotten close enough to see his face. He's always wearing dark glasses, and I think he even called me once. It was weird, that voice on the phone. If it was him. Kind of robotic."

"What'd he say?"

"That I can run but I can't hide. Isn't that cliché? Sounded like something straight out of some cheap gangster movie. I laughed but only so he'd think he didn't scare me. But he did." Bremmer shivered so hard it sent her hair ruffling over her shoulders in a soft, foamy wave. "Never mind. You don't believe me, and why should you? I'm nobody. My house is gone. So's everything I own. I've got nothing."

Which was an outright lie. She had the insurance money from her first kill and possibly from the second. Which made Shane wonder about her parents' allegedly fatal accident. Had she had something to do with that? Was she covering for someone else? Did she have a partner? That'd explain a lot.

"Are you armed?" Shane asked as he took hold of her left arm while Everlee took her right.

"Not with anything that'll hurt us," Everlee snorted. She glanced at Shane when she said that. Where Bremmer seemed fragile, helpless, and acted as if she were in over her head, Ev was decisive and capable, her body fit and toned. She'd taken Bremmer down with a damned good running tackle, evidence she'd kept in shape despite her sprained ankles. The message in her big, brown eyes was clear: Don't trust anything Bremmer says.

He nodded a curt but unnecessary message received. A person didn't need guns or knives to kill. Bremmer's weapons of choice, if she truly was a black widow, were seduction, sex, deceit, and disguise. Ev wanted him to remember that. Like he'd forget?

With her P365 Nitron Micro still in her right hand, Everlee set a course away from the burning house. Shane had no idea why she'd opted for the longer, scenic route. Their ruined rental car was behind them and their gear bags were getting farther away with each step. The police had his pistols and the EMTs had his holster. Only weapon he had left was the knife in his boot sheath and three useless magazines in his pockets.

"Our car's back that way," he reminded her.

"No worries. I've got us covered, but if Bremmer's telling the truth—"

"Tuesday Smart," Ms. Bremmer interrupted, still looking over her shoulder with every other step away from her burning home. "Please. My maiden name's Smart. I don't know who Tuesday Bremmer is, but I'm not her. I'm Tuesday Smart. That's the name on my birth certificate, check if you want. You'll see. I was named after my mom's sister, and my parents called me Tuesday. Just Tuesday. Please. At least call me by my real name."

"Why not Ms. Lamb?" Everlee asked testily. "Or isn't that your name, either?"

"B-because…" Their prisoner sucked in a shuddering breath. "That's not who I am anymore. After Freddy died, I went back to my maiden name. I'm just Tuesday Smart now."

Shane froze at the tremor of real terror in her voice. He knew fear when he heard it, and this woman was a walking, quivering mess of it. At least she was playing the part well. Her parents were both dead, and right then, Ms. Bremmer, err, Ms. Smart sounded more like a frightened little girl than a savvy killer on the run. Was she him all over again, a victim of circumstances that had forced her to make decisions that may or may not've been in her best interest? Like marrying a guy forty-two years her senior. Like Shane joining the Corps too soon after his mother's funeral. He should've waited that one recommended year before he'd dumped his old life and enlisted. Ms. Smart had only been seventeen when she'd married Lamb. Had she simply hooked up with an older man who—

She. Murdered. Her. Kids.

Allegedly.

Shane shook off the sensual allure of the *femme fatale* at his hand. But despite the fact that he'd read Ms. Bremmer's complete file, he still wasn't sure what he knew. Was it possible for a kid who'd done as well in high school as she had to turn into a cold-blooded killer overnight? Yeah, sure. Maybe. Her life had been turned upside-down, and who knew what emotional distress she'd gone through when she'd lost her mom and dad?

Shane. That's who. He'd been there, done something just as impetuous, just as foolish. Had the drab, OD-green, USMC t-shirt to prove how easily grief messed with a young, inexperienced kid's head and forced him—or her—into making crazy decisions. But that didn't explain why she'd killed an old man, her second husband, or her kids. Just for insurance payouts?

"If you're telling the truth, *Ms. Smart*" —Ev added enough sarcasm to that title to choke a horse— "and if someone really did blow up your house to flush you out… and if you're not Tuesday Bremmer and are innocent of killing whoever was in your house tonight…"

Ms. Smart stumbled, then stopped walking altogether. "Someone was in my house? They're d-dead?"

Shane had to give her credit. Bremmer was believable. She had that surprised but innocent routine down pat.

"Yup, saw the charred body with my own eyes. Looked like you bagged another male, judging by how tall it was." Everlee kept dishing out the bad cop routine.

"But I… I told you. I haven't killed anyone. I didn't do any of it. I… I…"

"Yup, that's what they all say."

Shane jumped in with, "If you know who did, give us a name so we can help you."

Before Ms. Smart could answer, Ev ordered, "Later. Let's walk a little faster, people. Oh, look. A dark alley. We're taking it. You still got your phone, Shane?"

He slapped a hand over his rear pocket. "I do."

"Good. Call us a cab. If they can't get here in five minutes, call an Uber. We need to be gone before the police start looking for us. We'll talk more later."

"You are going to tell me what's going on, right?" he asked, his fingertip already on his Google Search app.

"Safe house, Shane. Alex said take Ms. Brem, oops, I mean, *Ms. Smart*" —*heavy on the sarcasm*— "some place where no one can find her. He's got a safe house nearby. Let's wait until then to ask more questions."

"Copy that," he replied. Shane had their next ride ordered in seconds, and the cab pulled up within the allotted time. Once they climbed in, Everlee directed the female driver to take them to the nearest convenience store, which ended up being less than five blocks due east of what was left of

Smart's, aka Bremmer's, home. Once in the parking lot, they all climbed out, and Shane took his jeans with him.

Ev paid the cabbie, and as soon as the car was out of sight, she told him, "Now get us an Uber. We want someone here pronto."

He nodded like the good troop he was. While Shane tapped their location into the Uber app, then waited outside with Ms. Smart for their ride, Ev ran into the store and came back out with two bags. "Kill your phone, Shane. You too, *Ms. Smart*," she ordered, dropping hers to the asphalt parking lot and stomping her boot heel onto it, grinding it to pieces.

"Why can't you guys just call me Tuesday?" Ms. Smart whined.

"Because you're not our friend," Shane said clearly. "You're our prisoner, and we don't call wanted criminals by their first names."

"And this isn't a game," Everlee bit out as she handed a plastic-encased cell phone to Shane. "I've got two burners, one for me, one for you. Wait a sec, I bought something that'll cut through all that plastic security shit." She stuck her hand into the bag and pulled up a retractable utility knife. "Here. Use this. We'll get a couple more burners once we're at the safe house."

Everlee didn't give Ms. Smart a phone, but she did use the knife to remove the flex cuffs behind her back. After she shook her hands and scrubbed both hands up her biceps, Ms. Smart complied without argument, probably because of the pistol once again in Everlee's right hand.

She tugged a cell phone in a rhinestone-crusted case out of her trench coat pocket and dropped it on the ground. When she did, her long hair fell over her face like a tumbling waterfall of darker browns and golden blondes. Shane couldn't help but notice. Who could miss the way the parking lot lights caught that ultra-feminine move? Tuesday was a slender, good-looking woman, and all that hair looked sleek, soft, and touchable. It was no wonder she attracted husbands as quickly as she had. Ms. Smart was walking, talking, maybe stalking, sex on two long legs. Tempting.

Shane shook off the tender feelings for the woman growing in the back of his mind. He had to remember that she was nothing more than a killer. A pretty predator, but, in her case, with the evidence stacked against her, guilty until proven innocent. He'd seen the security footage. She *had* locked her husband and children inside a burning apartment. She had walked away while her kids cried for their mama. That alone was damned heartrending proof. Didn't matter how she looked. She couldn't be anything but guilty. Yeah, she might get off on a technicality—heaven forbid—but right here and now, he was the long arm of the FBI law, and he'd take her down by whatever means were necessary.

She seemed calmer since they'd left her burning home behind. But she was so damned small, almost fragile, more like a frightened rabbit caught in a snare, than a conniving black widow spider who spun webs of lies to catch gullible men.

Which he was not. Shane didn't trust Bremmer, err, Tuesday Smart, just because she was easy on the eyes and seemed so much younger than her twenty-five years. For all he knew, she could've been one of those nasty mean girls all high schools groomed to take over the world. Personality traits like that didn't just vanish overnight.

He'd seen the innocent, femme fatale act before, and that day still gave him nightmares. The black widow then had been a pretty, dark-eyed, dark-haired woman in a blue burka, holding what Shane now knew had been a two-year-old little girl on her hip. A child who never would've lived to see her third birthday if Shane hadn't been in the same busy Afghanistan hotel lobby. All because her radicalized mother was wearing enough Semtex underneath that burka to blow herself, her daughter, and half the hotel to kingdom come. It was where American contractors often stayed. She'd been sent to kill as many of them as she could.

She'd failed, and her sweet daughter was still alive somewhere, but only because Shane had sent her pretty, "Infidel!" screaming mother to her eternal reward with a precisely placed double-tap.

He always wondered what eternal reward Muslim women received after orchestrating their own martyrdom and murdering their babies. Zealous Muslim males who waged war against alleged enemies of Islam were rewarded in the afterlife with seventy-two virgins. What did mothers get out of sacrificing their children in the name of Allah? Besides dead? What on earth could possibly be worth that kind of sacrifice?

Damned if Shane knew, but he was going to Google that one of these days, maybe when he actually gave a shit. The heinous crimes committed in the name of Jesus Christ and Allah were the real sins. *Those* truly used the Lord's name— or names—in vain.

When the Uber driver rolled into the parking lot in a silver Toyota Camry sedan, Smart's head came up. She'd caught Shane studying her. He turned toward Everlee to catch his balance. He wasn't looking for love in all the wrong places, and he wasn't dumb. There was just something about Ms. Smart that sparked the protective instinct in him. That had to stop.

"I don't have shoes," she said softly, bringing his attention back to her. Her eyes seemed bigger and sadder than they'd been before. They were red-rimmed, her eyelids swollen, and there was a good-sized scrape on her chin, probably from when Everlee took her down. "Would you mind stomping my phone for me? I don't want anyone to find me, not ever again."

See? Right there? She said the right words, but was that softly spoken, innocent-sounding plea just a bait-and-hook tactic to get him on her side? Did she see him as just another mark to manipulate, or was she sincere? Shane wasn't sure, and he didn't want to care. Ms. Smart was a job. Just a job. He didn't have to like her to get her safely back to DC.

But he did care, and that was a problem. He was beginning to like Tuesday Smart. God bless him if she really was the child-killer, Tuesday Bremmer.

"Sure." He replied gruffly to reinforce his indifference. "I'll take care of it." Letting his cell fall to the ground beside hers, he mashed both in a boot crunch of shattered plastic, lost contact lists, and photos. That hurt more than he'd expected. He should've removed his SD card first, damn it. Oh, well. He had the Cloud. Guess he'd have to learn how to use it.

He opened the rear door of the sedan and, like a gentleman, gestured for Ms. Smart to climb inside. She'd no more than ducked her head like an obedient child to enter the car, when a white boat of a 1970 Lincoln Continental careened around the corner on two wheels, tires squealing, and streaming black smoke behind it. Someone in the car yelled a mouthful of blistering, racist profanities. Two AKs bristled from the front and rear side windows. Thunder and death spewed across the parking lot in crystal sharp rat-a-tat-tats.

Ms. Smart stood frozen in shock. "He found me! See? Just like I said he would!"

Shane dove for her, flattening her to the asphalt beside the sedan. He covered her quivering body with his. Made sure no part of her was left exposed. He was big enough. Greater body mass. He could take a hit and probably live through it. She couldn't.

Another flurry of bullets blistered the storefront. Plate-glass windows shattered. An alarm screamed from inside the store. More random shots kicked up dust and concrete shards. The screaming profanity continued. Nothing definitive. Nothing that singled Ms. Smart out. Just random, "Die motherfucker!" and other senseless crap.

The Uber driver took off like his pants were on fire. Smart man. But that left Shane and Ms. Smart in the open. Even Everlee had left them. Like a maniac, she was chasing after the damned Lincoln, returning fire with practiced skill. She hit the car. The rear window shattered, and she might have hit one of the punks inside. But the Lincoln didn't slow down.

"He's going to kill me," Ms. Smart whimpered, her body racked with hiccups and sobs. "You have to believe me, Agent Hayes. He wants me dead, but I don't know why. I don't even know who he is."

Out in the street, Everlee dropped one empty magazine and slapped another home without taking her eyes off the fleeing vehicle or missing a beat. Shane was smitten all over again. But not with the one whimpering in his arms. Nah. His heartbeat raced for the one in the street swearing a blue streak at the asshats who'd gotten away. The spunky woman who so obviously had his six. The bossy, gutsy one. Everlee was definitely something else. And the way she handled her piece? Sexy as hell. There was just something about a woman who knew how to handle firearms and swear. The vicious Jiminy Christmases she was flinging at the gangbangers were cute as hell.

But he still had a job to do. He palmed the back of Ms. Smart's head and forced her to stay flat against the still warm-enough-to-fry-an-egg asphalt beneath them. Less chance of a body getting hit that way. Less elevated body mass meant less of a target if those gangsters circled back. And him without his pistols.

Heat radiated into his kneecaps as he crouched protectively over Ms. Smart. She was damned small and trembling and crying, and shit. He couldn't help it. She was still a woman, and he was an idiot. Shane rolled to his side and pulled her into his arms, putting her back to his front, and his back to the street, making him the bigger target. Her head fell against his biceps, and stupid caveman that he was, he put his cheek next to hers and whispered, "Shush. No one can get to you while I'm here."

She shifted around until she faced him. "B-but you believe me, don't you?"

Her stammering nearly did him in. Damn, as smart as he was, she might just be smarter. "Not my job to believe or disbelieve you, ma'am," he told her with as much indifference as he could muster. Which wasn't much at the moment. "My job is just taking you back to DC and turning you over to the FBI."

Her lower lip quivered. It took her a minute to settle under his chin. He felt the soft flutter of her eyelashes like frightened butterflies on his neck. Her breath was warm over his skin and she smelled of feminine sweat and breath mints. As much as he knew this was one helluva stupid mistake, Shane wanted her there now that the immediate danger was past. He could and would keep her safe, damn it. This—she—*was* his sole purpose, and all he was doing was his job. Tuesday Smart, Bremmer, whatever, was mission one.

"He said he'll kill me," she whined, her fingers knotted into the front of his polo and her heart pounding hard. He could feel each hammering beat through the soft, plump breasts pushing against his chest. It truly felt as if she were trying to crawl inside of him to hide.

God, if she'd only be honest, just once. "Who?"

"The guy who called me. The guy I told you about, the one with the robot voice."

"Whoever he is, he can't get to you while I'm here," Shane assured her gruffly. He'd meant to include Everlee when he said, *'while we're here,'* instead of just *'while I'm here.'* But he'd said the first thing that popped into his dumb head and, unfortunately, it ended up making this interaction sound more personal than businesslike. And too damned kind. Apparently, his big brain wasn't in sync with his little brain. In another time and place, this position with a woman could've led to a night of sex and pleasure. Yeah, right. In another time and place, the woman in his arms wouldn't have been a murderer.

There was no way to know if that drive-by shooting had even been meant for Ms. Smart. It could've been a warning or a payback aimed at the convenience store owner. Or just the neighborhood gangsters flexing their muscles to prove how tough they were. By then, sirens were again headed in their direction.

"We need to move. Now, big guy. Get up," Everlee snapped at Shane.

"Copy that." He pulled Ms. Smart to her feet as he stood. "We should talk to the police first. Alex will under—"

"Nope," Everlee bit out. "Not talking to the police. Tonight we just do what Alex said. Follow me."

Well, okay then. She seemed to think she was in charge. Who was he to disagree?

She waved them around the convenience store, past a row of Dumpsters. The stink casting off them reminded him of the obnoxious scents that hit a guy's nose the second he stepped off the tailgate of the C-130 that dropped him in Afghanistan. Nothing quite like the nose-curdling sting of raw sewerage, rotted animal carcasses, and week-old wet garbage to bring on a guy's gag reflex.

Shane ran alongside Everlee but kept Ms. Smart sandwiched between them. Into the night. Away from the police. Away from whoever was gunning for her. Two blocks down, Everlee stopped beside a full-size, rusted pick-up truck that had seen better days. Without a word, she reached into one of the bags from the convenience store and pulled out three pairs of knitted gloves. "One for you, Ms. Smart. One for you, Shane. Put them on. We leave no fingerprints. Ever. Understood?" She looked directly at Smart when she said that.

Tuesday's head bobbed. Everyone put their gloves on. Everlee climbed up into the driver's seat, which was a sight all by itself. She was much shorter than Ms. Smart, and there were no running boards. But Everlee was limber, and Shane had a feeling she'd never ask for a boost up. She was one of those independent women. Good to know. He made a mental note to never hold the door for her again.

With a hand gripping the armrest built into the door, her other hand clutching the lower part of the doorframe, she hoisted herself off the ground like a gymnast and plopped her backside in the driver's seat.

"I could've helped you, you know," Shane told her.

"I don't need any help," she shot back at him.

Again, good to know. He'd pegged her right.

Everlee flipped the visor down and keys fell into her lap. She turned to Shane with a mischievous glint in her eyes. "Why are you guys still standing out there? The keys were where I thought they'd be. Get in. We've got to keep moving."

Once again, Shane did as he was told. He held Ms. Smart's elbow while they walked to the passenger side, but ended up having to lift her onto the seat. As before, he had her in his arms, up close and personal. It was hard not to notice how delicately she was built and how small-boned she was. How tiny her waist was. That she weighed next to nothing. That her hair smelled like powdery roses, and somewhere along the way, she'd stubbed the big toe on her right foot, and it was bleeding. But she hadn't pitched a fit, hadn't even complained or drawn attention to herself.

Very interesting.

There was no console in the old truck, just a long bench seat. Smart scooted all the way over, closer to Everlee, lifted her left leg over the stick shift, then turned to Shane and patted the empty space beside her.

As much as he wanted to keep her in the guilty-until-proven-innocent column, Shane was beginning to like

Tuesday Smart—a lot. Maybe there was something else going on. Maybe she hadn't killed anyone.

Yeah, right. Not only no, but hell to the no. Security tapes didn't lie, gawddamnit. Neither did his eyes. He knew what he'd seen on that video clip. She *had* killed her kids and her last husband. Her legal name *was* Tuesday Bremmer, per the marriage certificate to Atchison Bremmer on file in the New York borough of Manhattan registrar's office. If she'd switched back to her maiden name, she hadn't done it legally. But she *was* an arsonist and a killer.

"Hang on to your asses," Everlee ordered.

And he knew without a doubt that former LT Yeager *was* bossy.

Shane climbed up beside Ms. Smart and away they went.

Chapter Thirteen

Everlee didn't have to go far, just far enough to ditch the piece-of-shit truck she'd borrowed and locate a more respectable getaway car. It was a good thing she'd found the truck's keys on the driver's side visor just when she'd needed them. Shane might've been surprised at her good luck, but she knew men, and most guys who owned POS trucks and cars, if they were anything like her ex, were over-confident and lazy. Guys who owned cars worth stealing might be just as overconfident, but they didn't leave keys in their vehicles. But drunks and do-nothings? Their loss.

She found the ride she was looking for in the small, rectangular parking lot beside Uncle Luigi's Italian Dining on the corner of Seventeenth and Oxford. A silver Lexus. Recent model. Perfect. Handing over the bag from the convenience store, she told Shane, "Hold this. I'll be right back."

"Copy that," he replied obediently.

She wanted to tell him to keep his hands to himself, too. That he was getting too chummy with an alleged murderer, but that conversation had to wait. Him holding Smart like he had during that shootout rankled Everlee in a way she hadn't expected. She didn't know Shane. Wasn't sure she even liked him anymore. But in no way was she jealous of a woman who'd torch her children. If he was crushing on Smart, Shane was as worthless as Butch.

While Shane stayed in the truck with their apprehended killer, Everlee hurried into the eating establishment and headed straight for the bathrooms to tidy up. A woman had to look put together to be believable, and Everlee intended to present a polished image instead of the red-faced, sweaty one looking back in the mirror at her now. It wouldn't hurt to look decent the next time she saw Shane, either. Not that he cared. And she couldn't care less if he did. After a short-lived marriage that had totally sucked, she'd had enough of men to last the rest of her life.

Soaking a handful of paper towels under the cool running water, she wrung them out gently and wiped the chaos of the night off her face and neck. Another few towels dried the excess moisture from her skin. She slicked her hair behind her ears and pinched her cheeks to add a little color. Licking her lips, she tossed the towels in the trash receptacle and headed for Luigi's fine-dining room.

Outside the restroom, with a yummy mixture of scents to her left and a feast of quintessential Italian dining on her right, Everlee paused. Actually sitting down and dining at Luigi's would be the perfect way to end this hectic day. Inhaling the savory aromas of tomato sauce, oregano, parmesan cheese, olive oil, and all the wonderful seasonings that made Italian dining a feast for the senses, was almost sinful. Almost enough to make her stay.

But not tonight. Before long, Everlee was holding a large paper bag filled with three take-out orders of piping hot, salted, buttered bread sticks, three slabs of luscious, parmesan covered lasagna, and bottled waters.

She was inventive, if not always efficient or coordinated, and a little proud of herself for procuring dinner. Too bad they'd end up eating it cold.

Everlee marched back to where she'd left Shane and their prisoner. His eyes opened wide when he saw the oversized takeout bag, and man, the guy knew how to smile. He still looked like he'd just survived the zombie apocalypse. His jeans were sooty and singed, his clean shirt just as bad. But that ruggedly handsome, if somewhat ash-lined face, lit up when he spotted what she held in her hand.

Everlee liked that a lot. She lifted the bag to tease him. "I've got dinner."

"I see that." By then, Shane had climbed out of the truck and had one hand on Ms. Smart's elbow. She winced as she set a dainty foot to the sidewalk, grabbed Shane's biceps for balance, then bent over and brushed something off the bottom of her bare foot. Poor thing had no shoes. Everlee nearly snorted. *Like I care? Poor thing, my ass.*

Shane held still and let Smart use him to catch her balance. Annoyed at the nice-guy feelings this female killer seemed to invoke in her fellow agent, Everlee jerked her head toward the lot beside Luigi's. "Over there, guys. See that Lexus? That's our new ride. Hurry it up. This food's hot now, but *we've got promises to keep and—*"

"*'And miles to go before I sleep,'*" Shane finished brightly for her. There was that same light in his eyes again. "*'Stopping by the Woods on a Snowy Evening,'* by Robert Frost. My favorite."

Despite the devious but charming prisoner at his side, Shane was totally grinning now. His eyes were focused on Everlee, and so was that handsome, mega-watt smile. She could almost feel the warmth radiating out of him. How great was that? This big, gruff guy knew poetry. The night just kept getting better and better.

"I never would've guessed we'd like the same poet," she told him coyly.

"Here, Agent Yeager. Let me take that for you while you drive," Ms. Smart offered as she stepped alongside the Lexus and reached for the takeout bag.

"No, thanks. I've got it." Everlee didn't want Smart touching their food. The woman wasn't who Everlee expected, but she also was not who she seemed.

Everlee turned to Shane instead. "Want to do the dirty deed this time?"

"Sure." He stepped up to the driver's door of the Lexus, still smiling. The power of that smile destroyed the brooding moodiness he usually led with. Laugh lines radiated out from those midnight blue eyes like rays of golden sunshine over an indigo ocean. All because they both liked Robert Frost? Or maybe he just enjoyed breaking into cars.

The smile faded as quickly as it came. "You don't want to steal this car, Ev. Uh-uh. It's got *On-Star*. We take it and the police will be able to track us." He stuck his chin at the next one over, a crappy-looking 1980s Dodge Challenger parked crooked across two parking stalls. The car's once-shiny black paint was scuffed to a flat, dingy black. The wheel wells were pitted and lined with rust. The wheels weren't much better, the tires were bald, and the windows were streaked with dust and speckled with bird shit. It might've been a hot car in its time, but it had obviously been driven hard, put away dirty, and neglected. "That one'll be easier to get away with."

"Go for it then," Everlee urged. "Don't forget your gloves. I bought that extra-large pair just for you."

Shane grunted as if he didn't need to be reminded. Well, too bad. That was her job. It took him less than five minutes to open the driver's door, less to hot-wire the sad, old relic. This time he took the wheel, and their take-out order rode in the back seat between Everlee and Ms. Smart. They didn't talk much, not with Everlee sitting with her pistol on her thigh.

"Head into Dallas," she told him.

"Copy that," Shane said as he eased the Challenger out of the parking lot and onto the quiet street.

A real car thief would have swapped plates, but in Everlee's mind, the Challenger was an honest borrow, not grand-theft auto. Pulling up the map app on her cell phone, she gave Shane directions to another quiet neighborhood just east of Dallas. It took him half an hour to drive to the empty church parking lot. Everlee had already called an Uber driver and written a four-word note on a napkin from the take-out order. She left it on the Challenger's dash. All it said was: Thanks for the ride!

The night was dark and quiet by then. Not much traffic on the streets. They walked a block north to meet the Uber driver. From Dallas, they hop-scotched between Uber drivers and cabbies, until the final driver took them out of town to the middle of Nowhere Cattle Country. Like before, Everlee paid the final fare in cash, told the driver goodbye, and stood in the middle of the dusty road, watching his taillights grow smaller and farther away.

"What's going on now?" Tuesday Smart asked Shane.

Once again, they were standing side by side, Smart almost snuggled under his arm while he leaned down to answer. "Basic SERE tactics, ma'am." He ticked the four components of SERE training off his fingers. "Survival. Evasion. Resistance. Escape."

Of course, she offered up one of those weak feminine laughs that sounded sincere and breathy at the same time. "Evasion? Really, Shane? How could anyone find us? I don't even know where we are."

"Agent Hayes," Everlee corrected her sharply. "I'm Agent Yeager and he's Agent Hayes, not Shane. You need to address us accordingly, Ms. Smart. We are not your buddies, and this isn't a party." She left off Shane's junior agent title. Smart didn't need to know any more than she already did.

"Good," was all Shane replied.

He might not trust Smart, but Everlee had seen the spark of attraction between them. Smart might be a pleasure to look at, and that was most likely how she'd been able to seduce and kill two men for their insurance money. But Everlee didn't trust Smart at all, and she needed Shane's head in the game, damn it.

Rocking back on her heels, Everlee was on high alert, ready in case Smart tried anything and Shane missed the cues. Smart hadn't tried anything yet, not after Everlee mentioned the safe house. If anything, Smart was too damned compliant, and that rang every last one of Everlee's ADHD's overpowering warning bells, whistles, and buzzers. A true black widow knew how to act innocent, when to deceive, but also when to strike. They were intelligent, psychotic women who plied stupid men with the sugar and honey of their bodies, until they'd finally seduced them into their sticky, deadly webs. Once trapped, this kind of woman paralyzed her prey with her poisonous bite, then sucked his assets dry.

Everlee refused to let that happen again.

After the last cab drive, which had cost her a small fortune, they'd ended up so far west of DFW there were no big city lights visible in any direction. But she knew where they were. Safe. Finally. The night air was cool and full of the sweet perfumes of wild flowers, freshly cut alfalfa, and even some already-been-chewed-and-left-behind hay. Yup, cow shit.

"Here?" was all Shane asked once their ride left them in a cloud of dust and dark.

"Yeah. We're here, Agent Hayes." Everlee had her phone in one hand, the take-out bag in her other, and her patience on hold. She thumb dialed a number and said, "Hey, Smoke... Yeah, we made it. Glad Alex gave you a heads-up that we'd be late. Which place is yours, the one without trees or the other... ? Okay, good. I see the green light now. Sure. See you soon." Ending the call, she turned to Shane and snapped, "Follow me," as she set off toward the ranch without a single tree in sight.

Obediently, Shane followed. Smart did, too. Why not? Everlee knew how to lead, but she also kept their suspect within sight every step of the way. Not like there was anywhere for Smart to run, but Everlee wasn't taking chances.

Smoke Montoya stood waiting for them on the doorstep of his home. The black jeans and tight-fitting t-shirt he wore seemed molded to his lean body. Made him almost invisible in the dark, just another shadow beneath the dim green porchlight he'd turned on. Didn't need to. Less light, less risk. Smoke knew the drill. Civilians needed bright porch lights. Not former SEALs.

Everlee stuck her hand out when she cleared the fancy brick walkway that led from the gravel driveway to his doorstep. "Hey, Smoke, good to see you again," she whispered. "Sorry to bother you so late, but Alex said come, so we came."

Without a welcome or a *'go to hell,'* he stepped aside, opened his door for his late-night visitors, and ushered them inside with a wave of his hand. After everyone shuffled in, he engaged a deadbolt, then pressed his palm to the glowing panel alongside the doorjamb. The hushed sounds of metal screens sliding and unseen locks clicking into place filled his quiet hacienda-style home.

"Sure hope we don't wake Jess or your little girl," Everlee said quietly.

"No worries. Jess is in San Antonio this week. She took Carrie with her."

"She must have a good personal assistant."

"Yeah, she does. Also has a nanny and two bodyguards with her. Plus" —he shrugged— "she's Jess."

Everlee took that to mean Jess knew how to take care of herself. Jessie West, the widely acclaimed supermodel, was no weakling. She'd once lived with her parents and brother on the ranch east of Smoke's place. They'd been childhood sweethearts, had even competed in rodeo events until the never-ending war in Afghanistan came along and stole Smoke from his family. By then, Jessie had already made it big in the fashion world. They'd lost touch. Then along came the F5 tornado that brought them both back home and together again. But only because the twister had taken Smoke's parents, Caleb and Caroline Montoya, as well as Ethan West, Jessie's brother and Smoke's best friend.

Smoke and Jessie now owned quite a chunk of property that included his parents' ranch, the Lost Chaparral, the West's family ranch to the east, as well as what had once been Clem and Betty Hardy's ranch to the west. Last Everlee knew, Smoke's wife Jessie was breeding champion Appaloosa horses and Texas longhorns, in between photo shoots for her teen cosmetic line, *Western Stars*. An odd combination of interests, but hey. Smoke certainly had enough room for Jessie to do whatever she wanted.

If you asked Smoke how he was doing, he'd always say, "Good." Just like every other American warrior on the planet. Didn't matter if they were shot to hell, half-dead, or bleeding out, special operators were all the same. They were good, at least good enough to fight until they couldn't. Course, by then, they might also be good and dead.

Everlee had never been in combat, but she respected the hell out of men and women who had. They were the heroes. Unknown, underpaid, and trashed by the press, but tried and true. You didn't see reporters or politicians getting medals of honor. Just warriors, the men and women on the front lines, the ones who'd actually sacrificed blood and limbs and friends. Firemen, nurses, doctors, EMTs, teachers, and warriors, those were the other real heroes in America.

She turned a sober smile to the silver-haired gentleman kicked back in a corner of the dark leather couch beneath the curtained, now secured behind metal armor, picture window. "Hey, Jared. How's Sunnyvale treating you?"

"Damned if I know or care, Agent Yeager. Not a big friend of city folk drama, so I don't get into Sunnyvale much. But out here where the air's clean, I'm still kicking butt. How's my best girl?" Jared Powers was an older, wiser, and yet still flirtatious gentleman. He'd been Caleb's foreman until Caleb died and was Smoke's foreman now. A stern-faced cowboy with a mustache that matched the shade of his shaggy, silvery-gray hair, Jared managed the ranch, while Smoke handled the sixteen oil rigs scattered across the southernmost portion of the ranch.

"I'm good, you old snake charmer," she replied, then gestured to Shane, who still had a good grip on their prisoner's arm. "Smoke, Jared, meet my partner, our latest and greatest, former USMC Corporal, now Agent Shane Hayes, scout sniper extraordinaire."

Ms. Smart's eyes widened at that sensational intro. Good. Everlee meant to surprise their pretty little killer. Which was all Everlee saw. This woman was guilty. Her innocent act was just that, an act, damn it.

"Ha," Shane grunted, but leaned over and grabbed Smoke's hand. "Not sure about all that crap, but I am at your disposal for as long as I'm here. Damned good to meet you, Mr. Mon—"

"Smoke. Just Smoke."

Everlee had to smile. Smoke Montoya was quiet, yet as deadly and to the point as ever. He might look like a sexed-up playboy with his deeply-tanned skin, a by-product of his proud Mexican heritage, and all that lush, black hair, cut short on the sides and left longer on top. But he was still a former Navy SEAL and one of America's most lethal snipers.

Seeing these two men shake hands felt like watching matched bookends coming together. Both were the same height, damned near the same heft and confidence, both tall, dark, heavily muscled through their shoulders and chests, and handsome as hell. Only difference was Smoke's eyes were deep, dark brown, and Shane's were midnight blue. Smoke was obviously of Mexican descent. His skin was naturally dark. Shane's was not; he was just tanned in all the right places. Not like that made them different where it counted. The same haunted shadows still stalked behind their eyes.

Everlee wished she knew Shane's story and what put those shadows there. But she also sensed the instant brotherhood these men shared that she never would. It was an exclusive club combined only of special forces operators and men who'd survived combat. Not a sisterhood, but a rock-solid brothers-in-arms thing that defied politics, distance, or public opinion. There was no safer place for Ms. Tuesday Bremmer, aka Ms. Tuesday Smart, aka Ms. Whoever, than right here on the Lost Chaparral.

"Smoke, then," Shane said gruffly, nodding his respect.

Smoke crossed his arms over his chest, his obsidian black eyes as dark as his jeans. "Afghanistan?"

As if responding to some unspoken guy code, Shane released Smart's arm and assumed the same position as Smoke, his feet spread, his arms crossed over his chest. "Laos and Chile, too. Heard you were in Cambodia a while back."

Between the two of them, there was a wealth of nonverbal communication going on. Was this a contest or something?

Smoke lifted one shoulder. "Cambodia. Thailand. Vietnam. Wherever the bastards sent me."

Just that fast, the competition was over. Shane ran a quick hand over his head. "Shit, this is insane, me being here. Never guessed Alex was sending us to your place. You have no idea how long I've wanted to meet you. Best damned thing I've ever done. You ranch horses or cattle?"

"Both. You ride?"

"Oh, hell, no. I'm one of those awkward city boys zipping around town on rented scooters. Never been on horseback. Wouldn't know where to start."

"We can take care of that while you're here," Jared cut in. He stretched over the coffee table to shake Shane's hand. "If you're anything like this guy here, and I know you are, I'm damned proud to know you, son," he said as he gave Shane's hand a solid shake. "Take a chance on one of our horses while you're here. Even got a couple sturdy mules if you'd rather. Big man like you might like them better."

Emotion flared across Shane's face, like a wicked flash of lightning against the pitch-black backdrop of an approaching thundercloud. It vanished as quickly as it came, but Everlee wanted to know the reason behind that flare. She'd seen him crash and burn, knew PTSD pretty much trashed the person you were before you went to war. Shane was exactly like Smoke, a war hero with relentless demons locked inside. Maybe something ordinary like a horseback ride in the country would do him good. Fresh air wouldn't hurt, either. She intended to make that happen, somehow. But not now. Maybe later.

"Thanks, another time," Shane replied. And there it was again, that disquieting tone in his answer.

Everlee changed the subject. "And this—" she turned to their too-quiet, too pretty to be a real prisoner— "is alleged murderer, Ms. Tuesday Smart, also known as Tuesday Bremmer. She's a wanted fugitive, which is why we're here."

"She's not restrained," Smoke said matter-of-factly.

"Couldn't keep her cuffed as fast as we switched vehicles getting here," Shane answered, then added, "but she's not armed. Ev already patted her down. You wouldn't happen to have a spare pair of tennis shoes she could borrow?"

"Ma'am," Smoke said politely to Smart. Not friendly like he'd greeted Shane, and he didn't appear to be smitten by Smart's dewy, doe-eyed looks like Shane, either. Without a second glance at Smart, Smoke looked back to Shane. "Jess has a shit ton of shoes. I'll see what I can find."

"'preciate it," Shane replied.

Smoke turned to Everlee and nodded his chin toward the back of his house. "Follow me."

"Breakfast at six," Jared called after them. "You need anything before then, dial one for room service."

"Are you serious?" Everlee had to ask. Room service? Really? In a safe house?

"Hell, no. Just making sure you guys aren't dumb enough to believe everything you're told. Goodnight, folks."

"Goodnight, smartass." She lifted her take-out bags where he could see them. "And for your information, I brought room service with me. We'll be fine for the night."

While Jared chuckled, Smoke led the three of them through his kitchen. He paused at a panel beside the rear exit to release the lockdown panels that covered all windows. Then he led the way to his patio, the edges lined with beautiful, brightly painted Talavera pots in graduating sizes. A motion-activated light flashed on overhead, and Everlee could see the pots were filled with yellow and orange flowers. She stopped to take in the wide-open landscape behind his place, looking for any bushes or trees that could serve as sniper hides or fast getaways. But the Texas night was dark, and Everlee couldn't see much past his backyard, except for the barn and corral and what looked like rows of sapling trees.

"You planted a forest back here?" she asked.

"Live Oaks, yeah. They're slow growers."

"I heard you lost most of your trees a couple years back. These replacements?"

"Something like that," Smoke replied as he led them across the lawn to what looked like a tornado shelter, if that's what the slanted wooden doors in the middle of his backyard concealed. Sure enough, he reached into his pocket, pulled out a little black remote, and voila. The two doors slid to the sides, like pocket doors, to reveal a lighted concrete staircase that led below ground.

She gestured at Shane to head down with Ms. Smart. "You two get settled. Thanks, Smoke. I'm serious. We really do appreciate this."

"Yes, thanks for everything," Shane said, his foot on the top step and his left hand on Ms. Smart's elbow.

Everlee winced at how protective—and gentlemanly—Shane was with Smart. But that was just him, a gentleman, polite and courteous with everyone. Right? Even with Everlee after she'd spit coffee all over him. Even then, he hadn't been an ass, and he could've very easily called her names, could've blasted her for ruining his shirt and his interview, his one chance at a decent first impression. But he hadn't. Hadn't belittled her, and…

Jiminy Christmas, he prayed over his food. She'd never seen anyone do that before. So maybe that was all he was doing, being gentlemanly and decent to their prisoner.

"There'll be a vehicle here tomorrow for you guys, and I'll find a couple pairs of shoes for your friend. Don't bother saying goodbye. I won't be here, and Jared'll be too busy working to see you off."

"Thank you for the shoes, Mr. Montoya," Ms. Smart spoke up, her voice so damned gentle that Everlee wanted to smack her and tell her to shut it. "I'll pay you back as soon as I can."

He didn't answer, just nodded at Smart before he turned back to Everlee and said, "Too bad you guys can't stay long enough to reconnect with Jessie. She would've liked that."

"Yup, not this time," she told him. "We've got to get our client back to DC, the quicker, the better."

"Understood." Smoke handed over the remote. "The green button's for these doors, the red's the weapons vault. Take what you need. There's a wall phone down there that instantly connects with mine and Jared's cells. Call if you need anything. We'll be here till sunup."

"There's a kitchen and a microwave down there, too, right?"

"You bet. Sleep tight."

"Goodnight, Smoke."

Without another word, he walked away and left Everlee standing there, looking down at the hole in the ground that would be home for the night. She couldn't help but feel that where one adventure ended, another was beginning. Just like Alice through the looking glass. Only this rabbit hole had steps.

Chapter Fourteen

The storm cellar dropped Shane into a small living area with a couch and loveseat to his left, a tidy kitchenette to the right. The furniture was pleasant but nothing special. Generic. Two bedrooms lay opposite the steps. He caught a glimpse of twin beds in both and nightstands between them beyond their open doors. Another doorway revealed a shared bathroom connecting the bedrooms, complete with a shower/tub combination and individual overnight kits on the counter. Made Shane wonder how many other guests Smoke put up for Alex. The secure overhead steel door was concerning. Shane would've preferred at least two points of egress, but there he was, stuck in an underground hideout with only one way out and a woman who'd had no problem burning her children to death.

As soon as Everlee activated the remote, the overhead doors closed them in for the night. Despite the bright lighting in this comfy underground dungeon, Shane's claustrophobia kicked in, and right on its heels, the sneaky tap, tap, tap—slam! of hypervigilance. A man like him could go crazy locked in here with a murderer like Smart. He swallowed hard, forcing the panic back where it belonged, down deep in his gut. But Smoke said there was a phone—

Oh, there it is, on the wall. Not like that helped much, but relief flooded Shane's insides anyway. He fingered the burner phone in his pocket, the one he'd nearly forgotten. It was another way out, of sorts. At least another way to yell *'fire!'* if things went to shit down here. Sure'd be nice if his heart stopped yammering up his windpipe. But hypervigilance didn't back off easily. He took another slow breath, and…

"You can let go now," Ms. Smart whispered, her other hand's fingers gentle on the tight hold he had on her wrist. "I'm not going anywhere. Are you okay, Agent Hayes?"

What a lie. Looking down at her wrist, he noticed how dainty and slender it was. He also noticed where his much thicker fingers had left marks from him gripping her too hard, too harshly, too—

He let go. Just dropped Smart's wrist like it burned. But the lines left by his fingers remained, and wasn't that just great? He couldn't even treat a prisoner right.

"Yeah, sure. Never been better. Just looking the place over." And fighting off another freakin' panic attack. Would that be pathetic, him, the biggest guy here, crying like a damned baby?

"You didn't hurt me," Smart whispered. "I'm okay. I'm tougher than I look. Really. I am."

Everlee seemed oblivious to him and Smart, which was just as well. Shane didn't want or need the kind of attention she'd poured all over him back at TEAM HQ. She was at the kitchen counter, emptying the takeout bag, which was good enough for Shane. He'd made a big enough fool of himself that first day, didn't need to do it again.

"Where do you want me to go?" Ms. Smart asked timidly.

He nodded at the sofa. "For now, take a load off or go take a shower if you want. The flex cuffs go back on after we eat."

"I'd like a shower, yes, please." Her voice was extra-soft, or maybe his hearing wasn't as good as he thought. Shane almost leaned into her and asked for a repeat. But he got the message when she looked longingly at the open bathroom door and shoved a chunk of her mussed hair over one ear like it annoyed her.

Hurriedly, he snapped to and scouted the bathroom for anything she could use as a weapon. He left one cosmetic bag on the counter for her, but removed the razor and fingernail clippers and took the other two bags with him. The mirror was unbreakable polished steel, not glass, which was damned smart thinking on Smoke's part. There were no windows. No glass shower door. No way to escape. The worst she could do was drown or hang herself with the shower curtain, but Shane didn't think Smart was that kind of desperate. If anything, she'd kept up her lost and afraid demeanor pretty well so far tonight. He'd expected more drama from a black widow, instead of the little girl routine she did so well. Unless it wasn't an act. Unless she really wasn't the murderess he'd seen in that apartment security footage.

Damn it, no. The innocence *was* an act. Had to be. That was what she did best, pretend to be nice when she was anything but. As much as he wanted to believe that a woman as fragile as Smart could be innocent of murder, Shane knew better than to give her free run of this crowded space. She would most certainly be cuffed to whichever bed she ended up sleeping in tonight, so they could all get some rest. Not that he wouldn't still sleep with one eye open.

He took another look around the bathroom. No hairspray in sight. The drawers were empty, and there was nothing in the cabinet under the sink. When he was sure she had access to nothing that would serve as a weapon, he waved her inside, and he stepped out.

"Place is all yours," he told Smart indifferently. Even then, he knew it was risky leaving her alone.

"Thanks. I won't use all the hot water. I'll be quick so you and Agent Yeager can shower."

See? This damned killer was messing with his head, sounding innocent. Hell, acting damned innocent. But he still had to check the rest of the place for flammable fluids, matches, cigarette lighters, anything she could use to start a fire. Murderers could be damned creative. That was all her innocent routine was, a twisted form of creativity.

He made a beeline for the living area, shutting the door behind him. No more talking with Smart. She was the killer genius; he was just a hired hand sent to haul her to DC. With one eye on the closed bathroom door, Shane set the remaining travel kits on the coffee table, then strode over to the busy woman at the sink.

"I need a weapon," he told Everlee out of the corner of his mouth, his eyes still fastened to the bathroom door.

"Seems you also need to remember that Smart's a master of disguise, Agent Hayes," Everlee snapped. "She's a wanted fugitive, a killer, in case you forgot. Not exactly girlfriend material. The FBI could've tasked the US Marshals to bring her in, but they didn't. They came to Alex. We can't let him down."

"Copy that," he answered softly. There was a terse kind of tension in Everlee's voice he hadn't heard before, like she was pissed at him. Like she was scolding him. "I've seen the security tapes. I know what I'm doing."

"Yeah, well I've seen you in action today, big guy. You were snuggling a damned wanted criminal after that shootout."

"I was just keeping her from getting shot. That is my job, right? To keep the client alive?"

Everlee huffed through her nose. "You had your arms around her, Shane. If that's not snuggling—"

"It wasn't," he told her firmly. "She's not what she seems, Ev. I know that as well as you do, so knock it off."

For some reason, Everlee wouldn't look at him. Not acceptable. Shane took hold of her shoulders and turned her to face him. "What's this about? Am I not performing up to TEAM standards?"

Those brown eyes of hers were bigger and brighter. Was she going to cry? God, he hoped not.

She jutted one hip forward, staring at him without blinking, her hands dripping water from the sink. "Just want your head in the game, *Junior Agent*."

Man, this woman could pack a shit ton of sarcasm into very few words when she wanted. She just made him sound like a snot-nosed kid in junior high.

"The remote's in my front pocket. Take it. The red button opens the vault beside the stairs. What you're looking for is in there."

If this was a test of nerves, it was a damned good one. Shane slipped two fingers into that warm pocket, just enough to tug the remote up and out, not one inch more, and he didn't take his eyes off her while he did it. He had no idea if there were TEAM rules about fraternization. Hadn't thought to ask.

Hadn't thought he'd need to. He and Everlee were two agents on a job. That was all.

Earlier, they'd had a moment that could've led to something more if they'd been civilians. But they weren't. He was former special ops, and she was every bit as good and as dangerous an opponent as Jessie Krankowski. Which made Everlee just another guy as far as Shane was concerned. If anything, he was The TEAM's latest FNG and he needed to prove himself. He'd already fought hard to get this job. He refused to blow it on any woman. Which, by the way, was not Tuesday Smart.

But this wasn't the time to tell Everlee that, either. Yeah, he'd felt something sitting in his truck that evening at Farmer Boyz, with his hand on the small of her back. He was pretty sure she'd felt it, too. They'd been locked together in a moment that he was certain would've turned into something more. Maybe would've ended with just a kiss. If not for Hailey interrupting them with their order, he'd have taken the chance and he'd know now, wouldn't he?

But Everlee had turned her back on him, and damn it, another chance gone. Another opportunity wasted. Shane let the small sigh in his heart go between his pursed lips. He had a job to do. Now was not the time for high school crushes. Palming the remote, he pressed his thumb to the red button and got back to business. A hidden panel to the right of the stairs lifted away from the wall. Its partitioned doors split to the left and right, revealing a helluva high-tech weapons stash.

A motion-activated light flickered on inside the sunken compartment at his approach, revealing seven McMillan bolt-action, TAC-338 sniper rifles. All were equipped with Leupold Mark 4 LR/T scopes with illuminated reticles attached to their overhead rails, and black, retractable Harris bipods folded flat to their undersides.

"I think I'm in heaven," he muttered to himself as he cleared the space between the kitchen counter and the vault. "Look at these weapons, those knives. Everlee, come see."

Shane couldn't believe the quality or the quantity of what he was looking at. He knew damned well the rifles alone cost over fifteen thousand apiece. He'd priced them online one time but had quickly decided the cost put them out of his league. Tack on those scopes for another three thousand each, the bipods at several hundred dollars apiece, and he was easily looking at twenty grand for one of these weapons. That didn't include ammo, slings, or tactical forward grips.

Lovingly, Shane lifted one of those babies out of its butt slot and pulled it away from the magnetized barrel rest. As a scout sniper, he'd carried a beat-up Remington M40A5. The tan, cerakote-toned baby in his hands now was an entirely different weapon. He guesstimated it weighed around fifteen pounds, geared up like it was. Add ammo, a sling, and a forward grip, and he'd be as close to heaven as any warrior could hope to get. Of course, he'd also be flat broke and owing some bank an arm and a leg. But hot damn, he'd be one happy camper.

His chest inflated with another sigh, much like the one he'd breathed the Christmas before his mom had died, the morning she'd given him his grandfather's Winchester rifle. His grandfather had actually used it to hunt deer, bear, and small varmints, but to this day, Shane hadn't fired the Winchester, not even once. He'd been too busy. The cancer, the funeral, and the Corps had taken all his time and every last brain byte. But now...

A smile cracked his lips as Shane scanned the rest of the treasure trove. Dozens of loaded magazines stood alongside a light anti-tank shoulder cannon, aka a LAW, on the shelf behind the rifles. Next to that, two sawed-off shotguns, phosphorous grenades, and more tactical gear, including vests. The shelves built inside the doors were deep enough to hold night vision goggles, plastic wrapped fingerless knuckle-gloves, stacked boxes of carabiner clips, tactical binocs.

Shit! He couldn't believe he was looking at anything and everything a spec ops guy could ever dream of or ask for.

Flashbangs, pistols, knives, holsters, take your pick. Smoke had built a veritable arsenal and was offering it for free. Shane's nose twitched. He could almost smell the acrid tang of expended gunpowder in the air on the range after hours of practice. Smoky sulfur with a twist of burnt charcoal. Nothing better.

"You have got to see this," he told Everlee again over his shoulder.

Finally, she came to stand beside him, wiping her hands on a bar towel. "You find what you need? Wow, guess you did."

"Sweet, isn't it?" he breathed as he removed a hip holster, strapped it on, then filled its cups with two Glock pistols, both which used .380 ACP. Most over-shoulder rigs needed straps buckled to a guy's belt for stability. Not the ones Shane used. His were custom-made of stiffer material that held its shape and clung close to a guy's ribs. Problem was, there weren't any of them in the closet. No problem. The rig he'd just claimed was a damned good second best.

He tagged a couple carabiner clips to his belt loops and attached empty pouches to them for extra ammo. Two empty mags went into each front pocket. He'd load them later.

Oh, look, IFAK bags. As in individual first-aid kits. He selected one and ripped its Velcro sleeves apart to make sure items in the tri-fold kit weren't expired. Yup. Epi pens, preloaded CELOX applicators full of enough hemostatic granules to slow arterial bleeders, one tourniquet, prepackaged burn dressings, a twin pack of chest seals, self-adhesive gauze, Israeli pressure bandages, two pairs of nitrile gloves, two bags of Quick Clot, sutures, nylon thread, and enough hemostats to get the tough jobs done right. All of it fresh. All of it plenty short of its expiration dates.

"You think you've got enough, big guy?" Everlee teased.

"Almost," he replied even as he strapped a minimalist woven holster around his thigh and slid a Browning Black Label 1911-380 pistol smoothly home. The holster fit that particular weapon like a glove, and Shane liked the versatility and flexibility it offered. The trigger guard was made extra stiff so it didn't flap back over the grip when a guy needed quick access to his weapon.

Shane already kept a knife in one boot. He selected another sheathed blade and slid it into his other boot. Never hurt to be doubly prepared, and redundancy was a proven rule in combat. Finally done weaponizing himself, he stepped back and blew out a breath of pure satisfaction. He'd been a defenseless sheep for most of this mission. Not anymore. Even though he'd have to remove nearly everything he'd just put on before bed, it felt damned good being a guard dog again.

He lifted an arm up and around Everlee to seal the compartment. "You need anything?"

When she didn't answer, he looked down at her. She was standing nearly inside the bend in his arm, her body aligned with his. Nearly touching. Close enough to feel the heat between them. Her pupils were big and black, her irises shrunk to narrow rings of dark brown. She licked her lips, making them shine. Making Shane hard. Something crackled between them. Felt like electricity.

Had to be his imagination. Everlee didn't need a broken-down has-been like him. She was tough, former security, a cop, and an officer. A woman to respect. Former AF Lieutenant, for hell's sake. He'd seen the footage from that Virginia Highway Patrol officer's dashcam the day she'd taken down Finch. She hadn't held one thing back. Just went after the murderer with no-holds barred. Alone. Everlee was strong-willed and most likely a better shot than Shane. Frost that humble pie with his chicken-shit meltdown at TEAM HQ, and, yeah. There was no way she could be attracted to a loser like him.

It took a minute before he forced the lust running in his blood like molten lava to back the hell off. So why couldn't he lower his arm to his side? Why didn't he want to? And why was she frozen in place, still looking up at him like he meant something to her? Her, a woman who could have any man she set eyes on. Why was his throat so dry he could barely swallow?

She blinked up at him, her thick fringe of lashes velvety butterfly wings. Her eyes were two dark wells of mysteries he wanted to explore, relish, and solve. "Do you have everything *you* want?"

He didn't miss the emphasis she'd put on that second *you.* "No," he said quickly. Then added, "I mean… Yeah. I've got enough gear, but…" *No. I don't have what I really want. What I need. What… who… I honestly, truly would love to have in my life. I have no real home. No real family. And that song, "I'm so Lonesome I Could Cry," is the story of my life.*

She blinked again, her silence telling. Was she really waiting for an answer?

The air between them thickened. Her eyes were blown wide with what sure looked like lust. Time stopped, just as it had during that moment back at Farmer Boyz. There was something incredibly sexy about a strong woman who handled firearms the way Everlee did. She hadn't run from those asshats back at the convenience store, either. Had instead given chase, ran straight into trouble, and peppered the rear of their getaway vehicle with lead. Then she'd turned on a dime and provided dinner, like any totally domestic badass would.

Shane tucked his bottom lip between his teeth, worrying. Wondering.

They were within kissing distance. Mere inches separated her mouth from his. So close their breaths mingled. He was no alpha predator. Would never be as fearsome as Alex Stewart. Didn't have the personality dominant males did. Wasn't even in the running. Hadn't wanted to sell that much of his soul to be the baddest killer in the tent or room or… shit, not even on The TEAM. If anything, Everlee was tougher than he was. And yet…

Shane was man enough to know that whatever he'd felt for Everlee these past couple days had changed, grown into something else, possibly even that indefinable something more.

The longer their breaths mingled, the more sure he became. Did he dare grab this chance and find out? Ms. Smart was still in the bathroom. How long would it take her to finish showering? Ten, fifteen minutes? Twenty? Thirty? She said she'd be quick, but he had yet to hear the faucets running. Better question, did he have enough time to break yet another TEAM rule? Was Everlee brave enough, dumb enough, to break those rules with him?

Shane hit the red button, and the vault doors hissed shut. The hydraulics locked into place behind him. He squared his shoulders, planted his boots, and prepared to find out.

Chapter Fifteen

This man. This wonderful, foolish man was taking too long to decide his next move. *Operational awareness, big guy. Aren't you paying any attention to your surroundings?* The vault was locked up tight. The shower had just turned on. Ms. Tuesday Smart was out of their way for now. She wouldn't be back for a good ten, fifteen minutes. But, hello, big guy! Once she opened that darned door, Everlee would miss this once-in-a-lifetime opportunity. She could almost hear the squeaky gears grinding in Shane's hard head. What was he waiting for? Permission? Didn't he know that, sometimes, thinking was over-rated?

He was so close, way inside her comfort zone. The moment she'd tipped her head back to look up at him, his gaze fell to her mouth, and she'd known she had him. There was no flirty exchange between them. No manly glint in his eyes. Only heat and desire so thick she could taste it. Lucky for him, Everlee wasn't a sit-patiently-by-the-hearthside-and-pine-for-your man kind of woman. Not that he was any woman's man—or hers. Stretching up on her toes, she grabbed hold of the sturdy knit collar on his TEAM polo, jerked his ruggedly handsome face down to her level, closed her eyes, and slammed his mouth over hers.

Finally!

His lips were soft and warm, pleasantly responsive. Moist. Ready. The heavy five o'clock shadow around his mouth abraded her lips and chin. Everlee didn't care but dominated the move. Her nose filled with the delicious up-close and personal all-male scents of his skin: sweat, smoke, and spicy aftershave. Not cigarette smoke, but the smells of ash and soot and open flames from the disaster that had darned near claimed Shane's life today. Maybe he wasn't the chain-smoker she'd previously suspected. She hadn't seen him smoke yet. Not like she cared at the moment. Not when a groan broke free from deep inside his throat and vibrated up into her mouth. Or was that a purr?

Not when Shane took hold of her jaw between both hands and cocked her head for better access to her mouth, either. Nor when his lips locked onto hers, like two moving puzzle pieces suddenly joined. He didn't jerk away, nor did he grab her hands to hold her still. That freedom of choice was all the encouragement Everlee needed. Sliding her fingers carefully around the back of his head, avoiding his burned neck, not manhandling him too much. Not wanting to hurt him, but needing to be crystal clear that—

Jiminy Christmas, yes! She wanted this man, and he wanted her. Her. Not the devious bimbo in the bathroom who killed men and babies. Just her—just boring Everlee Yeager—the woman most men avoided.

The shower was still running.

Shane pulled her tight into him, until her breasts were flat against his broad chest. Everlee thrilled at the tingling sensation of her nipples turning hard. He wanted more? Well, good, because she had a helluva lot more to give. There was so much more to her than just her rank. So much more she needed; so much more she had to give. She was freaking tired of the double standard that branded female officers. She'd worked damned hard to get where she was. Hadn't once slept her way to the top like the rumors declared. Didn't have the time, not with her stinkin' disability. If anything, because of her ADHD, she'd had to work too hard, harder than anyone else to get where she was today. And she wasn't a slut. Either he wanted her for who she was or he didn't. Everlee needed to know.

She licked the seam of his mouth, and Shane opened for her. That was all the answer Everlee needed. He thought that closet full of weaponry was heaven? Uh-uh. He was. This man. Them tasting each other and breathing each other's air. Her luxuriating in the hard, swift stroke of his tongue sliding inside her mouth, tangling with her tongue. Over and under. Around.

The shower was still running.

Needing friction in another part of her anatomy, she rubbed her knees together. His hands were now firm on both sides of her head, holding her still. His long fingers were in her hair, his thumbs on her cheekbones. Shane had taken control, and he was making a growling feast of her mouth. *Jiminy Christmas*, one kiss wasn't going to be enough. Not even this warm, wet kiss that was making her feel alive. For once in her life, Everlee wanted all of this man. He could be her safe place to land. Maybe the promise of forever. Was that asking too much?

Maybe. Ever since she'd first seen him, he'd been wound tight and about to explode. With every fluttering beat of her wild, impulsive heart, she wanted that passionate explosion to be with her, inside her. When the sensual exploration of mouths and fingertips led to palms smoothing over clothed, forbidden body parts, Everlee's fingers strayed into his hair and scalp. She'd expected prickles, but she found soft waves. Once combed back, those silky strands now fell over his forehead. She brushed them back, loving the warmth of his scalp on her palm and the slide of his silky hair between her fingers.

A rumbling moan escaped his throat. Swiftly, his hands slid down her neck to her shoulders, then to her biceps. One hand slipped around to the small of her back, pulling her in tighter against him, the other slipped under her shirt and—

"Yes-s-s-s," she hissed at the startling sensations his callused palm over her warm sensitive skin created. He was touching her. Kneading her breast. Strumming her nipple. Flicking the tender, begging tip of it. Making it sing.

The muscles in her core clenched and cried for his fingers. His mouth.

She lost track of the damned shower.

But oh, the problems this sizzling connection would create back at TEAM HQ. Everlee knew that but she couldn't make herself say no or step away. Not yet. Maybe not ever. Finally she and Shane were skin against skin, and she was going up in flames. Please, please, please. More of his mouth and his air and this once in a lifetime moment of pleasure and—

Enough thinking! She grabbed hold of his belt and unbuckled it to make room for her hand. He growled something when she unbuttoned his jeans and slipped one hand inside. No way was she stopping. Not holding back either. Not anymore. Not now. Deftly, she maneuvered past the elastic band of his jockeys and through a forest of thick, curled hairs and—

Yes. Greedily, her fingers circled a quivering spike that had to be the largest cock she'd ever touched. Her heart thudded up her throat at the daring danger in this plan. Just when her brain kicked back into thinking mode, Shane's hand slid from under her shirt to her ass. He lifted her against him as if she didn't weigh anything, then pushed her back against the vault. Certainly better than the table.

"Hurry," she growled, her fingers pumping eagerly down, then up, then down, again and again.

"Birth control?" he mumbled against her kiss swollen lips.

"Covered," she answered frantically. "Don't stop."

Everlee didn't remember how Shane got her pants down and off her legs, or her feet out of her boots. Or if he was still a weaponized gunslinger, still armed, still packing all that heat. That delectable other heat.

By then, her bare legs were wrapped tight around his hips. She didn't feel any holsters, so somehow, he'd divested himself of his weaponry. His jeans were around his knees. The stiffer hair on his thighs prickled her tender backside. His hips had her pinned to the wall, and they were close, so close to takeoff.

"You're beautiful, Ev," he whispered into her temple, one long elegant finger now slipped inside her slick folds, and—

"Ahhh," she huffed at the warm, wet sensation of that single curled digit stroking where he obviously knew it'd do the most good. Against the feminine ridges created for mutual, maximum pleasure, his and hers if he kept that up. Her body arched into his, begging for more.

"Flattery later, big guy," she whispered huskily, opening her legs wider and grinding her core against his hand. "Action now. I want action."

"Yes, ma'am," he answered, and with one hearty thrust forward—

Jiminy Chrissssstmasssss! Shane slipped deep inside, to the hilt, all the way. They were pelvic bone to pelvic bone, and he was right where she wanted him. Needed him. He was big. Thicker than she'd expected. And he was in deeper. Talk about hung. This guy was a stallion and Butch was a Lilliputian. Ha! The contrast nearly made her laugh.

Instead, she hissed as waves of exquisite pleasure pounded through her blood and stole her breath. Automatically, her hips gyrated to accommodate his impressive girth. Everlee groaned as the massive thing she'd just welcomed home slipped in and out with quick, slick heat and focused vigor. And in again. So far in that she was sure he was hitting her tonsils. Her head thrashed from side to side as she stretched. Her breasts were on fire, aching for his hands. Ah! They'd have to wait. She growled again, her heart thumping like a beast as she held onto Shane for what was fast turning into the ride of her life.

"You okay?" he breathed in her hair, still pumping with sure, long strokes, still holding onto her ass as he pounded her into the wall.

"Yes-s-s-s-s," she hissed again, her eyes tightly closed, her fingernails dug onto his taut, muscled backside, urging him to be quick about this quickie.

Not like Shane needed encouragement. He'd set a good hard rhythm and was hitting all the right spots. Oh, man, was he nailing it, err, her. But they really couldn't get caught having sex like this. Not in whoever's house this was. Oh, yeah, Smoke's. Everlee couldn't even hear the shower, only the buzz in her body. Was the water still running?

What was she thinking?!

At the moment? Of nothing and no one but Shane. The work roughened coarseness of his palm on her ass. His hot and heavy breath in her ear. The overheated, very masculine muscle coursing deep inside of her.

She'd never been half-dressed nor driven crazy like this before. Not once in her mixed-up youth. Had never been with a man like Shane, either. He was gentle but rough and wild at the same time. Wild, like her. He was kind, but damned decisive once he made his mind up. And strong. So strong. Everlee melted into indescribable pleasure of him holding all of her weight. Its slick incline deep in her core flashed urgently, then morphed into a racing tsunami. And she came. On an orgasm that crested high, so high, she was tossed into a mix of radiant starlight, tinged slightly with lead agent torment.

The torment fled when a cataclysmic explosion of pleasure took over. Shook her down to her wanton core. Her body stiffened under the engulfing onslaught from the powerful man joined with her. His legs had turned into obedient pistons that seemed to never tire. Her legs clenched into a manacle around Shane's hips. She didn't want to hurt him, but she'd never felt anything like this before. Not once.

Her legs had turned into vises, gripping him while more waves of pure pleasure zipped through her like another lit fuse. Its detonation came just as swiftly as the first and tossed her higher, blinded and blessed, into a second, brighter universe of never before seen stars. Real stars. Real pleasure. She was fireworks. She was stardust.

So this was that elusive beast called Orgasm. Twice in a row. *Damn.*

"Do it again," she ordered, her voice as raspy and ragged as shit.

Shane's pounding turned fiercer. Harder. Within seconds, he groaned a hearty, "Fuck!" His entire body stiffened. His hips and his thighs and his knees. His release kicked loose and Everlee felt its unique, scalding heat pulsing inside of her. For the first time in her life, she wished she weren't on birth control. That they weren't wasting the essence that might've become a child. Their child. A dark-haired, smiling little son with sparkling blue, mischief-filled eyes. Or a daughter. A blue-eyed daughter would be just as good. Make that perfect.

What a foolish thought! Where had it even come from?

Everlee wasn't good enough to be a wife, never a mother.

Stupid damned tears!

Shane stilled, and they were both panting like draft horses after a tractor pull, or something like that. Draft horses pulled tractors, didn't they? Maybe racehorses would have been a better analogy.

They were still at the same wall. Her back against it. His breath hot and heavy on her neck. Their clothes were undone enough, yet not nearly enough. Both were slick with sweat. Sated? Momentarily, yes. But explaining the scent in the air and their current state of dishevel would be a challenge. Not like Everlee cared what Ms. Smart thought.

Shane took her mouth in an all-encompassing, gentle kiss that prickled her skin while it stole the last of Everlee's heart. He ran his nose down her neck to the top of her breast and kissed her there, too. "I want a real date," he whispered against her sensitive skin. "A real, sit down to dinner date. No one but us. Clothes are optional."

"Towel, now," she deflected shakily, which made Shane grin.

"You're so bossy," he teased as he drew close for another kiss, this one on the top of her nose. "I love that most about you, LT."

Love? Did he say the L word? Already?

"Shut up and hurry!" she clipped, shushing him to step on it before—

The blow dryer revved on in the bathroom. *Oh crap!*

Their heads pivoted to the still closed door, the only barrier between them and Ms. Smart.

The spell was broken. Like a lightning strike, the logic card in Everlee's impulsive brain cycled back online. The damned thing. Along with it came the corrective zap of what would be a well-deserved reprimand from the *Energizer Bunny* called Alex, reminding her that a true hardass owned The TEAM. And her. What would he say if he knew what they were doing now? That they were this kind of distracted while on a mission? That they weren't even thinking about their jobs—or him? At all? Tonight, of all nights? Here, of all places?

Oh, damn.

Just as fast, a rugged blast of ice-cold censure slapped the front of her cerebral cortex and shut down her impetuous plans for the handsome man worming his way back inside her arms. Initially, Shane had let her assume command of this mission, probably because he was a newbie of only two days. Anyone would have done that. But he was in control now, and as much as Everlee wanted more time with him at the wheel, she was about to wrest that control back. Now was not the time and this was not the place. She never should've led him on.

"Shane," she murmured around the warm, wet suction of his tempting lips.

His answering, "Hmmm" vibrated against her mouth like a sexy complaint.

Man, it was hard to think. She tried again, this time with, "Tuesday."

The tender onslaught ceased. Yeah, that was the perfect mood-buster.

"I know, I know," he agreed hoarsely, still licking her lips, still breathing her air, and holding on tight to her partially clad body. "But understand, Agent Yeager. I've wanted to make love with you since we met. We *will* be doing this again soon."

"You did?" A breathy sigh of satisfaction huffed out of Everlee. Knowing Shane was on board with the attraction between them was enough. It had to be. For now.

Clearing her throat, she pressed a gentle palm to the center of his magnificent chest. Man, he ought to have a likeness of that chest sculpted in marble. She wished they'd done this right, with him naked. On his back. What a waste that she hadn't gotten to see him, all of him. She felt cheated.

But later. Yeah, that piece of eye candy would have to wait. Everlee pushed him away, trying to gently remind him who they were and why they were in Smoke's storm cellar. Setting a boundary she knew she'd destroy the first chance she could.

Shane eased out of her body with a sweet, grumbly growl and set her feet back on the floor. Everlee found him staring down at her. Like a schoolgirl in love, she was smitten all over again. They were so close, still in each other's arms, yet suddenly, too far away. For the first time in her life, she found herself looking up at a man she respected and could actually see herself living with. A man she could live for. Maybe even die for.

The tenderness in his eyes shone down on her like a full moon setting over the Pacific, blessing her with comfort and tenderness and, okay, yeah, lots of sex and steamy hot romance. A storm of tender emotions was hidden there. Shane was a gunslinger at heart, but what a heart. He didn't want to let her go any more than she wanted to let go of him. His fingers were still tight, only they'd drifted to her waist. His gaze was steady, as if he'd found something he wasn't willing to lose.

"I shouldn't have done that," she admitted meekly. "I know better."

Lifting his hand, he smoothed it over her head, ending with his palm cupping her cheek. "I'm so damned glad you took the first step."

Everlee leaned into the strength of that warm hand and those strong, capable fingers. "Yeah, well, already told you I have no impulse control. Ask Alex. He'll confirm it."

A smile lifted the corners of Shane's mouth. "Alex isn't here and I wouldn't ask him if he were."

The hum of the blow dryer cut off, and Everlee shoved the man she was beginning to have serious feelings for, away. Sort of. Needing one last touch before he got too far away, she traced her fingertips along his square, whiskered jaw, and said "We'd better clean up and get dressed. I'll check under the sink. Maybe there's a can of air deodorizer down there."

"Don't move. Stay here," Shane said as he pulled himself together, buckled his belt, tucked his shirt in, and went to the kitchen. He doused a handful of paper towels under the faucet, then checked beneath the sink, and grabbed an aerosol can of lilac-something or other. He came straight back to Everlee, dropped to one knee in front of her, and signaled her to put her foot on his other thigh. He was so kind. So incredibly thoughtful. It was so out of character with every other male she'd ever known. She could have cried when he wiped between her legs and helped her get dressed and decent again. Yeah, he was one in a million. A trained sniper and a heartthrob.

"We should report in now that we're at Smoke's," she told him quietly, her hands on his shoulders while he slipped her feet into her boots. Everything he did, he was doing for her. She had no one to compare him with.

With a soft grunt, Shane lifted to his feet and tossed the used paper towels into the trash. Instead of letting Everlee go and pretending nothing had just happened between them, his hand slid around her wrist. With a quick tug, she was back against his chest, and he was pressing a warm, wet kiss to the center of her forehead. "God bless your lack of impulse control," he whispered. "Don't ever change, Ev. You're perfect just the way you are."

She wanted to spend more time savoring the sweet sentiments coming from this warrior. She could have stood there until she'd breathed every last molecule of him into her heart for safekeeping. Gallant moments like this one never happened to someone like her, mainly because most men steered clear of strong, capable women. They didn't want to compete, and they resented female authority. She'd worked with enough airmen over the years to know most of them had talked behind her back. They'd all seemed to honestly believe the only way she could've been promoted was on her back, by literally kissing ass. Untrue, but still wildly proliferated. If any one of them had truly taken the time to get to know her, they'd have laughed at the idea that she was that desperate for the next rank. Damned crybabies. But that was reality. Double standards were alive and well, even in this so-called 'enlightened' age of women's lib and 'alleged' social equality.

The bathroom doorknob turned. The door opened. A fragrant cloudy fog of steam announced Ms. Smart's re-entry into their private moment. Damn, she was back. Her long, blonde hair was clean and dry, sleek and shiny and curled just right. And she was smiling. At Shane. Of course.

Everlee took a full step out of his comfort zone, put her hands on her hips and glared at the cold-blooded baby-killer once again in their midst. She stabbed her finger at the four-person dinette between Smoke's formidable weapons stash and the countertop that passed for a kitchen, and ordered, "Sit down. First, we'll eat, then we'll hit the sack."

"I'll take the couch," Shane offered.

"Fine." Everlee's gaze was still fixed on their prisoner. "Shane'll keep guard, Smart, so don't try anything. You get the bunk to the left, I'll take the right. It's closer to the door. No funny business, understood?"

"And then you'll cuff me to the metal headboard, right?" Damned if Smart didn't look like a high school cheerleader. Double damned if there wasn't a glint of compassion—or something—in Shane's eyes. That had to stop.

"Right," Everlee snapped, mad at herself and the gullible male beside her. "We have a long day's drive tomorrow. Might not stop between here and DC, and—"

Damn it! Everlee was so sick of this woman's poor, innocent me routine. Looked like Shane was falling for it. "Never mind. Let's just eat."

Chapter Sixteen

Shane had no idea what he'd done to set Everlee off. One minute she was warm and cuddly; the next, she was back in bad cop mode. Downright rude to Ms. Smart. Downright bitchy. The lasagna Everlee had brought to the table was hot and good, rich and cheesy, though. Between that and the buttery garlic bread sticks, everyone was droopy with carb overload by the time their paper plates were clean and dinner was done. Before Everlee took over like she was prone to do, Shane jumped to his feet, cleared the table, and tossed the containers into the trash bin beside the kitchen sink. Then, because he'd been taught right at home, he located a clean dishcloth, filled the sink with hot, sudsy water, and wiped the table and countertops. He'd already divested himself of most of his new weaponry before he ate, just kept the knives in his boots and the pistols in his hip holster.

By the time he'd finished clean-up, he discovered Everlee and Smart were gone. The bathroom and bedroom door was shut. Darn. They were already locked down for the night. Which meant Everlee had cuffed Smart to the bedframe and that was Ev in the shower. Naked. With suds sliding over her bare shoulders and down her back and—

"No," he hissed at himself. Not going there. She was probably still mad at him.

But that kiss. The totally unexpected, slamming sex against the wall. Everlee was damned hot when she took control. Just thinking of her bossy mouth jazzed up his body again. It had been so long since he'd—

No. Just no. He refused to revisit what just might have been a once in a lifetime, hot damned sexual encounter. Shane was still armed. No doubt Everlee was, too. He didn't need to get himself shot. Even one pistol seemed overkill against a woman who acted as helpless as Smart. In no way was she savvy enough to get out of her flex cuffs. He understood the need for caution. People were not always who they seemed. But still... Shane had his doubts.

The bathroom door opened and Everlee leaned out with nothing on but a thick, white towel wrapped under her arms and around her body. Water dripped from her wet, slicked-back hair into her eyes. My God, she was small fully dressed, so much smaller—undressed. *Day-um.* Just when Shane thought he'd finally relaxed, he wasn't.

"Shower's all yours," she said as she dashed to the bedroom door, her voice breathy and her eyes bright, the tease.

"If we'd showered together, we would've saved water," he complained hoarsely.

A smile lit her face when she ducked into the bedroom, then peered back around the edge of the door and whispered, "We're on duty, big guy."

"Yeah, well…" He was at her side in an instant, leaning in, savoring the taste of her squeaky-clean skin and loving the flowery scent of shampoo in her wet hair. His tongue traced over his bottom teeth. Shane was thinking he deserved another taste. And another. "You sure we're done? I mean—"

The door closed in his face.

But he'd seen the heat in her eyes, the way she'd dragged her teeth over her bottom lip, the way she'd bitten it. The way her breath caught the moment he'd drawn close. And there he was, fighting another hard-on, wishing he were on the other side of her door. And that Ms. Smart was somewhere—anywhere—else.

Shane blew out a gust of pent up, sexual frustration. No sense getting excited when he couldn't do anything about it. He unbuckled his holster, draped it over the back of the couch where it was still within reach, slipped his dogs out of his boots, and headed for the shower. It was still steamy, still smelled like Everlee. He swiped the condensation off the mirror. One look at his reflection and he nearly laughed out loud. No wonder she'd turned him down. The explosion had turned his normally thick, dark hair into a singed, feathery mess that only a decent haircut would cure. His eyebrows hadn't fared much better. They were feathered into gray, singed ends. He looked ridiculous. And him without a decent razor.

Still thinking of Everlee, he cranked the shower faucets to hot and steamy, then shucked out of his dirty clothes. Folding his pants and TEAM shirt carefully, he left them on the narrow counter by the sink and stepped into the confining space of a four-by-four-foot stall.

Smoke had built a damned nice storm cellar. The entire bathroom was tiled: smaller cream-colored ceramic tiles on the walls and ceiling, twelve-by-twelve earth-brown tiles on the floor. A vent overhead funneled the steam to places unknown, and the ceiling heat lamp was a nice touch. The towels were thick and plush. The plumbing was sound and water pressure was great.

But size mattered. Every time Shane turned, he nicked his elbow on the faucet handles or the built-in, hard as a rock, *damn it,* ceramic soap tray.

Scrubbing quickly with the crisp new bar of soap Everlee must've left in the shower caddy, Shane let the hot water rinse the problems of the day away. For a guy who'd been blown off Smart's front porch just this evening, he wasn't feeling too bad. Yeah, the burns on his face and the front of his neck were tender but no worse than a good sunburn after a day at the beach. All things considered, his first day of TEAM work had gone well. Ms. Smart was now in custody, and he and Everlee were on their way home. Maybe on their way to another adventure if the stars aligned.

Cranking the faucets off, he grabbed one of those plush towels, wrapped it around his waist, and stepped out of the shower. Damn, what he wouldn't give to have Everlee with him in this crowded, steamy space. The possibilities made his mouth water. Them in the shower. Slick and soaping each other up. Suds and water making every part of her slippery and wet and...

"Everlee," he breathed into the steamy silence. She was a spitfire and a damned competent agent. A joy to work with, maybe a joy to work on, too. There was nothing hotter than a hard-charging woman who knew her way around weapons like she did.

Swiping a palm across the mirror again, he slapped on a thick layer of shaving cream, then extracted an actual razor from the courtesy shave kit, not a disposable piece-of-shit, and gingerly cleared the heavy five o'clock shadow from his cheeks and chin. Then his neck.

Come tomorrow morning, he'd have to shave again, but that was heredity for you. His deadbeat father must've had a dense beard, too. But Shane had no photo or proof to verify that guess, and as a boy, he'd never thought to ask his mom. He could've taken after his maternal grandfather for all he knew about his relatives. His mother never talked about her side of the family or the sperm donor who'd trashed their lives. But maybe not.

Shane grew up loving his mother. Her name was—*is,* he reminded himself—Erin Marlowe Hayes. Or Em. She'd often given just her initials when asked her name. She'd taken back her maiden name, though Shane had no way to know if she'd done that officially.

She'd been dark-haired, olive-skinned, and pretty; quick to smile, just as quick to forgive the jerk who'd deserted her and her toddler son when they'd needed him most. She'd always been a delicate thing, never should've had to raise a boy on her own, or work as hard as she'd had to make a decent life. But she'd done all that and more. They'd been a damned strong team all by themselves until cancer came along. It was too bad strength in character didn't equate to strong constitutions.

The only thing Shane knew about his mom's parents was they'd died years before she'd married. He'd never met any of his extended family, neither on his mom's nor his dad's side. For that matter, he had no proof she'd legally married his old man. She hadn't left any pictures. No, his bastard father had taken every photo and trace of his existence when he'd left. For all Shane knew, he might've been Mafia.

Shane had no recollection of Gary Tulane. Didn't plan on looking him up. No need. But for two cents, he'd gladly beat the shit out of the creep for what his desertion had put Erin through. Still, despite the hardships of those lean years, Erin and Shane had built a life full of what truly mattered, first and foremost, each other. Secondly, the simplest rule of life, the golden rule. *Do unto others what you would want done unto you.* Not a hard concept. More people ought to try it.

He swiped more condensation off the mirror and stared at the man looking back at him. The next time he kissed Everlee, he'd leave no whisker burns on her lips or chin. Although, there was a measure of pride in marking a woman like her. Shane tossed a cocky grin at himself in the mirror. That guy might not be much to look at, but he might be enough for beautiful, intelligent Everlee. Then, just because of her…

He tipped his head back and took one last long swipe up his neck to make sure it was clean and smooth. Using the comb and razor, he trimmed what he could of the ends of his burned hair. He would've shaved it all off, but he'd felt Everlee's fingertips on his scalp when she'd played with his hair. He wanted her to do that again. It was such a simple thing, no big deal, yet intimate in a non-sexual way. He just plain liked it, wanted her to touch him again.

After working his hair over, Shane utilized the deodorant stick, then splashed a healthy dose of aftershave on his face, just to feel the sting. Too damned bad they were still on the job. He'd love to sneak into her bed tonight and make love again, horizontally this time. He dressed in fresh underwear and the jeans she'd brought from his gear bag. Back in the common space, Shane turned out the lights, settled into one corner of the couch, and prepared to research a way forward while the women slept.

The night was quiet. Taking his burner phone out of his pocket, he brought up the map app, and plotted the straightest course to Washington DC. It was good knowing Alex had already provided tomorrow's transportation. A US Marshal's escort would've been nice, but Shane doubted Alex would offload his responsibility. Getting Ms. Smart back to DC was his gig, and he'd sent Everlee and Shane to make sure it happened.

A straight shot across the country seemed the surest route. Shane set a pin from Smoke's ranch in Texas, another one up in Arkansas, then another in Tennessee, then Kentucky. Since Everlee had gotten them this far by hopscotching between taxis, Ubers, and stolen vehicles, Shane felt confident they hadn't been followed by the unnamed guy Tuesday claimed was stalking her. But in case things still went sideways, he explored alternate routes that circumvented interstates and big cities like Little Rock and Memphis. He committed those byways to memory, not risking their core mission for speed or convenience. Their only mission was to get Smart to TEAM HQ alive, not fast. As long as he and Everlee stayed in touch with Alex, the rest of this road trip should be a breeze.

Should be, not would be. Shit still happened, even with the most detailed preplanning. A guy could always count on something to go FUBAR, as in fucked up beyond all recognition, the moment the first shot was fired. His efforts now were simply to minimize the possibility.

Once he filled his brain with different routes, Shane sent a text to Mark at TEAM HQ, telling him their planned route and possible arrival time, also copied Mother, whom he still needed to meet. Ms. Kennedy hadn't been in her office when

Mark took him around and introduced everyone, and she hadn't been at Alex and Kelsey's dinner, either. Shane wondered why not. He would've liked meeting The TEAM's genius techie. Since Everlee seemed impressed with Sasha Kennedy, Shane was, too. Someday, he might even call her Mother. Not Mom though. That tender title overstepped the loving relationship he'd known with his mother. She was and forever would be his only Mom.

His phone pinged a thumbs-up emoji from Mark and right on its heels, a message from Ms. Kennedy, stating that he should call her if he needed any help. With those messages received, Shane shut down his phone, punched into shape the pillow Everlee had left on the couch, and settled his longer than the couch frame down for the night. Sleep didn't come easy. While he lay there staring at the darkened ceiling, he thought of that kiss. That sizzling sex just a few yards from their client. He'd never taken a woman so quickly. For that matter, no woman had ever taken charge of him like Everlee had, either.

Impulsive. Bossy. Determined. That was Everlee. Yet, at the same time, she was a puzzle, vulnerable when he least expected it. Like when he'd been lying in the street singed from the explosion. She'd been so tender handling him, so worried. But the best would forever be making fast and furious love beside Smoke's vault while Ms. Smart showered. Talk about risky. But that had added plenty of fuel to their fire.

Everlee was willing, all right, maybe even as overdue for a true and loving, committed relationship as he was. He was, wasn't he? Overdue? Shane didn't know. He'd never been in one. Sure, he'd had friends in high school and a couple were girls, but there'd never been time for frivolous things like dates, dances, or homecoming games back then. He'd been too busy working. Once he'd teamed up with old man Swanson, if Shane wasn't in school or at home, he was at Swanson's store, trying to be all he could be. The Army's motto seemed to be the theme of his entire life, even during his time in the Corps. Shane had worked since he'd turned twelve. What would it be like relaxing after hours instead of going to a second job or out on patrol? Maybe with Everlee tucked under his arm? Better question, was she feeling the same wonderment he was from that frantic, wonderful moment between them? Had their lovemaking touched her the same way it did him?

A yawn came out of nowhere. It had been a helluva first day, and it was past time to catch a few winks. The night was quiet. Shane scrubbed a hand over his face and let his body go slack and…

Morning broke to the delicious aromas of Everlee and Ms. Smart fixing breakfast. Bacon, for sure. He lay there with his arm over his forehead and watched them working together in the small kitchen space. The women were efficient and quick on their feet. Ev's ankle didn't seem to bother her, as she rotated between refrigerator and stove. Once again, Ms. Smart sported flex cuffs, this time in front so she could use both hands. She didn't seem to mind, still managed to arrange silverware and plates on the countertop, then retrieved several pint-sized bottles of orange juice from the refrigerator. Damned if Ms. Smart wasn't humming quietly, too. Like she was content.

Which took Shane back a few years to before he'd lost his mother. She used to hum. Strange that the woman voted most likely to kill again, the gal with the most to lose, seemed happy this morning, not worried. Not rude. Also strange how easily these two women were working together. Everlee could like it or not, but right then, she was getting along with her prisoner. One might even say they treated each other respectfully, like sisters instead of adversaries. They were good together. At least while they made breakfast.

That bacon smelled tempting, the coffee, too. But Shane had a problem. Morning wood. With two women in close proximity. Time to spring into action before anyone noticed the tent stake in his pants. Thank heavens he'd worn jeans to bed. Gathering the pillow against his lap, Shane lifted to his feet and turned his back on the ladies. He dropped the pillow and grabbed his next bit of camouflage, the blanket.

"Breakfast is almost ready," Everlee announced quietly.

"Thanks. Sure smells good. Save some for me," he replied as he sauntered as casually as was possible into the bathroom. Sure was different waking up with women in the same room, instead of a bunch of raunchy, smelly men.

After eating quickly and cleaning what little mess they'd made, they dressed and were close to getting back on the road again. Everlee was back in TEAM black as was Shane.

But Ms. Smart had left everything she'd worn the day before in the bathroom garbage can. Her ensemble today included simple Rider jeans and a t-shirt, finished off with white anklets and bright-red Converse tennis shoes. Smoke, for all his taciturn attitude, had texted Everlee earlier that he'd left a bag for Ms. Smart outside the saferoom door. Which made Shane smile. Every military guy or gal knew the value of taking good care of their feet. That Smoke had gone the extra mile to take care of Smart's feet was just plain nice of the guy. The clothes he'd chosen fit her well.

Smart had grinned when she'd slipped the shoes on. "They're perfect. I love them. I'm writing that nice man a thank-you note the first chance I get."

See? She had to be innocent, didn't she? What black widow would think of sending thank-you notes? A damned smart one, Shane thought soberly, determined to keep her in the alleged-murderer column until this mission was over.

"Whatever," Everlee growled. "We're burning daylight, folks. Step on it."

For some reason Tuesday Smart jump to her feet like an excited little girl on a road trip instead of a woman on her way to prison. "Then let's go!"

Chapter Seventeen

They were traveling north-by-northeast. Their new ride was a dark-gray Toyota Land Cruiser with heavily tinted windows, courtesy of Alex Stewart. Smoke had outfitted the SUV with a large enough ice chest to carry supplies for a week, everything from prepackaged sandwiches to frosty bottled waters. Individual-sized bags of fruit or vegetable snacks and a good supply of protein bars. The tasty kind, not those damned stick-in-your-throat MREs the military bought.

Shane had the wheel. He'd stored his and Everlee's new and heavier backpacks in the rear cargo hold with the cooler. Those sturdy packs were now loaded with new weaponry. Both Shane and Everlee now possessed spanking new McMillan bolt-action, TAC-338 sniper rifles, both equipped with Leupold Mark 4 LR/T scopes and retractable Harris bipods. Along with tactical gear, including vests and ammo. He'd contemplated bringing along two pairs of NVGs and at least one sawed-off twelve-gauge shotgun. But in the end, he and Ev could only pack so much. So he'd settled for an additional two Glock pistols for Everlee, two Browning Black Label 1911-380 pistols for him, holsters and extra ammo. Along with a few other incidentals that might come in handy. One never knew what they'd need.

Shane planned on making it all the way through Arkansas, possibly as far as eastern Tennessee by dusk. Again,

Everlee sat with Smart in the rear seats, one of her pistols on her thigh. Smart sat directly behind Shane, which put her in his rearview mirror. For an alleged black widow, she didn't flirt or attempt anything coy, just stared at the scenery flying by.

But damned if she didn't look content. Happy. At peace. For the life of him, Shane couldn't reconcile the serious charges against Ms. Smart with the calm demeanor of the woman in the mirror. Either she was a damned good actress, or she was schizophrenic with some serious multiple personalities. Neither of which settled as right in Shane's gut. It was talking to him, telling him she wasn't a killer. He just wanted to be sure what it was telling him was right.

They'd no sooner crossed the northeast corner of Texas into Arkansas when Ms. Smart turned to Everlee and said, "I thought we were going to talk last night, Agent Yeager."

Shane caught the sudden exhaustion in her voice and the lack of excitement in her green eyes, which were almost as deep as evergreen pines. Apparently, the joy of those red shoes had worn off. He hit his blinker and moved into the slow lane. "Last night we needed food and rest more than we needed information," he answered. "So talk. What do you think is going on?"

"Yeah, Smart. If you didn't kill Atchison Bremmer, your three-year-old son Toby and your two-month-old daughter Betsy, who did?" Everlee's snotty sarcasm was no help, but it did serve its purpose. It hit a damned tender nerve with Ms. Smart.

"I don't even know who those people are!" she yelled at Everlee.

Which surprised Shane. But Everlee deserved the comeback. Didn't she realize she'd get more flies with honey instead of vinegar?

"And I'd never kill a baby, any baby, especially not mine! All I know for sure is that my face was all over the television screens at DFW airport when I landed in the States last week. The news says I'm a wanted fugitive, that I killed that man and his two kids. That I burned them alive. But there I am, strutting through DFW without a care in the world like a damned idiot! Does that sound like something a murderer would do? For Pete's sake, people were looking at me like I had two heads! I had no idea what was going on. I had to leave my baggage at DFW just to get a cab home because some guy started following me. He had his cell phone out. He was talking to someone, probably the police. Or maybe he was an undercover cop looking for me. How would I know? Maybe he works for whoever's framing me, did you ever think of that?"

Ms. Smart shook her head, her cheeks flushed and red. "The second I got to my Aunt's house, the one I just bought, I called the local TV station and asked what they were doing running all those lies about me. I told them to stop, that they had the wrong woman. That they were slandering me. That I'd sue. But they wanted me to come in for an on-the-spot interview. I told them no, not until they stopped running lies about me, that I didn't kill anyone. But they don't care about hearing the truth. They're nothing more than a pack of pushy, rabid dogs."

She took a deep breath and flipped a chunk of blonde hair over her shoulder. "Since then, someone's followed me every time I've left my house. Maybe it's the same guy from the airport. He's always in a dark suit and dark glasses, and he never gets close enough for me to really get a good look. Both times I've seen him, I tried to confront him, but he took off. Then you two came along and ran me down just when I thought I finally had him. He was in that crowd last night. He was there when my house blew up. He might be the one who blew it up, did you ever think of that? That's why I was dressed like a reporter. I needed to be hidden, to be safe, yet visible enough to be able to watch for him."

Shane was inclined to agree, but Everlee cut him off with, "You expect us to believe that BS?" She caught Shane's eyes when he glanced over his shoulder and gave him a chin lift like he had better agree with her. "I downloaded the video of you coming out of your New York apartment." She shoved her cell phone into Ms. Smart's face. "Want to tell me how a woman who looks exactly like you, isn't you?"

Shane kept glancing at Tuesday in the rearview mirror. As the short security clip ran, all color leached out of her face. She blinked. Took a deep breath and blinked again, like she couldn't believe what she was seeing. Which was interesting, considering she was looking at herself running a chain through both handles of her apartment doors, looping it twice, then padlocking it, barring the only exit from the home she'd lived in at least four years. With her husband and kids, for God's sake. He could hear them screaming, someone banging on the door to get out. Not just someone, but the man she'd vowed to love and honor till death do they part. She had to be guilty. That woman was her, damn it.

Wasn't she? Damn it, Shane wasn't so sure anymore. The longer Smart stayed in their company, the more his certainty diminished.

She raised one hand to her mouth and cried, "Turn it off! That's so, so terrible. Please! Turn it off!" Tears brimmed her eyes and her face was deathly white. Could anyone mimic that shade of pallor?

"Enough, Ev," Shane admonished.

With a glare at him in the rearview mirror, Everlee shut off the video clip and ended the torture. But damn. Shane hoped he never had to hear those babies' cries for their mama again.

"That's… That's…" Ms. Smart dashed a hand across her face, but there was no hiding the pain in her eyes. Or the tears running down her face. Or her snotty nose. She wiped both hands over her face. And again, Shane felt torn. Was she telling the truth? Sure felt like it.

"That wasn't me, I s-swear. That h-h-horrible woman who did that to those kids isn't m-m-me. B-but…" She gulped loud enough Shane heard it from the front seat. "Sh-she sure looks just like me, doesn't sh-she? She's… she's awful. God. Who does that?!"

Tears that looked authentic still dripped over her chin and down her neck. "How… how could she? To her own family? To the man she loved? To her children? Her b-babies?!"

Everlee was leaning far enough into Smart to shoot Shane a look of disgust in the rearview mirror. "She's you, Ms. Smart. Same heart-shaped face. Same long, tinted bleached-blonde hair." Everlee said that with a shit ton of head swagger. "Hell, look at her fingers. No nail polish, just like yours. Want to run that innocent routine by me again? Because I'm not falling for this stupid act of yours. How would anyone, even your twin if you had one, know enough about you to masquerade as you committing cold-blooded murder?"

Ms. Smart turned both shoulders toward Everlee and screamed, "I'm telling the truth, Agent Yeager! That despicable woman is… Not! Me! Not unless I'm schizophrenic and can't remember who I am or where I was when this crime happened. But I'm not, and I do. I'm the real Tuesday Smart, darn it. The news said the fire happened in January. Is that true?"

"Of course it's true," Everlee snapped.

"Well, for your information, I've been out of the country for the last three months on a job for Robert Freiburg. Maybe you've heard of him? He's the millionaire who produced all those documentaries about the catastrophic effect of carbon emissions on the planet. I've been too busy shooting footage across the world to watch TV. I was gone January, February, and most of March. I'm a freelance photographer. I can prove it. Every photo I take is date-stamped, and that stamp includes the locations where I was when I took them. Only…" She bit her lip and turned to the window.

Shane had been studying her body language as much as he could without taking his eyes off the road for too long. Ms. Smart's act was damned convincing. If it were just up to him, he'd believe her. But again, that was what made black widows good at what they did. They suckered stupid men. Like him.

Sucking in a deep breath, her eyes connected with his in the rearview mirror. Ms. Smart looked at him pleadingly. "You have to believe me, Agent Hayes. I did not kill those children or that man. I wouldn't do such a heinous thing. To anyone! Only I can't prove it because every picture I took was in my house. All my equipment and photos. My cell phone. And now it's… it's gone."

"How convenient." Everlee's continual use of sarcasm was getting old.

Shane nodded, not so sure which woman he was agreeing with. "You were out of the country for three solid months?" Yeah, he caught Everlee's cocked brow at his question, but he ignored her snark and focused on their prisoner. For the life of him, if Smart was lying, he couldn't detect any tells or the usual subterfuge, and his gut was screaming for him to believe her. Was she telling the truth?

"Yes, three months." Her head bobbed. "I spent six weeks in the Serengeti at the end of last year, then mid-January, I flew to the Arctic. I've been photo-journaling the effects of climate change on wildlife the world over. My next location is… was Mongolia in May, after that, the southern tip of South America and maybe Antarctica." She scrubbed her knuckles over her lips. "I can call Robert. He'll vouch for me. You'll see. He's got digital copies of all my photos, I know he does. I always forward copies the same day I shoot the footage. You'll see. I'm telling the truth. I promise."

Man, Shane wanted to believe her.

"Let me guess, he's out of touch at the moment." Everlee couldn't seem to stop playing bad cop.

"Yes, he's in Australia, probably unreachable," Ms. Smart bit out. "He's documenting the damage the wildfires did to the outback last year. Because he's a damned good photographer!"

"Hey, don't get your panties in a twist—"

"Please, do that, Ms. Smart." Shane headed off the rest of Everlee's comeback. "Contact Robert Freiburg as soon as we get you safe. The sooner you prove your innocence, the quicker the FBI will drop their charges. We can help you reach out to your friend if you'd like." He caught the spiked brow Everlee tossed at him, but Shane focused on Ms. Smart's startled glance in the rearview.

"You… you will?"

Shane nodded. He could almost hear her heart pounding from the back seat. Maybe it was time to cut her some slack, and, if she were guilty, give her enough rope to hang herself. "Yes, ma'am. We're not your judge, jury, or executioners. We're here to help you and the FBI, aren't we, Agent Yeager?"

If looks could kill. Everlee's cocked head and death glare told Shane all he needed to know. He'd stepped out of line, and she didn't approve. Well, too bad, Agent Yeager. Sometimes, stepping out of line was the right thing to do.

Ms. Smart's cheeks ballooned with relief. "Oh, thank you, thank you so much. I won't let you down, Agent Hayes, honest. The minute we get somewhere safe, I'll call Robert, and you can talk with him yourself. Hopefully, we'll be able to reach him. But will you still turn me over if we can't? To the FBI, I mean?"

Shane glanced at Everlee for that answer.

"If Alex says yes, you bet your ass we will," she replied tartly, avoiding Shane's eyes. "So, get your damned story straight, because once we hit TEAM HQ, you're not our problem."

Shane shot a quick look of censure over his shoulder at Everlee. "I need to stop for gas. Anyone need a break, maybe some lunch?" The landscape had changed from Texas arid to Arkansas green, scattered with rolling hills, intermittent rocky ledges, and granite outcroppings. The interstate was smooth, traffic was fairly light, and it'd been hours since breakfast. He was hungry.

"Sure. Pull over," Ev huffed. "That'll give me a chance to call Alex."

Smart said nothing, just stared at Shane in the rearview. Damn, she kept wiping tears out of her eyes.

"How about you, kiddo?" he asked her directly. "There's a rest stop ahead. I can pull in there or I can aim for the next town. It's twenty miles away, but it's fairly large, and we should find a better choice of restaurants there. Better bathroom facilities, too."

"I don't really care," she told him, her teary gaze direct and her tone heartbreakingly quiet. "Just keep me alive long enough to prove I'm innocent. Can you do that?"

"Absolutely," he promised. "You have my word, Ms. Smart."

She seemed to be relying on him more than Everlee, and Shane got that. He did. That was how the good cop/bad cop routine worked. The accused related to whichever law officer seemed the weaker or nicer of the two, and Shane was content playing the part. Not that he'd let his guard down, but he would honestly investigate any and all information Ms. Smart provided. She sounded damned credible. Plus he'd get Mother to research that Freiburg fellow.

Shane had to give Ms. Smart credit. Everything out of her mouth so far sounded believable. Was she playing a part, too? If so, if her honesty was just a ruse, a distraction, she was in for a helluva surprise. Because he might know how to act gullible and smitten, but he was no pushover.

Flipping the left turn signal, he put them back in the middle lane and stepped on the gas. Because of their early takeoff, it was now past noon, and Smart's flex cuffs were the only hindrance to them going inside anywhere to eat. Her hands were still cuffed in front of her, but that didn't make her less of a flight risk. Maybe Shane would be the food delivery person today. Then, after he gassed up, they could find some out-of-the-way place to eat and stretch their legs.

The sign for the rest stop flashed by. They'd just crested a hill and had a long stretch of interstate winding straight ahead of them when—

BANG! Felt like their left rear tire had blown.

"What the shit?" Everlee exclaimed while the SUV bucked across the far left lane, then took a sharp right down the center lane. Shane battled to keep the Land Cruiser clear of other traffic and on the interstate. Forget that. He cranked the wheel hard to the left, striving to not over-correct and make this recovery worse. He aimed for the grassy median between east and westbound lanes. But that small correction sent the SUV's rear end into a wicked three-sixty drift that propelled them toward the right shoulder. Which was gravel. Which should've given the tires something to latch onto, allowing him to brake safely.

Instead, the SUV's rear end slid sideways and dumped them onto the slick, grass-covered slope that led to the fenced field alongside the interstate. Which posed a different set of problems. Like rolling. Totally losing control of the SUV. The gas tank possibly exploding. All of them being trapped and burned alive and…

Fuck. No.

But who the hell was gunning for them? Because that blowout was not due to a worn tire. No way. Shane had checked their ride thoroughly before take-off. He spared a quick glance in the rearview to see which cars were behind him. Could someone have been following them all this time?

Before he could lock onto any specific vehicle, the rear window spiderwebbed, and a hailstorm of chipped safety glass rocketed through the SUV.

"Duck!" he ordered, as instinctively, he jerked sideways just before those chips spattered into the dash and the back of his headrest. Everlee and Smart were crouched low on the backseat by then. Son of a bitch! Who was after them?

Shane didn't have time to sort it out. He cranked the wheel a hard left, then a quick right, aiming to get back on the road. At last, he had the SUV somewhat under control, but he was driving too fast on one rim, the rubber from the blown tire completely gone. Things went from bad to worse. An old farm tractor blocked the shoulder ahead. Just ahead of that were the banked concrete walls of an overpass. A white-haired man in a cowboy hat sat inside the enclosed cab of that damned tractor. With every yard closer the SUV sped, the slower the tractor puttered along. Until—

There was no way to avoid hitting its substantially heavier rear end. Shane didn't dare go back into traffic and if the SUV hit the incline to that overpass, they'd roll. He switched gears and gunned the motor. Struggling to control the wheel, he aimed the SUV back to the bar pit near the fence. No such luck. Another shot rang out and his side mirror shattered. A third shot peppered the rear of the vehicle. The bastard had gotten close.

Shane floored the accelerator. The Toyota hesitated until, finally, its front tires engaged. But because of the missing tire, its rear end fishtailed in a widening arc that was taking them all the way around the tractor until the front of the Toyota was facing the front of the tractor. They were still spinning, hurtling closer to the overpass. He didn't want to hit the concrete wall that fed the incline. Shane's choices were bleak to none, but he damned well refused to hurt the old guy on the John Deere. Just as the Toyota's rear tires hit the ridge of the shoulder, the SUV bounced. The momentum sent the remaining tires churning up clouds of grit and dust. And—

The steering wheel seized.

"Hold on!" Shane bellowed as chaos took over. The SUV rolled and he flattened his palms to the ceiling just as it became the floor. Everything not belted down shifted from being cargo to lethal weapons. The first frightening rotation tossed the giant ice chest and their gear bags upward and over the rear seat. Shane's holsters flapped away from his hips.

"Jiminy Christmas!" Everlee yelled. Which was so damned appropriate. Hail Marys were running a mile a minute through Shane's mind.

Another bone-wrenching spin. Another plea for divine intervention.

Holy Mary, Mother of God... Ouch!

Then again...

Pray for us sinners.... Damn it!

And again...

Now and at the hour of our death...

Each wicked rotation jerked Shane's body against his harness which was damned near cutting him in half. He had no idea how Everlee and Ms. Smart were faring.

New grown vegetation slashed the dash where windshield had been. Stalks and dirt whipped Shane's face. At last, the vehicle settled on its roof with a creaky groan in the middle of a shit ton of dust. A husky *"Amen"* whispered out of him.

He coughed to clear his throat, then yelled, "Everlee! Tuesday!" needing to know they'd survived. That they were still with him. Still somehow breathing and not hurt, damn it!

No answers came back to him. Nothing but the whining sound of a vehicle gunning toward them. "Move your dumb ass, Hayes!" he growled as he jerked at his harness, struggling to get the damned latch loose.

No go. He was locked in, trapped. The light from the sun faded. Storm clouds maybe? God, he hoped. He'd willingly take a twister bearing down on them rather than the killers taking Tuesday. Or him dying without a fight. Fuck! He was so damned helpless!

Until total darkness flooded the SUV's dusty interior. A purplish fog stole into the ruined vehicle, covering everything. Obscuring his vision. Blocking light and sound. His upside-down body was heavy. He went slack against the harness that wouldn't let him go. Shane knew then he wasn't meant to survive. Not this disaster. It was the end of his road, and nothing could change what was happening now. Not cursing. Not praying. Not the women behind him. Not divine intervention.

"Everlee," he whispered, wishing he'd told her how much she meant to him.

But he hadn't. So he whispered again, just, "Everleeeee…"

Chapter Eighteen

Everlee rolled her pounding head on her poor swizzle-stick neck, slowly, very slowly. Wondering why a tiny movement hurt as much as it did, and why she couldn't hear anything but buzzing. Lots of buzzing. Plenty of vibrations, too, like she was inside a giant beehive. She came to in slow, dopey increments of stifled, dumb awareness. Her mouth was dry, her throat drier. As in dusty, nasty dry, like someone had stuffed a dirty rag in her mouth, which—what the hell?—someone had.

She wasn't in the SUV. Wasn't anywhere near where she should've been if she'd been thrown from their vehicle. And not only was there a rag in her mouth, the tip of her poor desiccated tongue was stuck to its noxious threads. She had a bag over her head, the open end of it cinched under her chin with what felt like twine. It was scratchy. And tight. She couldn't see where she was or where she was going. Or the dumbass who'd done this to her.

She was thirsty and blind and didn't want to breathe the stink inside the bag one second longer. But there was no way out. Her hands were bound behind her back, and her elbows were jerked back so far that her shoulders were on the verge of popping out of their sockets.

There were no bees and this was no hive. The steady vibration of rotors overhead caused whatever was next to her to buzz. Like a piece of plastic-wrap stretched too tightly over a broken window or *Tupperware* or… or something. She was in a helicopter, on the floor, on her side, and she was pissed. Angrily, she kicked one leg out straight, hoping to strike the nearest A-hole within reach. She did. Her point. Her game. Until—

OOMPF! Said A-hole retaliated with a swift boot in her gut.

The kick knocked the wind out of her, made her rethink her odds of survival. She was a woman and someone's prisoner. Maybe now, when she could barely breathe or swallow, was not the best time to strike back.

Where was Shane?

Everlee lifted her head, listening for his voice. Hell, striving to hear anything besides the whump, whump of rotor blades and that incessant buzzing. Had he survived the SUV rolling? Had Smart? Was she behind this? Was this her plan all along, to lure whoever came after her into another deadly trap, separate them, and—? And what?

No, just no. That wild-assed conclusion didn't hold a stitch of water. Smart wasn't intelligent enough to construct a plan this complex. Plus, she'd had no idea where she'd been stashed last night and no way to communicate her location to anyone. She hadn't known Smoke or Jess Montoya or—no. Just no. Smart might be guilty of murder, but she wasn't this kind of 'smart'. Okay, so her last name might be Smart, but a stitch of water?

Everlee almost giggled at the way her poor, aching head was working… Or wasn't working.

Until she realized that tiny side trip from reality might mean she'd been hurt worse than she thought. Concussions were traumatic brain injuries, and she must've been tossed clear of the Toyota. Her fault. She'd slipped off her seatbelt when she'd turned around to shoot out the radiator of the car gaining on them. But her grandiose plan came too late. Before she'd gotten one shot off, the Toyota rolled.

Needing more air, better air, and determined to escape this flying machine, get back on the ground, and rescue her junior agent, Everlee growled at her captors. Shane had only been hired a couple days ago. Helluva welcome to The TEAM, big guy, this continual baptism by fire.

"Can't you shut her up?" an ugly voice bellowed from somewhere overhead. The pilot maybe?

"Can do, Mister Smith," another male voice answered.

Mr. Smith? How cliché. Who did A-hole think he was, Mister Jones?

Too fast, said A-hole smashed something into the side of her head. Smelled like a boot. Something cracked inside her skull. Might've been a tooth. Or her jaw. Roaring, flashing cannons exploded behind her unseeing eyes. The tiniest, girly whine escaped into the grimy rag in her mouth. Then…

Nothing.

Shane came to on his back with a wrinkled, grizzled face staring down at him out of the blue, blue sky. He was out of his seatbelt, but the lower half of his legs and his feet were still inside the shattered driver's side window of the steaming, upside-down Land Cruiser. The rest of him was sprawled perpendicular to the wreck until the old guy tucked his hands under Shane's arms and dragged him a good ten yards or so away from the vehicle. Which was good sine the air was full of gasoline fumes.

His ribs protested the move. God, that hurt. His lungs squeezed out ragged gasps and coughs that sparked shuddering waves of lightning in his chest. He sucked in a jarring breath that shouldn't have felt like he'd inhaled thumb tacks instead of fresh air. Closing his eyes to the bright sky overhead brought instant relief. Dazed and battered, he lay there panting through the pain, struggling to get his brain back online.

Road trip.

Everlee.

Arkansas.

Everlee.

Someone's house—can't remember whose—exploded.

Everlee.

Lasagna…

"Everlee!" bellowed out of his mouth. He jolted upright but had to stick both palms into the dirt behind him to keep from blacking out and tipping over. Would've helped if he could make his eyeballs focus and his bones stop quaking. "There were three of us in the car. Where's Everlee?" he asked the older gentleman... err…

That can't be right.

"Tuesday? Err, Ms. Smart?" he asked, feeling more like a mixed-up, drunken fool than an intelligent special operator. Holy shit, he'd mistaken her for an old man? Three hits to his head within forty-eight or so hours might have guaranteed that concussion Doc Fitz was worried about.

"Yes, Agent Hayes, it's me," Smart replied evenly, now kneeling beside him, her fingers running soft as feathers on his chest and up his neck. "You're hurt, you're bleeding, and you need to go to the ER. Can I use your phone?"

"Not happening." Shane took hold of her fingers to stop the pleasant sensation skimming over his skin, fighting to keep this particular woman in the suspect column. She was not his friend, damn it. Sucking in another deep breath that didn't hurt as much as it had moments ago, he asked, "Where's Agent Yeager?" *Please don't tell me Everlee died in the rollover.* "Is she... okay?" *Did I kill her?*

"I don't know. A helicopter touched down as soon as we stopped rolling. You and I were both still upside down in the SUV, but I watched what happened through the broken window. Some guys dragged her away."

That didn't make sense. Shane had been sure the shooters were after Smart, not Everlee. He glanced over her shoulder at what was left of the Toyota. Its fancy plastic trim and all of its windows were missing. Most of its shine. Some of its paint. Not one part of it wasn't dented.

"A car pulled alongside us, Agent Hayes. Two men with guns got out. I think they were the same ones who shot at us. Agent Yeager must've been thrown clear of the vehicle when it rolled because she wasn't inside when I came to. They walked straight over to where she was and they took her with them in the helicopter. That's been about ten, fifteen minutes ago." Smart lifted a hand and shoved her thick, dust-laden hair out of her eyes and over her shoulder.

A helicopter? Some guys? Everlee? Abducted? That made no sense. Could this have anything to do with her ex, Butch? Or was Smart behind this? Was anything she said true?

But why would she lie? If she wasn't, then everything she'd been saying all along was true. Shit.

Shaking his head to clear the residual fog in it, Shane lifted slowly to his feet, straight-arming Tuesday Smart the moment she moved in closer to keep him from falling, not needing her help. At least, not wanting to admit he needed it. But definitely not wanting her up close and personal now that he was wounded. This easy op was making him look weak, when, until he'd joined The TEAM, he'd been one of the toughest men in his squad.

Gripping his pounding head between both hands, he shook off the burgeoning migraine creeping up on him. For now, no aura threatened to take over his vision. Those suckers were the harbingers of certain pain that would all but render him blind for a few hours, another complication he didn't need. Cussing his failure to prevent Everlee's abduction, he pushed the very real expectation of a killer migraine aside and planned on getting Smart out of sight and Everlee back. "How many men?"

"Two in the vehicle that stopped" —Ms. Smart nodded at the sporty, silver car butted up against the left corner of the Toyota's damaged rear bumper— "one guy in the chopper. But it stirred up a lot of dust when it landed, so I'm not really sure. I was still hanging upside down like you and—"

"It took three big tough guys to kidnap one little lady? What kind of helo?"

"Umm, a white one?"

Shane nodded. Shouldn't have asked. Smart was a civilian, had no experience with choppers, and it was a stupid question at best. "Which way'd they go?"

"That way." She pointed eastward, "but I stopped watching where they went once I got out of my seatbelt and got to you. You were so pale, and I... I thought you were dead."

Staring off into the direction where she pointed, he grunted at the tenderness in her tone, needing to shut that sympathetic connection down. She was just a prisoner, not his friend. "Not yet, sorry to disappoint."

Her breath caught in her throat, but not in one of those breath-hitching moments women made during all those cheesy, made-for-TV, Hallmark moments, either. The gasp was more as if she'd been slapped. Made Shane feel like an ass. All she'd done since the rollover was help. She hadn't run, and she could have.

Swallowing hard, he finally noticed the fresh blood on the side of her neck and darker red trailing into her shirt collar. She was still wearing those fashionably torn jeans and the red shoes Smoke gave her. But dirt and grass stains smudged her knees, and the scuffed, dirty toes of those shoes proved she'd crawled out of the SUV like she'd said. Dust and debris had settled everywhere. In the air. In his eyes. In her hair. Tuesday Smart was injured, yet she hadn't deserted him. She was still there. Her flex cuffs were gone, though. He should've noticed that a helluva lot sooner.

"Where are your cuffs?"

"There was lots of glass all around me, Agent Hayes. And a knife. I don't know where it came from, but I used it to get out of those cuffs and then, out of my seatbelt. It was hurting me."

Shane let his gaze scroll over her, then to the SUV. What Smart described was the truth. There was a knife in the dirt by the driver's door. Not in her hand. But right where she'd obviously used it to free him from his restraints. Again, she could've used it against him, saved herself and run.

"Where's that old guy on the tractor?" Who I made damn sure I didn't hit. "Where are the other drivers who were on the freeway? Why the fuck hasn't anyone stopped to render aid?"

"Shhhhh," Smart whispered. "It's okay, Shane. The guys who took Everlee scared them off. They had guns and fired at everyone. I think they'd already shot some of those cars before we crashed."

"Well, damn." That made sense. Shane stuck his chin at the SUV and told her, "Thanks for everything you've done for me. I hate to ask, but would you mind reaching inside that wreck and turning the engine thing off?"

"You bet," she replied easily. Lifting to her feet, she backtracked to the Toyota, climbed in through the driver's door window and onto the ceiling of the vehicle, leaned forward, and...

Thank God for silence.

Shane couldn't help but watch her backside as she completed the task he'd asked of her. Smart was still as compliant as ever, and those rear pockets were taut and, yeah. He noticed how they barely jiggled when she backed out of the missing driver's side window on her knees. It was getting harder to dislike her. Getting a big guy like him out through that shattered driver's side window had to have been damned hard. She was a woman, for God's sake, and he was a much bigger, wider load. Yet she'd dragged his dead weight all the way over here.

Pushing to her feet, she dusted her hands on her thighs and returned to his side. There went another chance for her to take off. Why hadn't she? As banged-up and slow-witted as he was, she could be long gone by now. Only she kept coming back.

When she knelt alongside his legs, he noticed her once sleek, blonde hair was thoroughly decorated with bits of weeds, dried grass, and tiny sticks. She needed a comb and a brush, an hour or two of rest wouldn't hurt. Damned if Shane's dumbass hero complex didn't jump up and want to provide all that crap to this woman. Right here. Right now. Not because he liked her that much, but because she deserved someone in her corner. Like it or not, she still looked every bit as innocent as she'd made herself out to be at the start of this nightmare. If that was all pretense, she was one helluva actress. Which was precisely what a black widow was, right? An actress? A liar? Shane had yet to see that side of her, but he'd sure as hell seen her compassionate side.

He shook those questions out of his head. He honestly didn't know who or what Smart was anymore. Photographer or killer? Innocent caught up in some other person's demented scheme? Practiced scam artist? Like an idiot, he brushed the strands of some dead weed out of the silky tangles hanging in her eyes. "You're hurt, too."

Brushing that same frazzled hank of hair over her shoulder, she leaned her cheek into his palm. "Not as bad as you. It was a helluva ride though, huh? But I was never completely unconscious. Just dazed and dizzy and mad when I couldn't get my seatbelt off."

He winced at her direct assessment of his failure as TEAM agent. Helluva ride, nothing. He'd nearly gotten them both killed. Possibly Everlee, too. Where could she be? For that matter…

"There was a first-aid kit in the rear of the Toyota, next to Smoke's cooler. See if it survived, then we need to grab it, some food, water, our gear bags, and get moving. We can't be here when the police arrive. We'll bandage whatever wounds we have once we get out of sight."

Like a female in distress, Smart looked up at him, her soft green eyes wide and so damned misty. "Why not, Shane? The police will help us. They'll believe you, I know they will."

She'd used his first name, not his title. For some dumb-jock reason he didn't want to examine too closely, he liked the sound of it on her lips.

"Sure, yeah, but we need to find Everlee, and we won't be able to do that if you're in police custody or if I'm in the hospital. Understand?" He hoped she did because Shane wasn't sure why he was suddenly relying on a baby killer to help him locate his partner.

The light of their dire situation finally dawned in Smart's eyes. "Oh. Okay, sure. I guess you're right. Everyone still thinks I'm a killer. Got it."

Shane had the good sense to withdraw his hand from her warm cheek. Like it or not, they were not friends and determining her guilt or innocence was not his job. This mission was a pick-up and deliver order, and he was the delivery man with a missing partner. "Come on, let's get rolling, Ms., err, Tuesday." He gave her that much.

"Thanks for using my real name, Shane. It helps to know you at least want to believe me, like maybe we can help each other. Where to?" she asked, her voice nothing more than a whisper in the hot, dead air between them.

Interestingly, this woman didn't do a thing for Shane's libido. There was no desire to kiss her or push her onto her back beneath him. Despite her very obvious feminine charms, a definite sadness shadowed everything Tuesday did and said. An unabated loneliness. That was what had initially drawn him to her. Tuesday Smart was a kindred spirit, a person who had, like him, suffered unimaginable loss at a young age. Also, like him, she was alone in the world. No family. No roots to go back to. Not a castoff. More like a solitary ghost nobody missed, ached for, needed, or saw. Until that debacle at TEAM HQ, Shane had been exactly like Tuesday. He had no idea how to help her. Hell, he couldn't even help himself. But he believed he honestly had a family now, or at least, the makings of one.

He'd never been in Arkansas before. Guess this was as good a time as any to fade into that new crop of baby corn and disappear. He glanced over her shoulder at the miles of lime-green rows running alongside this stretch of highway. "East," he told her with conviction. "We'll go east as far as we can today. Once we're a few miles away from this accident, we'll take a break and assess our injuries. I'll contact my office while we walk. Can you make it that far" —again he chose to use her first name— "Tuesday?"

"Yes, Shane. I can do anything you need me to do. Let's go."

God, he hoped she wasn't a liar.

Chapter Nineteen

Everlee woke in the dark again, upright and sitting this time, her forearms tied to the armrests of a chair, her poor butt flat and dead on a narrow wooden seat. Her muscles screamed for a bit of get-me-the-hell-out-of-Dodge exercise. There was no bag covering her head, not like she could see anything in this pitch-black darkness anyway. The rags in her mouth were gone. So were her boots. Her lips and tongue were still as dry as cotton, but breathing was easier without smelly fabric mashed over her face and mouth. But without light, her eyes were useless. She couldn't make out any points of reference, and there was no way to know which way to go or how to escape. Or if someone was in this dark hole with her. She didn't think so. She'd at least hear them breathe, right? She strained to pick up any other hints of life nearby. Usually, she could sense vibrations of other bodies. But now? Nothing. Until…

Plop. Something landed in her hair. Spiders!

Oh, hell, no. Fighting indescribable panic, she shook her head, needing that thing off her head, out of her hair, and far, far away. Maybe having a bag over her head wasn't a bad idea.

After a good shiver and a few minutes of head-tossing wiggles, Everlee stilled, more hyper-alert than before, in case whatever landed on her was now building a nest in her hair or sliding down the back of her shirt or—

No, no, no! She tossed her head harder, back and forth, side to side, shaking her hair to make sure she'd lost the unwelcome hitchhiker. At last satisfied it was gone, she listened again, striving to detect her kidnappers. The dirtbags, Mr. Smith and Mr. Jones, possibly Mr. Asshole, too. Nothing came back to her, not a squeak or rustle, not the murmur of a television from another room. Just the panting sound of her breathing. No conversation, no defining, stinking, manly smells, no crickets chirping, no flies buzzing, either. Nothing but stark empty silence that almost hurt her ears, it was so loud.

Dare she trust it? *Hell, yeah.*

Trembling with a burst of adrenaline, Everlee leaned to the left, then to the right, as far as she could without tipping over. Thank God, the chair wasn't bolted to the floor. It moved. Good enough. It was just wood; she was invincible. It wouldn't take long to smash this piece-of-shit furniture to smithereens against the nearest wall and be long gone before anyone missed her.

Despite the need to hurry, she froze as the oppressive lack of sound wrapped around her like an iron fist. It was so quiet. Too quiet. She couldn't detect anything, no distant street noises or sounds of kids playing or dogs barking. No hum of planes overhead. Just the dull thud of the chair's legs digging into what now felt like packed dirt, not solid flooring. Not even concrete.

Man, she wished she had her boots. "Where on earth am I?"

Panic slithered up her spine like a slimy cold rattlesnake at the hollow sound of her voice. This wasn't a shipping container. Couldn't be. But a deep, dark well in the ground would explain the lack of ambient noise, well, except for her too fast heartbeat and highly anxious breathing. Stashing a kidnapped victim in an abandoned hole in the middle of nowhere made sense in a frighteningly scary way. Her kidnappers could leave her there until they got what they wanted—which wouldn't be much if they were after ransom. Or they could simply walk away if their demands weren't met, and who would know the difference? Who could find her then? This might very well be a grave. Her grave.

Which made no sense. Why kidnap her just to let her die? She didn't come from money or fame, and maybe that was her fault, too. Blame that and a million other character defects on her father and her ADHD. She'd never been able to sit still and do nothing; didn't intend to now. But it'd sure be nice to be able to see or hear. Or run.

Her toes wiggled with anxiety. She wasn't sure if the GPS locator hidden inside her TEAM phone worked below ground level. Would it? Could Mother find her? Could Alex? Was her cell phone even in her pocket for them to track her by? Everlee used to know important minutia like that. Anything that had to do with her job, she was on it. But between the oppressive darkness and that damned spider attack, panic had lifted its ugly, unreasonable head, and she was running on pure adrenaline.

It struck her then. Mother might've been able to track her TEAM phone, but that was smashed back at that convenience store. Shane's too. There was no way Mother could track them now. Shit!

"I've got to get the fuck out of here," she told herself. Would've sounded better if her voice hadn't trembled. If that expletive hadn't sounded so weak. "Settle down and think, Everlee." Wasn't that what Alex always told her to do?

"I am thinking, Boss," she whispered.

But there really *were* spiders in this place with her. She could hear them. Not the cute little *spee-i-der* that landed on *Megamind's* eyeball in that Dreamworks Animation movie, either. But real, no-kidding, black widow arachnids that came with poison in their fangs and bright red, telltale hourglasses stamped on their bellies. The kind that lived in dark places, like wells and caves. The kind that spun man-sized webs to catch their prey before they sucked it dry and—

Shivers raced over her shoulders. All the more reason to… "Hurry," she hissed. "Come on, girl. Get your fat ass moving. Get out of here!"

Leaning her cheek down onto the binding wrapped around her right biceps, she felt rope, just simple, scratchy jute, not smooth nylon. Which was a good turn of events. Lifting the chair off the ground, she tilted forward and planted her feet, which, thankfully, weren't tied together. With baby steps, as in really quick baby steps because of her hunched-over posture, she toured the limits of her confinement with her butt still stuck in the chair. The first square corner she came to brought a wave of relief. Corners were good. Curved walls were bad. Another good thing, these walls sounded like wood. Not concrete. Jute and wood she could work with.

Walking faster, she mapped the boundaries of her prison. Four ninety-degree corners. Four straight walls. She was inside a square room. She'd counted her steps. Each wall was ten steps long, which equated to a ten-foot square wooden box. Approximately. Kinda like a coffin.

Whatever. Not one to wait and wonder, Everlee planted her feet, dug her bare toes into the dirt, and prepared for war. She turned her body as far to the right as she could go. In her mind, she was a pitcher in the World Series, using her weight, winding up to deliver a fastball—her chair and her body—into that wall.

Strike one! Okay, so she bounced back, but she didn't fall. She counted that a good first attempt. If she fell, getting the chair back on its feet wouldn't be easy. But she was still upright and her butt was still in the driver's seat. With more vigorous hip action, Everlee swung her rear end around faster and hit that wall harder.

Strike two! Damn it. She'd also bit her tongue. Well, too bad. More determined than ever, Everlee put more spin into her hips, needing this chair to shatter. That would be perfect, but even a creak from its glued joints would be better than the beating she was giving herself. She stilled and listened to her rapid breathing and her crazy fast heartbeat. But okay. She was still the only one making noise. That much was good.

Try, try again. With a deep breath in, Everlee assaulted the wall.

Strike three! Didn't matter. She was in this game to win it.

Strike four!

Strike five! Hammering those legs into the wooden walls. Sweating up a storm. Cursing. Calling the wall names. Stupid names. Ugly names. Just not willing to quit, damn it.

The thought of being caught and further abused—or worse—hurried her desperate escape plan along. She refused to give up and die in this man-made tomb. No way! She flung herself, her hips and her butt into attacking the wall. She gave the fight all she had. If anyone could get away from these jackholes, she could. By hell, she *would!*

"I can," she gasped, sweat dripping off her forehead and stinging her eyes. "I have to. I'm no princess, you asshats. I'm sure as hell not waiting in here until I'm rescued. Screw that! I mean fuck that!"

BLAM! BLAM! BLAM! those stiff, wooden chair legs went. Wood against wood. Something had to give, damn it. Maybe the wall. At least one of the legs. They weren't steel. And she was Everlee Yeager. Woman. Invincible. And all that shit.

At last, after a couple dozen more mega-hip gyrations, plenty of well-seated determination, and a whole lot of sweaty fucks, the chair's seat cracked down the center, then splintered into two separate halves. Okay then. Not precisely what Everlee was going for, but beggars couldn't be choosers. At least her butt was free. Well, almost.

Jerking the armrests apart, she easily busted the loosened slats from the chair's back and set her ass free. The armrests gave up next, and she was awash in scratchy jute and plenty of splintered wood that would make a damned nice fire. Later. Once her kidnappers were trussed up like turkeys. Skewered on a nice pointed post. Over a crackling fire where they could roast all night. *That'd serve them right.*

Tired as hell, Everlee scraped the circles of jute off her arms, then kicked the crap away. She was free to move all right, but that wasn't nearly good nor free enough. Back to the wall, she pressed her ear against the wood, hungry to know where she was and who was outside this damned box.

Still nothing. Not a single noise but her heavy breathing. Okay then. With her palms spread wide, she searched up and down the walls for doorknobs or latches. A window'd be nice. Or a loose board. When it became apparent there was no way out of this pitch-black room, she cast her gaze upward. Was it daytime or night? She had no way to know if she even had a ceiling. And the sky, if it were up there, was just as blank and black as everything else.

For hell's sake, there wasn't even a bucket in here to use as a toilet. Did they intend for her to dig a hole with her bare hands, just to pee in? Well, yeah. So she did, quickly did her business and buried it like a good little Girl Scout.

Wiping her now dirtier hands on her extra-dirty pants, Everlee leaned against the wall to rest. After ten minutes of that stupid idea, she felt around in the dark again this time for the remnants of that chair. She built a nice, tidy pile of rope and broken pieces, then selected one leg and began another round, tap, tap, tapping the walls. First at waist level, then knee level, then, when those revealed solid zeroes, she tapped higher up on the walls. She was on her second go-round when she caught a distinct difference in the sound her tapping made, about a foot above her shoulders. She reined her tapping into a tighter pattern. Sure enough. That part of the wall didn't sound as solid.

But how to reach up that high and what to do when she finally did. Hmm. Back to the drawing board. She needed more of that chair. It just might save her life.

She found what she was looking for, well, was feeling for. Two legs were still attached to half the seat. Making sure that half was solid enough to hold her weight, Everlee dragged it against the wall, balanced the flat end to the wall, then climbed aboard with a spare chair leg—her one and only weapon—and balanced herself on her splintered get-out-ofjail-free contraption just below the targeted space. With one hand on the wall to keep upright and her makeshift weapon under that same arm, she reached her free hand up and let her fingers smooth over the different sounding portion of the wall, searching for a joint or a crack or—

There. Just below the hollow-sounding space. At last. An edge she could get her fingertips under. The bottom edge of a piece of wood. Maybe a door? It was long enough to be a very small door, but was it big enough to be her way out? Man, oh man, her spirits soared at the prospect of freedom. Of escape!

Securing her chair-leg weapon under her arm so she didn't lose it, she used her fingernails like knife edges, tracing the bottom length of what had to be a small trap door. Leaning to one side but keeping her balance, she encountered one corner. That led her to a second corner and a tiny bit wider vertical space, like all doors had on their hinged sides. Yes! She could feel the cool of metal hinges. Okay, so it wasn't a trap door. It was an actual trapdoor. Even if it'd been shut tight, there'd still be space between the jamb and the door. Right?

Licking her chapped top lip, she backtracked, palming her fingertips over what absolutely was a way out. It *was* a door, damn it. Had to be. How else had her abductors gotten her inside this creepy dungeon of a room? Through the roof. Did it even have a roof?

Trembling and worried she'd fall off the unsteady stool, Everlee edged her fingernails up along the door's other vertical edge, the one opposite the side with what she thought were hinges. Digging her nails into the wood, she pulled that portion inside, toward her.

The damned thing gave, creaky centimeter by creaky centimeter, until, at last, dim light spilled into her hidden prison cell from the crack she'd created. Ducking low, she pulled the door over her head and stopped moving to listen to—absolutely nothing. At last, freedom! Best of all, no Mr. Smith or Mr. Jones.

Sunlight shone down on her sweaty head from above. This was almost too good to be true. Hoisting herself up onto the bottom ledge the open door offered, while still holding onto her weapon, Everlee worked herself into a sitting position and took quick stock of her surroundings. Okay, this was weird. She was sitting on the edge of a square door to a big wooden box inside what looked like a round, concrete silo.

The silo itself was inside a large dilapidated barn with a roof overhead that looked like it was ready to fall down. That was why she hadn't been able to hear anything. She'd been stashed inside layers of wood and concrete, hidden so well that no one would've ever found her. The small door frame she was now sitting on was cold but solid. Whoever'd built it intended it to last.

A creepy feeling that she wasn't the first person trapped inside what was essentially a coffin—or a torture chamber—slithered up Everlee's spine. Others had died here, she damned well knew it. Talk about sinister. It was time to get gone.

Like a ninja, she dropped off the nearly fool-proof and very sturdy box-of-a-torture chamber and landed on her bare feet. Still inside the silo, she dusted her hands together, then tipped her head back on her shoulders and peered straight up. She was looking at sturdy, wooden rafters and beams of sunshine overhead, but the rest of the roof was pretty much see-through.

"Jiminy Christmas. I've been trapped inside a box that's inside a silo that's inside a freaking old barn. Who thinks of this shit?"

Oh, look. A ladder. Metal rungs laced the far inside wall of this thirty-foot-plus dungeon. She was halfway up those rungs when she heard the hearty screech of squeaky hinges, followed by an angry woman screaming, "You stupid idiots. You grabbed the wrong one. That woman is not Tuesday Smart!"

"You got that right, bitch," Everlee breathed as she ceased climbing and clung to the rungs inside the silo.

"Get rid of her!"

I'd like to see you try.

"But you said grab the woman he was with," some guy muttered. "You never said there was two—"

"I meant the blonde in the picture, not the redhead. Don't you guys know the difference? Shit, I should've hired former military. At least they know how to follow directions."

"But I—"

"But nothing!" A single gunshot blasted outside the silo, maybe even outside the barn. Everlee wasn't sure.

"Jiminy Christmas," she whispered as she climbed faster. She needed out of this nightmare before it got worse. Right. Damned. Now.

Chapter Twenty

Still stumbling eastward through acres of dry, scratchy weeds now that they were well past the cornfield, Shane tugged the burner phone out of his rear pocket and thumb-dialed TEAM HQ. He hoped to bypass Alex Stewart and speak with Mark Houston. Shane didn't want to have to explain to his new boss on his first mission that *some guys* had mysteriously known where Everlee was, had flown in, kidnapped her, and taken her away by chopper. Her being targeted didn't make sense, and Shane didn't want a confrontation with his boss until he had solid intel. She wouldn't have left voluntarily, no way. She had to have been badly hurt if she hadn't fought back. And there was no way her ex had orchestrated this high-tech abduction. Not knowing who he was up against wasn't a good bargaining position for any new hire. By then, Shane was ready to drop, so he did. Just folded up and fell on his knees at Tuesday's feet.

She crouched onto the parched, furrowed ground beside him. "Oh, my gosh, your ear's bleeding. I'm sorry I didn't notice that before."

"D-d-damn," he stuttered, realizing she could still run away, or worse, overpower him. Maybe kill him. Killing men was a black widow's specialty, wasn't it? But something else told him Tuesday wouldn't have stayed in the first place if she'd meant to kill him. Black widows didn't kill anyone until they got what they wanted, right? Wasn't that how they worked?

"Tip your head back and drink," she ordered, a bottled water already pressed against his bottom lip.

"Shane, Shane! What's happening? Can you hear me? Pick up!" some unknown woman's voice barked from the phone in his hand, her tone laced with worry and panic. Almost motherly. If your mom was in need of a cigarette and her first cup of coffee for the day.

Hmmm, coffee…

Shane chose the cool taste of water over conversation but took the bottle from Tuesday to keep her from thinking he was a complete weakling. Running the hand with his phone in it over the top of his pounding head and down the back of his stiff, sweaty neck, he refused to fall apart again.

The woman yelling at him had to be that Mother person, the one Alex had tasked to make travel arrangements. "Mother? Err, umm, Ms. Kennedy?" he asked when his tongue was finally wet enough that he could sound halfway intelligent.

"Call me Mom. Everyone else does," she clipped. "Where are you guys?"

"Arkansas. Closest mile marker is… err, was…" He pressed the cool plastic water bottle against his forehead and closed his eyes, striving to pull that precise detail out of his scrambled brain. It finally came to him like a lucky shot out of the dark, but it arrived too late for him to pass it along.

"Never mind," she snapped. "You didn't ring in on your TEAM phone. Where is it?"

"Ah…" Shane pulled the phone in his hand away from his ear and looked at it. Oh, yeah. Burner. Not TEAM. Man, his head was mixed up. Placing it back to his ear, he told Mother, "We tossed them. Didn't want anyone tracking us or Ms. Smart. Sorry, I—"

"Where'd you get the burners?"

"Umm… Everlee bought them at…" He honestly couldn't remember the name of the convenience store back in Texas. Until Tuesday whispered it into his other ear. Oh, yeah. Then he recalled the bright, flashing neon sign over the front door. Shane passed the info to Mother.

"Good. What's Everlee's number?"

"Ah…" Shane shook his head, going to disappoint Mother again.

"Never mind," she bit out. "But the next time you two decide to go dark, you'd better call me as soon as you can with your new numbers. I can only work so many miracles in a day, Shane. And for God's sake, give each other your burner phone numbers. Shit happens. Understand?"

"Yes, ma'am." Jesus, he'd never gotten his ass reamed by so many women in the same day.

Clattering sounded over the connection. Had to be fingernails. At last, Mother returned with, "Okay. No problem. I've got you now. And Everlee, too, if she bought both phones at the same time, which I'm assuming she did. Just a matter of tracing the purchase, the vendor, and serial numbers."

Okay. That made sense. Kind of.

"Is Ms. Smart still in custody? How's Everlee?"

Shane bowed his head, ashamed, but going to admit another failure. "I, umm, lost Everlee, ma'am, but Tuesday's right here, and she's not exactly in custody because—"

"I said call me Mom."

Yeah, well... Shane swallowed hard. The woman on his burner phone sounded like she was grinding her teeth. But calling Sasha Kennedy mom seemed too familiar a title to use with someone he'd never met. Besides, he already had a mother. Erin was Mom. *Is Mom! Sheesh!*

Shane offered what little he knew. "We were in a gunfight on the interstate and—"

"What do you mean, you lost Everlee?"

"We crashed. Some guys were shooting at us. The SUV rolled. More guys came along in a helicopter. The first guys ditched their car and took Everlee. Don't know who they were. She must've got knocked unconscious like I was. Tuesday watched it go down. She and I were still trapped by our seatbelts inside the SUV. Neither of us could get to Ev in time." God, where could she be? "But yeah, Tuesday's here with me and we're—"

The shriek of sirens approaching from the west interrupted his rambling. Finally. He wasn't sure he was making sense or thinking logically anyway.

Mother kept talking. Shane heard her, but the world went wonky, and he lost track of the burner phone—not his TEAM phone—the burner phone in his hand. One moment it was there, the next he was looking at empty fingers. He was mostly upright, still kneeling, and Tuesday's soft, cool hands were on his face. She smoothed his hair out of his bleary eyes. The tenderness in her forest green eyes was so damned unexpected for the serial killer she was supposed to be. Shane blinked to focus his vision and get his brain to work better. Man, he felt like shit.

"Lie back," Tuesday told him firmly. "Your pupils are dilated. You're in shock. Let me help you."

Again? He shook off her advice, unwilling to yield—not like he had much of a position of power. "I'm not in shock. Can't be. Hafta find my partner. We can't rest until we get Agent Yeager back."

Because once I stop moving again, well, after I get back up on my feet and get going, and if I stop moving again, I'm done for. Hell, I might be done for now. Did that even make sense? He had no idea, but it sounded good when he thought it.

Tuesday leaned into him and used her weight to push him off-balance and down to his side onto the fragrant earth. Not like it took much effort to get him there. He went easily, just relaxed into an embarrassing lump, with her, apparently. Tuesday's sweaty face was now aligned with his, both of them on their sides, facing each other in the middle of nowhere.

He swallowed hard. This was not how junior agents measured up. They manned up, damn it. Which wasn't happening, since he couldn't even stand up.

With one hand she ran her fingers through his hair and over his head. "Don't worry, Shane," she whispered, as she took hold of his hand. "I'll stay with you as long as you need me. I've got more water if you want. When you feel better, I'll help find Agent Yeager. We'll get her back. I promise. You'll see."

"Scout's honor?" he choked. God, he sounded like an idiot. Should he believe her? Would that in any way be the wise thing to do? He no longer knew. Just couldn't go any farther, and the scrawny weeds around them were now closing in like a noose around his neck.

Jesus, he wasn't making sense, not even to himself. Shane sucked in as deep a breath as he could, fighting the threatening shadows between each menacing weed and new stalk of corn. Tuesday nodded like the good little liar she was. But what else did black widows do? Yet the thing in his gut that had told him to trust her earlier, murmured the same advice now. Too beat up to think clearly, he blinked once, just once…

Then he was waking up with a killer headache and a shadow leaning over him. The soft, sweet breath of Tuesday was in his face. Still. She had a bunch of crushed, dirty antiseptic wipes in one hand and her other hand was pressed over his left ear. In short, the diabolical murderess responsible for three, possibly four deaths, the FBI's most wanted black widow, the accused killer who could've run and left him to bleed out, had instead stuck with him without cuffs or coercion and was right then doctoring him. Without being asked.

Yet there she was, sitting beside him in the dirt, calmly blocking the sun as if she did that kind of thing every day, giving him shade and a much-needed rest and, oh yeah, first-aid. Were black widows ever this kind and thoughtful? Was she or was she not a cold-blooded killer?

"I talked with your friend while you were asleep," Tuesday said quietly, peering at him from beneath lush, dark golden lashes, so thick they looked like tiny, feathery fans. "Her name's Sasha by the way, and I explained everything that's happened since we met in Dallas. Here." Tucking the used wipes into her pocket, Tuesday reached beside her, picked up the burner phone, and handed it to Shane. "Call her back if you don't believe me. I'm not going anywhere. Just cleaning up the nick on the tip of your ear and the dried blood trail down your neck. I couldn't bandage your ear, but" —

lifting her hand away from the side of his head, she leaned in for a closer look and all that long hair came with her— "it stopped bleeding. I think you'll live."

Shane clapped Tuesday's hand with the phone still in it onto his chest as her hair turned into a silky curtain. "No, I…" He gulped, putting his neck on the line, but finally sure she wasn't dangerous. "I don't need to check with Sasha. I believe you."

"It's about time," she replied with a tiny sarcastic huff.

She pulled away but her fingers stayed wrapped around his cell, and Shane's fingers stayed around her hand. He didn't mind that she helped him, and he didn't let her go. Her fingers were cool. Considering the chaos of the last twenty-four hours, she was calm and quite collected. He hoped Everlee, wherever she was, was as solid as Tuesday was now. Which was an odd thought, considering who Tuesday was accused of being. Her calm? Was that the tell of a psychotic killer? He blinked at the quandary he found himself still trapped in, trusting a client who was supposed to be everything but trustworthy. Were pigs going to fly next?

"Anyway," she continued evenly, "the police are at the scene of our accident. I told Sasha, but I forgot to tell you before that, when the helicopter that took Everlee away first touched down, its blades sliced off a semi-circle of the nearby crop. You know, the tips that'll have tassels on them later in summer. It came in really low and scary, and I think that field was last year's crop. Anyway, its blades clipped the tops of the corn and shot them all over the place. I'm not sure the driver really knew how to fly. But I've been thinking, between your shot-up, wrecked SUV, and the damage to the corn, won't the police chalk everything they find back there up to a gang war or something like that? Maybe the Mafia? Do they even have gangs in the middle of Arkansas?"

Shane kept blinking. Now that he'd had time to breathe and really think, not once had Tuesday acted the part of a black widow. Sure, she'd been defiant at first, but since then, she'd been nothing but compliant. And helpful. And here she was, almost holding his hand, but not really. He was the one holding onto her and… and he was only doing that as an act of friendship, which she hadn't turned into anything more. She had yet to rub up against him, offer sly, sexual innuendos, or do anything a flirty, sexual predator would. Shane had met plenty of them in taverns and bars outside bases where he'd been stationed. Tuesday wasn't anything like those greedy, grasping women. Not once had she teased or used her very nice assets to seduce him. If anything, she'd been angry she'd been apprehended before she could identify the man stalking her. Also sadder for the children she'd allegedly murdered than more worried about herself.

"Maybe," Shane replied from his still prone position. He needed to get his ass in gear, but right then, he needed to be able to sit up and get his brain to focus. There was no sense getting up only to fall back down.

"Well, whatever they're doing back there, I don't think any police officers are coming after us. I mean, I haven't heard anything for a while, no shouting or sirens, and I don't think they brought dogs with them, or I would've heard barking. Maybe they still will, I don't know. Are K-9s allowed to bark?" Tuesday shrugged her shoulders like she didn't care, her gaze on the ocean of weeds around them. Funny how those weeds weren't threatening now.

But Christ. He hadn't once considered the police might bring dogs to track them. Or had he? Shane honestly didn't know or remember. But how cock-eyed had the pilot landed if the chopper came down low enough to slice corn stalks that were barely three feet high? Who was behind Everlee's capture? Idiots? Again, Shane considered her ex for the crime, but Butch couldn't even tie his shoes. He flat out didn't have the brain power to orchestrate an elaborate abduction like this.

Tuesday eased her hand out from under Shane's, leaving the burner phone on his chest. He lay there breathing, angry that he was the weakest link. Hell, even this alleged murderer was stronger than him, and she was a woman. Might sound sexist, but talk about making good first impressions, this wasn't how it was done.

Since he and Tuesday were still out of sight, he took a long minute to analyze his physical condition and his staying power. Besides a good strong headache behind his eyes and a wounded ear, which didn't count, he wasn't feeling too bad. Of course, he was still on his back, which was a weak statement all by itself. But standing up and walking might make him a liar if he fell down again.

"Anyway," Tuesday breathed, "Sasha knows where Agent Yeager is."

"She does? Where?" That brought Shane upright in a hurry. The ground beneath him waved like a beach towel in the wind. He planted both hands in the dirt behind him to stay upright and balanced.

"Sasha wouldn't say. She said for you to call her back and she'll tell you."

Shane hit redial and gathered his wits.

"Shane?" that same motherly voice led with instead of hello. "Are you okay? Do I need to send an assist, honey? How bad are you hurt and what do you need? Talk to me."

Ah, so she did have a softer side. Good to know.

"No, ma'am, I'm good. Just took a quick, err, umm, combat nap, you know how it goes." He had no idea if Mother knew what combat naps were or if she'd ever served, but that was all his brain came up with. "Tuesday said you know where Ev is?"

"I do. It doesn't make sense, but she's only two clicks directly east of your location. Her GPS signal's holding steady, but be prepared to be disappointed. You might only find her burner phone when you get there."

"Understood. Yes, ma'am." Shane wanted to ask Sasha why everyone called her Mother or Mom. She didn't sound old enough to have kids his age, but he held back. Something about her tone was intimidating.

"You sure you don't need help? I can send someone. Just say the word."

Shane appreciated the shift in her personality. A little kindness really did go a long way. "Yes, ma'am, I know you can, and I appreciate the offer, but no. I'm good." To prove he meant what he said, Shane climbed to his feet using the tried and true three-point method of sticking his free hand firmly to the ground until he stove-piped both legs and got himself back on his feet. Once upright, he was dizzy but good. Well, good enough.

"Ms. Smart doesn't sound like a deranged killer, does she, Shane?" Sasha asked quietly.

"No, ma'am, she doesn't," he told The TEAM's technical wizard.

"You need to know that while you were out, she told me you were hurt and she wasn't leaving you behind. That she'd stay with you as long as you needed her. Don't you think that's an odd thing for a cold-blooded murderer to say and do?"

Shane nodded, aware that Tuesday could probably hear everything Sasha said. "Wait a sec, I'm putting you on speaker. And no, she's not what I expected. Listen, would it be asking too much for you to digitally backtrack Ms. Smart's whereabouts for the last year or so? She's recently been in the Arctic photographing effects of climate change. Before that, she was in Africa, the Serengeti. Also, check into Robert Freiburg. Tuesday works for him or with him and—"

"With him," Tuesday whispered. "We're partners."

"With him," Shane clarified, "and I don't know how good you are with the Cloud, but—"

"Just tell me what you need, and if there's anything to find, I'll find it," Sasha said with a definite twist of arrogance in her tone.

Okay then. Shane put his neck on the line for the woman at his side. "Tuesday's a freelance photographer, and I believe her. She didn't kill her husband, and she didn't kill Mr. Bremmer or his kids. She didn't even know them. The first she heard of her alleged crimes was when she saw a news broadcast at DFW. But her equipment, cameras, and computer were lost when her home exploded, so she can't prove anything. Could you possibly—?"

"Yes, I can download her files. Just need her user ID and password."

Shane held the phone out to Tuesday. "Mother needs your—"

"I heard. Sasha, my user ID's *TooSmart*, all one word, capital T, capital S. Password's *MomandDad*, all one word, M and D are caps."

"Got it," Sasha replied, and Shane was pretty sure those clattering background noises were her fingernails on a keyboard. But he'd also heard the quaver in Tuesday's reply. That more than anything else made his mind up for him. She'd loved her parents. She was innocent and she was being framed. That was the God's honest truth, because what kind of woman used mom and dad for a password? An innocent woman, that was who.

"Also, while she and I locate Everlee, could you track down any airport security footage of Tuesday's departures and arrivals?"

"You're thinking she's got a stalker? Where was her last arrival?"

He turned to Tuesday and said, "Dallas/Fort Worth?"

She nodded. "Yup. DFW. Three days ago. I flew in from Anchorage on Alaska Airlines. Do you want my flight number? My itineraries?"

"Don't need them," Sasha replied, "or any other flight information. Understood? I can find those details easy. No trouble at all. I'm on it."

"Are you sure you don't need—?"

"I said I'm on it, Shane," Sasha snapped. "Now go do your job. Get Everlee."

"Yes, ma'am. Two clicks east? What'll be there when I, err, I mean when *we* get there?"

Tuesday shot him a small smile of gratitude.

"A Piper airplane and a helicopter last time I checked my satellite feeds. It's a deserted private airfield with a barn close by, a single hangar, and several smaller outbuildings. It's off the interstate, though, behind the ridge of granite outcroppings running east alongside the field you're in now. I'll help you get to Everlee once you're closer. Can you accurately determine where you need to go?"

Tuesday pointed down the rows of corn.

"Still East?" he asked her, the pad of his index finger on the phone's microphone.

She nodded at the same time Mother said, "Exactly. Keep the ridge to your right and your phone handy. I'll check back in twenty to see how you're doing, understood?"

"Copy that. You're the best."

"Damned right I am. You do understand that it's not how many times a man falls off a horse that counts, don't you? It's how many times he gets back in the saddle and keeps trying."

God, she reminded him of his Mom. "I do know that, yes, ma'am, and thank you for reminding me. Sounds like you're a horsewoman."

"Not exactly, but I recently discovered I like to ride, and Maverick's got some gentle mares I like, and he's taught me a few things, and…" Her voice trailed away. She seemed to have run out of things to say.

Shane filled the silence between them with a heartfelt, "Thanks, Mom."

"No thanks necessary." She cleared her throat. "Helping my TEAM is what I do. I'm only a call away. Talk to you soon."

"Copy that." He ended the connection. Shane was beginning to like Sasha Kennedy. Turning to Tuesday, he asked, "Are you sure you're ready for whatever comes next?"

She gave him a tired smile. "Doesn't matter if I'm ready or not. It's coming at us either way. Let's go get Agent Yeager back. And thanks for treating me like a person instead of a killer."

"Like I told Sasha, I believe you, Tuesday, and I trust you." *Please don't make a liar out of me.* He nodded sideways in the direction they'd be walking. "And I'd be honored to help you clear your name."

That earned him another smile.

"Come on, then. We need to be a helluva lot closer to Everlee's location before Mom calls back."

"You call Sasha mom?"

"Yeah, I guess I did," he admitted. *And from now on, I always will.*

"Why? You didn't call her that before."

Shane had to chuckle. "I have no idea. It just feels right."

Chapter Twenty-One

With that shot still reverberating inside the over-sized, empty barn, Everlee took a chance and leaped off the silo's wall with her chair leg in hand. She was determined to get out of this whacked-out version of Crazy Town before someone shot her. With a heart-pounding whoosh, she dropped to all fours, the distance to the barn floor deceptively farther than she'd guesstimated. So far, so good.

But damn. A thick, hefty male body in gray pants and a bloodied dress shirt lay sprawled on his back to her right, blocking the barn door from closing all the way. No one else was in sight. The silo itself was a wide, squat concrete thing that took up one entire corner of the front of the barn. At least, she thought that was the front corner, given that was where the only door was that she could see. Taking advantage of the silo's curved wall, she ran around it and tucked herself between its far side and the barn wall, hidden in the shadows from the dead guy and his killer. That woman.

Breathing hard, she took stock of her new predicament. Sturdy rafters ran the length of the roof, but the roof itself was no more than a see-through conglomeration of missing and broken timbers, laths, and shingles, all pieced together by a ton of rusty nails.

An empty hayloft stood on twelve eight-by-eight wooden stilts across from Everlee. No windows anywhere. Below the loft, wooden-slatted stalls stood in a single row along the rear of the barn, just as old, unused, and forgotten as the rusted farm implements parked nearer the partially closed door. Dusty tack that looked like it had been hanging there for years, decorated the half-wall to the right of the door. Ropes. Chains. Bridles. Halters. Leather-wrapped poles Everlee had no idea what they were used for. No farmyard animals, just sparrows and swallows coasting between the desiccated walls and roof. This place wasn't a barn as much as a disaster waiting to fall down. One good breeze and it'd be rubble. It'd be damned nice if she'd found her boots before then. Who knew what she might step on?

Keeping out of sight, Everlee crept far enough toward the door to take a quick peek at the dead guy. Another muscle-bound man, dressed in an identical black business suit had arrived by then. Leaning in from outside the barn, he grabbed hold of the dead guy's ankles while telling someone at his right, "Understood, yeah, you bet. Yes, ma'am. Get the right woman. Kill the one we got. I'll handle it from now on. Uh-huh, yeah, no problem. Never shoulda left these two numbskulls in charge in the first place."

Everlee found it interesting that these guys, including the dead one, fit the description of the man who'd followed Ms. Smart in Texas. Heavy weight. Black suits. Black polished dress shoes. It didn't take much to connect the dots between the victim burned to death at her house with the guy murdered here. Was that guy just expendable muscle? Was he killed by the same hot-tempered woman? Made sense. But that meant Smart was telling—the truth.

Everlee let that take root for a couple seconds. She guessed it was possible, but the evidence against Tuesday was damning and eyes didn't lie. Neither did security cameras. Yeah, no. Everlee chalked these new revelations up to coincidence. Smart *was* guilty, damn it.

No one answered the guy now in charge, at least no one close enough that Everlee could hear. He must've been on the phone. Did that mean the woman was already gone? Didn't matter. This might be her only chance to escape. The thug outside the door would have to climb into the silo to kill her, right? She'd escape then, and, somehow, she'd find her way back to Shane. Wherever he was. He'd probably been hurt in that rollover, maybe Ms. Smart, too. They needed her, and Everlee meant to get back to them as quickly as she could. *If* she could figure out where they were. Hell, if she could figure out where *she* was.

Her pockets were empty. She had no phone. Plan B. Rush the creep, hit him over the head with her trusty chair leg, steal his phone, and run for her life. Nothing to it. Sounded impossible, but she'd been in impossible situations before.

Stealthily, she inched forward, keeping her back to the silo, the chair leg on her shoulder, and her body obscured in shadow as long as possible. She could almost taste the freedom beyond that open door. But *Jiminy Christmas!* Now that she'd gotten closer, she could see that door was narrow, damned narrow. Weren't they supposed to be wide enough for tractors and wagons and horses and stuff like that to fit through? Not this one.

Her unspoken rant stalled when another big, burly gorilla stepped over the raised door sill and into the barn. Shit. Now it was two against one, maybe three if that demented woman was still out there. Everlee had no way to know for sure how many she was up against. Whatever she did next would be risky. And these guys were big and wide and mean and…

Jiminy Christmas! Freaked out at the odds stacked against her, Everlee ran a quick hand over her short-cropped hair. Too bad Shane wasn't there. He'd know what to do and, for sure, he could take down both these men, easy. But he wasn't and Everlee was, and—

"I ain't gonna do nuthin' with that bitch you and Rick took," Thug One told the new guy now at his side. "Dumb asshole. Talk about a rookie move."

"Rick's who grabbed her. Not me!"

"I don't fuckin' care! You want her, you climb down into that shithole while I stash Ricky boy outta sight. Far as I'm concerned, she's already dead. Ain't no way outta that fuckin' box you built, and I din't leave her no food or water or nuthin'. She won't survive long once we leave, but if you wanna play, Ringo, make it fast and make it lethal. Maeve's already plenty pissed. She'll kill both of us if we let her down again."

By then, he'd dragged Ricky Boy mostly outside, but left one arm with its ham-sized hand draped over the door sill.

"Just make sure you kill her when you're done messing her up, then take pictures of what's left of her and send 'em to Maeve. Maybe that'll keep her off our backs."

"I ain't gonna just mess 'er up, Bud. I'm gonna fuck her every which way I can till she dies screaming or choking. Makes no difference to me. No one can hear anything what goes on inside that toybox. Those concrete walls are a foot thick and that box is damned near airtight. No weak little bitch is gonna escape what I've got planned."

When that rat bastard palmed his junk and sniggered, Everlee cringed. He meant to kill her. All the more reason to run.

"Which is why I built it as tight as I did, and why I put it where it is. Simple solutions are best, and I've had a lotta fun in that box you call a shithole. You oughta try it some time." He blew out what sounded like a disgusting satisfied sigh. "Messing up a bitch is what makes a man a man, know what I mean?"

"I don't, but thanks for the creepy visual, you perv. Maeve ain't coming back, but if you wanna get on her good side, don't forget she likes trophies. You got ten minutes, Ringo. Get the hell down there. Do what you gotta do. When you're done, cut a finger or something off that dead bitch for Maeve's collection. Then we gotta get gone. I like my hairy balls where they're hanging, not dangling off Maeve's rearview mirror like fuckin' fuzzy dice."

"Start counting," Ringo replied almost cheerfully, now hanging by one hand off the silo's ladder, like the long-armed ape he was. Not that Everlee wouldn't have used that ladder if she'd known about it before. Turned out that jump had probably saved her life.

With every noisy step Ringo took up, Everlee's time was running out. She didn't recall if she'd shut the door to that *toybox* behind her. As soon as he saw the open door, he'd—

"She's gone! Shit, you hear me? She's gone!"

Too late. Time was up.

"Then she's still inside this here barn," Bud growled as he tossed Ricky Boy's arm outside and slammed Everlee's only escape route behind him. "Oh, girleeeey," he crooned like the sick bastard he was. "Come out, come out, wherever you are."

When Hell freezes over.

Jumping off the ladder, Ringo hit the barn floor with a clap of thunder. He crouched low, a switchblade now gleaming in his right hand. "You still got that lighter, Bud?"

"Yup." Bud dug it out of his pants pocket, along with a pistol that… no, make that a Taser. Guess they wanted her alive for their idea of fun and games. So what was the lighter for? *Shit, shit, shit!* These morons meant to burn her out.

Everlee shrank deeper into the dark corner. She didn't have a proper weapon, only the broken chair leg, but no real way forward, and from the way Bud kept flicking the lighter, luck wasn't on her side. The second he set fire to anything in this place, even the tiniest scrap of leaves scattered across the floor, the dry, dusty air inside the barn would explode. This day was going to get uglier before it was over. But by hell, she'd go down fighting, and maybe she'd get out alive.

Maybe…

Miracles still happened, and Everlee prayed for one now.

"You go that way," Bud ordered slyly, like he thought she couldn't hear them breathing. "I'll check the stalls, start a few small fires in there, get the place burning, and flush her your way. Catch her fast though. Once this place starts burning, it'll go quick."

"Let the fun begin," Ringo whispered.

"Just don't lose her."

"No worries. I like a good chase before a barbecue."

Everlee heard a click that could've been a lock. Which spelled doom if her only escape was now lost. Sometimes discretion was the better part of valor. Only problem with that philosophy was Everlee wasn't born with discretion or patience or a think-twice chip in her brain. Slow and steady were not her modus operandi—never had been, wasn't going to suddenly start happening now. She acted and reacted, that's who she was. She was impulsive and she was on the verge of going toe-to-toe with these assholes. Either die trying to escape or be tortured and burned alive. There was no in between. No time to wait. She might just get a sandwich out of these guys before they made a meal out of her, but by hell, she refused to hide like a sissy coward crying for mercy.

Not me, damn it! If I'm going to die, so the hell are you two!

Stepping into the open, she kicked a half bale of old hay out of her way and came face-to-face with Ringo's killer grin. Man, he was an ugly sucker. A wicked scar ruined one of his cheeks, then hung a sharp curve into his mouth, making his lips a gnarled mess that twisted his face into a huge, creepy grin. He could've played the *Joker*. Wouldn't have needed make-up.

His eyes lit up and his ugly lip quirked higher, adding to the whole *Chainsaw Massacre* vibe he had going. "There you are," he purred, then yelled over his shoulder, "Found her! Come get a piece of her before I end her."

That brought Bud to his side. Big, dumb Bud, still flicking his lighter in this tinderbox of a barn.

"You guys want a piece of me? Then come and get it!" Everlee barked, the chair leg swung over one shoulder like a baseball bat. She would go down fighting, damn it.

Aim for their heads, then balls. Throats next. If Bud wants to play with fire, fine. But he'll have to wait his bloody turn, because I'm killing Ringo first. It'll get bloody before I burn to death. Damn you guys to Hell!

Planting her feet, she growled, determined to get the first swing in. Yeah, these guys were bigger and stronger, but she was a woman! Pissed and righteous and—

The damned barn door burst open with a thunderous clap. Into the sharp, white beam of sunlight stepped a monster of a man. Her one and only exit was blocked.

God, why me? Everlee thought, but then she thought better. *Son of a bitch! If I can kill two, I can kill three!*

Maybe.

Whoever this creep was, he had a chest that made Bud's and Ringo's look puny. He was so big and broad that he had to slant sideways to clear the doorway. She would've laughed at the shocked expressions on Ringo and Bud's faces, the way they'd frozen in their tracks when they saw him. But there wasn't time to waste and nothing about her desperate situation was funny.

So strike first and hit hard!

Everlee screamed like a banshee and ran straight at Ringo. Quick, while he was looking the other way. She lifted the chair leg high over her head, the battle for her life now begun. With hate in her heart for cretins like these two dirtbags, she screamed her one and only war cry. "Come get some, assholes!"

She was nearly within reach. She had him, by God. Righteous rage fueled her every footstep. She swung the chair leg high over her head. She would win this fight, damn it! At least one of these guys would die at her hand.

Until—a shot blasted from the doorway and something gooey splattered across her bare feet. Ringo dropped dead.

Just keeled over, on his face, stiff as a board. A widening puddle of blood pooled under his chest. What the hell?

Before she could lift her chair leg for another attack, a solid *THUNK* hit the center of Bud's skull. Thin, red mist swooshed out the opposite side of his head, like his brain was in a hurry to get away from him.

Everlee froze, her best-laid plan shot to hell. She stood there in shock, waiting for her turn to die. Holding a short, stubby chair leg against the damned precise weapon that had just ended Ringo and Bud. Had the witch who'd given the order for her to die changed her plans? Had her executioner come back to silence Bud and Ringo instead?

Her poor heart pounded at the very clear knowledge that her time was up. There was no way to best the hulking shadow at her one and only exit. Her stomach lurched, threatening to upchuck. So much gore lay between her and her last opponent—the assassin whose face she still couldn't make out against the sunlight blasting behind him. Almost seemed like a halo. Damn, he was good.

This was not what she'd expected, not how she thought she'd die. Not by another killer. Two she could've taken. But three? She lost her nerve. The last thug standing was quietly waiting for her to make her move. Then what? Did he honestly think she'd scurry beside him like a scared rabbit trying to get through that narrow door? He was the only way out. Those two big pistols were still smoking. He was too big. Too thick and too deadly. There was no other way.

Still, she licked her lips, determined to fight to her last breath. That shouldn't take long. Everlee's heart sank. The asshat was toying with her, that was what he was doing, like a cat with a stupid mouse. She was trapped, and he knew it. The light squeezing into the barn behind him made him look bigger and blacker, just plain evil and—

Damn him! She refused to back down. Hadn't backed down to the two dead guys, wouldn't to this bastard, asshole, whatever! What was he waiting for?

"Through you or over you, Mister," she declared defiantly, her voice quavering just a little. "I don't give a shit who you think you are, but I know who I am, and I'm leaving right damned now. Get out of my way. Move it or lose it!" she screamed.

"Everlee?" the last killer asked, his voice deep and quiet, as even as the sunlight behind him.

"Shane?" she croaked, not daring to drop her weapon, but willing to hope.

Her miracle came back to her with a raspy, "Yeah, babe, it's me. But I can come back later if you're busy."

"I'm not busy!" she yelled. Tossing that stupid chair leg aside, she ran to Shane and crashed into his wide-open arms. Craving the safety she knew she'd find in his embrace, she burrowed her face into his magnificent chest, so damned thankful he was there. "It's you! It's really you!"

He was there! Lifting her head, she took possession of his handsome, sweaty face with both hands and climbed his body until her legs wrapped around his hips. Tightly. As tightly as she could. Tighter than before. Everlee wanted more than a hug. She wanted all of him. Somehow. Right damned now. He was there!

"You came for me," she cried, hiccupping like a damned girly girl.

With a delectable, throaty grumble, Shane took a half-step backward to reinforce his balance, then cupped her ass with both gun-wielding hands. A shiver raced up her spine at the intimate contact. Talk about him taking possession. The barrels of the weapons he'd just fired were warm against her backside. But she was more attracted to the smoking hot barrel pressed against her core.

She was out of control, not her usual smug self. No longer aggressive or ready to fight. Just the opposite. She felt inexplicably wanton for the first time in her whole, messed up life. With stupid tears in her eyes, Everlee grabbed hold of Shane's jaw and mashed her mouth over his.

He came for me. Somehow, he found me. Shane being there in the nick of time proved it. *Miracles did happen. Shane saved me! He did! And he tastes so damned good.*

Everlee pressed in closer, smacking her lips and ready to devour him. Man, this guy could kiss. He was making a meal of her mouth, and Everlee would've given him everything, right there and then. Instead, she offered her tongue and her air and every last bit of her wild, crazy heart—if he'd have it. If he'd take her and help her forget what a loser she was.

But as fast as she'd taken possession of his mouth, he took it back. Angling her away from the dead men and the gore, he carried her out of the barn and into sweet, clean sunlight. Might as well have been starlight. She was so much in lust and love with this sexy man.

Once outside, Shane took a sharp about-face and pressed her back against the barn, and held her in place with his hips. Growling like a beast, he plundered her mouth, the in-and-out actions of his tongue mimicking what his hips seemed to be doing with her core. She had no idea that dry humping was a real thing or that it could feel so good.

Holding their bodies tight against each other, Shane ravaged her mouth, lips, chin, and cheeks with a pent-up passion that put whisker burns everywhere he kissed. And she loved every last one of them. This was as close to indecent exposure as Everlee had ever been with any male. If she was what and who Shane wanted, she was ready to bare all, give all. Standing against the barn wall. Lying in the dirt. Any. Where.

The more their physical connection overheated, the more the air between them buzzed with feral electricity. Her body wanted this man inside of her, now. Again. Every tingling part of her hummed until—

A polite, feminine "Ahem" broke the spell.

Shit! "Bremmer?" Everlee gasped, literally gasped into Shane's mouth, almost swallowing her tongue at what their prisoner had just witnessed TEAM agents doing to each other. Pulling far enough away from Shane's up-close and oh, so ruggedly handsome face, Everlee glared at the alleged killer in their midst. "What are you doing here, Bremmer? I mean Smart?" Shit, she couldn't think straight. Was she Tuesday Smart or Tuesday Bremmer?

Everlee settled for Tuesday.

Tuesday's shoulders lifted in a shy shrug that almost—almost—made her look innocent.

Yeah, right. "Where's your damned cuffs?" Everlee growled even as Shane breathed like a sexy beast in her face and told her, "No worries. She's with me."

Like that was supposed to make her feel better? "She's what? With you how? What's that even mean?"

"Hi again, Agent Yeager," Ms. Smart offered quietly. "Yes, I'm here. Guess Shane forgot to tell you that before he dragged you outside to kiss you, huh?"

Swiping off the tears dripping down her face with a quick hand, Everlee glared at the woman and snapped, "Damn it, Smart. You're a convicted, err, suspected—oh hell! You're a child-killer and murderer and a—Shit! I don't know what you are anymore!"

"She's not a killer," Shane declared huskily, the sensation of his warm breath tantalizingly heady on Everlee's sweaty neck.

Her stare snapped from him back to Smart, then back to him. Hot damn, that sexy rumble of his was a distraction Everlee didn't need. Normally, she wouldn't've been bothered by a male. By any male! But this was Shane, and he was here, and he had come expressly for her, and...

He was holding her and loving her like she'd never been held or loved before. With his entire body and both hands. With his mouth and his tongue and his lips. With his breath. With everything he was. He *had* risked his life to save her. She was alive because of Shane. Not because of Alex or Butch or... or anyone else. Just Shane.

A wave of humility rolled over her, dousing her self-righteous snark. Everlee buried her face in the warm, sweaty corner where his shoulder joined his neck and took a deep breath of him to help her think. Until Smart ruined everything, all Ev wanted was Shane. On his back. In bed.

But now, the position she and he were in was inappropriate on so many levels. Did she care? Sort of, yeah. Not about what Smart had seen or about TEAM rules, though. Only about Shane. No way was she letting go of the man in her arms. She refused to push away just to make Smart feel more comfortable. Everlee didn't care what offended the alleged murderess or what she wanted. Only Shane. He was here and he could hold onto Everlee all day if he wanted to. She wished he would, and they could—

But Alex would care. *Oh, yeah. Alex. Damn.* The brittle warmth of embarrassment flamed up her neck, her face, and on up into her scalp. She was prickly all over. Probably looked like a sweaty, red-faced troll. True, some of that red was probably the blowback from one of those dead guys' heads. And sweaty or not, Tuesday Smart somehow managed to look fresh and kind and…

Shit.

Turning away from her sharp, green eyes, Everlee bumped her forehead against Shane's scruffy cheek. "I needed you and here you are," she whispered. "How'd you know where I was? I know you're smart, but how—"

"No, babe," Shane mumbled into her mouth, his incredibly sexy five o'clock shadow abrading her already tender lips. "She's Smart. I'm just some guy."

Everlee couldn't help smiling. "I know she's Tuesday Smart, smartass. But how… how'd you find me, and why isn't she locked up? Did you have to bring her with you?"

"Of course. She knew the way. Where else would she be? We were in the same Toyota when it rolled, remember? She's the one who saw those asshats fly off with you in their chopper, not me. Not sure I'd even be alive if she hadn't pulled me out of the SUV."

"You're hurt?"

Shane pressed his forehead against hers. "I think we're all a little dinged up, but I'm good, and you're here and…"

He took a breath and purred. "I like this, Everlee. I like you. You're perfect."

Oh, man, he was killing her with every sweet word out of his mouth.

"She saved your life?" Everlee asked, incredulous that a black widow would do something so noble—unless she had ulterior motives. This could all be a trick.

"No, I just—" Tuesday started to explain.

Shane interrupted Ms. Smart's quiet rebuttal with a firm, "Yeah, she did. She saved my life, Ev, and she even talked with Mother. Err, Mom."

"I only did what anyone would do after an accident," Tuesday said evenly, which made Everlee look closer at her dirty hair and the smudges on her chin and cheeks. The model-worthy lady Everlee who had taken down just last night, looked more like a battle-worn soldier just come in from a firefight now. Her t-shirt was filthy. Her fashionably tattered, stone-washed jeans were so torn up they showed more skin than before, and some of that skin was scraped and scratched, dirty and bloodied.

"Really, I just did what anyone else would've done, Agent Yeager. I'm sure sorry I couldn't get out of my seatbelt before those men took you away, though. You were dazed and hurt, I could tell. You took your seatbelt off before we rolled, didn't you? Do you remember anything? Did you hit your head when the SUV rolled?"

That seemed to be the question of the day, hour, minute. Still clinging to Shane, with his hands still clamped under her butt, holding her to him, Everlee shook her poor aching head and replied, "No. I can't recall the rollover or even what kind of car we were in. Shane said Toyota? Where the hell did we rent that? Only thing I remember when I came to is being on my stomach inside a buzzing machine with a rag stuffed down my throat and a smelly bag over my head."

Fragments of what happened came back to her. The Toyota rolled. A Land Cruiser, "Oh, yeah. The vehicle behind us was a POS sedan, but I couldn't make out the model. POS sedans come in so many different flavors these days. I never got a shot off because—"

"We blew a tire," Shane interrupted.

"Yes, and I undid my seatbelt. I was going to shoot out their radiator. But I didn't, did I?"

"I have no idea, babe," he answered, letting her slide slowly down his body until she was on her feet. But still in his arms.

Pursing her lips, Everlee blew out a stream of fresh air—just because she could. She peered around Shane and faced Ms. Smart. Shane hadn't let go yet, and Everlee was afraid she'd fall down when he did. But he probably should. They were, after all, trusted TEAM agents. Nothing more. And that kiss probably didn't mean as much as either of them thought. It was just an impulsive reaction to seeing each other again and hormones and adrenaline and being alive and…

Yeah. All that.

"One of the guys you just took out punched me when we were in the chopper. I remember that," Everlee told Shane, her gaze still fixed on Ms. Smart. "He knocked me out. Next thing I knew, I woke up tied to a chair inside the big wooden box that's inside the silo in there." She jerked her head toward the now closed barn door. "There was a woman with them, though. Here. I heard her but couldn't see her. She was in charge. She didn't come inside the barn, but she wasn't happy.

She screamed they'd taken the wrong woman. She ordered them to get rid of me. I think she killed the dead guy outside the barn."

Everlee craned her neck around Shane's beefy body to see the body she was talking about. But Shane quickly blocked her view, and Everlee didn't push for control like she usually would. Shane was protecting her, and for once in her life, she let a man stand between her and trouble.

"That woman killed her own guy, Shane," she told him, her voice growing squeakier with every word. *Why do I sound like a frightened little girl?* Clearing her throat, Everlee tried again. "That woman—"

"Relax, Ev. I've got you. It's okay to let go." With the tip of his index finger, Shane forced her chin up. "Breathe. Just breathe, babe. Cry if you need to."

"I don't cry," she growled. But she might now. No one had ever called her babe before. Bitch, yeah. She'd heard that behind her back plenty of times. Skank. Whore. But an actual endearment? Rare as flying pigs.

Everlee all but fell into Shane's ocean-blue eyes. The tender light swamping her was so hard to bear. She'd never been weak. Never wanted to be a sissy, prissy, pretty girl. Had always had to rely on herself. Because, *hello*. Until Alex's TEAM, there hadn't been anyone in her life to count on. Murphy might never know but he'd saved her life the day he'd hired her.

Sucking back a shuddering breath, she relented. On the verge of breaking down beneath so much gentle, male kindness and concern—both rarities in her life—she gave that inch where most men would've taken a mile. She let go. Just took a cleansing breath and decided to believe Shane. If he trusted Tuesday, she would, too.

The way he held onto Everlee wasn't so much possessive as just plain comforting. There'd been damned few times in her life when any guy had been this careful of her body or her feelings. And she had feelings, damn it. Sensitive feelings. And right then, they were about to pour out of her big mouth and her eyeballs if she didn't calm down and man-up and—

Oh, hell. She was so sick of having to *'man'* up. Just once, it'd be nice to be soft and feminine and just be who she really was, a strong female. A woman! For a minute or two, it'd be nice if that part of her didn't scare guys away. Was it asking too much for a man to let her be what and who she was? A little worn around the edges. A lot of trouble, okay, sure. A challenge because of her unpredictable ADHD. Clumsy. Pushy. But so damned willing to always step up and give a hundred fifty percent, no matter what. Could she help it if her enthusiasm pushed others away? And sometimes helped her fall on her ass? And sprain both ankles? And look bad in front of her boss? Although he was as OCD as she was. Maybe Alex truly did see something in her that others didn't. Maybe he really was just teasing her when he joked about her falling down. Maybe he did like her. As an agent, not a wannabe girlfriend or anything outrageously foolish as that. Because he loved his wife and Everlee adored Kelsey and…

Jiminy Christmas, where the hell am I going with this?

"Not sure I'd be alive without both my partners," Shane continued easily. "Tuesday, may I introduce my companion agent and my very best friend, Everlee Yeager. And no, she's not related to Chuck."

Your very best friend?

Everlee had never had one of those, not like she wanted him to be just a friend. Not as deep as her feelings were for this big guy. But she had a feeling he was just taking the attention off her so she could regain her self-control and common sense, which was getting harder to do by the minute. But she was his very best friend? No one had ever said that before. Everlee let her head fall against Shane's chest, sure she looked like a sweaty, bloody mess. But she was past caring. He'd just admitted, in public, well, at least to Smart, that Everlee was important to him. She'd take that to the bank and worry about the details later.

Shane didn't seem to mind her snapping out orders or bossing him around, or acting like she knew more than he did. But Everlee knew better. Of the two, he was the true warrior, the one who'd come home from years of combat, with real scars on his body and on his soul. Good soldiers, airmen, and scout snipers were each entitled to every last one of their scars, wounds, and bloody messes. Those scars were the true medals, each backed up with stories of valiant struggles to survive, of true heroism, and tons of outstanding courage.

And—*Thank you, God*— Shane was here. That alone declared what kind of man he was. And if he trusted Tuesday Smart, well, Everlee would, too.

She stuck her arm around Shane and extended her hand in friendship to their prisoner. "Good to see you again, Ms. Smart. Thanks for taking care of my buddy. My friend."

"I think. No..." Shane started, "I'm absolutely sure we've got the wrong woman, Everlee. Ms. Smart could've taken off after that wreck. She had the chance, but she didn't leave me. She gave aid when I needed it, and she gave credible intel on what happened to you."

"How'd you know where to find me, though? There's no way you could've known where I was." *Or what they meant to do to me when they found out they'd kidnapped the wrong person.* Everlee shivered as Ringo's ugly plan for her came back. Ringo and his torture chamber. Bud and his lighter. *Geez!*

"Easy. We talked to Sasha" —he toggled a finger between him and Smart— "and Mom tracked your burner phone. Don't ask me how. I just told her where you bought the burners and she worked some kind of magic. Want to bet your burner's either still inside this barn or in that chopper over there?" Shane jerked his stubbled chin at the open hangar across the yard.

Everlee hadn't thought once about her missing phone not being her TEAM phone. Holy shit. She'd been in a more desperate situation than she'd realized. And that chopper? The hangar? Two more things she hadn't noticed until Shane mentioned them. She'd been too close to falling apart to see anything beyond Shane and Tuesday. And, okay, she only had eyes for him. She was smitten with the guy. But she was noticing the white, turbine-powered, six-seater helicopter resting on its skids near the hangar across the weed-filled yard now. The damned thing looked like a giant mosquito sitting there, waiting to suck the blood from some other defenseless woman.

Pissed that she'd been abducted by idiots the likes of Ringo and Bud, Everlee wanted to squash the shit out of their chopper. With the heel of her boot. Then stick a block of Semtex in its carcass and blow it back to Hell. With them! After too much adrenaline, she was still feeling unusually aggressive. She needed to hit something. Or cry. But whining and bawling were her least favorite things to do, so yeah. Her hands clenched into fists in anticipation of a brawl.

"They were going to kill me," she growled. "I don't know where that big-mouthed woman went, but Ringo said he would fuck me up until I died screaming or choking. He said he liked to play games. I think these creeps have killed other people here before."

Shane pulled her in tighter. Man, his arms were the best medicine in the world. "You and Tuesday wait here while I go inside and get what I need to identify them. Tuesday?"

"Sure thing, Sha—"

"No!" Everlee spat, thumbing her chest in case he forgot who was in charge. "*My* job! If anyone's going back inside, it's gonna be—"

Before she could spit out the rest of her threat, Shane whirled her around and got straight in her face. "No way, Agent Yeager. They're already dead, and you're compromised. Stay out here. Neither of you ladies need to see what I'm going to do to those asshats in there."

He thought he could boss her? Just because he was male, bigger, stronger, and wider? Forget that bullshit. Everlee opened her mouth, prepared to dress him down and spit him out when—

Shane's warm, wet mouth crashed over hers, silencing her out-of-control rant and swallowing every last bit of her angst and her rage and...

Oh, hell, he tasted good. Her fingers tightened over his biceps. *Jiminy Christmas,* he was solid and she loved the way his muscles flexed under her fingers. His hands were hard and his fingers long and right then digging into her upper arms, reminding her that he truly was all things male. That males were instinctively dominant fighters and winners and protectors of all they held dear. Never mind that he was also holding her again like he'd never let her go. Like he truly, honestly cared about her.

Best friend, nothing. She wanted this friendship to be the kind that came with benefits. Everlee's eyes rolled back in her head at the delicious power radiating off this intense man. The taste of his bossy mouth was so damned sweet, and this time he was demanding in an entirely different—better—way. He was right, damn it. She didn't have to be in charge all the time. She could let go like she wanted to. She already trusted him.

Her out-of-control need for vengeance dissipated in the passion that was right then owning her mouth and her lips and… yeah. Her poor battered, tenderized heart. Maybe her soul. Succumbing to the animal magnetism running like a steaming hot current between Shane and her, she huffed through her nose. Her hands moved from his biceps to the strong cords in his neck, then to his stubbled cheeks. Damn, he had one helluva five o'clock shadow going for him. What time was it anyway?

"For once, do as I say," Shane murmured around their nearly indecent kiss. Then he added, "Please? For me?"

Smart, smart man.

Everlee hadn't realized he had her off the ground again. Like he could've held her all day. Like she weighed next to nothing. If she were a braver, gentler, girly woman, Everlee would've told Shane she'd fallen in love with him. She'd never felt the wonderful sensation zinging between them like sparking electricity before. It left her breathless. Maybe a little brainless, and—

Yes, her silly heart whispered. *Tell him. You do love him. You know you do.*

Instead, Everlee eased out of his arms and let Shane go. He'd been in combat; she hadn't. He just might have skills she didn't. Might even know a few things she didn't. Like what to do with three dead morons. Maybe there *were* things men did better than women. She was willing to explore the possibility. For now. She decided to obey, but only because Shane asked. He wasn't some guy with a dick bigger than his brain. No, Shane was smart. He put her feelings first, and more than anything, Everlee needed that kind of thoughtful, positive reinforcement.

Pursing her lips, she blew out another deep breath and whispered, "Yes, sir. Yes, for you. Okay. I'll stay here."

"This won't take long," he assured her, his voice less stern, but so rough and hoarse that wet heat pooled between her thighs again. What was that about? She was hot and bothered just because he'd bossed her? Apparently.

"Come on, let's find some shade." That was Ms. Smart and she was holding her hand out for Everlee to take. As if she were the adult in charge, and Everlee was just a civilian, a child. Also as if she might've already suggested that more than once and had been trying to get Everlee's attention.

With her heart pounding, Everlee turned to Ms. Smart. They weren't besties or BFFs, didn't even like each other. Ignoring Smart's silly act of female friendship, Everlee turned her back on Tuesday and walked over to the far side of the barn all by herself. Meanwhile, Shane was busy dragging the first dead guy into the barn.

There were no chairs in sight, not even a dried-up tree stump to sit on, but hey. Beggars couldn't be choosers. Everlee sank down against the barn's cool, stone foundation and let her head fall forward to her bent knees. She was free. She was alive, and there really were times in a woman's life when the sound of her own breathing was all she needed. There was no way this dilapidated barn could keep out the rain, but its stone foundation was solid, and its east side offered a ton of cool shade this late in the day. If shade could be measured in tonnage. *Totally useless, random thought, probably caused by all that fading adrenaline. And lack of sleep. And dehydration.*

She tempered her snark and aimed to be, well, pleasanter. More pleasant? Aww, who knew? Everlee didn't. Turning to Ms. Smart, she huffed, but only because the short walk had left her breathless. "So, *Tuesday*." She managed to sound civil for a change, and she used the name Shane used. "You and Shane are on a first name basis now, huh?"

"Yes, ma'am, we are. I'm here to help you guys, Agent Yeager. Any way I can. Shane said he'd help prove my innocence. It's a fair trade, us helping each other." Her statement ended sounding more like a timid question.

Helping each other sounded like a great idea, and because Everlee was too tired to get spun up over Smart's apparent loyalty to Shane, she simply nodded. "Please, just Ev. Shane's right. We've been through enough shit to trust each other."

"That'd be nice," Tuesday replied without a trace of attitude. "He likes you. I'm glad. But he's always so polite. I didn't think he had it in him to do what he just did with you."

"What? Kiss me?" Everlee ran her tongue over her bottom lip, savoring the delicious taste that lingered. What would it be like to be able to kiss him any time she wanted?

To make love with that rugged, handsome body. To put her hands all over him, morning, afternoon, or night time?

Tuesday's head bobbed. "Yes, and he killed the men who hurt you. He cares for you. A lot. You should've heard him swearing before he kicked in the barn door."

Why did Shane's caveman act make Everlee grin? Shane kicked in a door to save her? *How sweet is that?* "What'd he say?" And now she sounded like a junior high teenager bonding with her girlfriend.

"Well, he heard what those guys were saying they'd do to you, then he dropped a lot of F-bombs. You should've heard him. He was already a walking, talking, cursing maniac with Sasha. She helped us locate you. But he went ballistic once he knew you were in trouble."

"I was in trouble."

"That man looks at you like you're his whole world. Haven't you noticed?"

Everlee cleared her throat and shook her head, afraid if she acknowledged how much she cared for Shane, she'd only fall deeper in love with the guy. Which was not smart for agents who worked together. Connor and Izza Maher seemed to make it work, but they'd been married before they'd worked together. Rory and Ember Dennison, Walker and Persia Judge made it work, too. But Everlee had already proved she sucked at the marriage thing. She'd been burned before. Once was enough. Wasn't it?

"He's just pumped full of adrenaline right now," she explained, needing to set Tuesday straight. "It's simple biology. Intense situations create dramatic feelings of loyalty and duty, and sometimes, those feelings get confused with lust and love, especially between males and females. Especially when one of them gets hurt. Not that I'm hurt. I'm not. But because of what happened inside the barn, and when he saw me, and he knew they'd hurt me, but I was alive, and…"

Jiminy Christmas, I'm rambling.

Tuesday's hand on Everlee's shoulder was all that shut her up. "Trust me, Everlee. I've photographed thousands of people all over the world, and in my job, I've seen true love up close enough times to recognize it. I've seen it in the middle of famine, warfare, battle, and peace. It's more a feeling than talk. It's actions, not words. It's him going back inside this barn to do whatever he thinks he has to do to make sure you don't. Love is stepping up to be more than you ever thought you could be. Sometimes, it's simply showing up, not saying anything, just being there for someone. That man adores you. It's written all over his face, but especially in his eyes. Don't you see it? I sure do."

Everlee had no idea what to say. So she grunted because, well, grunting was kind of an answer, wasn't it? Not a denial, not exactly affirmation, either.

But Tuesday had just confirmed everything Everlee had felt in Shane's arms. He'd become important to her in a brand-new, exciting, and unexpected way. If this was love, and even if it wasn't, she wanted to see what happened next between them.

But she was still afraid to take that risk. What divorced woman wouldn't be? That realization astounded Everlee. There was a day—like yesterday—when she wasn't afraid of anything or anyone. Wouldn't admit it, didn't consider it a conceivable option. But now? Getting close to this guy, only to wake up some day and find out he'd stepped out on her?

That he'd played her, only needed a good time, short time fuck buddy?

No. Way. She refused to go through that again. And yet...

Like the temptress it could be, her tongue traced her sore bottom lip, still searching after the deliciousness of Shane's mouth. She smoothed her fingers over the tenderized abrasions his passionate kiss had left on her chin and lips. Her buttocks remembered how it felt having his hands in charge of her body, his big, capable fingers gripping her ass as if he'd never let her go. Her core heated with need.

If this strange new feeling was love, she wanted more of it. But fear of failure had planted itself firmly in her way, and for the first time in her life, Everlee didn't know what to do.

Chapter Twenty-Two

"I killed them," Shane explained honestly to Alex from where he'd crouched alongside the hefty body of the dead man he'd dragged into the barn. He'd hoped to speak with Mark or Sasha, but got his boss. "They meant to kill Everlee, so I killed them first. No identification on any of these three guys. Sending mugshots and fingerprints now." He texted the two pictures he'd already taken, along with two sets of blackened fingerprint cards from the kit he carried. "Will send the third set as soon as I'm done. But Everlee said some woman's in charge, not these guys. She heard her order them to kill her."

"How's Ev? She hurt?"

Shane twisted his neck and stared at the closed barn door behind him. "A little banged up is all. Tuesday's taking care of her right now. They're outside the barn. I didn't want them anywhere near these dead bastards."

"Good call. How about you?"

"I'm good." Said every man ever.

What surprised Shane was Alex hadn't asked why Tuesday was taking care of Everlee. Instead, he said, almost casually, "Tuesday, huh?"

"Yeah, Tuesday. She's not who the FBI said she is. They're wrong, totally off-base. After the SUV rolled, she stayed with the wreck, Boss. With me. I was unconscious, still hung-up in my seatbelt. She got me out of the SUV and dragged me away from it. She could've run. Most criminals would've, but she stayed, also gave credible intel on Everlee's condition and which direction these jackasses went. So I need you to double-check her prints, too. Make sure we've got the real Tuesday Smart." He dipped into his rear pocket for his wallet and pulled out the card with the prints from the water bottle she'd tossed in the garbage the night before at Smoke's.

"She know why they took Ev? She hear anything?"

"No, Tuesday was still hung up in her seatbelt when they touched down. She wasn't close enough to hear anything before they took off with Ev. But Everlee said the woman behind the kidnapping was pissed at these three for taking the wrong woman."

"Not professionals then."

"Not even close. These three jerks look like wannabe thugs, all dressed up in identical black suits, packing plenty of muscle, but no brains. Found two Dirty Harry specials, knives, and knuckle gloves on them. Their boss is framing Ms. Smart. I'm almost sure of it."

There was a quiet grunt from Virginia, as if Alex were thinking. "But why impersonate Tuesday? Is that what you're thinking? That the woman behind Ev's abduction and all these false accusations intentionally set up Tuesday Smart? That this mystery woman deliberately assumed Tuesday Smart's appearance, which means plastic surgery, to frame the real Tuesday Smart?"

Well, since you put it like that... Shane wasn't sure what to think. Other than he believed the real Tuesday Smart was the woman sitting outside the barn with Everlee. He'd never have left Everlee if he hadn't believed Tuesday. And believed in her.

"Sounds crazy, I know," he admitted.

"Think about what you're saying," Alex said. "To get away with everything she's done, the woman you're accusing would have to look exactly like Tuesday. Yet it's definitely Tuesday Smart's signature on her marriage certificate with Atchison Bremmer. Every medical file for those two dead children, from their birth certificates to their well-baby doctor visits, supports the FBI's evidence that the woman you're protecting killed her husband and her kids. It's her face in that hallway security footage. When her little boy had to have tubes put in his ears, Tuesday Bremmer, the woman you're protecting, signed for the procedure. She had to provide proper identification at the hospital. They have her face on their security footage, too. It's not just that the FBI is hard set to arrest Ms. Smart, Shane. It's that they have rock solid evidence she's a killer."

"Then you'd better check those signatures against this Tuesday's handwriting, Alex. Because I'm telling you, the woman who killed Mr. Bremmer and those kids is not this Tuesday Smart. Trust me. I'm not wrong."

A grunt came across the connection. "You honestly believe someone who looks exactly like Tuesday Smart is who we should be after. Is that right? If you believe Smart, the woman in your custody, then you also believe an unknown mystery woman, the same one who had Everlee kidnapped, killed Lamb, Bremmer, and the... the others."

Shane caught the hesitation in Alex's last two words. Which was interesting for a man as driven as he was. It was a tell, an unconscious outward signal that Alex had, or knew someone, who had prior experience with other child murders. But that was a mystery for another day.

He answered his boss with a loud and clear, "Yes. Absolutely. I believe the Tuesday Smart in my custody. She is not a killer, and she did not murder Atchison Bremmer or his kids. Whoever the real murderer is, she has a hard-on for Tuesday, else why destroy her life like she has?"

"Not a serial killer, though."

"No, more like a woman who's obsessed. Someone who believes with a frightening intensity that she's been slighted. I don't know why or how. Maybe it's jealousy. Fake Tuesday Smart is pissed that the real Tuesday Smart married Frederick Lamb. Fake Tuesday Smart planned on being his wife."

"But the woman with you and Ev didn't really marry Mr. Lamb, did she? Not like a wife marries her real husband."

Shane cocked his head at the very astute observation coming from a man on the other side of the country. "All I know is that I've seen some pretty whacked-out sickos overseas, and some of them were women. But I'm not getting that vibe from the Tuesday Smart traveling with us. I believe she's innocent. That she's exactly who she says she is, and you do, too, don't you? That's why you sent me and Everlee to track her down. You want us to prove you right and get to her before the FBI does."

"No, I sent you and Everlee to protect a woman the media has slandered since the day this story bubbled to the surface of their alleged free-speech cesspool. Common people don't stand a chance against the machine called free press these days." Alex made *press* sound like a dirty word. "Lawyers willing to fight that kind of slander cost money most common folks don't have, damn it. I do. This is who we are, Shane. We fight for the little guys, understood?"

Shane smiled at the vehemence coming loud and clear through the connection. "I'd say *'yes, sir'*, but you'd probably make me walk the plank, wouldn't you?" *You son of a bitchin' Marine.*

"Damned straight," Alex growled.

And just like that, a faithful, devoted servant was born. Shane grinned, because that servant was him. He already knew Alex Stewart was one of those rare leaders who never sent his people into battle without proper equipment, intelligence, or air support. This was his way of flying cover. He might show up in person and lead when needed, but more often, he'd delegate with authority, and lead them in spirit. Shane knew he'd follow Alex Stewart into Hell and back.

"Hold on, Shane, ahh, yes. Here's your answer, once and for all. Mother just informed me that the set of prints you just sent belong to the real Tuesday Smart. Mother validated them against Tuesday's high school and college records. The woman with you is who she says she is."

"So, why'd the FBI give us her location? Why'd they offload this particular operation to you? Why didn't they track her down and arrest her themselves? They already knew where she lived. Why put all this work and rework on us, I mean, you?"

Alex cleared his throat. "They may or may not have known they gave up that information," he deadpanned.

Which made Shane smile. "You hacked the FBI, didn't you? You're the reason they wanted a TEAM contract because you manipulated them into asking for help. Am I right?" *How is that even possible?*

"I will neither confirm nor deny. Let's just say that Mother's still accumulating all security footage and information on the woman in your custody," Alex replied smugly.

Yup, the cocky bastard knew all along he'd sent Shane and Everlee to rescue the real Tuesday Smart.

Alex continued with, "Tuesday's departures last year and this year were either from SeaTac in Washington or DFW in Dallas. Mother's also tasked her overseas contacts to assist. So far, they've turned up sightings of the real Tuesday's infils and exfils as far north as Canada, Norway, Russia, and Sweden. All from private, off-the-grid runways, flying into and out of the Arctic Circle. She's been a busy woman, but we still may not find the person you believe is stalking her."

"Someone waiting for her arrivals at stateside airports would make better sense. Not sure about those far north sightings," Shane said. "Anyone going into those extreme places would have to be determined as hell. Does that sound like any black widow you've come across?"

"Never underestimate women. They're smart, and they can be as cruel as any man. Ever hear of Catalina Montego? Ethel Durrant? Son of a bitchin' Lucy Delaney?"

"Can't say that I have," Shane replied, not sure what those women had to do with Tuesday.

"Good," was all the snarky comeback Alex offered. "What's your plan going forward?"

Shane glanced down at the dead body at his knee. He'd been inside the silo. He'd found Everlee's boots tossed aside in the dark, and he'd seen the evidence of her courageous escape. But he'd also seen blood spatter on the walls inside that wooden death chamber. Everlee was right. Others had surely died there. She would've been next if not for Mother's astute tracking ability.

Shane's first instinct was to burn the barn down, the dead assholes with it. Instead, his strong sense of justice prevailed. "The FBI needs to process this building, Alex. There's DNA evidence all over the walls inside the silo. I'm positive others were murdered, maybe tortured, here. Their families deserve to know what happened to them."

"Consider it done. What else?"

"I'm taking Everlee to a hospital." *Somehow.* "She won't like it, but she's been through a ton of shit today. She needs to speak with a counselor and…" Shane paused. "I'll need transportation to make that happen, but…"

There he stalled. There were two women counting on him, but he couldn't take Everlee into a hospital without risking Tuesday's freedom. Police officers tended to visit hospitals and emergency rooms. It'd only take one observant, conscientious officer or doctor to ruin everything. He changed his mind. "Never mind. I can't risk Tuesday to save Everlee anymore than I can risk Everlee to save Tuesday. I'll figure something out."

"How? You have no car. You're in the middle of nowhere."

"Yeah, well…" Shane pinched the bridge of his nose, the firestorm beginning to rage in the very center of his skull. Which meant a migraine would soon dictate complete rest, total darkness, and a nearby bucket for projectile vomit. "I've been in worse situations. I'll figure it out." *Somehow.*

"You're one stubborn son of a bitch, you know that?"

"Remind you of anyone?" *Like you, you bastard?*

"Stay where you are," Alex growled. "The FBI won't be there for hours even after I contact them. Keep the women hydrated and cool. You do the same. Help is on its way."

"No," Shane said firmly. "Ev and I started this. We'll end it. We'll be in touch."

Silence. Then a curt, "Then I want a son of a bitchin' sit rep every twenty-four hours."

"Can do." Shane ended the connection before Alex could give him more hell or force him to stand down. There was no way he'd hang around waiting to be saved. Marines were first in and last out. It was past time he proved he was just as tough as, maybe tougher than, his boss.

Shane recognized the differences in the women with him. Whereas at first glance, Tuesday seemed more timid and feminine, a people pleaser who wanted to be left alone, she was also resourceful, sincere, and loyal. She'd stayed with him after the crash and helped him until he was back on his feet. That spoke volumes. The woman had empathy. She cared about those two dead kids and their father, and she'd been authentically shocked at the way they'd been murdered. There was no disguising emotion like that.

Everlee, on the other hand, was a no-kidding ball-buster from the ground up. She thrived on adrenaline, and the woman was tough as nails. She didn't want nice or quiet like Tuesday. She wanted in-your-face action. Only, at the same time, she didn't.

Shane looked over his shoulder at the closed door. That kiss of hers was the hottest thing he'd handled in his entire life. The moment he'd wrested control from her, Everlee had damned near melted in his hands like a brick of butter. She might be a hellcat on the surface and while on the job, but he had a feeling there was a completely different woman beneath that former AF Lieutenant façade. She desperately wanted someone on her side, someone strong enough to back her up and call her on her weak or foolish moments. And he wanted to be that guy.

Sure, she led with plenty of bluster and bravado. What former military leader didn't? Especially officers? Even he tended to lead with his chin, a definite Devil Dog trait. That was what years in the military did, it created leaders. Go-getters. People who stepped up and took charge when needed, and sometimes, when it wasn't needed. But he had a feeling the woman behind all that over-confident, in your face, you-want-a-piece-of-me persona that Everlee did so well, wouldn't mind having the right male on her six. Maybe in her bed. She'd demand respect, that was easy enough to read. And in Shane's mind, a given. Women should be respected, damn it. Least until they proved themselves unworthy of it. Like the shrew impersonating Tuesday.

His gut told him to tread easy with Everlee, though, especially since her ex still stalked her. It was obvious she had needs that Butch-the-whiner never understood. What a mismatched pair, her, the ultimate competitor and winner; him, a total loser. What had she ever seen in the guy?

Lifting to his feet, Shane looked down at the three dead men one last time. He hadn't come back in here to desecrate their bodies. Their mortal injuries were desecration enough. All were facedown. All were deceased. He'd double-checked, and regardless of their condition, he would've administered first-aid if they'd required it. But they hadn't and he was thankful for that. He wasn't the monster. They were. He didn't need to prove anything, other than he was the one walking out of there.

For now, he needed to do precisely what Alex said. But a sparkling aura had swarmed his vision, blocking the clarity a sniper required. Squaring his shoulders, Shane left the dead to their eternal damnation, and aimed for the exit and the only two people in the state of Arkansas who mattered. They needed to know what to expect while he battled with what he hoped was the final demon of the day. And he needed Everlee to take control of their two gear bags.

Shoving the door open, he winced when the brutal light from the setting sun stabbed his eyes. Closing them to forestall the pain, he let his chin drop to his chest. Shit. This was going to hurt.

Chapter Twenty-Three

Shane stood stock still at the open barn door. He had her boots in one hand, his other hand on the door, but he was looking down at the ground.

Everlee jumped to her feet. "What's going on?"

Tuesday was already at his side. "He's had a headache since the crash. He's hurting," she murmured as she took hold of his wrist. "What do you need, Shane? Tell us what to do."

Everlee snagged her boots from him, dropped to the ground, and put them on. "He's not hurting, he's a Marine for—"

His shoulders sagged. "Get my bag. Pill bottle. Inside zippered pocket."

"What'd they do to you in there?" Everlee barked, her hackles up as she tied her laces.

Tuesday had led Shane into the shade by then and was forcing him to sit and lean back against the stone foundation. She pulled a bottled water from one of the bags she'd been carrying, opened it, and tipped it to his lips. "Drink. You're dehydrated."

Shaking his head, he told her again, "Uh-uh. My bag first. Please. Need the pills in there. Migraine prescription. Three of them. H-hurry." By then, rivulets of sweat were running out of his hair and down his neck.

He shouldn't have had to ask twice. Everlee snapped to and eased the bags off his shoulders and out from under his arm. Man, they were heavy, still full of Smoke's state-of-the-art weaponry. But no prescription bottle. Then she remembered. The bags they'd flown with were both back in their rental. In Dallas.

"Ah, Shane."

He held a hand out. "You got them?"

"No, they're still in our rental. In that bag."

"Shit."

"There's ibuprofen in the first-aid kit," Tuesday said. "Would they help?"

"Won't even come close," he replied as he tossed his head back and gulped the rest of the water. "Secure both backpacks, Ev."

"Copy that, big guy. What else?"

"Shade. I'm gonna need to be somewhere totally dark, maybe until morning."

"The hangar," both Everlee and Tuesday said at the same time. It took a few minutes, but together, they got him back on his feet and across the yard to the hangar. His eyes were tightly shut the entire time. He was stumbling and he was blind, or he wanted to be. By the time they had him sitting on the concrete floor inside the empty, plexiglass office just inside the hangar door, his stomach was making unpleasant noises.

While Everlee worked the winch that lowered both doors, she ordered Tuesday, "Find a bucket. Quick. He's going to be sick." She'd worry about those backpacks later.

Tuesday was as obedient as a spanking new airman. In seconds, she'd found a dusty metal bucket, had somehow rinsed it out, and set it beside Shane. He was gray by then, sitting cross-legged, his elbows on his knees and his head in his hands.

"Please go," he whispered. "Leave me alone."

"He needs total darkness and silence," Tuesday whispered as she padded across the hangar to a jumbled pile of dust-covered canvas in the far corner. It ended up being one large prefabricated cover for a small plane. Between the two women and the aluminum ladder Everlee located in the hangar, they maneuvered the canvas over the exposed office walls, as far as they could get it to go. Since the office took up the entire front corner of the hangar, and because there were plenty of bare two-by-four metal studs reinforcing the corrugated metal walls, they were able to maneuver the edges of the canvas between the studs to keep it in place while it shrouded the office in near total darkness.

"Sure glad this was built into a corner," Tuesday muttered, as, at last, they succeeded in blocking most of the light from where Shane now lay flat on his back with one arm over his eyes.

Tuesday was at ground level. Everlee was still on the ladder. "It's going to get stuffy and hot, though," she worried, not sure of the best way to help Shane.

Right on cue, the sounds of gagging, coughing, and retching came from the covered enclosure. Everlee's gaze went to Tuesday, her mind pinging for solutions she didn't have.

"You're right. It's too warm in there. I know what he needs, but I'll need your help to get him to agree to it. He'll listen to you."

Quietly, Everlee dropped to her feet. "Tell me. Hurry."

Tuesday nodded at the canvas-enclosed space. "Let's go inside with him, but be quiet."

There was still enough light inside the now-covered office for Everlee to see poor Shane on his knees, his head over the bucket.

"Damn it, get out of here," he growled, spitting. "Go away. Please."

"We're here to help," Everlee admonished quietly.

"I've got more water if you want it," Tuesday whispered.

"Leave me alone!"

Everlee felt helpless, but she couldn't let him suffer. So, when Tuesday knelt on Shane's left side, she knelt at his right, eager to do whatever he needed.

"Don't you two know how to listen?" Shane spat into the bucket again. "It stinks in here. I stink. It's only going to get worse."

"Not if we help," Tuesday said matter-of-factly. "When you're done throwing up, lean back so we can reach you better."

"Whatever." Angrily, he shoved the bucket away and rolled to his butt, his eyes still closed, and his hands on his knees.

Shifting positions, Tuesday knelt behind him and put her hands on his shoulders, her thumbs on the back of his stiff neck.

He winced the moment she touched him. "Your hands are cold," he told her grouchily.

"Because you've got a fever. I'm going to use acupressure on you, Shane. Our bodies have specific pressure points. I'm going to manipulate those points to relieve your migraine before it gets worse. On a scale of one to ten, how bad is it now?"

"Nine going on a hundred," he grumbled.

"Okay. Not ten, that's good. Try to relax while we work on you."

He stopped arguing, but Everlee had no idea what Tuesday was talking about. Acupressure sounded like some weird, quackery that people in tie-dyed shirts did. So she watched and she learned as Tuesday dug the pads of her thumbs into the muscles at the base of Shane's skull. He let loose a few vehement curses, but Tuesday didn't stop, didn't even slow down. "Breathe Shane," she ordered softly, tipping his head forward and his chin down. "I need you to focus on breathing. That's all. Slowly in. Slowly out."

"Ow, ow, ow, damn it! Stop! That hurts."

"I know," she soothed, "but I promise, what Everlee and I are doing will help. Be patient. We won't take long. Now breathe like I asked."

He chuffed like a big, mean cat, but he also let her do her thing.

Jiminy Christmas, Tuesday was being so kind, more evidence she was not the cruel murderess the FBI claimed. There was nothing sexual about the way she touched him or about her idea of help. Nothing unusual about her at all, not in Everlee's book, nothing except… All at once, she'd morphed from being just an unfulfilled FBI assignment into an efficient, practical nurse who just happened to also be pretty. So pretty, she could've passed for Nicole Kidman's kid sister. But it was the kindness that radiated in everything she was doing to Shane that convinced Everlee.

She'd tried her damnedest to see Tuesday through her Agent-in-Charge, follow the rules lenses. But everything had changed. Tuesday wasn't who everyone said she was, and Everlee wasn't so sure who she herself was anymore. Paradigms. It was all about those hard, fast ways a person looked at the world. Only they weren't so hard nor so fast anymore.

Tuesday moved in front of Shane. She took hold of his hands and dug her fingertips into the muscles between his thumbs and forefingers.

His gorgeous brows slammed together. He bared his teeth and growled.

"Just a few seconds more. Okay, now breathe," she told him as she released his hands.

He slapped them to the ground beside him, his chest heaving.

"Slow and easy," she murmured as again, she shifted around him, squeezing other specific targets: points under his jaw, at the sides of his neck, even alongside his nose and eye sockets. When she finished, she moved down to his knees and gently told him to, "Straighten your legs for me, please."

Shane was breathing easier by then. He obeyed, his eyes still tightly closed. It seemed the more she handled him, the more compliant he became.

"That's really good. I'm proud of you," Tuesday whispered sweetly, almost as if he were a little boy instead of a full-grown, combat hardened, badassed Marine. "You're feeling drowsy, aren't you?"

His head bobbed. "Yeah, I guess."

"Thanks for helping me help you, Shane," she whispered back. With each word, she'd spoken softer, until Everlee had to move in closer to hear her.

"Help me get his boots off," Tuesday said.

Without a word, Everlee unlaced Shane's boots, then tugged them off and set them aside.

Very calmly, as if she'd done this before, Tuesday slid her hands up under his pant cuffs and took hold of his shins. Without asking for Everlee's help this time, she performed the same type of squeezing massage. Shane seemed calmer this time around. Didn't cuss once.

"I need your help with this next part, Everlee," Tuesday whispered when his head fell back on his shoulders. "We're almost done. Measure one palm width below his kneecap. Do like this." Tuesday showed Everlee precisely where she needed to grip the lower part of Shane's leg.

It seemed such an intimate thing to do, grab a man's well-muscled leg while he was suffering. But Everlee focused on how relaxed Shane became at her touch and did what Tuesday asked.

"Yup, right there. Perfect. Now press the pads of your fingers, not your fingernails, into his leg muscle. Press hard. Squeeze as tight as you can. Right there. Like this." She illustrated on his left calf. "Not gently. He's a big guy. He can take it. Keep the pressure up until I tell you to release. It'll hurt him a little, but it'll also break the negative energy flowing through his body."

That actually made sense. "Got it," Everlee whispered, her hands now flattened around Shane's hefty calf. This wasn't exactly how she wanted to touch him, but he was breathing easier, so Everlee focused on that. If a simple massage lessened his migraine, she was all for it.

"Good job, Ev, now quick. Release." Tuesday let go of his other leg and pulled her hand away.

Everlee did the same, almost. Inexplicably, her fingers fluttered as if she were sprinkling fairy dust. Which was such a girly thing to do. She hoped Tuesday hadn't noticed. Tuesday hadn't sprinkled anything. Nothing but—kindness. Which was damned humbling after all the mean things Everlee had said to her.

"Now, Everlee," Tuesday whispered. "Let's repeat what I did with the pressure points of his hands. Squeeze hard, then… quick release."

Everlee shifted positions from Shane's feet to alongside his hip and did what Tuesday asked. Squeeze hard. Quick release. This time, without fairy dust.

"You ladies have magic fingers. I do feel better," he said groggily.

"That's why we're here," Everlee whispered contritely. How does anyone admit they were wrong? How could she ever ask Tuesday's forgiveness?

Tuesday took hold of Shane's shoulder and leaned him forward. His body was now slack enough that he tipped into her for support. Something about the gentle way Tuesday put an arm around Shane and held him against her bugged the hell out of Everlee. Yet Tuesday didn't seem affected by Shane's close proximity the way Everlee would've been, nor did she take advantage of the man almost laying in her arms. Taking hold of his hand closest to her, she pinched between his thumb and index finger, hard enough that he grunted.

Everlee followed suit with his opposite hand. "Does this hurt him?"

"Nah," Shane grumbled, his chin on Tuesday's shoulder and his face in her hair. "Feels kinda good."

"Everlee," Tuesday whispered, bringing her attention back to the matter at hand. "I need you to find something that will make a soft landing for this man once I lay him down. Please, hurry. He's a big guy."

"He's out cold?"

"Like a rock."

"Okay, sure." That she could do, and she could do it fast. Anything to get Shane out of Tuesday's arms, damn it. Suddenly, irrationally jealous, Everlee scurried from under the draped canvas and into the open hangar. Taking a big breath of fresh air, she quickly grabbed their gear bags and dragged them into the now blacked-out office. But all she had to offer was her roll of dirty clothes from the day before. Oh well.

"Thanks," Tuesday breathed, as, between the two of them, they cupped the back of Shane's head and neck, and lowered him onto the makeshift pillow. Everlee straightened his long legs and removed his socks. Tuesday grabbed the bucket and ducked out, leaving Everlee with a decision to make. Either she followed Tuesday to make sure she didn't run, or she trusted her like Shane did, and stayed with him to make sure he didn't vomit in his sleep and choke to death.

Aww, who was she kidding? Shane was out cold and relaxed enough that he was snoring. It was stuffy in there. He didn't need her. Not really. It was more the other way around. Everlee needed to be near him. To touch him and watch over him. But he wouldn't have known she was there, would he? Shane was sound asleep. What was she waiting for?

Decision made. Reluctantly, Everlee eased away from Shane and followed Tuesday, but not because she didn't trust her. She crawled under the canvas and flipped it back into place to block any light left in the evening sky from reaching Shane. She'd just climbed to her feet, when Tuesday walked back into the hangar, swinging the now rinsed-out bucket, as if cleaning up after a sick man was no big deal. Which it really wasn't. Everlee had done that often enough for both her dad and her ex. Cleaning up after men came with being female, didn't it?

"There's an old well behind this hangar," Tuesday said, keeping her voice low. "I saw it on the walk in, but this time I tried the pump, and once I primed it with what was left of that bottled water, it actually works. The water tastes better than what comes out of my kitchen faucet. Err, what came out of my faucet." A shadow darkened her face, probably because that faucet and kitchen no longer existed. "Anyway…" She sucked in a breath and went on. "Shane and I saved our empty water bottles. Now we can refill them."

"You saved plastic bottles?"

"Sure. I don't throw anything away. Pack it in, pack it out, my motto for life in general. Leave no trace behind. Especially in the Arctic."

"Why?" Everlee demanded to know. "Why'd you decide to photograph the Arctic, of all places? It's cold up there."

A hint of shadow flittered beneath Tuesday's bright-eyed demeanor. "Once you've lost everything, what does it matter where you go or how cold it is when you get there? You're still alone. And alone is the loneliest kind of cold."

"Well, yeah, but…" Everlee knew she was finally seeing the real Tuesday. "Is that why you work for Freiburg, so you can go to far-off places alone?"

She heaved a great sigh, still headed into the hangar. "Mostly, yes. When I'm working, I forget what I've lost, at least for a while. Up North I was cut off from mankind, and yes, Mother Nature could've killed me anytime she wanted. But it's also a uniquely perfect experience to stretch out under all those stars at night and know you're the only living being within miles. Well, except for an occasional polar bear or seal, which I took plenty of photos of. But, for a few days or a week or a month if the weather's decent, it's just you and God and the infinite sky."

"And the cold."

The corners of Tuesday's mouth lifted into a sad smile. "But frigid cold ensures solitude, doesn't it? In my experience, coming back home where it's warm and living with mankind is the bigger challenge. People are the real predators on Earth, not polar bears. War. Hunger. Oppression. Climate change. Mankind is behind all those. I wish I had my camera. I'd show you the last photos I took."

"Of the sky?"

"No, of a mother polar bear and her yearling cub. It was by far my best naturally monochromatic shot, all grays, blacks, and shades of white. Took those the morning I packed up and hiked to my rendezvous point. Hooked up with the bush pilot who'd flown me in. And here I am, back in America, the land of selfies and idiotic reality shows, where nobody listens to what anyone else says, but where everyone's shouting like their opinions are the only ones that matter."

"You'd rather be at Mother Nature's beck and call?"

"Always. You know where you stand with her. She's the ultimate serial killer, and her *'survival of the fittest'* law is the greatest test for mankind. Either we wise up and obey her, or she'll put us back in the primordial ooze we crawled out of. Even polar bears know how deadly she is. One mistake in the Arctic and—" Tuesday snapped her fingers "—you're dead."

Everlee sucked in a breath. She'd never, not once in her life, had a sister or girlfriend. But Tuesday sure felt like a friend now. She had to ask, "What *are* you afraid of?"

Tuesday cocked her head as if Everlee had just asked a sixty-million-dollar question. "Losing the people I love. Cold and darkness are simply physical challenges to be met, to be studied, and to be overcome. But loving someone, then watching them suffer and die, and not being able to save them…" Her gaze strayed to the canvas-covered office in the corner. "That's the hardest loss in the world. I wouldn't wish it on my worst enemy."

"You mean your parents."

"And the only man I've ever loved. But you have to understand, Freddie was my hero, not my lover. He was my knight in shining armor, but mostly, he was my best friend. I was lost, ready to kill myself after my parents died like they did. I was thinking about suicide the day he came along. I was mixed up and hurt, confused and so alone. God, I was sick, mentally sick. I know that now. Everyone says they'll be there for you when they hear the bad news, but then they leave and get on with their lives. But you're still stuck in the same place, trying to pick up the pieces of lives that no longer exist. That's where I was when Freddie showed up. He just knocked on my door, gave me a big hug, and told me I was going with him to New York. He literally came to my rescue, Agent Yeager. I know it sounds corny, but he swept me off my feet. He held onto me and let me cry until I was all cried out. Not once did he tell me to get over it or buck up or any of that stupid stuff. He sat with me on my parents' front porch and listened. I had no one. I didn't know what to do, how to even begin putting my life back together. But from day one Freddie heard me. He listened and he cared. He let me cry and he" —both her shoulders lifted— "he took me home with him that very same day. He gave me a safe place to hide, and he let me heal. He made all my financial problems go away."

She sighed. "He let me lean on him and he put me through college. He loved me, Everlee. Without me having to do anything at all. Like my parents, he honestly just loved me."

Tears filled Tuesday's eyes and Ev's were already overflowing. She ran a finger under her eyelid, her heart breaking with empathy for the poor high school girl from Minnesota who'd had to deal with her parents' deaths all by herself. Reminded Ev of herself. She'd had to handle her mother's funeral alone. Sure, the funeral director helped, but he was just doing his job, wasn't he? He got paid to care. How uncanny was it that she and Tuesday had so much in common? She wished she'd believed Tuesday from the start.

"You actually loved him back?" she asked cautiously, not wanting intimate details, but needing to figure out how a young girl had ever found love with a man so much older.

"Not like everyone thinks, but yes, I loved Freddie. I still do," Tuesday answered quietly, her gaze direct and fixed on Ev. "There was never anything physical between us, nothing more than hugs and maybe a kiss on the cheek. Anything else would've been weird, and believe me, I wasn't in a good place back then. Freddie understood. He was more like the grandfather I never had. Trust me, I didn't believe him at first, that he wanted to take me to New York, to his home. I tried to argue, I did. But he refused to walk away. He said he'd never leave me alone. I think that, all by itself, is the greatest gift we can give anyone who's suffering. Just being there for them. Just showing up and really, truly caring."

She took a deep breath. "At first, I hated the city. New York is noisy and big. There are way too many people there. Everywhere you go, all you see are walls of brick and glass and concrete. Sirens howl all day and every night. But yes, eventually, I grew to love the city, mostly because it was Freddie's. He was my best friend, Everlee. He empowered me, and everything he did made me stronger. How do you think I graduated from Columbia? I had nothing when Mom and Dad died, nothing but funeral expenses and debt and debt collectors and…"

She ran a hand over her head, sweeping her long blonde hair over to the opposite side of her neck. "He said it was what Dad would've wanted. He was my dad's friend, and until he died, Frederick Lamb kept me safe and gave me something to live for."

Swallowing hard, Everlee knew then why Shane trusted Tuesday. Shit, he'd even let her hold him when he was at his weakest, and that still bugged Everlee. But because of Tuesday, Shane was now passed out and snoring. Sleep and, apparently, acupressure, were precisely what he'd needed. "How'd you learn acupressure?"

"Freddie had horrible migraines. He showed me what to do, how to help him. It's easier when someone else manipulates your pressure points for you. Better yet, two people working together are always better than one."

"I've never had many friends," Everlee volunteered. And why that blurted out of her mouth, she had no idea.

Both Tuesday's shoulders lifted. "Me either. But people can change. I mean, it's up to you and nothing's impossible. Not if you really want something. Freddie taught me that. He was a great believer in positivity. He had a magnificent library in his place, and I could've sat there and read all day because it was so quiet and peaceful. He helped me get back to normal. My new normal."

"We need to talk," Everlee told her new friend. "Because Shane's right. You *are* innocent. Now let's prove it."

Chapter Twenty-Four

"Yeah, migraines," Shane admitted to Sasha. After the onset of his migraine, he'd slept three hours, and while he'd been passed out, Everlee and Tuesday had ganged up on him. In a good and helpful way. He vaguely remembered their gentle hands on him, and he did feel better than after most killer-migraine episodes. *So acupressure, huh?*

Once he'd come to, he'd found himself lying on a fuzzy blanket that smelled moldy, with something else rolled into a pillow under his hard head. Since then, Ev and Tuesday made sure he had a bottle of water in his hand and something in his stomach. At the moment, the three of them were sitting cross-legged inside the abandoned hangar's office, under the tarp that now kept the chilly Arkansas night at bay. Everlee had set a flashlight bottom-up on the floor so they could see.

She and Tuesday had somehow become BFFs while he'd been out of commission. The way Everlee now advocated for Tuesday, even explaining how much she'd loved Frederick Lamb and why, told Shane these two women had gotten a lot out in the open. Which made life simpler. Everlee wasn't shooting daggers at him with her eyes every time he spoke to Tuesday. At last, they were a team of three.

He was on his cell now, with Sasha Kennedy, aka Mom, who seemed to control every last security camera in the States if the wide scope of her intel was any indicator.

"But you're feeling better now?" she asked. "Are you sure?"

He nodded, then, because this wasn't a video chat—*Duh*—he spoke up and told Sasha, "Yes. Ev and Tuesday are keeping me well fed and hydrated."

"With what? Trail mix, protein bars, and bottled water?" she scoffed. "Never mind, I don't care how they take care of you, only that they are. I've already sent Heston to your location. He's bringing emergency supplies. You'll be better off then. But you were right, Shane. Tuesday has a stalker, a woman named Maeve Astor. She stole Tuesday's identity after Frederick Lamb died by forging her birth certificate, which allowed Astor to apply for a copy of Tuesday's Social Security card. Once she had that, she requested a copy of Tuesday's driver's license, which gave her all the ID she needed to access Tuesday's bank accounts and the trust fund Lamb set up for her. Astor can get her hands on, well, everything that belongs to Tuesday."

Unbelievable. Shane switched his phone to speaker so everyone could hear. "You're on speaker now. Could you say that last part again?"

"Sure," Mother replied, then repeated everything and added, "So Tuesday, none of what happened to Atchison Bremmer and his children is your fault. Maeve Astor's a certifiable nutcase."

"But she killed her own children," Tuesday told Mother quietly. "I don't care about the money she stole or even her stealing my identification. She can have it. But how could anyone hurt a little boy and baby girl?"

"Because she's a stark raving psycho, girlfriend," Everlee cut in.

"I know but…" Tuesday's gaze dropped to her clenched hands in her lap. "Everyone said those little kids were *Tuesday Bremmer's* children, and the press made sure everyone thought I was *Tuesday Bremmer*, and I kinda feel" —she shrugged— "responsible. Like that little boy and that baby girl were, at least could've been, you know. Mine."

Shane's heart sank. Here was a woman of exceptional worth, thinking of those poor dead children instead of her diminished financial status, obviously touched and hurt by the cruelty of their deaths at the hands of the woman who should've sheltered them. It seemed Tuesday had made the same spiritual or emotional—or whatever—connection with the Bremmer family that Shane had with the Stewart family. Death really was a twisted, sickening bitch—like this Astor woman. They both hurt everyone they touched.

"Honey, of course you feel that way. You're a decent human being. You're full of empathy. I can tell." It was obvious Mother was staunchly in Tuesday's corner.

"Why didn't you notice your bank account balances shrinking?" Shane asked Tuesday to get his brain out of the pit of remorse it sank into whenever he dwelled too long on the past. "Sounds like Astor's been bleeding you dry for years. Didn't you notice?"

"Not dry, Shane. Not even enough for anyone, except maybe Tuesday's CPA, to notice," Mother corrected. "Like I said, Astor's smart. Smart enough she hasn't skimmed much off those accounts. Why would she? All she has to do is wait until Tuesday goes to prison. After that, she'll have free access to the rest of Frederick Lamb's assets, and she won't have to worry about being caught. She only marries millionaires, and she was Atchison Bremmer's sole benefactor. She's already wealthy. Why take more risk than she has to?"

"But I'm still in her way," Tuesday added, reaching out for Everlee's hand. "Else she wouldn't have targeted Agent Yeager."

"Yes, but she's done this before," Mother told them with authority. "She killed at least three other husbands, all under suspicious circumstances, but nothing as devious as what she's done to you. As of this morning, those deaths weren't on any law enforcement radar, but they are now. Like I said, that woman is not stupid, but neither am I."

"Yes, she is," Shane said softly. "She traded her children's lives for money, Mother. She's a pig."

Tuesday cocked her head and finally looked at him. Her eyes were wide and glimmering.

"What she is, is a brilliant gold digger," Mother cut in. "You guys already know it's very likely she killed Frederick Lamb. Can't say for sure. Still waiting on the FBI to do their thing. But now that I've found this wacko, I'm backtracking her whereabouts for the last ten years. And Tuesday, rest assured, we're going to prove every last crime she's committed and nail her butt to the wall."

"W-w-wait. What?" Tuesday shrieked. Her hand trembled as it covered her mouth. "She killed Freddie?"

Shane winced. How had she not picked up on the fact of Freddie's death yet? *Shit.* He reached across the space between them to pull her in close before she fell apart. But he was too late.

"She killed my Freddie?" Tuesday barked. Her gaze pivoted to Shane, then to Everlee, then back to Shane. "But I thought… you guys never said… I thought she was just after me."

Wisely, Everlee did what Shane couldn't. She reached over and put a hand around Tuesday's shoulders. "Sorry, girlfriend. We thought you knew."

"Tuesday, I am so, so sorry," Mother added. "It's been all over the news. I thought you knew, too."

"How could I? I've been out of the country. I only saw the lies about me killing Mr. Bremmer and those babies when I flew home. Does everyone think I killed Freddie, too? Oh, my God! Why me?" Shaking like a leaf Tuesday wrapped an arm around her closest supporter, who, ironically, had just that morning been her snarkiest adversary.

"Good question, people," Everlee growled possessively, shooting daggers at Shane. "That bitch killed the only man Tuesday ever loved, and now she can get at all her money. Why does she want Tuesday dead?"

"Yeah, what Everlee said," Tuesday muttered quietly. "What'd I ever do to her?"

"Listen, honey," Mother replied sternly in what Shane now recognized as her *motherly* voice. "Astor's a heartless killer. It might be because Lamb chose you to marry, not her. Psychopaths don't operate on logic. They're seriously mentally ill."

"You can't take anything Astor did personally," Shane added. "Yes, she killed Freddie out of spite, probably to hurt you. And yes, she's also orchestrated identity theft so far-reaching even the FBI believes you're guilty of the murders she committed. They aren't even looking at her. But she didn't kidnap Everlee on purpose. Her hired help did that. Does she sound like a person with normal coping skills? With any sense of right or wrong?"

"He asked me to marry him in the middle of the Hudson River under the Statue of Liberty," Tuesday whispered. "It was the first Fourth of July we were together. He said it was the best place to watch New York's fireworks, and he was right. He was wearing his captain's hat that night, and we were on one of his boats. Freddie owned a shipping company, did you know that? I can still see the sparks in the sky and their reflections on the river. It seemed like stars were everywhere. I was seventeen. Of course, I said yes."

She almost smiled. "He even got down on one knee. He was such a romantic. But he also wanted to make certain his two sons didn't run roughshod over me if something were to happen to him. He wanted my future ensured." She swallowed hard. "But after he died, I did sign over the three skyscrapers he owned in the City to his son, Jeff, and the entire Lamb fleet went to his other son, Henry. It made good business sense to do that, and I trust them. I mean, I didn't know anything about managing millions of dollars-worth of prime real estate or shipping empires. Still don't. And Jeff and Henry aren't mean or greedy. I've been to both their homes. I've met their wives and children, and I really like them. They almost feel like… my family." Her voice broke.

Gah, she was tearing Shane's heart out. The more Tuesday revealed, the more he understood why she hung out in far-off, barren places like the Arctic Circle. She wasn't just photo journaling. She was him. Forever the outsider, cast by circumstance into a life of solitude. A wanderer and a person without anyone in the world to care what happened to them. Without anyone to rely on. Except in her case, maybe Jeff and

Henry Lamb, possibly Robert Freiburg. God, he hoped so. She deserved someone good and decent in her corner. Poor damned kid.

Mother jolted him out of his mental wandering with, "Don't you worry. I have plenty of evidence, enough to convict her. I've caught Astor coming and going on dozens of traffic cams along Billionaire Row in New York City, most often near One57, the Tower condominium."

"That's where Freddie and I lived before…" Tuesday's voice trailed away.

"Yup, I know, honey," Mother replied evenly. "But your money and identity isn't all Astor stole. She wanted to look like you, too. And it makes sense. How else could she convince the world you were a killer?"

"Which is why she looked directly into the security camera when she chained the door of her apartment that day," Everlee whispered. "She needed you to look as cold-blooded as she is. The bitch!"

"Right, Ev. She was brunette when she started working at One57 roughly seven years ago, right before your parents died, Tuesday. But now she's the same shade of blonde as you, and, call me crazy, but I think she's bleached her skin. For sure she's had plastic surgery. A nose job. Probably liposuction on her rear end, too, because that caboose used to be a wide-load coming through. But lately, it's been trimmed to a firm size ten like yours. I'm sure you've noticed, Shane."

Shane damned near choked on his tongue. Of course, he'd noticed Tuesday's backside. Good looking women naturally hit his radar. He was a guy, for hell's sake, not a robot. But it wasn't Tuesday who'd captured his attention these last couple days. It was Everlee. Not that he'd ever, ever tell Sasha. She was a little too nosy.

"Nice segue, *Mother*," he bit out sarcastically, hoping Everlee and Tuesday wouldn't encourage her sass.

"Wait, guys. Hold up a second," Everlee ordered. "I'm confused, can't keep all this info straight. Do you have a, umm, a timeline, Mother? Something to the point and, uh, brief?"

Shane cocked his head at his bossy companion agent, wondering what was really going on. She hadn't had any trouble keeping up before. In fact, had been damned sharp during that quick exfil out of Dallas.

But by then, Tuesday had untangled herself from Ev, and Shane had another woman to worry about. She'd drawn her knees up, wrapped her arms around them, and her chin was on her kneecaps. She wasn't making eye contact. She'd effectively built a wall Shane wanted desperately to knock down.

"You bet," Mother replied with enthusiasm. "Let's go by Tuesday's ages when everything happened. At sixteen, her parents were killed in an automobile accident. At seventeen, she married Frederick Lamb, then he died of a heart attack when she was twenty. At twenty-one, Astor enters the scene, assumes Tuesday's identity, and, while the real Tuesday is still in mourning, the fake Tuesday marries—"

"Never mind. Enough!" Shane ordered, ending Mother's accurate, but insensitive reply. "Text it to Everlee, Mother. We'll go over it when we have time." He couldn't bear what those details were doing to Tuesday. Her face was now stuck between her kneecaps, and, even in the muted lighting, he was smart enough to know she was crying.

"Oh, sure, you bet," Mother answered. "I'm, umm, sorry Tuesday. I got ahead of myself and… I tend to forget…"

"It's okay," Tuesday squeaked as she lifted her face and swiped a quick palm over her cheek. "This is what you guys do, and you're helping me, and I'm grateful for everything. Really I am."

"It's just hard, isn't it?" Shane asked quietly.

Oddly, Everlee's eyes were glimmering as bright as Tuesday's now. The women had bonded, and he was glad for that connection. There were moments when it seemed Everlee needed a BFF as much as Tuesday did. But what the hell were those tears about? Was something else going on?

"But I should know better," Mother said meekly. "Sometimes I talk too much. I'm really sorry, honey. I hope you know that."

"I do," Tuesday replied hoarsely. She wiped her other cheek, but still didn't meet Shane's eyes. Damn it. He'd let Mother rattle on too long.

Shane thumbed the burner phone off speaker and asked Mother, "Do you know for certain that Astor stalked Lamb?"

"Yes. There are hidden cameras all over One57," she answered. "I've got tons of video showing Astor following him. But the kicker happened the day he died."

"Keep talking." Like Shane could've silenced Alex's loquacious techie.

"She delivered a giftbag to the doorman on ground level that day. Got her on One57's security film, clear as day. She was all dolled up in a shorter-than-shit black mini skirt. A flouncy red blouse with ruffles, one of those sheer things that showed a black bra beneath it. Bright red Jimmy Choos, or maybe they were Louboutins, I don't know. Whatever. But she was wearing black silk stockings with those fuck-me-darling shoes, and like Tuesday Smart, she has damned long legs to go with that getup. She was every man's wet dream that morning, I'll tell you, and she started to cry when the doorman denied her access. Made quite a scene. Keep in mind I only have video, so I have no way to hear exactly what either of them said. Wanna bet he was telling her there was no way in hell he was letting her in Lamb's condo?"

"Smart man." Shane cleared his throat to keep Mother's monologue moving along.

"Want to bet that gift is what killed Lamb? What caused his heart attack?"

"Possibly. Please tell me NYPD has the bag and its contents in their possession, and that they wore gloves when they examined it."

"I have no idea if they even looked for it. Why would they? But Tuesday was with him. She called the EMTs. Why don't you ask her where the bag is?"

"Please hold," Shane answered. Resting the burner phone face up on his thigh, he asked, "Tuesday? Sorry, but do you recall a gift being delivered the morning Frederick passed? Someone from the hotel would've delivered it."

A blank stare gazed back at him, and Shane felt bad for her all over again. There was so much little girl inside Tuesday, and that little girl had lost so much.

"Y-yes. Freddie was excited to get it. He thought it was an antique book he'd ordered. Only it was one of those fake books with a tiny silver key instead, the kind that's really a safe. You can get them on Amazon. But when he unlocked the book, it was empty."

"Not even a card or note?" Shane asked.

She shook her head. "No, nothing."

"Do you know where the bag and book are now?"

Her shoulders shuddered with a sigh. "When I came back from the hospital, you know, after he died, I put the book back in the bag and set it in his bedroom closet. He was my best friend!"

Her last comment was thrown out with plenty of pain, and Shane caught the defensive flash in Everlee's eyes. "Sorry ladies, but I had to ask," he explained contritely. "If the FBI can prove Frederick Lamb's death wasn't caused by a cardiac event, but by whatever he touched or inhaled that morning, then the gift Astor delivered to his condo holds the evidence we need to prove she murdered him, not the real Tuesday."

Devastation flashed like a thundercloud across Tuesday's already beleaguered countenance. "I had nothing when he rescued me after Mom and Dad died. Then Freddie died, and now, and now… I have nothing all over again."

Everlee tugged her back into a lopsided hug. "You've got us, Shane and me."

"It's godawful hard to lose people you love, isn't it?" Shane asked.

"You understand?" Tuesday asked, big fat tears running down her cheeks again.

He nodded, not wanting to go down this road again, but doing it nonetheless. "Yeah, I know. My mom… she died. Cancer. She was all I had. Started out as breast cancer; ended up in her bones, eating her alive. It was" —he swallowed hard— "the toughest thing I've lived through. We didn't have any other family, so" —his heart was beating like a robin caught in his ribcage by then— "so, yeah, I know how you felt that day. How you still feel. But then…"

God, why was he doing this? To help her understand that she wasn't alone? To somehow redeem himself from the guilt he carried for ever thinking she could've killed her husband or Bremmer or those kids? Shane honestly didn't know if he was being selfless or selfish. He just wanted her to stop feeling alone.

He cleared his throat and started again. "But then" — another deep breath that brought no relief or enough air— "I was in an accident the morning after Mom died, and I... I killed two innocent people."

"Oh, Shane," Everlee whispered.

But he didn't want pity. He'd just wanted Tuesday to understand that shit happened. That life sucked sometimes, but it did go on. It was still worth living.

"Jesus Christ, this is hard," he hissed, wiping a quick hand over his face before he lost it completely. "But Tuesday, I promise you that Freddie wants you to keep living, just like my mom wants me to keep going. They loved us when they were alive. They still do. We honor them by living the best way we know how."

But he'd forgotten Mother was listening. Deliberately, his thumb pressed the OFF button, ending the connection. As smart as she was, Mother had probably already put two and two together, was no doubt researching the exact date of his mother's death. Possibly already knew he was the reason behind Stewart's rage at the world. A rage he hid very well, just not well enough that another bastard who'd lost everyone he'd loved wouldn't recognize the same black pit of grief and despair when he saw it. And Shane saw it every damned time he looked in his mirror.

All the anger he'd patiently stored, day after day and year after year, was nothing but a mountain of grief for all he'd lost that morning and the pain he'd inflicted on an innocent man. Shane was that greedy dragon *Smaug* in Tolkien's novel, *The Hobbit*. But instead of gold, Shane had hoarded enough self-hatred, disgust, and anger to fill an ocean. Surprisingly, he was recognizing that very obvious shortcoming now. *Shit,* he was as broken as Tuesday.

He cast his eyes to the dusty floor between him and probably the only two friends he had in the United States. He was his own worst enemy, and he'd banked those embers of rage and grief for years, until the fire they created had nearly consumed him. It was only in his reaching out to Tuesday that he'd inadvertently discovered the answer to his own riddle in life. *How to let go.*

Shane let his chest expand with the stifled air in this, his most recent hideaway. He almost felt good. Well, better. Alex didn't hate him like he'd expected. Neither did his mom, Sara, or Abby. He sucked in another deep, cleansing breath and faced his truth.

Maybe it was time to stop beating himself up for something he could neither change nor forget. Maybe it was time to truly live again.

Chapter Twenty-Five

Everlee couldn't help it. Without thinking, she flung herself at Shane, and thankfully, he caught her, just like she knew he would. He settled her sideways on his lap while she cried, "I'm sorry," into his neck. "I didn't know your mom died like that. How awful. How sad!"

"Yeah, well…" His chest rumbled with a throaty growl. "It's not something I talk about. In fact.…"

Everlee pulled back enough to look up at Shane as he ran a hand over his head, standing the short strands on end before bringing his hand back to rest in the middle of her back. "I've talked about it more since I joined The TEAM than I ever have before. Must be something in the water."

She almost laughed at his attempt at levity, but choked instead. He was so much like Tuesday and her, left alone in the world at a tender age, still struggling to get back on his feet. Could she bare her own secrets like Shane and Tuesday had? Could she tell them how her race-car-driving dad, who she still idolized like a stupid little girl, had treated her and her mother? How she'd married the same kind of man, a selfish, narcissistic loser? A user of women and children and…well, of everyone he'd thought he could get something from?

Yeah, she loved her dad, still did, always would. But she knew now he'd never loved anyone but himself. Which he'd proved that fateful afternoon in her mother's kitchen. Her father was the reason she'd left home and joined the Air Force as soon as she could. They'd actually needed her. He'd only ever needed himself.

Here Shane had bared his personal tragedy to connect with Tuesday, to make her feel like less of a leper. Only problem, that valiant effort made Shane and Tuesday the healthiest two people under this raggedy big top. There was only one leper left. Everlee. And she had no idea how to take that precarious first step toward freedom.

She snuggled closer into him, wanting his touch, craving the steadfast feel of his hand on her back. It had been a long damned time since any man had held her so kindly, like he cared. Truth be known, she was starved for touch. His touch. Shane was real and true and honest, and so damned handsome, it hurt to look at him sometimes. Especially when he smiled.

And there Everlee flamed out. Because he was everything she wasn't. She was the big pretender, the fraud. But he'd been brave enough to say grace at his boss's TEAM picnic, with everyone watching. Even Alex. But she was just a workaholic wannabe, busting her ass to keep up with the guys, running too fast, talking too much, always trying to prove she was just as good as any guy in the world.

Yet here was a man brave enough to confess that he'd killed two innocent people.

"I'm fine, ladies, really," Shane assured them both. Taking another deep breath, he let it out between his pursed lips, and Everlee believed him.

"Yes, you are. You're fine. I mean, not fine, like fine, *fine*, but more like better fine because you had the guts to share something that must've been horribly hard to live through." *And I won't. I can't. I'm not that brave.*

Struggling for composure, she pulled herself together, wiped her face, eased away from Shane's embrace, then turned back to Tuesday. "I guess we're all broken somehow, and I can't imagine how hard it must've been for you to go back into Freddie's condo all by yourself after that. But you've already proven you're a fighter. Look at you, Tuesday Smart, a wildlife photographer who braves the Arctic and polar bears and killer walruses, and who's going to be famous someday."

Tuesday snorted. "I'm already famous, well, infamous. Just ask the national news."

"And we're going to set that shit straight." The words were no more than out of Shane's mouth when the phone in his hand buzzed with an incoming call. He answered with, "Hey, Mom. Knew you'd call back. What else do we need to know?"

With a crooked smile at Everlee and Tuesday, he'd flicked the phone on speaker just as Mother blurted, "You were driving the delivery truck that day that" —Shane slammed his palm over his phone. But by then, Everlee and Tuesday had heard everything— "Alex's wife and daughter were killed. Sara and Abby. You're that guy."

Everlee's breath caught in her windpipe. *Jiminy Christmas!* Sara and Abby? The tattoo on his chest? That was who they were? Shane killed Sara and Abby Stewart?

Ohmygod. Ohmygod. Ohmygod! He was the unnamed man behind the wheel. Because he'd legally been a juvenile, not yet eighteen years, his name hadn't been released to the press. He was that man. The guy who'd destroyed Alex's life. And yet Alex hired him? Did he know who Shane was?

Not one iota of emotion shone in his eyes as he told Mother, "Yes, ma'am. That was me. I did it." Shane's face turned to stone when he looked down at Everlee and saw the shock on her face.

A tortured, "My God, Shane!" breathed over the distance between Virginia. And Arkansas.

His entire body cringed as if Mother had just slapped him. And just that fast, Everlee tipped back against his chest, trusting this man with all of her crazy heart. There had to be more to the story. He'd never purposefully kill any innocent, especially not a mother and child.

But Mother wasn't done. "Your poor mom hadn't even been dead twelve hours!" she nearly yelled.

A breath sniffed out of him. "You think I don't know that?"

"That had to have been so hard for you. Losing her to cancer, watching her die, being there with her until the end, then involved in an accident the morning after."

"It was." His reply was softly spoken. Everlee put her hand on his chest and spread her fingers wide, sending him strength instead of shoving him away.

Mother kept going. "Trust me, Shane, I know what prolonged illness does to your soul, honey. You poor, poor kid! But there you were, back to work, trying to make enough money to pay for your mom's funeral and your college tuition, and for food and rent and" —her voice cracked— "You were just a kid! I wish I'd known you then. I would've paid for everything for you! I would've given you anything you needed!"

He cleared his throat, his gaze still fastened on Everlee despite Mother's emotional declaration of support.

Everlee looked him in the eye. She was right. Mother made it sound as if he were a victim too. He'd been old enough to have been held responsible, maybe tried for vehicular homicide as an adult despite his age. But he wasn't. Why not? What were the extenuating circumstances? He wasn't anything like her father, who believed in bribes and lies and dodging the truth when things didn't go his way. Shane was the exact opposite. And any man who prayed over a meal like he had at the Stewarts' shindig couldn't be a murderer. He just couldn't.

She knew he'd enlisted in the Corps right out of high school. Or had he? No, Mother said something about him trying to pay for college tuition. So he'd given up college to join the Corps after his mother died? By then he'd been a man by most standards. Not able to vote or buy alcohol or cigarettes, but he'd been legally bound to register for the draft, able to enlist in any armed forces, old enough to die for his country. Also old enough he could've been tried as an adult, and—

"Your mother died, then you were in an accident the very next day? *That* accident?" Everlee asked, her heart breaking for the tense warrior beneath her.

His head dipped, just once. Quick and sharp, as if he had no idea what she'd say next. As if he didn't care. There wasn't a part of Shane that wasn't shut down and closed off. Mother had just outed him in the worst possible way, at the most inconvenient time. To his companion agent during a failed mission. In front of the woman who was supposed to be their prisoner. Just when Shane had mostly recovered from a migraine he'd obviously been seeing a doctor for. Just when the three of them had become that undefinable *more*...

Everlee brushed aside these new, tragic facts and relied on what she knew and believed about this man. What he'd done and what little she knew. He was like most guys coming back from the sandbox, traumatized and suffering from PTSD.

Yet Alex trusted him enough to send him on this mission with me.

That Mother had revealed this new information about Shane told Everlee that Alex already knew, yet hadn't shared Shane's secret with anyone, except probably with Mark because Mark hired Shane. He'd been there that first day when Shane flipped out. Which meant Alex and Mark knew.

But Alex still trusted Shane.

Everlee stretched her palm to Shane's face and cradled his bristly jaw, resting her thumb on his chin, now darkened with one helluva five o'clock shadow. Despite the questions whirling through her disorganized brain, she knew this man was as honorable as Alex. She also knew what it was like to be judged by assholes who didn't care about facts or truth. Who jumped to conclusions and lied behind your back. Well, she wasn't one of them.

"You poor thing," she whispered, as impulsively, she tugged his mouth down to her level and kissed him like she'd never let him go. Just cracked that stern, but so damned vulnerable mask he was hiding behind and poured everything she had into him. Her trust, her heart, maybe even her soul. Through his mouth, damn it, down his throat and into his broken heart. Because who could survive the loss of their mother and not have a broken heart? She hadn't. Well, neither had Shane, damn it.

It took a second, but at last, his rigid demeanor softened and he let her in. With their teeth clashing and their tongues melting together, Everlee showed Shane exactly what those secrets meant to her. Nothing. Were they important? Sure, maybe, yeah. Okay. Details considered within the context of truth were always important. But Alex was no dummy. He'd known precisely who Shane was when he'd hired him. That explained why Shane had been so stressed the first day in TEAM HQ. He'd faced Alex down, hadn't he? He'd confessed to murdering Sara and Abby. Everlee didn't have to ask; she knew to her soul that was what happened. Shane wouldn't have kept his true identity from Alex. In fact—

"That's why you collapsed in the lobby the day we met, isn't it?" she whispered into his mouth. "You'd just had the mother of all shitty mornings. You told Alex who you were, didn't you?"

He eased back from her far enough to gently bump his forehead to hers. "Yeah, shitty. But it had to be done. I owed him that much, maybe more."

At last—finally!—the light came back on deep within the midnight blues she adored.

Shane planted a tiny, wet kiss on the end of her nose. He'd just been unmanned by Mother, but Everlee had his back, would always have his back, and she'd keep every last secret he wanted to share. Because she had hers, too, and someday, she'd tell him what they were.

"All these years, I've suffered in silence," Tuesday commented sorrowfully from where she sat behind them.

Shane twisted Everlee around until they both faced her.

"Thanks for letting me share your burden, Agent Hayes. It's an honor to know that you're human, too. Like me. That you understand what I've been through." She huffed out a throaty sigh and tossed a chunk of her tangled, dirty blonde hair over her shoulder. "I know this sounds corny, but because of you guys, I feel better than I have in a long, long time. You both understand what I've been through. I'm not alone anymore. Thank you both so, so much. I like you guys. I really do, and I haven't had anyone I could talk with since Freddie died. But you two honestly get me, don't you?"

Everlee hit Shane's mouth with a small peck before she turned back and faced Tuesday again. If ever there was a time to reveal her own secret, this was it. Instead, she said, "You're all right for a civilian, you know that?"

Shane stifled a grunt, even as his arm tightened around Everlee's waist and his hand smoothed over her ass.

"And you…" she said as she stabbed her index finger into his chest. "Partners don't keep secrets. We share everything but underwear, got it?" Stab went her fingertip again. "And we always, always have each other's backs. We don't gossip behind each other's backs. We trust each other. You've got my back, and I've got yours, got it?" *Stab, stab, stab.*

He was smiling plenty by the time she finished poking him. Everlee took his hard head between her hands and pulled him into her face. "Anything you ever want to share is between you and me, got it? I won't even tell Alex. And I know Tuesday will keep your confidences, too."

"Well, duh," he murmured, his voice soft and low, more like a purr. "She saved me, remember?"

Ev would've stabbed his chest again, because, well, it was *his* chest, and she adored touching that thick set of pectorals and the ink on it—a lot. But he captured her mouth and her breath and… Everlee relaxed into the arms of the man she'd fallen for. They'd only known each other a few days, not even a full week. But yeah. She was starting to love this big guy.

"Hello out there! Hey, Shane! Everlee!" Mother called from Shane's cell phone, which he'd fumbled when Everlee had launched herself at him. "If you guys don't pick up in two seconds, I'm getting Alex on the line, and then shit's gonna fly!"

Shane grabbed the phone off the ground and told her, "Thanks for outing me, *Mom,* but—"

"I'm a millionaire, Shane," she sputtered, interrupting him. "I could've paid all of your mom's hospital bills and your college tuition. But I couldn't even save my only child's life. How's that for a secret?"

Everlee's heart skipped to a full stop as Mother went on with a tearful, "And the entire time I've worked for Alex, I've kept my beautiful baby girl a secret. I never told him or Mark or Zack or my best friend Ember or anyone else." By then she was sniffling so hard she could barely speak. Everlee was sniffling, too. Shane was still frozen like a rock. Tuesday just sat there, cross-legged, her eyes as big as saucers.

"After Dempsey died, I lashed out at everyone, even Justice, and I miss him so much, but I blamed everyone, and I was so, so mad, and..." Another round of sniffles, choking, and coughing came over the connection. "I'm not anyone's mother anymore, not really. But I love you guys, and that's why I take especially good care of you, all of you, okay?" She made that sound like a dare. "I can't lose you kids, too. Is that understood?" By then she was all but hysterical, and Everlee wished she could hug Mother. The woman surely needed it.

"Yes, Mom," Shane replied meekly. "You love us, and we love you, too."

Everlee looked up at him. Her hand was still on his chest, and she knew darned well she had a sappy look on her face. Somehow, Shane had just given Mother precisely what she'd needed to heal. "You're the best, Mom," she told Sasha quietly. "Shane's right. All us guys love you."

She came back with, "But I'm not the best. And I didn't kill my baby. If anything, I loved her too much." More sniffling. More throat clearing. More nose blowing. At last, Mother said quietly, "I also know where Ms. Smarty-Pants Astor is right this very minute."

"You do?" Shane asked. "Where?"

"Never mind. Get packed and ready to go. Heston's thirty minutes out from your location. He'll get you where you need to go. Stay safe. Bye." The connection went dead.

Shane was still looking down at Everlee. She was still sitting on his lap, her index finger tapping the ink on his left pec. "That's why the tattoo. Alex's family is part of you."

A tortured sigh shuddered out of him. "Yeah, Mom's in my heart, and their names lie over it. The ink reminds me that I might've given some, but they gave all."

"Aww…" she whispered. "You should tell Alex. He'd like knowing you love them, too."

Shane shook his head. "No, never. I've hurt him enough. Let's go meet Heston and get this job over with. I really want to go home."

Everlee scrambled out of the warmth of Shane's embrace, then reached for Tuesday's hand and helped her to her feet. "You ready, girlfriend?"

Tuesday brushed her hands on the back of her pants. "Yes, I want to meet this Astor witch who killed Freddie. And then, I want to meet Alex and Mother and…" She ran a grubby hand over her dirty hair. "I am so glad you guys found me instead of the FBI. Thanks for believing me."

Shane answered what Everlee was going to say, "It's been our pleasure. Now let's go kick ass."

Chapter Twenty-Six

The night was darker and colder by the time TEAM Agent Heston Contreras arrived and expertly landed the Bell 429 corporate helicopter in the decrepit, weed-filled airfield next to the hangar. Shane liked the guy on sight. Dressed in a navy-blue flight suit, Heston was black-haired and olive-skinned in the way of his Mexican ancestry, and he'd definitely been blessed with Hollywood handsome features. From the way the rotor's downdraft ruffled his short but thick black hair when he stepped out of the cockpit, to his tall, slender, but athletically muscled frame, he was one of those guys who made other guys look like clumsy trolls. He stood a good foot over Everlee, but only a couple inches taller than Tuesday. Everlee seemed a bit smitten if the sparkle in her eyes meant what Shane thought it did. Which irked him despite knowing Contreras had had his shot at Everlee and had obviously missed.

After she made quick introductions, and after Contreras stopped schmoozing the ladies, he assisted the women up into the helo and personally fastened them into the two rear, forward-facing executive seats. He took time making sure their protective aviation headsets fit securely, then offered both bottled waters and plastic-wrapped sub-sandwiches, along with individual-sized bags of chips. The guy was a gentleman to the max, and it was obvious he'd charmed them.

Even Tuesday's eyes were bright and sparkling. Funny how that didn't bug Shane at all, but how he wished Contreras would trip or stumble—or something—when he catered to Ev.

She was exhausted, Shane could tell. She hadn't ordered him around once since he'd rescued her from that mess in the barn. Well, except when she'd stabbed his chest. If anything, she seemed more subdued and thoughtful, maybe even introverted since Mother broke the news of who he was—not qualities he would've ever ascribed to Agent Everlee Yeager.

While Heston lingered, chatting with her and Tuesday, making jokes and just overall settling them down, Shane dropped Everlee's and his gear bags inside the rear compartment alongside her seat. She was running on empty. There were dark crescents beneath her eyes, so he made sure she knew where her gear was in case she needed something. Made him feel stupid for crashing like he had before, and sleeping those precious hours away. She was the one those bastards had battered, the one who should've taken a nap. She should've soaked in a hot bath, too, followed by a three-course dinner, maybe a bottle of wine. She needed a back rub, and—

"How you doing, Shane?" she asked, interrupting his salacious wayward thoughts. "Headache still gone?"

While Heston was busy impressing Tuesday, Shane leaned into Everlee and told her, "I'm fine, Ev. When we get back, how about a date? We could go out for dinner one night. Or breakfast or lunch, whatever you'd like."

The smile that broke out on her face and the sparkle in those deep brown eyes was like watching the sun rise in the middle of night. "I'd like that," she answered, oddly submissive considering the take-charge woman she was. "Name the time and place and I'll be there."

He shook his head. "Uh-uh. How about I swing by your place and pick you up instead?"

She demurred, dropping her gaze. "That'd be nice."

Shane tipped inside the doorway and put a finger under her chin, needing to look into those pretty browns again. "I've got your six, babe," he told her, running a hand over her shoulder to the nape of her neck. "You know everything about me, everything that matters. You can talk to me, Ev. Hope you know that."

A sigh lifted both of her shoulders, and at last, she made eye contact. "Someday, I'll take you up on that offer, but not now, okay? It's… it's been a really long day."

He winked and smiled, willing to wait until she was ready. "Whenever you decide." He stepped back. "All strapped in?"

She nodded. "Don't get hurt, okay? Alex will kill me if you do."

"Look who's talking, the gal with a chair leg."

"Hey, I could've taken both those two jerks down with that weapon, and you know it."

"But a woman shouldn't have to fight her battles alone, should she?"

"Are you calling me Chair Force?" she quipped.

He grinned. "Never, babe. Now lean back. Get some shut-eye. I'll wake you once we arrive."

Shane closed her door, then went up front and hunkered into the co-pilot seat, belted into the safety harness, and snapped a headset on. Tipping back into the luxurious headrest, he listened to the chatter between Heston and his guests. The man was precisely what Everlee and Tuesday needed—a diversion. He treated both like equals, kept everything professional but lighthearted.

The entire conversation came through crisp and clear, while at the same time, the high-tech headset muted the overwhelming power of the rotors humming overhead. Shane had traveled in plenty of noisy Navy and USMC choppers in the past, all rugged workhorses built for utility and combat. But this luxury bird of Alex's was something else. Sleek, clean, and downright comfortable, riding in the Bell 429 was a welcome change from the prospect of camping on the ground tonight and sleeping in the open.

Shane was feeling relaxed and a titch spoiled—until he noticed the six-barreled electronically-operated mini-guns framed inside sturdy racks just inside both rear doors. Also, two sets of monkey harnesses secured to industrial-strength eye hooks fastened to the floor by the rear seats. Then Shane felt even better. Those harnesses would keep a Marine safely inside the chopper if something ugly came up and he had to man one of those mini-guns. Leave it to Alex to think of everything.

After Heston finished securing his charges, he climbed out the side rear door, shut and locked it, then climbed into the pilot seat and told Shane, "You look like shit."

Shane extended a hand and replied, "Good to meet you, too, Contreras. Thanks for the ride."

Heston nodded back toward the ladies. Instead of shaking hands, he signed for Shane to change channels on his headset. Once Shane made the adjustment, he asked, "Everlee looks pretty bad. Do I need to stop at a hospital first? Maybe somewhere we can all get a good night's sleep before we finish this war?"

"No way!" she barked from where she sat behind Shane. "I read lips, you know. The plan is we attack now, before Astor gets away. Don't even think of taking me to some emergency room."

"Nope, we're good," Shane assured him, grinning at the vehemence in former LT Yeager's tone. Heston and he switched back to their original channel. "Besides she'll take both our heads off if we even think of babying her. She just needs a safe place to rest a while, and a trip in this helo will do fine. Mother said she knows where Maeve Astor is, so I'm assuming you're taking us to her. We'd really like to wrap this mission up tonight. That possible?"

"Absolutely," Heston agreed. "Yeah, Mom and I talked." He twisted around and faced Everlee, who was seated directly behind Shane. "Astor and her goons are at the Capital Hotel in Little Rock. Five stars all the way for that witch. God, I hate cold-blooded murderers, don't you?"

"You know it. How many goons are you talking?"

"A few. Five, six at the most. She's in the penthouse, top level. It's got four guest bedrooms and a master suite. I'd imagine her bodyguards are there with her. Might even be in those spare bedrooms."

"You think you can get Ev and me inside?" Shane asked.

"Abso-fuckin'-lutely." The cocky grin Heston shot Shane dazzled. Figured, he'd have bright white, perfectly straight teeth, too. "The landing pad's located right above her suite. There's a stairwell down to the penthouse, and the roof's soundproofed, so she'll never hear our approach. I can set this baby down without anyone in the hotel even knowing we're there. No offense, but I'm going in with you and Ev. Or did you want me to babysit Ms. Smart?"

"I trust Tuesday, but yeah," Shane said, "I'd appreciate you staying with her. She's been through enough."

A cocky spark danced inside Heston's dark eyes. "No problem, amigo. I'd pick standing guard over a pretty woman over combat any day."

Shane nodded his agreement. "Good, let's wake this troll up."

"My pleasure." Adeptly, Heston worked the controls, lifting the helo up from the hardpacked Arkansas ground like a dragonfly flitting off a lily pad.

"'Bout damned time," Everlee grumbled.

Shane turned around as far as he could and gave her a thumbs-up.

"I want a pistol," Tuesday said quietly. "You're not leaving me behind like some stupid Disney princess. I'm going in with you guys, and I want to be armed."

The silence in the chopper was damned loud. And awkward. Shane twisted within his safety harness far enough around to look into her face. Nothing but determination stared back at him.

Heston didn't miss a beat. "Works for me," he replied easily, still looking straight ahead. "You're not trained for this kind of infil though, ma'am. It'll be dangerous. She's a twisted piece of work but hell yeah, you need a pistol. I'll load it for you and teach you how to shoot it. But it'd still be safer for us if you stayed behind. I'd be glad to stay with you."

"I know how to defend myself," she replied crisply, "and I said I'm going in with you guys. If I can face down a mother polar bear defending her two cubs, I can face this bitch and her goons. Besides, that will make it a fairer fight, four of us against her and however many guys are dumb enough to be in there with her."

Shane shot Heston a grin, but had to ask, "Any TEAM rules about an *alleged* black widow taking down the *real* black widow responsible for killing her husband and maligning her good name?"

"Sounds fair to me," Everlee replied. "But Tuesday, Heston's right. You're not trained like we are, and with you along, we'll be worrying about your safety when we should be focused on Astor. You going in puts us at more risk, might even get one of us hurt. You've got time before we hit the hotel, so think about what you're asking."

"She killed Freddie, Everlee. I know she did and your Mother person has the evidence to prove it. I should be the one who puts a bullet between Astor's beady eyes. You guys are probably better shots, but this is personal, damn it. Freddie deserves—"

"To be avenged?" Heston interrupted quietly. He glanced briefly over his shoulder. "I agree, but making this about revenge makes you our weak link. I'm not telling you no, but please think about what you're asking. We'll surely all have your back if you decide to face Astor. But to us, this is just a job. She's trash and taking out trash is what we're trained to do. But you're an artist, senorita. A sensitive, classy woman. It'd be our pleasure to do this dirty job for you. Please reconsider. Taking a life puts a dark hashmark on your soul you'll live with the rest of your days. Be certain that's truly what you want."

Shane couldn't have phrased it any better. His gaze shifted to Everlee's hand. She'd reached across the short space between her and Tuesday's seats and now had hold of

Tuesday's wrist. "Heston's right," Everlee said. "Astor *is* a despicable piece of garbage, the worst kind, and believe me, all of us understand where you're coming from. Just be sure before we land, okay? Think about it. Because once we get there, we're going in fast and hard."

"And there will be blood," Shane added quietly through their shared communication link.

"With seven high-value targets, extreme chaos, too," Heston explained. "Surprise will only be on our side for a few seconds, but one of us could still get hurt."

"Will you have body cams?" Tuesday asked more timidly.

Shane hadn't thought of that. He looked to Heston for the answer.

"I have two helmets cams aboard. If that will keep you safe, whoever goes in can certainly record what goes down for you."

"Can't I watch it live? While it's happening?" This question was asked more hesitantly. Shane dared to hope that Heston's delicate touch was working on Tuesday's determination.

"Abso-fuckin'-lutely," Heston replied. That seemed to be his go-to cuss word. "I'll even make a copy if you'd like."

Shane heard the breath whoosh out of Tuesday. "No, that's okay. I don't need one. But please end her, Agent Hayes," she all but pleaded. "I don't care what she's done to me, but she killed Freddie. I know she did. Make her pay. Promise me."

"Everlee and I will take care of her." Shane couldn't promise Astor's execution, though. That was not who he was. But one way or the other, he would take Astor out of circulation. How she ended this day, dead or alive, was entirely up to her.

Heston turned to face Shane. "Helmets are in overhead storage. Gear up, amigos. Touch down in ten minutes."

Chapter Twenty-Seven

Aching from the top of her head to the soles of her feet, nonetheless, Everlee planted one boot flat to the reflective circle of the hotel's rooftop helicopter landing pad. It was go-time. Once outside the helo, she stood still as her neck acclimated to the weight of the helmet Shane insisted she wear. It was more cumbersome than she'd expected, though most of that extra weight was probably her stubborn need to take Astor down instead of letting her team, or herself, rest for the night. It was knowing where Astor was that pushed Everlee. So what if her head and neck ached tomorrow? Outing Astor's plan to destroy Tuesday, maybe ending Astor herself, would be worth it.

Man, this mission had been one helluva long damned drag. Everything had gone wrong since the moment they'd pulled in front of Tuesday Bremmer's cute little home back in Dallas. Only now, there was no Tuesday Bremmer, never had been. Only one darned intelligent Tuesday Smart. Everlee wondered how long Astor had planned to kill Atchison Bremmer before she'd carried through with it. Were those two kids physically, biologically hers? Jesus, had she given birth solely to trick Atchison? To get his insurance money? It seemed too bizarre to be true.

Everlee pushed that quandary to the back of her mind. It was bad enough Astor had duped Atchison for five years before she'd killed him. But that she'd gone through the pain of childbirth was pure abomination. What kind of mother could stoop so low? Ev would never understand, not if she lived to be a thousand. So yeah, Everlee refused to rest. She was driven, as much as Tuesday. The Bremmers, Freddie Lamb, and Tuesday deserved better. Everlee's helmet didn't feel so heavy anymore and the heads-up display was cool.

She'd worn a helmet cam before. That time on a joint training exercise with a group of Navy SEALs, at their Special Operations Forces Cold Weather Maritime Training Facility in frigid Kodiak, Alaska. It hadn't been easy working with them. SEALs were a different breed of spec ops from Air Force members Everlee knew. They'd been damned serious and totally focused, as if their lives depended on passing the course.

Talk about tough. Everlee respected anybody dedicated enough to survive Hell Week, then tackle Cold Weather Training the way those guys had. By the end of the course, she'd been run ragged and she had pneumonia. But by hell, she'd kept up with those bigger, meaner, sturdier men. They'd good-naturedly nicknamed her Squirt, which she still hated. But one of them, Chief Petty Officer Nick Coletti, had at least slapped her back when they'd headed to their helo for the ride back to San Diego. He'd told her she'd done good. She'd told him she never wanted to see him or his team again. He'd laughed, but she'd meant that, too.

Everlee had slept the entire flight back to Seattle, she'd been so sick. She still thanked her lucky stars there were no women on SEAL teams—yet. Because then she'd have to prove she could beat those types of guys, anytime, anywhere, too. Ah, the story of her life.

As agreed upon prior to landing, they left Tuesday with Heston. He'd cut the engine the moment they'd touched down to reduce the raucous noise of rotor slap.

"We'll be watching," he called to Shane, who was also on the ground. "Try to keep it PG."

"You bet," he replied.

But Everlee doubted Tuesday would mind seeing Astor's brains eject from the back of her head. She watched the silent guy-speak between Heston and Shane. The way they communicated with a nod, the thrust of their chins, or head bobs. Like the chin Shane had just directed toward Tuesday. "Keep her safe, amigo. She's the target here, not the killer."

"Copy that," Heston answered with a swift two-fingered salute.

Shane closed the side door, hitched his gear bag high on his shoulder, and turned to Everlee. "You ready?"

"Been ready since this shit show started."

Besides the helmets with cameras, they were both now armed to the gills, each with a McMillan bolt-action, TAC-338 sniper rifle slung over their shoulders and plenty of ammo. But this was no training exercise and the rifles were for just-in-case scenarios. Close quarter combat demanded pistols, Shane with a right nice pair of Browning Black Label 1911-380s, Everlee with two Glocks from Smoke's vault. Between them, they'd preloaded a dozen magazines and were more than ready to end Astor and her goons. Anticipation was palpable, and Everlee was on high alert, ready for this sprint to the finish line.

But what the hell? Shane had just stepped into her, blocking her way with that big, squared-off body of his. She titled her head upward, intent on staring him down if he'd decided to go all alpha male on her and insist she stay behind too. Not. Happening.

"You got something to say?"

"Don't forget our date once this mission is over."

"You gotta bring that up now?" She was impatient to be done with this never-ending day, didn't need the pleasant distraction he offered. Her head needed to be in the game and her reflexes sharp, not sluggish like they'd been since her encounter with Ringo and Bud. Shane needed to knock off the small talk. Multi-tasking took too much effort.

"Why not? I'm looking forward to it, Agent Yeager."

"Me too," she admitted grumpily.

"So?"

"So what?"

"So how do you want to go in?"

Everlee sucked in a lungful of the cold night air, her smaller body buffeted by the chilly wind raking over the rooftop. "Fast and quiet. Hard but without unnecessary roughness. No collateral damage. Alex hates that. Only one we take out is Astor and only if she shoots first. Watch your backstop and don't get hurt again."

He pursed his lips and blew her a kiss. "I love it when you talk dirty."

She slugged his biceps, meaning it to hurt. Which it probably didn't. "Stop yakking and move out."

He gestured for her to take the lead. Which Everlee loved. She stepped out ahead of him and aimed for the only rooftop exit, grabbed hold of the metal handle, and damned near pulled her arm out of its shoulder socket. It was locked. *Shit!* That newbie move made her look stupid, which she wasn't. Green and cocky, yes. But also smart enough not to challenge Shane when he dropped to one knee beside her and pressed a small shape charge—probably C4, something he'd obviously raided from Smoke's place but hadn't told her about—around the door handle and—

Poof! Open sesame.

Everlee wondered what else he had in those pockets. No time for that now. She clapped his right shoulder, then walked past him through the now open exit. Not much to see there, just the lighted stairwell. At the bottom of said stairs, Shane lightly tapped her shoulder, a signal for her to proceed through the fire doors ahead. Those should open to the private hallway that housed the penthouse entry and its private elevator. She hurried quietly, the Glock in her right hand, pointed down at the floor, adrenaline pounding through her veins at the audacious thing she was about to do. Into the hallway she went. Elevator to her right. Penthouse entry to her left.

Wordlessly, Shane stepped around her, reached one long arm up to the ceiling, and pressed a small glob of what looked like *Silly Putty* over the lens of the tiny security camera above the elevator.

Damn. Ev hadn't thought to look for cameras. "Thanks," she whispered guiltily.

"That's why I'm here," he answered easily, "and why we work in pairs. One is none, but two is one, Ev. Don't forget it. Let's do this. Ring the doorbell. See who's home."

"With pleasure," she answered, kicking the doorknob out of her way like the hardass she was. The door banged open because she'd meant it to. Or, she thought, it hadn't been locked. Or maybe, they'd been expected. Not a comforting feeling—all those doubts.

Once inside, she leveled her weapon and announced loudly, "Down on your knees! You're all under…"

The command died on her lips.

She'd expected resistance.

Not this.

Talk about an entire mission gone sideways.

The first whiff inside was so horrendous that Everlee wanted to puke. The stench of perforated bodies and heads. The horrific bouquet of blood spatter and perforated bowels would cling to her hair and clothes until she showered. A dozen times.

There. In the center of the expansive white carpeted room. Six men. Well-muscled, big-bodied men. As big as those SEALs she'd trained with. All in various stages of undress. All laying face up with ugly, black holes in the centers of their foreheads and chests. Looked like they'd been ready for bed, or in bed, when they'd died. Make that when they'd been killed. Murdered.

Some wore sweatpants and t-shirts, others just boxers. One was completely nude. But their bodies had definitely been posed, their faces tipped intentionally toward the penthouse entry. Facing Everlee. All those unseeing eyes were staring… Straight. At. Her. Daring her to relive her worst nightmare. A scream edged up her throat like that old familiar snake she'd never been able to swallow down.

Not here! Not now! Damnit! This is pure coincidence. Astor does not know one damned thing about me. Certainly not that!

The walls closed in. If she stayed with these six bodies, she'd lose her cookies and any respect Shane had for her. Everlee refused to bow to her body's natural aversion to gore, not in front of Shane. Throwing up and fainting like a sissy were out. Too bad she couldn't get her heart to slow down. Or her lungs to breathe right. Or her throat to swallow.

"Call the police," she ordered huskily. She'd honestly tried to relay that order with military precision and authority. She was former military police, damn it. So why'd that command sound weak and pitiful?

"Already did," he answered.

"You did?"

"Yes, ma'am."

And why's he calling me ma'am? Her brain refused to process another puzzle. It was already overloaded with what her eyes were seeing. Fighting nausea and the primal instinct screaming from the animal side of her brain to run, Everlee dragged her gaze away from the nightmare. She pointed the muzzle of her Glock to her right, at the bloody drag marks in the hallway. "These men didn't die here," she told Shane in case he hadn't already figured it out.

"No, they didn't," he replied grimly. "Cut your feed, Ev. Hurry. Shut it down. Tuesday doesn't need to see this."

"Oh, yeah, yeah, I… I f-forgot," she muttered, fumbling the helmet's butterfly switch under her chin. At last the feed to the helicopter ended, but poor Tuesday had to have seen everything. "Damn. I'm… I'm too late. Sorry." *So, so sorry. For Tuesday. For me. For Shane taking charge like he did. For my mom For his mom. For Lamb. God, for everything!*

The memory rolled over her like an attacking M1 Abrams tank. Her coming home from school that day. She'd been sixteen going on fifty. Too young to feel so old. Too young to have grown up so alone. So deserted. So betrayed. But that afternoon, when the high school bell rang dismissal at three fifteen, she hadn't expected to run home and find her mother murdered in the middle of their kitchen floor. She'd been staring at Everlee then, too. Just like these guys were staring at her now. Which made this death scene eerily familiar, and the thought that Astor knew everything about her, that the witch was really after her, scary as hell. That all of this was more about ending, torturing, and outing Everlee Billings. Not killing Tuesday Smart.

Because that afternoon, her mother's murderer had still been in the house. Everlee had never expected it'd be her dad. Which begged the question: Did Astor know the intimate details of her mom's murder? Was that why these guys were facing the door, to scare Everlee? Was her dad behind this mess? Or was Astor so smart that she knew the sight of these dead men would unsettle Everlee? Worse, Astor had killed one of her men after she'd declared he'd kidnapped the wrong woman. Was that a lie? Just another smokescreen to confuse Everlee? Had those despicable murders been about her, not Tuesday? Who was Astor really after?

Tuesday or me? Both of us? She dug her fingernails into the side of her head, shifting the helmet out of her way. *I don't know anymore!* So many questions, none of which Everlee could accurately process at this sudden shock. Her gloved hands trembled so hard that her pistols were shaking, too. Not wanting to appear weak in front of Shane, or, heaven forbid, unable to perform like the skilled operator she damned sure was, Everlee pressed both fisted weapons against her thighs. There. See? Better. Not falling apart here.

Not me. No way.

As if *looking* better could ever be the same as *being* better. Or being in charge of her heart and her body and that damned snake still edging perilously up her throat to… to unman her. Unwoman her? Was there such a word? There should be.

Before Shane could take over again, Everlee blocked his path to the smeared carpet in the hall at their right. "Don't touch anything," she ordered in the weakest damned voice that had ever come out of her mouth. "Understood?" she nearly yelled as she tried to recover her tougher-than-shit, LT Everlee Yeager, Chief of Security Forces, persona.

Shane stared her down. "Copy that," he replied with a nod of his head, showing her respect. Judging by the tender glint in his eyes, he knew she was close to falling apart. But Ev was damned if she'd admit it. And he'd better not ask.

His eyes were such a deep, bottomless ocean blue that… she had to get a grip. "Is… is there any way our helmet cams can record this scene without transmitting it to Heston and T-T-Tuesday?" Damn it. Her tongue didn't seem able to perform the simplest question.

"Yes, ma'am," Shane answered politely. Without another word, which was really good considering the half-assed way her brain was working, he reached both hands for her helmet and—

Everlee saw him coming. She knew Shane was good and honorable, yet still… Still! A terrified flinch vibrated up her spine when he cupped her head. She closed her eyes and jerked out of his reach. She knew he'd never strike her. He'd touched her before and that hadn't hurt. Not at all. Yet she couldn't stifle her reaction whenever a man's hands came for her. Especially not now. Cold, stark panic climbed up her throat. Adrenaline kicked in.

Fight or flight? Which will it be?

He took another step into her. She fought to not take a step back. Because she knew—she knew!—he wouldn't hurt her. And he didn't. Instead of knocking her around, choking her, punching her face, breaking her nose, or spitting insults, he simply cradled her head and her helmet and... *Click.* The heads-up display relayed what he'd done. *Recording. Not transmitting.* Why was thinking so damned difficult?

Because her poor brain was pinging through years' worth of physical abuse from her dad, then from asshat Butch. For God's sake, as much as she'd detested what her father had done, she'd still married a man like him. What was wrong with her? Had all those slaps and punches caused her ADHD? Had it messed up her brain? And why was she thinking about that crap now? Here?

Because she was the worst, biggest fraud in the universe. "Okk-kay then," she declared shakily, stretching her neck forward to get the cramp in it to ease up. "F-follow me."

"Always," Shane whispered as she led him into each of the four guest rooms and six horrific murder scenes.

One by one, Everlee documented the rooms, but didn't touch anything. She used her cell phone to capture as much as she could, just in case something happened to the coverage from the helmet cams. Extra backup never hurt. Redundancy was rule number two: Always take more pictures than you think you'll need. Someone else might see something you missed. Right after rule number one: Don't get Shane killed. And stop shaking. Too many of the pictures she was taking were blurred, another reason for redundancy. She couldn't even do this right.

Shane already had his cell up. Of course. He didn't need to be told what to do. He'd been capturing images before she'd thought of it, and his were probably crystal clear. But okay. He might just be smarter than her. Everlee didn't mind admitting that. Shane was her partner. She trusted him. She really, really did. She wasn't alone, and he always had her six. Maybe she should admit her shortcomings and let the real hero in this twosome lead...

Just that fast, the snake in her throat vanished. Her chest expanded. She could breathe again. If that wasn't an all-out nudge from the universe, nothing was. Okay then. As soon as this f'd-up mission was done, she was done thinking she had to be as big a badass as Shane. She was stepping back from being a fraud. Maybe then she'd stop hurting herself, falling and spraining her ankles.

Which took her full circle to the very real fact that she was a fraud. Always had been. It might just be time to come clean. To let someone in.

Chapter Twenty-Eight

Shane followed Everlee. There were only four guest rooms. The scene in each was the same. Two queen beds. Six bloody murder scenes in all. Looked like Astor had delivered cold-blooded headshots while the men she'd hired to do her dirty work slept. The shredded pillows at the headboards now held blood, brain matter, and bone fragments. There were no signs of resistance, not even in the shared bedrooms. Which begged the question: Why hadn't any these guys reacted once they'd heard shooting? Silencers were never as quiet as Hollywood portrayed. Had Astor drugged or poisoned them? That'd explain a lot.

Like Everlee, Shane snapped photo after photo. Of the rooms. The pillows. The blood splatter on walls and headboards. The darkening blood smears down the hall. By the time he and Everlee were back in the main room, his heart was pounding pretty hard. Quite frankly, the entire suite stunk to hell and the scene was beyond gruesome. But he was more worried about Ev than himself.

He'd seen worse than these carefully orchestrated executions during his deployments overseas. You put in enough hours in third-world countries, and it was a given. Most Americans, especially those loud-mouthed talking heads who'd never seen a second of combat, would be horrified at what most military members saw every day. The filth. The squalor. The physical abuse. Hell, the first time Shane had seen a small boy whipping his sad little donkey to make it walk, when its poor feet were lifted in the air by the over-sized weight of the cart it was trying desperately to pull, had been a huge wake-up call. There really was no place like home and when he wasn't in America, he was powerless to stop any kind of abuse. The poor were just as wicked and as cruel as the wealthy. There was no EPA, ASPCA, Family Services, or women's shelters. No compassion for elderly. No empathy for handicapped. No justice. Just gawddamned money. And pain. Yeah, always plenty of pain.

But Everlee hadn't been exposed to any of that, and there simply was no way to train a grunt how to react to their first kill or death scene. The Corps hadn't developed any how-to manuals to teach a guy or gal how to process the internal shock from violent, visceral imagery. You could talk to yourself all you wanted, but seeing truly was believing. Only then did you understand what walking through Hell meant, how it smelled and what it looked like. What Astor had done to her men was right up there with the atrocities committed during public executions in Iraq, Iran, and Afghanistan.

Everlee had panicked at first sight, and for a few moments after she'd so skillfully kicked in the door, Shane had fully expected she'd bolt. But she hadn't. She hesitated, but she'd stood her ground, and that said a lot. Everlee might be brash and in-your-face ready to fight, but she was also disciplined enough to control her emotions and finish the job. Even when it was uglier than sin.

But that flinch and the fear in her eyes when he'd taken hold of her helmet, that was something else again. She'd nearly freaked and he needed to know why. He'd held her before. Hell, they'd made love like rabbits back at Smoke's place. Yet he'd startled her now? Why? Had Butch slapped her around? Abused her? Punched her? Shane made it his next mission to find out.

"I can't believe she killed her guys," Everlee whispered once they were both back in the white room. "All of them."

That quietly spoken statement sounded as if it came from a little girl. Why was she staring at the bodies? Why was she standing over the closest vic, looking down at him like she knew him? Which Shane doubted. Something tremendously heartbreaking was going on inside Everlee's head. One moment she'd seemed able to overcome the senselessness of this gruesome discovery, but the next—

"In c-c-cold blood… Her own m-m-men…" Her voice had grown breathier, too. "All six of them. Err, seven, if you include the guy back at the barn, and I think we should. She's s-s-sick."

Little Rock's police department would be there within minutes. He'd given dispatch the basic details of the multiple murder scene, his name and TEAM badge number, as well as the identification number on his official FBI orders. He'd explained what authority he and Everlee'd had to enter the penthouse and go after Astor. Had also provided TEAM HQ's main phone number if Little Rock's police chief wanted to speak with Alex. He'd answered all dispatch's terse questions. And now they waited.

While Everlee stood over that one body, Shane cleared the rest of the rooms, something he should've done as soon as they'd breached entry. He'd barely put his gloved hand on the closet doorknob behind the entry door when—

"Don't kill her yet! She's mine!" Tuesday yelled from the open entry, where Heston stood at her back. She held a SIG P365, a slim 9-millimeter pocket pistol that fit her small right hand perfectly. Her stance was spot on, her feet spread, one foot behind the other for stability, the heel of her shooting hand cupped like a lover in her left palm.

"Tuesday, shush. Put your weapon down," Shane scolded. "Just me and Ev in here."

"Oh, sorry. Yeah. I-I know. I see that." She aimed her pistol at the floor and jerked her gaze off the murder scene at his backdrop.

"Couldn't keep her away?" Shane asked Heston.

"Not after the murder scene you guys transmitted. Thought you'd need help. Extra hands, you know." The charming Hispanic was gone. Heston's sharp, brown eyes were grim and his lips were thin, tight lines. He leveled the .45 caliber, full-auto SIG 1922 Emperor Scorpion pistol in his right hand down at the floor.

Shane admitted, "Just finishing what I should've done earlier."

Heston's pistol came back up. "You're just now clearing the place?"

"Yeah. Things went to hell as soon as we B&E'd."

The closet knob in Shane's hand rotated. The door slammed open, bounced off his chest, and—

Holy shit! Tuesday Smart was in two places at once. One with Heston. The other in the closet. Both pistols sprang to his hands. It was time Astor died.

"Back! Everyone get back!" Shane bellowed.

He couldn't believe his eyes. Sure as fuck, the woman in the closet could've passed as Tuesday Smart's identical twin.

Well, except for the sneer twisting her ruby red lips and her poor choice of an FBI SWAT uniform as a costume. Not once on this entire mission had Tuesday sneered like that.

Astor fired. Shane jerked back at wicked sting of a close quarter impact. Fuck! She'd hit him! High on his biceps. Burned like shit. Whatever!

Astor kicked the closet door out of her way and came face-to-face with the real Tuesday Smart. She blinked once. Twice. It was like looking at identical twins, only her eyes were cold, green fire and she'd thought she could pass herself off as FBI SWAT. Big fuckin' mistake. Because the real Tuesday Smart was still wearing bright-red Converse tennis shoes, and she'd just taken a quick step forward.

Heston was dead on her six, his pistol alongside hers. "No, Chica."

Everlee was no longer in Shane's peripheral, but he knew she was behind him, also poised to fire. Would sure make one helluva mess if they all shot Astor at the same time.

But he couldn't let Tuesday follow through. This was TEAM business, not revenge. Shane stepped between Astor and Tuesday. Blocked Tuesday's and Heston's shots. Going for broke. Needing to control what happened next. Willing to give Astor a chance to surrender despite her having shot hm. One last chance at justice in a court of law. That was what Alex would've wanted. Not an execution.

Sounded real damned fair in his head. Until Astor's pistol twitched the barest millimeter to her left, bucked, and the sickest "Ooomph" hissed behind Shane.

He pivoted to his right to shield his partner. "Everlee! No!"

Rage kicked in. He damn near swung back around to shoot Astor's fuckin' head off, but—

BA-BOOM! BA-BOOM! Tuesday and Heston pistol unloaded on her first.

Astor's body arched backward. A vivid spray of red and dyed blonde flew over her head. Her pistol cartwheeled, hit the wall, and came down harmlessly to the floor. She collapsed, just folded onto her knees like a sack of wet concrete.

But Everlee was down. *No! No! No!* Shane sank to his knees beside her. A bright red splotch blossomed high on her chest, just above her tactical plating. Might be her shoulder. He couldn't tell. She kept blinking.

Fighting time and physics, Shane dug his blowout bag out from the mini-pack strapped to his belt. Snapping his wrist, he unfurled the kit and spread it open on the floor beside Ev.

Heston was patting Astor down, checking her neck for a pulse, making sure.

Tuesday knelt at Everlee's other side. "What can I do?"

"Talk to her. Make her stay with us," Shane snapped. *With me!*

He barely heard Heston ordering, "Agent down! Request immediate assistance at…"

Too focused on Everlee, Shane stopped listening to any sounds not coming from her. Peeling her shirt open took his last hope. Sucking chest wounds were killers. Everlee's was higher on her chest than he'd expected. Not dead center, thank God, but he was looking at an exit wound, not entry. This bullet hole was too large, its edges too ragged.

Not until he stripped her tactical vest away did he realize that, somehow, Astor's bullet had struck Ev below her armpit and exited out the top of her shoulder. Which indicated Ev hadn't been facing Astor head on like he'd thought. She'd turned to her side, damn it. He should've taken better care of her. Everlee hadn't been herself since she'd walked into this shitting room full of dead men. Christ! He'd let her down!

Focus, damn it. Shane shoved the condemnation to the back of his mind. He had better things to do than worry about what couldn't be changed. Shoving the end of a plastic bag of QuikClot between his teeth, he ripped it open and poured the entire dose into that damned exit hole. Then he tore open another bag and did the same to the entry. Emergency triage, treat bleeders first.

Thick, absorbent, layered gauze came next. Laced with more clotting chemicals, he placed one entire package over the exit wound on her shoulder, another on her side over the entry. Cursing Astor with every breath, Shane pressed his palms over both wounds and applied pressure to slow the flows.

Blood still trickled around his fingers. He pressed harder.

Everlee groaned and squirmed. He pressed harder still.

She closed her eyes and that frightened the hell out of Shane. "Don't give up on me, babe," he ground out. "Fight, Everlee. You don't know how to quit, remember? So fight."

Tuesday had taken Everlee's other hand and was talking to her, but she was too quiet. Everlee wouldn't hear whispers. She needed loud and clear. So Shane gave it to her. "Stay with me!" he ordered, yelling into her face as he kept extreme pressure on her wounds. He knew he was hurting her. But she was *not* going anywhere but home with him, damn it. He was not losing this woman, too!

"You hear me, Yeager?" he challenged. "Don't you dare die on me, LT. You've got some explaining to do, *ma'am!*" He knew that title irked her, probably like being called *'sir'* irked Alex. Too bad! "We have a date, you chicken-shit *Chair Force* officer." His eyes watered. "You hear me, *ma'am.* Damned straight. I said *Chair Force* and I mean it. Meant ma'am and chicken-shit, too. Fight. For once in your life, fight like a motherfucking Marine!"

A single, chest-heaving breath huffed out of her nose.

Shane could've kissed her, but one breath was damned near nothing. He threw his full weight into his palms, pressing her life back into her. He needed to see those coffee brown eyes sparkle again. He needed to hear her endless supply of sass.

Somewhere in the back of his mind he heard the hubbub of police and EMTs flooding into the room behind him. But he blocked them out and ordered Everlee to, "Live, damn you. And we're going to talk, *ma'am.* For hours! Until I know what the fuck is going on in that hard damned head of yours. Because whatever you think you know about yourself, you're wrong. You're perfect the way you are. You don't need to change. Stop believing what you think you know. Because you don't know nothing. Listen up. Stay with me and—"

"Sir, you need to let us take over," a firm female voice said.

Shane shook his head, refusing an order for the first time in his life. He had so much more to tell Everlee.

The female medic beside him cupped her hands over his and pressed down on Everlee's exit wound just as hard as he was, squeezing his fingers as she attempted to take over. She was a pretty Black woman with shiny, short hair. Thin but strong for her size. She exuded the calm professionalism of most first responders. She looked like she knew what she was doing, but—

"I can't leave her," he told her. "Won't! She's got two wounds. You need two more hands!" The last time he'd turned his responsibilities over to a medic, they'd both died. Visions of Sara and Abby Stewart overlaid the too-damned quiet woman beneath his bloody hands. They'd been as pasty white then as Everlee was now. Her lips were just as blue.

Fuck! Shane pursed his lips and tried like hell to fight the relentless panic tapdancing up his spine. It was happening again. Like his Mom. Like Sara and Abby.

The medic slapped a square, heavily weighted package over the exit wound on Ev's shoulder. Damned thing worked like a compress. Just that fast Everlee stopped leaking blood. The medic tried again to take over the entry wound below Ev's arm. "What's your name?" she asked patiently.

He threw "Shane Hayes!" at the medic like a dagger. Why should his name matter?

She was on her knees now, just like him, right beside him, her full weight leveraged over Everlee, gently pushing him out of the way. "Good to meet you, Shane. I'm Dottie Kaminski. I know, Kaminski, strange name for a Black gal, huh? But Shane, honey, I can't help your friend if you won't let me do my job."

See what she did there? Made it personal, first name basis kind of personal. Personally challenged him to let her take over caring for Everlee. To give in. Shane was almost convinced when a strong arm snaked around his shoulder and neck, jolting him back to the present and away from Everlee. Whoever that was, they thought they could physically restrain him? Jerk him around? Put him in a headlock? Guess again, asshole. He pulled back, fighting mad, ready to bust that idiot's nose, until—

"It's me, buddy," Heston murmured against the side of his head. "Just me. Settle down. Let Everlee go. Help is here and these guys brought blood. Right now, she needs them more than she needs us."

Well, blood. Yeah. Any fool could see she needed that. Okay then.

Shane grunted, then tipped over onto one hip, his eyes still glued on Everlee. Not quite ready to leave her side, but willing to listen. Heston was right. These medics were efficient, and Shane could see they knew what they were doing. And Everlee needed their expertise, not Shane going caveman. The female medic was gentle and quick. She talked into the radio clipped to her collar, relaying short, medical-ese details Shane didn't understand, to another female voice, maybe a doctor. It was hard to differentiate. They both sounded so competent, so—medical. So much smarter than Shane. Like they really could save Everlee.

He shoved to his feet and found himself buttressed on one side by Tuesday, Heston on his other. Tuesday slipped an arm around his waist; Heston's hand was firm under Shane's elbow. They were both holding him steady. The two male EMTs who'd come with Kaminski were fast, just as good as she was. Shane was impressed. By then, there were two IVs in Everlee's arm, one clear with saline, the other dark red with...

"O Negative, universal donor," the one male EMT told Shane while he wrapped a warm blanket over and under Everlee, preparing her for transport. "I figured you were military, that you'd understand how urgent her condition is. We work with the local hospital. We're their Life Flight crew, which is why we carry blood. Most EMTs don't. Trust me, your friend here is in good hands."

"She's not my friend—" Shane swallowed hard, afraid if he said anything more, he'd break down. *She's my everything.*

"Which hospital are you taking her to?" Heston asked the medics.

Shane didn't hear the answer. He was too busy watching the room behind Heston fill with police officers and the coroner maybe, if that's who the white-haired guy attending Astor's dead body was. A couple gurneys. Several black body bags. He swallowed hard at the carnage in this ugly, crowded space. At sweet Everlee in the middle of it. At the somber backdrop and the stifling darkness of Death around her. Hell couldn't look any worse.

Shane managed to tell Medic Kaminski, "Wherever you take her, I go too." *Please don't fight me on that. I can't let you just take her away like you did last time, not again. Not this time!*

She gave him a quick smile full of perfect white teeth. "You bet you are, darlin'. We always have room for one more in our chopper. We ready?" she asked the EMT who'd told Shane about the O Negative.

"Ready to transport as soon as you are, Dot."

"We should go now," Shane ordered. "Hurry."

She shot him a kind, motherly smile. Just like Kelsey might have if she'd been there. It was that same kind of graciousness and open generosity. Lifting to her feet, Kaminski pulled off her blue latex gloves and held a clean hand out for Shane. "Like the gentleman said, we need to hurry," she told her EMT buddies. "And you are definitely coming with me, Shane Hayes, so I can dress the hole in your arm."

Shane looked down at his arm. He'd forgotten he'd been shot, too. The pain hadn't set in yet, too much adrenaline. Too much worry. But there stood Tuesday, at his side, pressing a clump of that same chemically-treated gauze to the bullshit wound on his biceps. Man, she'd even cut his shirt sleeve, and for some dumb reason, his eyes filled with blurry tears. That was the real Tuesday, the much-maligned woman standing there, helping out when she could've run and never been seen again. Judging by the tall policeman at her left, the guy with the clipboard under his arm, she'd been answering questions, explaining, and probably defending Everlee and Heston, hopefully herself, and—*me*.

"Come to the hospital with us?" Shane asked, needing his friends with him more than he'd ever thought he would.

"Well, of course, silly." The bright smile in her eyes was real and genuine and so much like the Tuesday he'd come to know.

"Get going," Heston cut in. "We'll join you later. Got to move the helo so Life Flight can land close enough to transport Ev. Guess they had to land across the street because I parked up top. My bad."

Shane nodded. "Okay. Whatever. I'll be with Ev."

"Where else would you be?" Tuesday asked, her green eyes tender and so damned pretty. "Now go. We'll join you as soon as we can."

Shane thanked them both, then turned and again told Kaminski, "Hurry."

The mission wasn't over yet. Everlee still had to live.

Chapter Twenty-Nine

Everlee was rushed into emergency surgery upon arrival, and Shane was directed to wait in one of those nondescript beige conference rooms. The kind where family and friends gathered and drank too much coffee, and worried and waited. Detective Senz showed up shortly after he arrived. For well over two hours, Shane explained, re-explained, then re-re-explained every step he and Everlee had taken since they'd entered Little Rock airspace. He showed Detective Senz the crime scene photos on his phone. Explained why and how they'd tracked Astor to her hotel suite. Which federal agency had assigned the duty to a private contractor. What gave them legal authority. Which contractor. Why. Over and over. Around and around. He and Detective Senz went over every last detail until Shane was sick and tired of repeating himself.

Enter Alex with two venti Starbuck coffees. Smart man. Everything changed then. Alex tackled Little Rock' finest head-on, almost confrontationally, as if he had a chip on his shoulder that Shane was being questioned at all. Told Senz he needed to check with his chief, get his son of a bitchin' story straight, that this was a federal affair, not local. That The TEAM had been contracted to apprehend Astor and ensure Ms. Smart's safety, and to stop badgering his agents.

Alex wasn't rude, just so damned direct that Shane felt sorry for Senz when he tucked his little paper tablet and pencil into his suit jacket pocket, told Shane not to leave town for the next forty-eight hours, and headed for the elevator.

"He's just doing his job," Shane told Alex after he'd handed him a coffee and settled into the chair opposite his.

"And we're just doing ours," Alex clipped. "Tell me what you know, what you think. How's Ev?" The man was a no-nonsense, hard-driving son of a bitch.

"She's tough. She received medical care the second she hit the floor because I had my blowout bag with me. I'd already started first-aid when the EMTs showed. Tuesday assisted. EMTs were prompt, gave Ev blood within minutes of her getting hit. Dottie Kaminski," he told Alex. "That's the medic who treated Ev."

"Good to know." Alex damned near smiled. "I expect your after-action report on my desk the day you get back."

"It'll be there. But one question."

"What?"

"Why'd the FBI pawn this mission off on you? Why didn't they pick up Tuesday Smart themselves? She wasn't hard to find. Hell, she was living in their backyard."

"Because..." Alex let that one word hang in the air for a full minute, then he sucked in a chest full of air, arched his back, stretched both hands over his head, and finally admitted, "Not everything is black and white in our world, but try telling the Bureau that. They have too many rules, too much bureaucracy, too much red tape and crap to wade through to do their job. I don't. Federal regulations hamstring them. When I found out from a reliable source they were going after Tuesday Bremmer like they usually go after criminals—like damned wrecking balls—I intervened. Got the contract assigned to me and my TEAM. Sounds like I made a smart decision, didn't I?"

"She never killed anyone."

"Exactly. From the start, there were too many red flags. Call it a gut feeling, but I've seen enough to know twenty-twenty vision can still make you blind."

"So how'd you finagle that contract? Just walk over and ask to speak to the Director?"

Alex's face lit up like a carved Halloween pumpkin. "You ought to know by now that I have friends in low places. Just a matter of working the right communication line. Knowing who to tweak, when to suggest, when to charge. Director Tucker Chase is a damned good man. I'll have to introduce you someday."

A nurse appeared at the door marked Do Not Enter. "Mr. Hayes?" she asked the room.

"Here," Shane answered as he and Alex both stood.

"Ms. Yeager is being moved to her room now. If you'll follow me, I'll take you there."

Shane and Alex followed the nurse to the elevator, then to Everlee's room. She looked pale after the staff transferred her to the bed and arranged a mass of medical equipment around her. The nurse explained that there was a drainage tube in Everlee's left side to prevent air pressure from compressing her lung. The tube would stay in for at least two days, possibly as long as five. Ev also had a couple IVs. A blood pressure cuff on her right arm. An oximeter on her left index finger. A noisy, beeping contraption at the head of her bed. Her oxygen stat was good, he could read that much, and her heartbeat was steady.

Her surgeon stepped into the room just as the last of the staff stepped out. He explained how both Shane's and EMT Kaminski's immediate first-aid had facilitated Everlee's chances of complete recovery. "If she continues to surprise us like she has, I'll release her in twenty-four hours."

"Ev never ceases to surprise any of us," Alex growled good-naturedly. "Thank you, sir."

The surgeon nodded, shook their hands, and left.

Alex cuffed Shane's shoulder once the door closed behind the guy. "Everlee's a fighter. Just wait and see. She'll be sassing us plenty before breakfast tomorrow."

Shane had no doubt.

"I've got to check in with Mark and Mother. Take good care of my girl while I'm gone."

Because a smart "Yes, sir" was forever on the tip of his tongue, Shane simply nodded. But Alex was wrong. Everlee was not his girl. She belonged to Shane, and he was finally where he belonged, at her side. The only light in her room came from the bathroom. He closed that door, left just the barest crack, for who he wasn't sure. Everlee might need the comfort of a nightlight, and he knew he did. Dark nights were not his friends, and because of her dog Blade, he guessed she felt the same. Was he killing two birds with one stone? Maybe.

With a sigh of contentment, Shane dropped on his butt to the floor on the other side of the room, out of the nurses' way, and watched Everlee sleep. Just being with her calmed him like nothing else ever had. He'd damned nearly lost her tonight. To be able to sit there and simply watch her sleep, to see her chest lift and know she was on her way to recovery, felt like a blessing. He'd lost so much in life, first his mom, then Sara and Abby. Several guys in the Corps. To be able to sit there and quietly study Everlee's sweet face was damned humbling.

Shane made himself comfortable. He didn't need pillows or blankets. Just stretched out on the floor and set his internal alarm for five AM. Doctors made rounds early, and he wanted to be awake by then. He needed to know how to take care of her once she was released. What she could eat. When she could resume normal activity. All the really important stuff a man should know about the woman he had grown to love.

Because, damn it, she wasn't alone anymore and neither was he. He just hoped she recognized that fact when she woke up. More than anything, Everlee was hard-headed and stubborn. She led with her chin more than she needed to. But he'd also noticed how she'd withdrawn into herself when Mother had inadvertently revealed his history. It was good to have that out in the open, at least between him, Everlee, and Tuesday. But not once had Everlee confided in him the way Tuesday had. Shane honestly felt he knew Tuesday better than Ev, and that had to change.

He closed his eyes. His first civilian mission had been one continual mess, but it was over. Astor was dead and Mother had a ton of evidence that would prove Tuesday's innocence. But damn, Maeve Astor had left a trail of unanswered questions in her wake.

Number one: Why kill her husband and children?

Number two: How could any wife or mother do that? Mother had tracked that marriage and those birth certificates down. Her marriage to Atchison Bremmer was authentic. She was Toby's and Betsy's biological mother. She'd delivered both of them naturally. If he lived to be a thousand years old,

Shane would never understand how women could mistreat their children.

Third question: How had Astor tracked Tuesday from Dallas, through the various vehicle changes Everlee had run them through, into Arkansas? It didn't seem possible. What'd Astor have, her own damn satellites overhead? He doubted that. Some kind of tracking device? A drone? But drones required technicians behind the lines to track and report, to deploy armament. Made no sense unless Astor had satellites. But satellites were expensive, were federally controlled, and Shane was certain Tuesday hadn't been wearing any kind of tracking device.

He seriously doubted Astor had more tricks up her sleeve since she was no-kidding dead. But if she did? If she had an accomplice, someone else in the shadows running interference, or worse, facilitating her ongoing crime spree against Tuesday? Shane wasn't worried. The Corps hadn't squandered time or money training him, and no Marine needed weapons to deal with Astor's lackeys. Astor's ghost and her ghost operatives could take that to the bank—or shove it up their asses.

Mental note to self: *Ask Alex. He'll know. Better yet, ask Mother.*

Shane fell asleep thinking about Everlee and Blade, Dolly and Molly, Mother and Tuesday and… something called forever.

Chapter Thirty

Everlee woke, groggy and disoriented, stiff and sore. But still breathing. Still alive. Which was more than she'd expected when Astor got that lucky shot off. Nothing hurt too badly. Her chest was tight and her side was tender and achy. But she didn't feel like moving just to find out how bad off she was. The room was dark. Slivers of sunlight slanted through the blinds where Shane and Alex were seated, maybe eight, nine feet away. Both had their heads tilted toward the other and were murmuring in voices so low she couldn't make out what they were talking about. Or maybe she'd gone deaf. Maybe she should sign for them to speak up.

Later.

With a sigh, she relaxed and gave in to the fog in her head. She was alive and safe. Shane and Alex were both there. That was all that mattered.

The next time she came to, her two favorite men were still there. Must've meant she was okay, at least going to be okay if they were hanging around. She vaguely remembered Shane getting shot in Astor's suite, not much of what happened afterward. The big dumbass had confronted Astor. He'd made himself a target, for Pete's sake! And he did that to save Tuesday. Which had left Everlee exposed. Which was damned dirty trick.

But not exactly damned dirty. Not Shane. The second her brain had jumped to that conclusion, it didn't feel right. He hadn't wanted Tuesday to kill Astor, that was why he'd shifted in front of her like he had. Shane was honorable. He'd rather carry the hashmarks on his soul for killing Astor. He'd trusted Everlee to have his back, which was why she'd gotten shot. Because he'd honestly thought she could take care of herself. And most times she could've. But most times, she would've been a helluva lot sharper than she'd been up in that damned penthouse suite with all those dead men and their dead eyes and—

She swallowed hard. Yeah, her getting shot was her fault. Tuesday probably could've taken care of herself, but Shane hadn't known that. He wasn't there when Everlee and Tuesday talked about how she'd survived the Arctic. He had no idea how good a shooter she was.

And like Alex said, Shane was built. The man was wider, thicker, taller by at least a foot, bigger boned, and heavier than either Everlee or Tuesday. Hell, than both of them put together. But sure as shit, the miniscule correction he'd made to protect Tuesday, a correction he damned well should've made, allowed Astor a shot at Everlee. For the life of her, Everlee didn't know if she'd fired at Astor at all. How embarrassing. Maybe she was the dumbass. She had been shocked seeing all those murdered men. Those bodies. Her reflexes were trashed that night and her confidence, too. Shane hadn't reacted to the scenes in that penthouse like she had, but he'd probably seen a lot of ugly stuff overseas. Right? Which made Everlee the weak link, the inexperienced. The fraud. As usual.

She ran a quick tongue over her chapped and cracked lips. Her poor tongue felt as thick and dry as cotton. She needed a good, long drink. But the second she lifted her head, intending to at least balance on her elbows, both Shane and Alex shot to their feet. All at once, Shane was on her left, filling a clear plastic glass full of water from a pink plastic pitcher with bright pink flowers around its neck like a lei. A bendy straw was sticking out of the hole in its top. He eased his free hand under her neck, just enough to tilt her forward as he put the straw on her lip.

Jiminy Christmas. Water never tasted so sweet. She sucked in a big gulp before he pulled the glass away. "Easy does it, Ev. Breathe a little. I'm not going anywhere."

"I… am… breathing," she rasped, her throat sorer that she'd expected. Damn, she was tired. Just sipping a tiny drink wore her out.

"What am I going to do with you?" Alex asked gently.

Like she hadn't heard that before. Everlee licked her lips, top and bottom, then licked them again because they were so tight, they hurt. Shane didn't ask, just popped the cap off a tiny tube of lip moisturizer with his thumb and smoothed it gently over her lips until they were nice and greasy and....

Ah. It was funny how the tiniest things mattered at times like this.

Everlee sagged back into the pillow, her energy spent. "Talk to me, big guy. What happened? Did you get her?" she meant to ask. But her voice came out hoarse and she sounded like an old woman. She cleared her throat, which hurt, damn it.

"Take it easy," Shane cautioned. "You had a tube down your throat. It's bound to be sore."

Alex had taken a seat on one corner of the bed, his knee bent toward her, one hand on his ankle, his other foot on the floor. As usual, he was dressed like a savvy businessman, his suit dark gray, probably bespoke. He could certainly afford it. The red silk tie at his neck was undone and loose under his collar, as were the top buttons of his black dress shirt. The exposed triangle of skin on his chest was tanned and smooth. Everlee could envision Kelsey snuggling there. Which was where she belonged. Kelsey, not Everlee.

His dark hair was clipped short on the sides, longer on top. Clearly, he'd run his fingers through it a time or two, probably in exasperation that she'd fouled up another mission. It was messy and spiked, not the usual tidy look of her OCD boss. He'd aged nicely. The only signs of stress in his life were the hints of silver at his temples. His eyes were still razor sharp and as startling blue as ever. She knew he had a photographic memory, which had made him the genius he was. Why he'd ever invited her to move to his new TEAM HQ, Everlee would never understand.

But there she was, the least valuable of all his physical assets.

Then there was Shane, the same height as her boss, but a few years younger. Both were lean, not massive heavy weights like Zack, Mark, and Beau. More agile like most agents on The TEAM. Shane carried more bulk in his chest than Alex, and he had the same commanding attitude. Guess that was what USMC training did.

Yes, she'd served, like Shane, but never in combat. Never in the chaos of firefights. She recognized now that was the biggest difference between them and her. She could talk a good story, but she lacked hands-on experience, the pain and struggle that honed good military men and women to be all they could be. It was time she admitted her deficits and started looking for a different line of work. She'd run this race as far as she could. She'd done good, but she'd never be as good as Shane. It was time she faced the truth.

With one last quick lick over her ragged bottom lip, Everlee gave up the fight and sagged into her pillow. Shane had stashed the lip moisturizer by then.

"What's the last thing you remember?" he asked as he took a seat alongside Everlee on the bed, in pretty much the same pose as Alex. Like bookends. Only Shane was closer and sexier.

Everlee's cheek puffed out a heartfelt sigh, wishing she didn't have to remember. "Bodies. Blood. So many eyes…" Dead men's eyes. All staring at her. Which was why she'd chosen to stand next to them, instead of by the exit. Because those guys couldn't stare at her then. They hadn't been positioned to see her beside them. Not like her mom…

She licked her lips again, trembling as the horrific memory from long ago crushed her.

"You left some things out of your personnel file," Alex said quietly.

"Ah, yeah. About that…" Alex rarely gave in or gave up. Unlike her, he was a winner. She might as well confess and beat him to the punch. "B-Boss, my, umm, name's not Yeager. Not really. It's Everlee, but my last name's Billings, only it's not anymore because I had it legally changed, and I'm sorry I lied to Murphy when he hired me, but I've got a good reason, and—"

Alex held a hand up in her face, not like he meant to slap her, but with his fingers spread, like he wanted her to stop talking. Like what she'd just blurted out wasn't what he'd intended at all. "We didn't know you're allergic to penicillin, Ev. That's all I meant. Take a breath. You're not on trial here. And anytime you decide to update your records is fine with me. Understood?"

He cocked his head at her, one brow spiked like he was so good at doing. Kindness and courtesy melted over her like a welcome home hug. Which she'd only ever gotten from her mother. And Shane. And yeah, Alex and Murphy and Zack and Mark and…

She nodded, ashamed that she'd jumped to conclusions, but that was her standard operating procedure. Jump the gun. Never let anyone see her stumble or fall. Never fall behind. Lead, damn it. Lead!

Alex sounded so nice, and his tone was so gentle. He wasn't angry. Just sincerely worried. About her. She blinked, then blinked again, struggling to get back in control. At least, not to be so damned emotional.

"Astor got off a lucky shot, Ev, that's all," Shane told her. "Her bullet hit you up high under your arm. Guess you had your arm raised. You were probably ready to shoot, but her bullet hit first. It struck a rib and fragmented. One piece ricocheted into your lung, the other exited out your shoulder. Scared the fuck out of me. But the EMTs got there fast and—"

"—and Shane had the bleeding stopped by then, at least slowed down," Alex added.

Shane blew out a deep sigh between his handsome pursed lips. "Always carry my blow-out kit with me, just didn't expect I'd need it for you. But then you developed pneumothorax in the chopper on the way to the hospital. You couldn't breathe. Air got into your chest cavity. If not for Dottie Kaminski, one of the EMTs, you might've died. She knew what to do. That's why the tube, Ev. Your doctor said it'll take days before you're completely out of the woods, but if you're good and do what you're told, he'll let you go home tomorrow."

She smoothed her free hand over her ribcage. "That's what I'm feeling." Sure enough, a thin tube was held in place there by a big square piece of paper tape. Which was also good since she was allergic to latex and hadn't put that in her personnel files, either. Ah, the tangled web she'd woven. All because of pride.

"Astor fired at me because she couldn't hit Tuesday. You blocked her shot."

"Yeah, my fault," Shane admitted. "I only did it because I didn't want Tuesday to kill her. I didn't want that on her conscience. But now I wish I'd let Tuesday have her way. In the end, she and Heston ended Astor. I was kinda busy keeping you from dying."

"You saved my life, big guy. Thank you."

Shane was up off the bed in a heartbeat, leaning over her, planting a kiss on her surprised mouth. She swept her tongue over his lips, and he opened for her. The kiss was wet and quick, and damn, he tasted good. Smelled good, too.

When the kiss ended, Alex was gazing at the window, then up at the ceiling. Everlee couldn't help but glance at the ceiling, too. At last, Alex shook his head, turned to her and Shane and said, "I'm going to tell you two something I've never told anyone before. Only Kelsey. But when I first found her—and yes, *found* is the correct word—she was a bloody mess, a battered spouse left to die in the woods where I just happened to own a piece of shit, rundown cabin. She'd been beaten, had amnesia, and was in damned rough shape. Her asshole husband had just killed her two little sons. Drowned them in her car. Then blamed her. The whole state of Washington was looking for her. But I'm the one she came to. I'm the one who found her."

Alex's fingers clenched into fists. "I thought she was dead. She sure as hell looked like it. Well, when Whisper found her, because he got to her first. Damned dog squared off with me, even growled, ready to fight me to keep her, can you believe that? Crazy mutt."

His fists loosened. He cocked one arm and rubbed a hand up the back of his neck. "Back then, I'd just lost Sara and Abby, and I was as worthless as that piece of shit cabin. Pissed at the world twenty-four-seven. Mad every minute of every son of a bitchin' day. On my way to killing myself with booze or a .38 special, didn't matter which. Nothing mattered, not the successful company I'd started, nor the loyalty of my friends. Not one damned thing—until the morning I found her. Even then, I treated her badly. Didn't want to be saddled with more responsibility. Didn't want to take her inside and take care of her and… Yeah. I was an ass. But I had a good mother and—"

"I'm so, so sorry I killed your family," Shane murmured, his face ashen and his eyes glistening. "Your wife and child. Sara and Abby. I can never repay you for what I took—"

"Stop, Shane. Just stop. It's over. It's done." Alex sounded like he was pleading, a damned rare thing to witness. "Nothing anyone can do to change it. Please. Let it be. 'Sides, I'm not telling this story to guilt you, just to give you two a piece of advice. Don't be so sure the sins you're packing are sins, for one thing. Most of the time, we blame ourselves for events we had no control over. In the long run, with Kelsey at my side, I've come to realize that the person I needed most to forgive back then was me. Myself. Yeah, I wasn't there that day and we both know what happened." He directed that calmly spoken fact at Shane. "Would things have happened differently if I'd been in town or if I'd been driving? Maybe. But maybe not. Do I miss Sara and Abby? God, yes. Every day. But you have to understand that Sara was a headstrong woman, Shane. She knew what she was getting into when she married me. She was born into a military family, lived it, breathed it, didn't know any other way. She knew the drill, that military wives left behind ended up handling every move, every deployment, every damned inconvenient thing Uncle Sam or life threw at us while we were gone. But that was who she was, Shane. Who she was born to be. Hell, Sara didn't need me hanging around. She had everything handled, and she was smart. She had Abby in tumbling the last time I was home, had set up a college fund, too. Had even refinanced our house at a lower interest rate. If anything, I was deadweight in her life. If I'd died instead of her, I know in my heart she would've gotten along fine without me."

"But Kelsey wouldn't," Everlee declared boldly.

"I wouldn't be so sure about that," Alex replied quietly. He swallowed hard, closed his eyes, then pinched the bridge of his nose between two fingers. Shook his head, then focused on Shane. "My point is, don't hide who you kids are from each other. If this" —he aimed a rolling motion with one hand in their direction— "whatever's going on between you two, amounts to anything, stop pretending. Man the hell up. Be straight with each other." He cranked his neck and looked over at Everlee. "Let him in, Ev. Don't be stubborn, so good at hiding who you are, acting so tough that you miss the best thing in your life. And just so you know, you are not a fraud. Clumsy, yes, but nowhere near to being any kind of a fake. Trust me, you're not even close."

Her eyes filled with tears. This was the man she'd foolishly lusted after for so long, even though she'd known he was beyond reach, that she'd never follow through with any of her foolish daydreams. Yes, Alex was smart and good-looking, downright handsome as hell. He'd always be her rock star. But he was also right. He adored Kelsey, and he'd never let her down.

Everlee turned to Shane, the man she'd grown to love. Maybe adore. She had been holding her truth back. It was time to reveal the real LT Yeager. "I have ADHD," she announced for the first time—ever. "And my dad killed my mom when I was in high school. He was drunk because he's an alcoholic, and he used to beat her, and sometimes he'd hit me. He'd get so mad, then tell her he was sorry. Mom always believed him, always took him back. He's in prison now, and he's why I changed my name. I couldn't stand having the same last name as him, and Chuck Yeager's the best hero a girl can have, even if he isn't my dad."

"Yeah, well… I drink too much and I'm having a son of a bitchin' hard time retiring," Alex announced just as quickly. His hand went over his head, brushing his hair down in some places, standing it up in others.

"I hate the dark, and I sleep with two dogs every night because my PTSD's killing me," Shane said softly. He jerked his chin at Alex. "But you already know that, don't you?"

"Bet you won't be sleeping with two dogs much longer," Alex chuckled.

Heat suffused Everlee's neck and cheeks. She could feel herself turning red. But he'd made her laugh. A little. And she hoped he was right, that Shane would move her into his place, or something.

Alex lifted to his feet, took hold of her ankle through the covers, and squeezed. "You need to sleep," he said sternly. "Come on, Shane. I'll drive you back to that empty room I'm paying for. Might as well get some use out of it."

"In a minute, Boss," Shane replied, his gaze still on Everlee.

"Okay then. Later." Alex stepped out, shutting the door behind him.

"I love you, Everlee Yeager," Shane said when the door finally closed.

"I love you, too," she admitted quietly. "I know it's early, and we don't really know each other, but I really want that date you promised me."

"Me too, babe. I want to see where this thing between us goes," Shane said as he carefully lifted her up from the mattress, enfolded her in his arms, and pressed her head under his chin. "I thought I lost you. Finally found the woman of my dreams and you nearly got away. Shit, you scared the hell out of me."

She wiggled one arm around him and splayed her fingers up his back as far as she could reach. "I'd like you to hold doors for me and help me get up into your truck. I like ice cream cones and dogs and kisses and… and I like this." She could feel his body relax beneath her as she held on as tightly as she could.

He was breathing into her hair by then. "I'm so damned tired of living alone."

"You've got Dolly and Molly."

"You know what I mean. Alex is right. I've been hiding who I am for years. Never wanted to be a Marine, much less a sniper. But I owed him that much. Now I owe you."

"For what?"

"For this." The moment she looked up into those deep blue eyes, he took her mouth. Kissed her and licked her and held her while she fell apart and cried. Then he kissed her through her crying jag. By then she was deliciously spent, so damned tired it was hard to keep her eyes open.

So she didn't. Just leaned into Shane, took a deep breath, and let his strength take her weight and her secrets. Finally. She was home. Didn't matter that she'd found her happily-ever-after in Arkansas. She knew it now. Her home was with Shane. Wherever he went, she would follow. *Yes. Follow.*

Chapter Thirty-One

"Hurry. They'll be here in ten minutes."

Everlee was hurrying as fast as she could, but no matter how much Shane scolded, she could still only do so much. Her energy hadn't fully rebounded since she'd been shot. Certainly not as quickly as her physical injuries. If anything, she felt like she was fifty-years-old today. Stiff and tired. But mostly, grouchy. Put upon. Not her usual peppy self. Yes, physical therapy was getting her strength back. The problem had more to do with what was going on with her heart, and what she'd seen the last day in the hospital, that intimate moment between Shane and Tuesday. That damned kiss he had no idea she'd witnessed. Sure, he'd packed a bag and moved right into her place to help her convalesce, without even asking. Which made things between them worse.

He'd been the perfect caregiver. Attentive. So damned thoughtful. Kind. He fixed all of her meals, even took the dogs for long walks, which made Blade a true believer. What dog wouldn't be thrilled following an alpha like Shane? Didn't hurt that along with Shane came two adorable, bouncing Springer Spaniels that were now Blade's best girlfriends. The three of them slept together in one huge puppy pile on the fluffy bed that had once belonged solely to her pittie. Only now, he'd turned into a grinning, slobbering pup who adored Shane and his girls.

But Everlee couldn't move beyond what she'd seen between Shane and Tuesday. Before that, Everlee thought she and Shane had been on solid relationship ground. Which would've been a first for her. Now? Not so much. Shane's subterfuge had spoiled everything. She hadn't kissed him once since she'd been home, didn't ask him about what she'd seen. Wouldn't dare. How could she ever prepare for that big of a letdown? If he told her they were through? She was already hurting enough.

She'd never be blonde or sexy or beautiful like Tuesday, and her legs would never be long. Men might fall like dominoes for Tuesday, but no one would ever for a short, stubborn, ill-tempered, pushy former Air Force lieutenant. And Butch didn't count! He hadn't fallen for her. All he'd ever wanted was a slave, some stupid idiot to mother him through his lazy-assed addictions.

So, yeah. Why ask for more pain? Even if Shane were polite and sweet while he told her they were through, that he was moving out and moving on, she knew she'd open her big mouth and say things she didn't mean. Or worse, she'd fall apart and cry like a damned sissy.

So, no. Flat no. She got it. She was the ugly step-sister to Tuesday's gorgeous Cinderella. So for one more day, Everlee pushed her confrontation with Shane into the future. Hopefully, when she could stand and fight back and do it with style. Like a boss!

But that day was probably closer than she wanted. Everlee could tell. Shane had grown even kinder lately, more thoughtful. Sweeter. More gentlemanly. As if he wasn't already choirboy perfect. He still said grace over their meals, which he insisted they eat at her dining room table because he'd said he wanted to recreate the connective family atmosphere he'd known with his mother. Which was all well and good—*if* she and he were a family. But they weren't. They were co-workers, two people who'd been temporarily welded together by a near fatal event that he obviously felt responsible for. They were ships that passed in the night. Nothing more.

He'd sure been surprised when he'd first stepped inside her apartment though, mostly because she'd furnished her place—not her Dad's place and not Butch's!—with expensive Stickley furniture that had cost an arm and a leg. At least it was classy. More's the pity that she'd forever be white trash with her father incarcerated at Washington State's Walla Walla Penitentiary. Every piece of her pricey furniture proved she could certainly *look good enough*. That just took money. But she'd never *be good enough*, would she? She'd never be classy or beautiful. And today, Everlee was positive no one could ever love a big-mouthed loser like her.

Living with three rambunctious large-breed dogs didn't help. Molly, Dolly, and Blade had bonded within minutes of meeting, then turned her apartment into one perpetual puppy playpen. At least they got along. But rubber balls, gelatin bones, and tattered chew toys were everywhere. Sometimes they were underfoot, more often than not, under the furniture. Not that she minded, because, hey, most of those toys belonged to Blade, and she'd meant for her home to be a sanctuary, not a showroom. Still, her prized pieces of Stickley were the only classy things she owned. Blade didn't count. He was more like her, rough around the edges, a gnarly chunk of coal more than a diamond in the rough. As if she, Everlee Yeager, a murderer's daughter, could ever be mistaken for something bright and shiny. Someone worth keeping. That'd be the day.

But this afternoon, Shane, darn him, had gone and invited Heston and the gorgeous Ms. Smart over to visit, like any minute now. Guess he needed reinforcements when he bailed on his promises. Guess he wasn't a gentleman after all.

"Stop feeling sorry for yourself. When it's over, it's over. No second chances. Good riddance," Everlee grumbled as she knelt beside her prized rocking chair and tipped it far enough back to reach the rubber bone beside the rear runner. As expected, her position caught the dogs' attention and the game was on. Suddenly there were three furry, drooling faces peering beneath the rocker, all of them panting dog breath into her face. Making her tear up. Reminding her how much she was going to miss these sweet Springer Spaniels when Shane left.

Suddenly, a big warm hand landed on her backside, cupped one cheek, and made her smack her head on the underside of the rocker's hardwood seat. "Ouch! Damn it, Shane," she complained when she jerked upright. "You startled me, you big ape!"

She'd meant for him to back off, to at least give her enough room to get on her feet. But next thing she knew, Everlee found herself flat on her back beside the rocker with Shane on his hands and knees over her. His chest was bare, and he was smiling. Despite what she thought she knew, he didn't look like he was going anywhere. His pupils were too big and black, and his handsome face was bright with mischief. His bare chest was drool worthy. Man, she was going to miss this guy.

Her breath caught when his strong, capable fingers smoothed over her skin beneath her baggy t-shirt, under her bra, and gently cupped her breast. Everlee closed her eyes as the work-roughened pads of his thumb plucked at her nipple. *Yes, yes, yes.* That was what she'd wanted for weeks, this intimate connection. This beginning. Only it was the beginning of the end. Wasn't it?

It was a first since her release from the hospital, though, and the sensory stimulation overwhelmed Everlee. Her heart pounded like it wanted out of her chest. He'd been so damned in control since her shooting. So careful handling her, and way too cautious. He hadn't even slept in her bed with her. Not once. Sure, they'd cuddled on the couch in her living room and watched TV, but as soon as she'd drifted off to sleep, he'd picked her up and carried her to her room, tucked her complaining ass into bed, and then gone back to sleep on the couch. Every time. Every night! Until Everlee wasn't sure about that so-called date he'd promised her. Because this wasn't it, neither was him being her caretaker her idea of a relationship. This was platonic, and he was too damned nice, and she was *not* that kind of a woman. She wanted rough and dirty and hot and heavy and sweaty. Right now! With the dogs watching!

With her body revved up and screaming like an LS engine caught in the four-second delay between the flash of amber and green on the Christmas tree before a drag race, she grabbed hold of his belt buckle and—

The doorbell rang. "Shit!"

Shane pulled back, his grin wider, his perfect, white teeth showing between his sexy lips, and... a dimple? Everlee hadn't noticed that cute little thing before, but there it was, tucked into his cheek like an adorable secret surprise. Everlee wanted that perfect little dimple to be just her secret surprise. *Not sharing, Tuesday!*

The bell rang again and Shane looked over his shoulder at the door. She wrapped her fingers around his belt. "Make them go away. Tell them to beat it," she ordered, her errant tongue licking up the side of his neck in anticipation of at least one good, wet kiss. That's all. And okay, maybe a little skin-on-skin playtime before he left her. She deserved that much. She did!

But when his head rotated back around to her, that sexy smile and those deep blue eyes were her undoing. Shane rested his forehead on hers and kissed the tip of her nose. She melted in the delicious, coffee-scented breath in her face. "Soon, Everlee. Very soon. I am going to make you mine, and you'll never doubt my intentions again. But right now we have company and—"

"Are you leaving?" she demanded to know. By then, her fingernails were stuck in his back like cat claws. "I mean me? Are you leaving me? Is that what this is all about?" She never could keep her mouth shut.

His brows slammed together and those adorable wrinkles she loved lined his tanned forehead. His hair flopped down into his eyes. He looked playful as sin, but upset. "Why would you say that?" he asked as his fingers eased out from under her shirt. "How could you even think I'd leave you?"

"Because this is the first time you've touched me like you want me," she bit out, still mad at him for inviting Tuesday over to her apartment. Hers. Not his. Not theirs. Not yet. Maybe never.

Those damned tears welled up again, making her blink.

Shane's eyes turned stormy. With his elbows dug into the thick Turkish rug beneath them, he bracketed her head between his big, warm palms. His thumbs smoothed over her cheeks, which had to be bright red if the heat coming off them meant anything. His long fingers laced into her short, spikey hair, which, for a split second, Everlee wished was as long and blonde as Tuesday's.

Without warning, he slammed his mouth over hers and French-kissed the temper out of her. Like a cleansing tidal wave. A tsunami. Her foolish indignation was swept away in the hurricane called Shane Hayes. He suckled and nipped, he bit her top lip, then the bottom one as he stormed over every last one of her childish, petulant defenses until—

Everlee melted like gooey caramel into the rug. Shane took possession of her lips and her tongue and every last one of her uppity, self-righteous senses. And she was drowning. Claimed and owned and so damned breathless for every atom of oxygen he exhaled. For his scent. His taste. For every single part of this man. This was what she'd been craving.

Somewhere off in the distance, the doorbell rang a third time. Someone pounded on her door as it tolled its final beat, and Everlee found herself upright, standing dizzily on her feet. Shane's hands were on her waist, and his lips were warm and moist on her forehead.

"Then I must be doing something wrong, babe, because I'm not going anywhere," he murmured. "Not without you. We should answer the door, though, and after our friends leave, you and me are going to talk. All night if we have too, got it? Because I love you, Ev, and you should know that by now. I thought you did."

"I did, err, I d-do," she stuttered. "And I love you, too, and I do know that. Most of the time." She knew she was smiling like a loon, but Shane had finally squashed her nagging doubts. At the same time, he'd staunched the bleeding, sucking hole in her soul that had come with losing her entire family the way she had. With her fingers on his bare chest, her nose against his bare skin, and her ass in his big, warm hands, she finally understood that maybe—just maybe—she didn't have to try harder than everyone else anymore. She didn't have to be like Tuesday at all. He loved her just like she was, and she was a silly, spoiled brat for ever thinking otherwise.

"You need a shirt, big guy," she told him breathily, still cocooned in his love where she wanted to stay.

He winked, let her go, and shucked the clean t-shirt hanging off the back of the rocker over his head. "No, babe, all I need is you. We good now?" he asked, his brow spiked like a beast, daring her to act up again, but that gentle glow back in his eyes once more.

"Yes," she breathed, running a finger over her ear and into her hair. "We're good, Shane. And you are so damned hot. I really like you like this."

That brought back his grin. "You mean undressed? Later, babe. For sure. But let's get rid of our visitors first, okay?" That was the most perfect thing he could've said.

"Yes, please," breathed out of Everlee. Her shoulders lifted. She smiled at how compliant one kiss from Shane could make her. How did he do that?

Chapter Thirty-Two

Shane could've cried at the sweet innocence pouring off Everlee. She'd had such a tough life, and she'd come so far from the insecure teenager she'd been. There was no reason on Earth she should be jealous of Tuesday. But look at the stars in her eyes now. Made a man proud, at some deep, dark, caveman level knowing he'd put them there and that her moods and happiness revolved around him. That he and he alone had the power to make her smile. Not that he'd tamed her. Oh, hell no. There was no taming Everlee Yeager. But loving her? That would be the challenge and highlight of the rest of his life.

With one final kiss on her forehead and one more sigh from her lips, he told their three dogs, "Places." They eagerly dashed across her open floor plan and whirled around to stand on their appointed mats beneath the bay windows. Those three dogs would stand there until he released them to join the conversation. Until then, Shane latched onto Everlee and headed for the door.

"What took you so long?" Heston grouched when the door opened. "We've been standing out here for hours."

"I wish," Shane grumbled back.

Tuesday giggled. "Shush. They've been getting busy. Can't you tell?"

A salacious grin cracked Heston's face. "Well, good! It's about time. Looking beautiful, Ev!" He opened his arms like he expected a hug.

Obviously, he didn't know Everlee. She shoved him away into Tuesday's side. "Knock it off, creep. I don't hug strangers, and man, you are one strange dude."

Heston tipped his head back and laughed. "Dude? Me? Honey, you have no idea."

Shane stepped to her side and put an arm around her shoulders. "Glad you guys could make it. Come on in," he said, gesturing Heston and Tuesday into the open living room area as he closed the door.

Everlee took a seat beside Tuesday on the couch, while Shane took the one rocker and Heston took the other. A quietly uttered whimper escaped one of the dogs. No doubt Blade. Shane didn't blame the hefty guy. He was the most spoiled.

Shane looked over his shoulder and gave those handsome dogs the quiet command to, "Come." Mayhem ruled for a few minutes while the rambunctious threesome raced to greet, smother, and slobber on their guests. But when Shane said, "Off," they promptly obeyed and each chose someone to settle down beside. Surprisingly, Blade dropped to his belly with a grunt at Tuesday's feet. Everlee just winked at him and let him be.

Tuesday bounced on the couch, her fingers tapping her knees restlessly. "Did you hear?"

Today she'd dressed in black jeans that hugged her long legs, stylishly distressed, brown leather ankle boots, and a fuzzy, soft pink sweater top. Her sleek hair hung in perfect blonde ringlets down her back. Pink blush brushed her cheeks and her green eyes were lightly shadowed, then highlighted under the brows to make them seem bigger. Shane's gaze strayed from Tuesday to Everlee. Look at her, sitting there with no make-up whatsoever. One glance at her made his heart sing. She looked like a mischievous pixie with stars in her eyes.

"Hear what?" he asked respectfully. After Everlee's out-of-the-blue question earlier, he was more aware of her insecurities. Tuesday might be gorgeous, but she was nothing compared to the imp with the tousled, copper hair beside her. Shane wasn't a hair, butt, or boob guy. He was Everlee's guy. End of story.

"I'm going to be on *Sixty Minutes*!" Tuesday gushed. "With my friend, Robert Freiburg. He knows one of the producers. We'll be two of six experts on a discussion panel about climate change. Isn't that great?"

"Congratulations!" Everlee crowed. "You know what you're talking about. You'll be perfect, girlfriend."

Shane eased back in his seat and relaxed at that one word: *Girlfriend.* Special praise for Everlee to tell anyone.

He'd read up on Adult Attention Deficit/Hyperactivity Disorder while Ev had been in the hospital and at home sleeping. He now knew she'd had to really work at everything she'd ever accomplished. That she'd always have trouble focusing, reading, and spelling, which made simple everyday things like listening to spoken instructions, writing after-action reports for Alex, even running simple mathematical equations in her head, extremely difficult. Which also meant she'd struggled in high school, then had fought extra-hard to become an Air Force officer. It had been tough for her to fit in with the guys and gals on The TEAM, the ones she wanted most to impress. It also explained why she'd been sitting alone that night at the Stewarts' impromptu dinner picnic, why she'd closed herself off. It explained her inability to restrain her reactions, like the day she'd spit coffee in his face, then called him *'big guy'*, and demanded he eat lunch with her, that she was buying. He'd found her cute but annoying. Her boundless energy and attention, all of it aimed solely at him, had been uncomfortable—then.

Not anymore. One only had to look into Everlee's brown eyes to see the sincerity that suffused every word she said and every thought that flittered through her mind. Yes, she was impulsive, prone to act without thinking, and semi-disorganized. But she was no dummy. She was smart enough to understand her limitations, and because she did, she directed every last ounce of her boundless energy into being all she could be despite them. That said a lot about her. Because everything good in her life had come extra-hard for her, Everlee took nothing for granted.

It also told Shane how strong she was, that she'd never given up. That she'd set higher goals than most airmen, and that Alex probably knew these same things about Everlee. That he'd chosen well the day he'd hired her. Or at least the day he'd approved Murphy Finnegan hiring Ev. Shane hadn't yet met Mr. Finnegan. Murphy was still in Ireland. Shane didn't know why. But he did wish he were sitting beside Everlee. She needed someone to hold her. To love her and always have her six. Because even among friends, he knew damned well that she still felt alone. He caught her eye and winked to let her know that he saw her. That he adored her.

She shrugged and smiled back.

"Mother figured out how Astor tracked Tuesday," Heston said nonchalantly.

Shane shook his emotions about Everlee off for the time being and asked, "Yeah? How?"

"The old battleax. Watch this, Ev." Tuesday leaned into Everlee's biceps with her cell phone, dabbed at the screen, and brought up a video clip from somewhere noisy. "Mother found it. See Astor? Right there, walking beside me. We were inside DFW's concourse. I was on my way to Montreal to meet Robert. He went with me on my first flight into the Arctic. Don't have a clue where Astor was headed."

Everlee squinted and pursed her lips, her neck stretched forward and her countenance one of serious concentration. Everything she did now humbled Shane. He finally understood how hard his woman had to focus just to watch a video. Just to keep up with the direction this friendly conversation was going.

She blinked. "Did that bitch just stab you? With a knife?"

"You saw it, too, huh?" Heston asked.

"No, but it sure looked like she did, didn't it," Tuesday replied. "I mean, that thing in her hand was shiny, but…" She thumbed her cell phone screen and—

"She hit you with a hypo?" Everlee growled. Tuesday must've enlarged the screen.

"That's how she injected a tracking device into your arm," Shane breathed. "That's how she did it."

"Yup!" Tuesday replied with a big smile and plenty of gusto. "I remember feeling the pinch, but it happened so fast that I never thought twice about it. I mean, honestly, who would've thought anyone would do something like that?"

"That's how she knew where we were in Little Rock," Ev said.

"Are we certain she couldn't locate Tuesday inside Smoke's underground bunker?"

Heston nodded. "Mother already ran diagnostics on all Alex's safe places, Smoke's included. There's no way Astor knew where Tuesday was that night."

"Good. But why?" Everlee asked. "Why track and try to kill Tuesday? Hell, why kill anyone?"

"Greed maybe," Shane replied. "Greed, revenge, and love are the three top motivators for most crimes of passion."

"Don't forget crazy. Astor was psychotic as hell," Tuesday added.

"Not psychotic," he said thoughtfully. "A psychotic is someone who's lost their grip on reality. It's not their fault they're sick. They need to be taken off the streets and cared for in safe facilities. But Astor was different. She was simply a stone-cold psychopath. She was intelligent, not impaired. She knew precisely what she was doing, and she deliberately planned—for more than five years—to murder her own children, her biological offspring, for hell's sake. Psychosis and psychopathy are two very different things. People like Astor have no feelings, no empathy. That's why she thought she could just waltz into Freddie's condo and kill him. I'm sorry, Tuesday. I know that brings up hard memories. Do we know what was in that gift bag of hers yet, Heston?"

"Ever hear of Batrachotoxin?"

Shane shook his head. "No, sniper here, remember? Not chemist. Ask me about high-velocity rounds, the HVTs I took down, not poisons."

"Same here," Heston agreed. "But the ME who performed the second autopsy on Mr. Lamb found traces of Batrachotoxin in his system, also inside the velvet lining of that fake book. An amount as small as two grains of Batrachotoxin will kill an adult. It affects the heart the same as coronary arrest, which is why the first autopsy concluded massive heart attack. The FBI has no idea how much she put inside that book, not like it matters now. Within seconds of simply touching Batrachotoxin, it causes fibrillation and arrhythmia, instantaneous cardiac failure."

Shane turned his attention to Tuesday. "How are you handling what happened in Little Rock?"

"She's as steady as a rock," Heston replied. Shane didn't miss the pride in his voice.

"I'm not that lonely little girl anymore," Tuesday replied evenly. "Sure, I miss Freddie. Just sorry I didn't shoot Astor in the face before she shot Ev."

"Wish I'd seen you take that bitch down," Everlee said. "That would've been priceless."

"It was" —Tuesday's chest expanded with a long inhale— "satisfactory, knowing I ended a predator like her. I don't enjoy killing, but I approve of justice. Call it the most extreme version of tough love, but there's a time and a place when we owe the victims in the world more than we owe a depraved killer. And Astor earned every ounce of the lead Heston and I put in her."

"She did," Heston agreed.

"How many?" Shane asked.

"Double tap from me but—"

"I only shot her once," Tuesday declared, her head up and her green eyes clear of any sign of regret or guilt. "No need to waste ammo. She wasn't a polar bear, for Pete's sake."

"Nope. She was an ass," Everlee deadpanned.

Which broke the tension that had stolen over the group of friends.

"Do we understand why she killed Atchison Bremmer and those kids yet?" Shane needed to know.

Heston shook his head. "No, and the FBI is upset that she died before they had a chance to question her. But self-defense was definitely warranted. No doubt about it."

"But babies," Tuesday murmured. "That she killed her flesh-and-blood babies makes me sick. I don't understand how anyone could do that."

"Me either," Everlee agreed.

Shane knew he needed to divert the attention away from how her mother died. "I've got teriyaki chicken in the oven," he announced. "You guys will stay for lunch, won't you?"

Everlee shot him a brilliant smile, either because she was hungry, which was good, or she knew precisely what he was doing, namely hinting. Which was even better. Yeah, they were going to make it.

"We can't," Heston replied, his palms on his knees. "Tuesday has to be in Manhattan early tomorrow morning. Just wanted to check in with you kids before we left."

"*We?* You're going with her?" Everlee asked.

"Yeah, sure. I'm still playing bodyguard. No big deal. Alex wants to be sure there's no Astor-related blowback."

"He thinks it's possible?" Shane asked.

"Not likely, but he gave me the week off, and I've never been to New York, so I figured, why not? With Tuesday as my tour guide, it'll be fun."

"Do you still own Freddie's condo?" Shane asked her.

She shook her head, which sent those golden curls bouncing off her shoulders. "No, I turned it over to the New

York police department after that mess in Little Rock. They've assured me they've gone over it with a fine-toothed comb and there's no danger of anyone else coming into contact with the toxin. After NYPD sells the place, the money will go to the New York Police and Fire Widows and Children's Benefit Fund. And that guy I *allegedly* killed in my home in Dallas before I *allegedly* blew it up?" Tuesday poured a ton of sarcasm into *allegedly* just like Everlee had done with her at the beginning of their mission. Shane couldn't help the grin that split his face.

"He was another one of Astor's minions," Tuesday said. "Do you believe that? He might even have been the guy who followed me when I got home from the Arctic. Who knows? Dallas PD found his and Astor's fingerprints in my bedroom, do you believe that?! That horrible woman meant to frame me for his murder, too. As well as those guys in the penthouse! What a lunatic."

"She was that," Everlee said quietly.

Her gaze had drifted to Shane. He was looking at her. Their simple across-the room connection sizzled and seemed to trigger a reaction from Heston.

His palms slapped his knees and he pushed to his feet. "We'd better get going."

"Wait, before you leave," Everlee said, "Does anyone know why Astor killed Freddie?"

"Oh, yeah," Heston replied. "About that. Astor worked at One57, the Tower, where he lived, remember? Her first job was at the swimming pool, but she was also at the grand opening, serving champagne and finger foods. Mr. Lamb was there, mingling with other guests. Astor made a play for him, which he politely ignored. When she kept after him, he turned her down again, told her *'no thanks'* loud enough that people heard. Then he walked away. Gotta give the man credit. He knew precisely what Astor was."

"I still don't understand. Why'd she need to destroy Tuesday if Freddie was already out of the picture?"

"Hard to know for sure, Ev," Tuesday replied. "But I think it's because I was Freddie's widow, the woman he chose over her. That might've made her jealous."

"And insane," Everlee murmured.

"The whole woman scorned thing," Shane added.

Tuesday shrugged. "Who cares? She's not going to bother me anymore, is she?" With a bounce off the couch, she grabbed Heston's open hand as if he'd just invited her to a party and they were late. "Bye, guys! We've got to go!"

Chapter Thirty-Three

By the time the front door closed behind Heston and Tuesday, Shane was totally focused on Everlee. She was chewing her bottom lip. Something was still bothering her.

He held out a hand. "Come with me?"

"I saw you kiss her," she told the floor.

Ah, so that's what's been bugging you. That silly kiss. "You mean Tuesday? In the hospital hallway? Yes, she kissed me," he confirmed without hesitation.

"Wanna explain?"

"Nope," Shane replied, popping the 'P' as he leaned over and snagged one arm around Everlee's waist, the other under her knees. "I've never lied to you. Not starting now. You saw what you saw, babe, but it was just Tuesday's way of saying thanks and goodbye. She's a hugger."

"And a kisser," Everlee grumbled. Her arms were around his neck, but hurt still shimmered in her eyes.

"And Heston was right there with us. Bet you didn't see him, though, did you? Couldn't have. He was beside your open door, and trust me, he didn't even try to kiss me."

Everlee let loose a half-hearted giggle. By then they were in her room and Shane was standing over her bed. He rested her backside on the edge of the matching nightstand while he tossed her rose-colored quilt and white sheets aside. Then he sat Everlee with her back to her pillow and told her, "You also noticed I didn't kiss her back, right? A kiss on the cheek is nothing. I didn't even do that. And, oh yeah, I'm sleeping with you from now on, babe. Got a problem with that?"

She was looking up at him by then. "You're right. I didn't see Heston and I do know you didn't encourage Tuesday. And that kiss was pretty tame."

"No big deal. I love you, Everlee. No one else. It's you and me from now on. Only us. Can you handle that?"

"Yes," she whispered. Her big brown eyes were wide with anticipation, and if she licked her lips one more time, he was going to need a cold shower to slow the freight train in his blood.

"Good. Take off your clothes."

Of course, she challenged him with a snappy, "You first, big guy."

Shane complied quickly. No reason not to. Her bossy expression changed to surprise when he yanked his t-shirt over his head and tossed it into her face. She caught it, and just like he expected, threw it back at him. He let it drop to the floor because he liked that her gaze was fastened on his chest. By then, he'd unbuckled his belt, but let it hang loose. He unsnapped his jeans next, and her lips formed a silent O. But when he dropped his pants to the floor and kicked them aside, her eyes lit up. She liked what she saw and he loved that she was looking.

"Keep going," she whispered hoarsely. Those coffee-colored baby browns were dewy, as they should've been. He was no small man and his body was pointing at her, making his intentions clear.

"Yes, ma'am." He shucked the briefs off and told her, "Your turn, babe."

But the moment she doffed her shirt, he changed his mind. "Belay that order, LT. My present. I get to unwrap you."

Sticking a knee into the mattress alongside her, he swung his other leg over her hips and pushed her shoulders gently back to her pillow. Her skin was golden against the white sheets, her hair a luscious coppery color that begged a man to run his fingers through it—just because he could. His bigger, wider body blanketed hers, letting her take just enough of his weight to know she'd soon be all his.

"You're my lucky penny," he whispered, his fingertips threading through those silky locks.

"Just worth one cent?" she teased.

"Just worth everything. Just mine," he breathed. The pads of his fingers slipped over her scalp. She shivered. Her body arched into him. It was time.

Nimbly, Shane climbed off the bed, slipped her out of her clothes, and tossed them to who-cared-where. Back on top, he pressed her into the mattress. But his blood was running hot, too hot, and he was fighting his cock for control. Pesky thing tended to take over, and it had been a damned long time since he'd been in bed with a woman he truly cared for. He was already leaking pre-cum like a damned teenager, and it was all he could do to calmly slide his hands over her silky-smooth skin.

He'd barely slid a hand around her and unsnapped her bra when she took hold of him. His woman had a firm grip. A determined grip. *Fuck.* He closed his eyes to control his body's natural drive to divide, thrust, and conquer. That might be the quickest way to get this job done, but Shane wanted more than just slam, bam, thank-you, ma'am. He wanted to take his time making love with the daring woman beneath him, the one who seemed to think she always had to be in control. He wanted to taste all of her secrets, to discover her ticklish spots, and to sink into her slowly. If it took all night, this first time would be about making love.

He wasn't having much success slowing that freight train down, though. Her busy hand was working wonders on his cock with that perfect up-and-down push and pull, the slick pad of her thumb busily flicking over the sensitive tip. Heat snapped up his spine like tiny bolts of lightning. Shane cringed. This was happening too soon. Too fast.

"You keep that up and I won't last," he told her in no uncertain terms, his voice deep and raspy.

"Too bad, soldier," she growled. "My bed. I'm the boss of you."

Ah, how he loved a good challenge. With a mighty heave-ho, Shane had her topside, straddling him, her knees beside his hips, and her busy hands now flat on his chest to keep her balance. Whether she knew it or not, she was now in the prime position of control. But he suspected her past sexual experiences hadn't anything to do with feminine control or pleasure or, hell, probably not even orgasms.

"Not fair," she grumbled, wiggling those full hips like she knew what she was doing.

"Marine, ma'am!" he snapped with true Devil Dog arrogance. "Not soldier. Soldiers are Army. Get it right. If you're gonna be in command, you damned well better know who you're ordering around."

"Is that a fact?" she drawled. But her face had lit up with a fiery glow that honestly, looked like the sun had just broken through those castle walls and that moat full of alligators she'd built inside.

"Damned straight! Now stop moving your ass, LT," he ordered gruffly, slapping one hand on her bare ass and sliding down over their bellies and between their bodies. "First things first," he told her with belligerent certainty, his thumb already working on her soaking wet clit, his fingers mapping the dripping cleft between her spread legs. Her breath hitched. She was so slick and damned warm. Tempting. Luscious.

"I won't last long, but you'll damned well be ready when we do this. We, understand? Not just you doing me, but… We. Do. This. Together. Got it, LT?"

"Yesssss, sssssir," she hissed, panting like a beautiful beast, her knees squeezing his ribs tighter with every unrelenting flick of his thumbnail. Her eyes were closed, but her voice was soft and sexy like the kitten he knew she could be. Yeah, right. A saber-toothed kitten with nine-inch claws.

With a sexy moan, she arched her belly and those succulent, full breasts fell forward and she all but stuck them in his face. Shane closed the distance, opened his mouth wide, and sucked her breast into his mouth as far back as he could, and—

Fuck! He was in over-stimulation heaven. Suffocating maybe, with his nostrils buried against her soft, fragrant skin, her diamond-hard nipple at the back of his throat. But a man should die surrounded by the woman he adored. Just like this. With his mouth and his hands full. But that truly wasn't enough, not for her, not for him.

Shane let her breast loose with a slathering wet pop and ordered her to, "Kiss me. Now, babe. Hurry your ass up, Air Force! Move it, move it, move it!"

"I'm moving it, already!" she declared with attitude, grinding her core onto his hand as she tipped onto his belly and…

This. Yes, this. He fuckin' loved the irritation grumbling up her throat even as she obeyed him. Him, a lower ranking nobody. She was irritated because he'd wrested control of their lovemaking from her? Too bad. She thought she could order him around? Maybe later. Not now. Not with her moaning like she was, not with her gyrating her hips and grinding her core against his hand. If that was her way of punishing him? *Guess again, babe.*

With a grin, Shane closed his eyes and inhaled her sweet breath and her lips. Ev's fingertips slipped from his chest over his head, into his hair. She grabbed a handful and tugged. The kiss turned feral. He kept his hands right where they were, one still on her ass, the other poised between her legs, not willing to sacrifice a second of prime real estate. Or that plump lower lip of hers. He bit down on it, ever so slightly. Just enough to sting. She tugged his hair harder, forcing his head into the pillow.

Just like he wanted. While she kissed and nibbled, he inserted one long finger into her and scraped a fingernail over that ridged erogenous zone just inside. Instantly, the kiss was over. She arched upright, and those perfect feminine muscles squeezed down on his hand like a clamp. Her head fell back. A throaty, sensual growl purred out of Everlee. Her sinuous arms lifted over her head. Her fingers delved into her hair, ruffling all that bronzed beauty while, at the same time, exposing full, blushing breasts that bounced like clumps of ripe, coppery-tipped grapes.

Shane blinked up at the golden, naked goddess straddling him. She was perfect, a combination of honey-flavored skin punctuated with diamond-hard nipples of russet and wine, and messy hair that matched. Honey and sass, that's what Everlee was. Right then, he had a perfect view of his woman. From the crisp, reddish-brown curls where his thumb still played, up her centerline, to the sweaty valley between her plump breasts, up farther to the strong column of her stubborn neck. Moaning like the sex goddess she was, Everlee cupped her breasts together, opened her hazy eyes and looked down at him. Her tongue took a succulent lap around those perfect, kiss-swollen lips.

Made Shane hard as fuck. His cock thickened with more blood. He replaced his fingers with what Everlee wanted. What she needed. What he needed to give her. And Shane lost control. Not that he'd ever really had it. Not with this impish dominatrix sitting on him like she was. Where she was. Not with all that heat in her sultry brown eyes. This was her pouring herself into him. Giving up her control.

Yeah, right. There was no tempting, teasing preamble to what he did next. Just snapped his hips forward and—

"Fuck. Yeah, Ev," he hissed as her heat enveloped him. Her core clenched tight, gripping his cock in a wondrous stranglehold. Then tighter. And tighter still. With every thrust, he met eager, slippery anticipation that held him fast.

A delightful, incoherent grumble wound up Everlee's throat, vibrating through his cock. Shane set a faster rhythm, thinking he could climax with her. With every beat of his heart, he pounded forward or pulled backward, in sync with Ev's body slamming down on him. With her legs growing tighter at his hips. With her body stiffening.

"Shane!" she growled.

And yeah, of course, she came first. That seemed to be the theme of their relationship. She needed to be first. Always. And it was no big thing for Shane to allow her the win. If it truly was a win. Everlee's need to be smarter, to run faster and farther had driven her all her life. So, yeah. Shane didn't hesitate making the sacrifice. Anything to make her happy. To please her. Anything.

"I see you, Everlee," he whispered, breathing hard as he took hold of her pretty face and brought her within kissing distance.

He shouldn't have looked up when she opened her eyes. Her pupils were blown, reducing the brown irises to thin rings at the edges of—forever. Her luscious body literally writhed against his. She was a woman undone.

Shane's entire body stiffened at the sight of the wanton creature in his arms. The final rush of blood burned up his spine. He stuck his heels into the mattress for better leverage. Then…

"Fuck, yes!" Shane slammed himself upward into Everlee. Into home and forever. Into her slick, wet heat and her clenching grip that refused to let him go. Finally. He closed his eyes and gave himself over to this, his one and only second chance. To warmth and love and laughter. To trust and joy. To Everlee.

The muscles inside her body were still strong. Very strong. They fluttered like tiny determined fingers around his cock, tugging, jerking the last of his orgasm out of him. He let her win again. She stiffened and came. Then again. Each time, she whimpered through the pleasure while her body undulated against his, teasing him for another round.

He stilled, his hands now clamped on Everlee's ass, holding her fast to him, his cock deep inside of her and already twitching like a needy addict who needed the fix only she could give him.

What a rush. What an eye-opening revelation. Her body was slick with sweat, and damned if another swell of wicked aftershocks didn't wash over his cock, still clenching, still holding him inside where he wished he could stay forever. He was the weakest man on Earth, and damned glad of it. Women's bodies were amazing. So much better than any man's. But Ev's was downright splendid.

Shane couldn't refuse the smile that blossomed over his face, hell, over his entire body. He nearly laughed, the pleasure was so intense. So pure. But instead, tears flooded his eyes. He wrapped his arms around the woman who'd just saved him. Who loved him in spite of himself. The woman he would gladly give his life for. "I love you, Everlee Yeager," he whispered into her ear. "So much. It feels like I've known you forever, babe."

Heavy breathing was the only answer Shane got. He swiped a quick hand over his face so she'd never know what a wuss she'd just made love with.

"You had enough?" he asked quietly, his fingers smoothing over the bottom swells of her ass, then petting designs of infinity symbols up her back.

"I never…" she whimpered into his neck. "Never… Not once…"

Shane kept silent. Verbal expression was hard for Everlee. It took her longer than others to understand her feelings enough to translate them into words. He moved one hand up to the back of her neck and held on.

"Till now… That was…" She sniffed through her nose. "Jiminy… Chrisssssstmasssss. That… was… so… so…" Her belly expanded, pushing against his. "That was so good I can barely talk."

"I see that," he whispered. "No rush, Ev. Take your time. I'm not going anywhere."

Then Everlee made it better. She eased back on her haunches and said, "You're so big, Shane, and thick and…" She licked her lips. "Wow. I had no idea making love could be so…" She blinked and her brows lifted nearly to her hairline. "So wonderful." Like the spontaneous, petulant woman she could be, Everlee collapsed on his chest and into his arms with an exaggerated sigh. Then she wiggled under his chin.

Shane took a deep breath of forever. There was a time he'd honestly believed he'd never be happy again. Never know this kind of peace. Never have the family he'd so desperately craved as a stupid, young man. Now he knew better.

They stayed tangled and sweaty together, the sheets somewhere on the floor. Shane tugged the comforter up and over them. "Time for a nap," he whispered to his sleeping beauty.

"I'm not ready for kids yet, are you?"

Not what Shane expected, but he should've known. Everlee's mind worked differently than his. "Eventually. Not twelve, but it's no fun being an only child. Maybe a couple. Four's a nice even number."

"Good answer," she huffed. "Four, yeah, Shane. I can see us with four babies."

"Well, not all at the same time," he replied softly. "But one at a time shouldn't be difficult."

Her body melted into his. She was warm and she was safe. Tomorrow would come and she might not remember this conversation, but Shane would remind her when he slipped the diamond currently tucked in the side pocket of his gear bag on her finger. Because he was marrying Everlee. He was keeping her. He took a deep breath, his nose in her hair and an ocean of contentment in his heart.

It was just the way things were. Bad things, like car accidents and murders, happened to good people. The rich got richer and the poor got poorer. People were born and people died. Some of those people were saints and some were devils. All in all, not a bad celestial plan for mankind. Not when Shane ended up with his arms around the woman he adored. Everlee would certainly give him a run for his money, but he wasn't worried. She was his everything, his angel. His reason for living. Everlee might never see herself that way, but he figured he had a lifetime to bring her around to his way of thinking.

For the first time in a long while, Shane closed his eyes and succumbed to a night of peaceful dreams. They were the real deal, the present and his future. The nightmares he'd once had were simply ghosts from a past no one could change. Dreams trumped nightmares every time. They were the stuff of life and love, of families and forever, and…

Of Everlee.

About the Author

Irish Winters…

…is a best-selling author who, when she isn't writing, dabbles in poetry, grandchildren, and rarely (as in extremely rarely) the kitchen. More prone to be outdoors than in, she grew up the quintessential tomboy on a dairy farm in rural Wisconsin, spent her teen years in the Pacific Northwest, but calls the Wasatch Mountains of Northern Utah, home. For now.

She believes in making every day count for something, and follows the wise admonition of her mother to, *"Look out the window and see something!"*

Connect with Irish online:
On Facebook: https:/www.facebook.com/author.irishwinters
On Twitter: https://twitter.com/irishwinters1
Or at http://www. IrishWinters.com

www.ingramcontent.com/pod-product-compliance
Lightning Source LLC
Chambersburg PA
CBHW030948190726
48285CB00004BB/1281